BURNING LITTLE LIES

A Novel

by

Christine H. Bailey

ISBN: 9781951122744 (paperback) / 9781951122751 (ebook)
LCCN: 2023947436
Copyright © 2024 by Christine H. Bailey
Cover illustration copyright © 2024 by Melinda Posey
Cover Image: Unsplash - Vadim Sadovski

Printed in the United States of America.

Kinkajou Press
9 Mockingbird Hill Rd
Tijeras, New Mexico 87059
info@kinkajoupress.com
www.kinkajoupress.com

Content Warning: This book contains descriptions of sexual assault and trauma that may be disturbing to some readers.

Prologue

THERE'S BEEN A MYSTERY for months surrounding who killed Ellie Stone. All anyone seems to know is that she was found dead at the edge of the Usman River with a blue flower placed over each of her eyes. No arrests have been made and nothing has been released about cause of death, only that it's been classified as a homicide. It's been consuming our small town ever since—the *who did it* and *is he coming for me next?* She was only sixteen... *as lovely as they come.*

People are saying it was someone she met online or the work of a serial killer. A few years back, two girls went missing from a town not too far from us. One of the girls was found buried in a small field of blue flowers. Some people think the wrong person is in prison and that the real killer is still out there. But there are other theories too, one of which includes Ellie's own circle of friends. I've heard the whispers, the rumors, people saying it was one of us. It's bizarre how small-town gossip spreads like wildfire, curling at the edges of our lives like crisping newspaper as the wicking flame catches.

But I know the truth. I know who did it because I was there that night. She didn't deserve to die. Not like that. I've been holding my breath ever since, knowing that eventually the person who did it will get caught. But I'm not telling which one of us killed her; whether it was boy-genius Nick Moore, his brother Hayes, Tori her best friend, or Piper the outcast. We're all guilty of keeping secrets, but one of us is hiding the biggest one of all.

One of us knows it all.

Part One: Tori

Chapter 1

THE HINT OF JAPANESE cherry blossoms from outside the classroom window smelled sweet in the chilled air, fresh after rain. To me, the flurry of pale pink blooms in late March always marked the real beginning of spring in our little Mississippi town. Waterford had always been known for its annual Cherry Blossom Festival, but lately, we'd been in the spotlight for something else—something none of us would have ever imagined. I glanced at the empty desk next to mine and slumped lower in my seat as our twenty-something Poli-Sci teacher, Miss Taylor, tried her best to get us back on track. She had just opened the window, trying to keep us awake during last period on a Friday afternoon.

"Let's talk about the global economic impact from the COVID-19 pandemic," she said.

Someone behind me groaned.

I slid an earbud under my hair. It wasn't that I didn't care about the global impact of the pandemic. I really did. It was more about her too-bright pink lipstick and the high pitch of her voice. No one should ever be that chipper discussing a virus.

A twinge of guilt swept over me, for a split second, before I hit play on my phone. Not even the deep, baritone voiceover on my audiobook could drown out my teacher's nasally voice, but *anything* helped. Besides, I was doing my AP English homework, listening to Tolstoy's *War and Peace*. So, the way I saw it, I was using my time wisely, knocking out both English *and* Poli-Sci by studying the impact of Russian literature on the rest of the world.

Miss Taylor droned on for the next twenty minutes, losing almost everyone in class except for freshman phenom

Nick Moore, who sat a couple rows over from me. The kid was brilliant. That's why he was the only freshman in a class with mostly juniors. But he was weird too, always staring at people—me, for one—like he was psychoanalyzing us or something. He probably was. His mother was a therapist after all. *My* therapist. I turned back to my notebook, shading Tolstoy's bushy eyebrows then adding a few more lines to his billowing beard, which kind of looked like swirls of cherry blossoms. My rendering of the literary genius wasn't half bad. Ellie, my best friend, would have loved it. She would have laughed, adding her own touches to the drawing. I leaned back, sighing at her empty desk. The girl in front of me turned around, bugging her eyes out at me. "What?" I asked, before peeking over my shoulder to see who else had heard me. Yep, Nick had. He was still staring.

When the bell finally rang, everyone bolted out of their seats, rushing for the door as Miss Taylor rattled off an optional homework assignment for the weekend. I'd probably do it, especially after my last test grade.

"It's contradictory, don't you think?" Nick asked, stopping at my desk. He slipped his backpack over his shoulders, securing the strap across his narrow chest until it wrinkled his shirt.

"What?" I hit the pause button on my phone and glanced at Miss Taylor, who was cleaning the whiteboard.

"It's contradictory seeing history as both predestined and yet determined by individual free will, you know, small choices, freely made?" He scratched the freckles dotting the bridge of his nose and squinted his hazel eyes, slightly magnified behind thick glasses.

I shook my head, slightly irritated. *What was this guy talking about?*

He pointed to the notebook on my desk, nodding at my drawing and chicken-scratch writing on themes in *War and Peace.* "Tolstoy?"

"Oh, right." I shoved the notebook in my backpack and zipped it, then started to head for the door.

"If you ever want to talk about it—"

"I'll let you know." I really wasn't trying to be rude or anything, but I wasn't in the mood to chat about literary themes with Boy Genius on a Friday afternoon. I'd *almost* made it out the door when Miss Taylor called me back. "Yes, ma'am?" I turned in the doorway.

"Have a second?" she asked.

Really? Right now? I gritted my teeth and forced a quick smile. "Sure."

Nick swept by me in the doorway. "Bye."

"Yeah, see ya," I said, moving toward Miss Taylor's desk. She was latching the window as a sudden, cherry-blossom breeze swept into the room. I cleared my throat to get her attention.

"Oh," she said, twirling around to face me. She paused for a second then said, "Your hair looks nice. Did you get highlights?"

She asked me to stay after class to talk about my hair? Weird. It was the same plain brown as always. Everything about it was the same from the color to the way I wore it: parted in the middle and long, straight, and loose. "Um, nope."

She fidgeted with the top button on her pale pink oxford shirt. "Oh, looks like you got highlights. Anyway, have a seat."

"I kind of need to get home?"

"Right, right. I'll be quick then. You seemed distracted in class. Everything okay?"

I was growing pretty tired of everyone asking me that. My answer was the same every time. No, everything was *not* okay. My best friend was still dead. Still gone from my life forever. "Yep, I'm good."

"It's just that your last exam, well, it wasn't up to your usual..."

"Yeah, sorry about that." I nodded, giving her the reassurance that she was wanting.

"I know things have been hard lately, but..."

Hard? That was the understatement of the year. "I'll do better," I said, being short. I didn't want to go there with her. Not now. She kept staring at me though, like she wanted to say something more or maybe she wanted *me* to say something more. But what else was there to say?

"I just wanted to check in with you. That's all, Tori."

"'Kay."

"Well, alright then. Have a good weekend."

"You too."

She was only trying to be nice and supportive, but sometimes all the asking about how I was feeling from what felt like literally everyone, well, it was too much for me. After I left her room, I took the less-traveled back hallway toward the faculty parking lot. No one ever used that exit except for a few teachers that I didn't know very well—and they *never* talked to me. I kept my head down anyway, just in case, and plugged in my other earbud.

Outside, the sun was starting to break through the patchy rain clouds. As the deep, baritone voice recited Tolstoy in my ears, I thought about what Miss Taylor had said. Okay, so maybe my grades had been horrible lately, but that was to be expected, right? I'd do better, just like I'd told her I would. I had to. There was no way I was repeating junior year. So far, it had been the worst of my life. And besides that, my parents would lose it if I failed all my classes, especially my mom. I crossed through the parking lot, making a plan that would catch me up in all of my classes, not just Poli-Sci. But then, it got me thinking, too, about what Nick had said after class. What had he meant anyway by our small choices determining our histories? I couldn't shake the feeling that there was more to it.

Ten minutes later, I still hadn't figured it out as I neared his house on Church Street, not that I had any intention of ringing his bell to ask him what he'd meant. It was just that his house was on the way to mine. That was all.

But I did slow down for a second.

I wish I hadn't.

The turn-of-the-century estate in the middle of town had always intrigued me. It was straight out of an eerie movie with its thick evergreens guarding most of the house from street view, but not all of it. You could still see peaks of the gabled roof and thick ivy that crept up the front stonework. Off to the side was a separate entrance where an old carriage house used to be. They'd converted it years ago into a garage before turning it into Dr. Moore's office. At least, that's what she'd told me once in a session.

I needed to go back. I'd cancelled the last four sessions with her, promising my mom I'd go "next time," but the thought of sitting in that room, talking about my feelings to Dr. Moore made my stomach twist. It didn't help, talking about it. Nothing helped. I rubbed the chill bumps sprouting on my arms. "Next time," I mumbled as I turned to cross the street... not looking.

How many times had my mom told me to "look both ways before you cross"? But I didn't look. Not even a quick over-the-shoulder glance.

It all happened so fast—the screeching tires and the front

grill of the silver SUV only a few inches from me. As it squealed to a stop, I lurched backwards and stumbled on the curb, losing my balance. I must have rolled, trying to break my fall, but I wasn't sure exactly what had happened. The next thing I knew, I was splayed out on the gritty asphalt with Tolstoy still going in my ears. "Okay, you're done," I said, slowly removing an AirPod. The other one—the left one—was gone. I tried lifting my head to search for it, but a bolt of pain shot right through my body from my right temple down to both knees. I closed my eyes, gritting my teeth. Why hadn't I looked before crossing the road? Why? Why? *Why?*

I didn't move. I stayed as still as possible as footsteps echoed near me on the pavement, getting closer and closer.

"Are you okay?" someone called out.

That voice—it was so familiar. I wanted to see who it was, see who had almost hit me, but even opening my eyes in the bright sun hurt.

"I'm so sorry. I— I didn't see you. You just..."

"My AirPod," I whispered.

"Tori? Are you okay?" he asked again, this time quieter, closer, and more panicked.

He knew my name. I opened one eye, but I couldn't see anything except for a shadowed face against the sun. It was blinding and bearing down on me full force. "You almost hit me," I said as I wiped what I thought was sweat from my right temple.

"Oh, man, you're bleeding."

"What?" I asked, squinting.

"You're bleeding," he repeated.

He was right. My fingertips were red. I was about to give him a piece of my mind that maybe he should slow down or watch where he was going when he shifted slightly, blocking the sun in my eyes. That's when I saw who it was. My heart raced, and the throb in my head worsened with every thudding beat. *Oh, great. Anyone but him.*

"I'm sorry," Hayes Moore said. He was Nick's older brother. My therapist's other son. "I didn't see you. I swear. You just ran out in front of me."

Heat rushed to my face, and my pulse ramped up as he squatted in front of me. All those kindergarten playground moments of me chasing him, giving him fruit snacks, kids singing

Tori and Hayes, sitting in a tree... it all flooded back as a couple of cars honked in the street, swerving past us.

How mortifying. I'd just been mowed down—nearly killed—by our junior class president, who was also my ten-year unrequited crush.

"Can you sit up?" he asked, reaching for my hand.

My throat went dry as he held my stare with those storm-colored eyes of his, the ones with flecks of gold and deep blue. "I don't know. I can try." I bit my bottom lip and winced as he helped me sit up. My head was suddenly spinning as I breathed in hints of exhaust and his cologne, which was faint but nice, like springtime.

He took off his gray hoodie and balled up one of the sleeves, pressing it to my temple. "Want me to call the police? Take you to the ER?"

"No," I said, glancing from the Nike swoosh on his t-shirt to the small crowd that had gathered behind us on the sidewalk. One of the gawkers was a kid from school, holding up his phone and recording it all. *Great.* That was all I needed.

"Are you sure?"

"What?"

"Are you sure I shouldn't call someone?"

"I'm sure."

He lifted the sweatshirt from my gash and leaned in to examine it. "It's not deep. Don't think you'll need stitches."

I raised my hand to it, accidentally brushing his.

He took a quick breath then handed me the hoodie. "Keep pressure on it." He stepped back, rubbing his bare arms.

"I lost an earbud," I said.

He opened his mouth like he was about to say something when someone from across the street screamed, "Oh my gosh!"

It was Rachel, his girlfriend, getting out of her Honda and racing toward us.

"What happened?" she asked, out of breath. She wrapped her thin arms around his waist then stepped back to examine him. "Are you hurt?"

"I'm fine," I mumbled under my breath. *Thanks for asking.*

Hayes cut his eyes at me.

What? I wanted to say. It wasn't like he was the one bleeding from his head. I grabbed my bookbag, wedged in the storm drain, and started heading in the opposite direction of them.

My knee stung as sweat and dirt trickled into a small gash, visible through a new hole in my jeans. Why did I have to stop? If only I'd kept walking. *What a nightmare*, I thought as I glanced over my shoulder at him one more time.

"Wait," he called out. He was reaching down in the road for something. He held it up—something small between his thumb and forefinger.

No way. It was my AirPod. I met him halfway, amazed that he'd found it.

As he handed it to me, he said, "I really am sorry."

"It's okay." It wasn't like he'd done it on purpose or anything.

"Let me know if you need anything, 'kay?"

Rachel huffed loudly behind him.

"Thanks. I will," I said, even though I never would.

Besides, it was just a little bump and a few scratches. Still, my head throbbed with every step against the asphalt. But it was what I did... smile through the pain.

As soon as I turned the corner, my phone buzzed in my back pocket. My heart sank. Surely that gawker from school hadn't already posted the video online. All I needed was the whole world to see me lying in the street cut up and bloodied. I pulled out my phone to check, but it was just Drew, my boyfriend, asking where I was. I didn't have the head space to explain what had just happened. I'd tell him later. Maybe.

Or maybe not.

It had been really hard talking to him lately—about anything—even though we'd been together for over a whole year. When we first started going out, I thought there was no way he could be interested in me. It had to be Ellie. Every guy at school had it bad for her. I kept waiting for him to say it—the line I'd heard a million times: *Do you think you could talk to her for me?* But Drew never said those words. Sometimes, l still wondered, *why me?*

Now, glancing down at his text, at the blinking cursor waiting for me to respond, I had no idea what to say. It wasn't his fault that we'd fallen out of sync. Every time we hung out, he wanted to talk about Ellie or school or baseball or whatever, but it was like I couldn't hold a conversation about anything anymore. Somewhere along the line, I'd forgotten how to be... me.

I slipped my phone back in my pocket and kept moving.

The sun shifted behind a thick blanket of rain clouds, still lingering, making the sky gray and sad. More rain was coming, but I kept going anyway, limping right past my house. Mom's car wasn't in the driveway yet. She usually got home from work around 4:30, which gave me just enough time to head over to Ellie's house for a quick visit. It was what I'd done every Friday since *that day*—go around the block to sit under Ellie's bedroom window. I'd stay a while and then get back home just before Mom did, before she could ask where I'd been.

The house hadn't changed. It was the same two-story white-bricked colonial with its massive Magnolia tree in the front yard. I took my place under her window, slightly shaded by a row of evergreens, and finally exhaled. "So, guess what, El? Listen to what happened to me today."

A car revved its engine on another street.

"You wouldn't believe who hit me with his car... Hayes. Hayes Moore."

I could see her apple-green eyes widen and her lips part in surprise. "No way... get out," she'd say.

"No, seriously, he did. Well, he *almost* hit me."

"Let me guess," I imagined her saying, "you were all like, I'm so sorry. It's all my fault, blah, blah, blah."

"No way. I told him to watch where he was going, and that he almost killed me."

"Uh huh. Sure."

"I did! He was all freaked out about it and kept apologizing... and then *she* showed up."

"Ugh, Rachel."

"Yeah, Rachel," I whispered, leaning the back of my head against the brick wall of my best friend's house. I sat there for a while longer, quiet with my head aching. I didn't stay too long though. I never did, afraid I'd somehow wake up Peaches—her tiny terrier—and alert everyone to a "stranger" in the yard. Afraid that Ellie's mom would see the small lump of a girl in ripped black jeans and a hoodie over her head and get her hopes up that it *hadn't* happened. That it had been all a hellish nightmare and that her baby girl was still alive. Then she'd realize it was only me. Pathetic Tori. The best friend who'd left Ellie alone that night at the bonfire. I didn't want to be around for that reckoning.

And so I left.

On my way home, I cut through the woods between our houses, thinking, again, about how I'd left Ellie that night. Small choices. Is that what Nick had meant earlier? Did he know something? The sun was out again, peeking through another break in the clouds and offering new little streams of light. But it didn't make any difference to me. I hadn't felt the tiniest glimmer of hope in weeks. Not since they'd found my best friend by the river, fully clothed, arms crossed over her chest, and with a single blue flower over each of her eyes. I wanted her back. Nothing in my life had been right since.

I stopped on my back porch and glimpsed her house through the woods. "I'm so sorry, El. I'm sorry this happened to you."

My phone buzzed in my back pocket.

What I wouldn't give for it to be her, saying *come over*. But it was Drew again, asking if I was okay. *Saw the video online,* he wrote.

Great. Just great.

Why didn't you tell me Hayes hit you with his car?

He didn't exactly hit me, I texted back. *But I'm fine. Just a few scratches.*

I'd been numb for weeks. What were a few scratches in the bigger scheme of things? Even if Hayes *had* hit me, not even the impact of a head-on collision with an SUV would make a difference.

Chapter 2

I **KEPT MY BEDROOM** window open all night, hoping the distant cries of spring peepers would lull me to sleep. It hadn't come easy lately, not since they found Ellie. Some nights were worse than others—the nightmares, the guilt, the dark thoughts. Usually, I'd fight it, toss and turn into a twisted, exhausted knot and eventually fall asleep. But that wasn't happening tonight.

I sank deep under my covers, picturing Ellie beside me with her dark hair spilling over onto my pillowcase. All those sleepovers when we stayed up until dawn laughing, talking, confessing our deepest secrets—all of it was gone now. I rolled onto my side and swept my fingers across the pillow beside me. "That video of me lying in the street," I whispered, "is posted online. It's so mortifying." I could see her wrinkling her nose. It's what she did when she didn't know what to say.

That wrinkle. I missed it. I missed everything about her, like how she always apologized first, even if it wasn't her fault. I missed the way she'd pull me to my feet and make me dance or sing along to her new favorite song, whatever it was that week. She was so vivacious. So full of life. She *was*, past tense. And now, her future was gone. No prom, no graduation, and no going to one of the colleges we'd applied to together. How was I supposed to deal with that? I closed my eyes and rolled over.

By five a.m., I finally gave up the good fight for sleep, shoving my toes into pink fuzzy slippers and making my way downstairs in the soft blue-gray light of predawn. Dad was moving around in the guest room, probably making the bed and trying to hide that he'd slept there again. I didn't have the heart to tell him I knew.

As my lemongrass tea steeped on the veined marble

countertop, I wished for it all back, for those beautifully uncomplicated days full of little nothings—of lemonade stands and lazy summer afternoons. If only. Then everything would be okay again... I'd have Ellie back and my parents would be happy again.

But as I swiped through my phone, trying my best to avoid the video of me and all of the comments under it, I landed on that same post I'd seen a million times—the one about Ellie's death—and I knew it would *never* be okay again. My stomach wrenched at the sight of her school photo, the one with that tiny, smart-ass smirk. The headline still cut like it had the first time I'd seen it weeks ago: **Waterford Teen Ellie Stone, Dead at 16.**

Almost two whole months had passed with no new information. All we knew, all that anyone knew, was that she was found dead by the Usman River after Sam Cox's birthday party at White Pines Farm. And the only reason we knew any of what we did, like the blue flowers over her eyes, was because a first responder had taken a photo of the crime scene and had leaked it. Other than that, we knew nothing.

Oh, there'd been theories, lots of them, from it being the work of a serial killer to a ritual cult killing. Some people even believed that the river was cursed and connected to other deaths—its "evil currents" flowing into Pine Lake, where other mysterious deaths had occurred. Everyone had a theory. But what good were theories without an arrest? The police weren't doing squat, and it was really starting to get to me, festering like a cancer.

"Morning, kiddo," Dad said, slipping into the kitchen.

"Hey," I said, trying not to sound too resentful for him being a cop, even though he wasn't the one working Ellie's case. He was in Narcotics, not Homicide, but still, he could do more, right? I sipped at my warm lemongrass blend as Dad opened the cabinet over the microwave for the Folgers.

"Can't sleep?" he asked while scooping tall heaps of coffee into the pot.

He'd make it too strong, as usual, and then Mom would come in later, dump the rest of the thick, black sludge into the sink, and make a smoother pot. That's how things went down lately.

"Not really." I cradled the hot cup of tea in my palms, staring out the kitchen window into the deep, dark woods behind my house. Who could sleep, knowing that whoever did this to her was still out there?

In the winter months, Ellie's bedroom was visible from my house, or at least a light coming from it was through the evergreens. But now, in the thickening throng of trees, it was hard to see anything. At least the sun was starting to come up, meaning the scary monsters in the woods would soon be retreating.

"You work today?" Dad asked. He was sitting at the table now, waiting for the coffee to brew. His shoulders sagged under his wrinkled t-shirt, gray and drab. Mom always preferred him in blues and vibrant greens to "accent his eyes," she'd say.

"Yeah, later." I sat beside him as he nudged a day-old box of donut holes toward me. The perfect cliché, a cop and his donuts. I popped one into my mouth, calculating the calories as the sugars sat on my tongue.

"What time?" he asked.

I shrugged. "Noon, maybe?" Or was it four? I reached for my phone, checking the schedule my co-worker Piper had sent me. She'd been nice like that, sending me texts here and there, asking how I was, and taking my shifts when I couldn't face the world. We'd been super close in ninth grade, Ellie, Piper, and me, but we'd drifted apart like friends sometimes do. Lately, we'd started talking and texting again, now that she worked at Blue's Café.

I'd tried quitting a few times, but Mom had always come back in that thick, Mississippi drawl of hers: "It's not right to leave them high and dry." But she didn't get it. It wasn't her best friend who had died, who had left her in the messy, tangled aftermath, and it wasn't her being asked the same horrible questions week after week after week.

"Any new leads?" *No.*

"Do you think her boyfriend did it?" *No.*

"Such a shame, don't you think?" *Yes.*

"She was a lovely girl, wasn't she?" *The best.*

"Your dad getting closer to finding the guy?" *He's not on the case. He's in Narcotics.*

More than one person had said that with every passing day, things would get easier. Liars. They were all a bunch of stupid liars. I really did want to quit, but it was all I had left of Ellie. Memories of us sneaking brownie bites, hot from the oven and scalding our tongues. Of closing the place and dancing to cheesy '90s country on the old-school jukebox. Of stolen breaks behind the dumpster, crying over boys.

The pipes creaked, which meant Mom was awake and in the shower. It also meant that at any second, Dad would make a move to leave. I waited for it—three, two, one—

"I should head to the gym before it gets too crowded." He grabbed another donut hole.

"Or maybe you should cut down on the sugar?"

"Funny." He kissed the top of my head, then paused, examining the cut on the side of my face again. "You sure you're okay?"

"Yes, Dad. I already told you it was no big deal. The car didn't even hit me."

"Okay, okay." He held up his hands then headed to the coffee pot to top off his to-go mug. "Just making sure." He turned toward the back door, stopping to grab his keys on the counter and rifle through a pile of day-old mail. "This one's for you," he said, holding up a cream envelope.

It was probably another college letter from another school that Ellie and I wouldn't be attending together. He handed it to me. "Love you," he said, then closed the door behind him.

The label on the front was typed. It didn't look out of the ordinary, but it also didn't look like the other letters I'd gotten from the universities Ellie and I had picked out online. We'd had big plans to leave our small town and go somewhere new. Anywhere but here. But as I tore it open and pulled out the letter, it wasn't from a college. It was a piece of paper torn from a spiral notebook. I glanced out the window at the dark woods then back to the letter. Taped on the frayed page was a typed message: *I know what happened to Ellie Stone.*

Chapter 3

WHEN I FIRST OPENED that letter, my whole body trembled at the thought of some twisted, maniacal person—the same one who'd killed my best friend—taunting me about her death. My first instinct was to run and tell my dad, but then, the way it was done, a typed message on notebook paper, it made me think that it was just a stupid prank. It was probably someone from school messing with me, and I was *not* about to play some clichéd teen-horror-movie game, complete with a letter saying, *I know what you did last summer* or whatever. It wasn't worth my time or my mental space. Whoever it was, he or she wasn't worth my effort. Or maybe I was in denial. Who knows? But then, a week later, when the second came, suddenly, I wasn't so sure anymore.

"I'm going for a run," I yelled to Mom, who was clinking around in the kitchen.

She popped her head around the corner. "Right now?"

"Yeah, why?" I glanced out the front window at the low hanging clouds, rolling and anxious, in a pewter sky. "Uh, rain again," I mumbled. "Why does it have to rain so much?"

She wiped a dusting of flour from her forehead with her sleeve then shrugged. "What time do you work?"

"Not until later."

Mom squinted at the window behind me. "Looks ugly out there."

"I'll be fine," I said, checking my weather app. The storms weren't supposed to come for another couple hours.

"Tori, *please* be careful."

"I know, Mom. It's just a little rain."

But that's not what she meant. I plugged in my ear buds and headed to the foyer before she had the chance to give me the speech. "Bye, love you," I called out, pulling the door shut behind me.

Outside, the cool, late-March air was wicked, lashing my skin as I started my run down the driveway. Every single breath was agony as I tried to fall back into my old habit. Plus, I was still a little sore from my run-in with Hayes a week earlier. Crash or no crash, it was as if my body had forgotten how to move naturally, easily. Even my favorite playlist didn't work like it usually did, pushing me faster with its steady, hammering beats. Not even the thought of a chocolate glazed donut helped. Sometimes Ellie and I would stop for one as a reward. Her idea, not mine.

A mile and a half in, I popped into Dee's Donuts anyway and bought two crullers.

Then, a block down the road, I tossed them both in the trash and turned to head back home. Donuts or not, I just wasn't feeling it.

I took the same route as always, which ended at Ellie's. I'd always loved her street. The houses were bigger, the trees taller, the traffic quieter. But now, the wind was also sharper, bending tree limbs against a murky sky.

Mom texted just as I made it to Ellie's mailbox: *Where are you?*

Really? She knew *exactly* where I was, tracking my every movement on my phone. But I stopped anyway to text her back: *Heading home now.* I hit send then glanced up at Ellie's house, her dark roof blending into the sky. The last time we'd gone running, we raced from her mailbox to the top of her driveway then collapsed on her front yard, arguing who had won. I swore I had. I wouldn't let it go.

"Okay, okay, fine. You win or whatever. I'm sorry," she'd said.

Now, I couldn't remember what I'd said back to her. I leaned on her mailbox with its faded yellow sunflowers and wished we could still argue about dumb little things that had no meaning. "I'm sorry too."

K. Be careful, Mom texted. *About to storm.*

The clouds had picked up some serious speed, rolling and volatile, but the sky was still holding. I had some time. "Race you from your mailbox to mine," I whispered.

A few minutes later, and with my lungs fully on fire, I made it to the edge of my driveway just as a big fat rain drop landed on my cheek. "You win," I laughed, tagging my mailbox. Then, even though it was still too early for the mail to have run, I pulled open the rusted hinge anyway, checking out of habit. And that's when I saw it.

It was just sitting there all alone, with no stamp or postmark.

I hit pause on my playlist and glanced over my shoulder.

The street was dead quiet.

I stood there for a second, alone and exposed, suddenly feeling... like someone was watching me. I glanced over my shoulder again then reached inside for the letter. Everything about the envelope was the same as the other one, from the color to the clear label on the front addressed to me, but this one felt different. Maybe it was because *I* had found it, not my dad? And that's when I thought: What if it *wasn't* someone from school pranking me? The last one had said: *I know what happened to Ellie Stone.* I'd thought it was just a silly game, but what if it was more than that?

Something moved in the thick woods edging my house. I held my breath, waiting, watching as every hair on my body stood. "Hello?" I called into the wind, now bending the trees.

I swore I saw it move again.

But this time, I wasn't waiting around for it. I sped across the front yard with the letter in my hand and practically ran over my mom as she opened the front door for me.

"Whoa. There you are," she said, pulling me inside just as the rain unleashed. "I was starting to worry."

Sweat from my palm seeped onto the letter.

Mom glanced at it. "Is that all that came today?"

I nodded.

"Another college letter?"

"Yeah," I lied, knowing she'd have a ton of questions if I told her that no, it wasn't. She'd freak, asking me: Who sent it? Why? What do you mean this is the second one? Why didn't you tell us about the first one?

I just needed a minute to process.

She leaned in to hug me. "I know it's hard without her," she said, her warm breath tickling my face. "Oh, hon, you're shaking."

I followed her into the living room, which smelled of cinnamon and honey ham. I'd been gone less than an hour, but the whole house smelled like Thanksgiving. "What's the occasion?"

"Feel like going with me to visit Lisa today?"

My heart lurched. "Ellie's mom?"

Mom nodded.

The smells wafting from the kitchen made sense now. Sort of. It was what we did in the South. We brought casseroles with condolences, but that was usually for funerals. Ellie's had been weeks ago. I wanted to ask her *why today*, when it hit me. It was two months to the day. Ellie had died on January 25th. The letter burned in my hand.

"Tori?"

I placed the envelope on the antique hallway table, staring at its menacing label. It was too much. All of it was too much, I thought, as I pushed the letter under some old, forgotten-about mail.

"It would mean a lot to her," Mom said cautiously. "We don't have to stay long. I know you have to work later."

I rubbed my sweaty forehead, swiping a few fingers across the small scab from my near-fatal encounter with Hayes. "I don't think I can," I said, finally meeting her eyes. I hadn't been inside Ellie's house since the funeral. I'd been under her bedroom window plenty of times since, but not actually *inside* her room. The thought of seeing her room, her things in it, or facing her mom or little sister Chloe was still too hard.

She pulled me into her arms again and bent slightly to rest her chin on my head. She was a good six inches taller than my five-foot-two height. "I understand," she said, finally letting go. "Here, wrap up in this." She handed me the blanket from the back of the couch.

I draped it over my shoulders and followed her into the kitchen, where the countertop was littered with sweet potato pie, green-beans, and a plate piled high with chocolate chip cookies. "When did you make all this?"

"Been at it all morning," she said, stepping to the pantry. She looked so young with her high ponytail and paper-thin Ramones t-shirt. A few seconds later, she was back with a bag of mini marshmallows. "Put these on the sweet potatoes, will you?"

I took the bag from her and stopped at the back window, watching the trees sway. It was probably a deer that I'd seen or a neighborhood dog. Nothing more than that. I turned back around and jumped as a loud pop of thunder rattled the house.

"You made it back just in time," Mom said.

"Yeah. Is it supposed to rain all day?"

She glanced at her phone on the counter, reading a text that had popped onto the screen. She started typing. "Hold on, hon." After she hit send, she swiped a few strands of caramel highlights from her face. "Sorry, what?"

"If it's supposed to storm all day, can I take the car to work?"

"What time do you go in?" she asked.

"In about an hour."

"Why don't I just drop you off on my way to Lisa's?" Her phone dinged again and she looked at it, smiling at the screen.

Could she be any more obvious? I thought as I tossed white puffs onto the casserole.

I'd seen a few texts here and there from her co-worker, Will. I pictured him with his expensive salon haircut and checkered collared shirt. That toothy grin in the photo that popped up every time he called my mom with a "work" thing. I hated that photo. And his stupid white teeth. And how he made my mom smile and act like a silly girl.

She silenced her phone then slipped it into her purse on the counter. "You off tomorrow?"

"Yeah, I told Drew I'd go fishing with him."

"That sounds nice."

I grabbed the aluminum foil from the drawer and rolled out a long piece to cover the cookies on the counter. The tiny, metal teeth on the edges of the box caught the edge of my finger mid tear. I cussed under my breath at the row of blood bubbles surfacing.

"Here, let me see." Mom reached for my hand, but I snatched it away before she had the chance to inspect it.

"I'm fine. It's nothing," I said, sucking at the wound.

Mom held my stare.

"What?" I asked.

"Nothing, Tori." She shook her head. "Why don't you go and get ready while I finish up here?" She put the casserole back in the top oven to brown the marshmallows as I headed upstairs.

No matter what I did, I couldn't knock the cold from my

bones. I took a hot shower and even put on winter clothes. But the letter, sent two months to the day, had made me sick. Literally, sick to my stomach. And now I had two letters. Who would do something like that? And why two months to the day? I thought about going back downstairs to talk to my mom about it all—the letters and the feeling that someone had been in the woods watching me—but she'd seemed so distracted with cooking and with Will. Besides, why worry her any more than I had to right now? I needed to talk to Dad first.

When are you going to be home? I texted him.

Not until late. Why?

No reason.

It was too much to put into a text. It would just have to wait until we were both at home. In the meantime, I'd check the door-cam app. Maybe it had caught someone lurking in the yard. The only problem was that I didn't remember the password. I started to ask Dad when my phone dinged again. This time it was Drew.

Come over later? he asked. *Parents are out of town.*

My stomach lurched. *Thought that was next week,* I wrote back.

Nope. This weekend. Come on, T. We need this.

I sat down at my vanity, shocked by how pale I looked. Even a few swipes of blush didn't help much. I hardly recognized the sad, gaunt girl looking back at me. I bit my bottom lip, tasting my fruity wax lip balm and thinking about being alone with him, just the two of us, at his house, in his room. We'd been talking about taking things to the next level for a while, but that was *before*. He was only trying to get us back on track, back to where we were... before Ellie died. But was *this* the best way? I took a deep breath. Could his timing be any worse? The cursor kept blinking at me: *We need this,* he'd said.

What I needed more than anything was something he couldn't give me: Answers about who was sending me those letters. Closure about who had killed my best friend. Peace about her being gone from my life forever. But I didn't want to lose him either. The last thing I wanted was to be all alone—no best friend. No boyfriend. *I'll text you after work,* I wrote.

I headed back downstairs.

Can't wait, he wrote as I landed on the bottom step.

"Ready?" Mom asked, breezing inside from the garage.

"I'm not sure."

She stopped mid-stride and stared at me. "What do you mean?" She felt my head. "Did you eat anything today? Anything at all?"

I shrugged, picturing the two donuts in the trashcan in town. After it first happened, I stopped eating. It wasn't on purpose. I couldn't feel anything, not even hunger. But then, after the numbing shock had worn off, every inch of my body hurt. That constant, deep ache in my gut, well, it was hard to tell if it was for food or for wanting my best friend back. But when my clothes started falling off me, Mom had started force-feeding me like I was a toddler.

"I'm fine," I told her.

She pulled a protein shake from the fridge. "Here," she said, handing it to me. "Drink this."

Right. Like a chalky, artificially flavored drink was going to make everything better. She waited for me to take a sip, then smiled after I swallowed. "Happy?"

"Yes, you make me very happy." She grabbed the sweet potatoes from the counter then swept by me. "What time do I need to pick you up?"

I followed her into the garage. "Drew's picking me up." I pressed my lips together, debating just how much to add.

She put the casserole on the back floorboard and ran back inside one more time.

As I got into the car, my stomach clenched at the sight of Ellie's seafoam bicycle, still propped against Dad's workout bench where she'd parked it that day—the last day I ever saw her. Her bike hadn't moved since. The flaking white wicker basket still had that one loose loop. She used to mess with it, tucking the strand back into place just to watch it unravel as she pedaled against the wind. I hadn't been able to return the bike to her house. Mom had said more than once, "All in good time."

Mom hopped in the car and handed me a huge plate of honey ham, still warm on the bottom. As she turned on the engine, my body tensed. Smells of cinnamon and honey collided with exhaust fumes, making me nauseous.

"Tori?" Mom placed her hand on my arm.

I kept my eyes focused on the dash. "Yeah?"

"If you're not feeling well, you can call in."

"No, it's okay. Probably the shake not sitting right."

As she eased down the driveway, my mind went from Drew back to the letter. It was still sitting there on the hall table with its menacing *I know who did it* taunts.

As we drove off, I watched our two-story house getting soaked by the rain. The historic colonial had seen better days, that was for sure, but it was still one of the prettiest homes on my street with its white columns and old gray stone. Plus, it still had all of its people—for the most part anyway—unlike Ellie's house.

Chapter 4

AT WORK, I PUT on my brave face, smiling while taking orders, running sweet teas and paninis to tables, and then bussing dirty dishes only to do it all over again. But I could handle busy. It was the quiet, slow times that were the hardest. I was just thankful no one asked me about Ellie. I wouldn't have been able to handle it with it being two months to the day on top of getting two sick letters and dealing with sparring parents and a boyfriend who was growing more impatient by the minute.

When the dinner rush died down, my mind started racing, especially with XM radio spitting out song after song about "wanting to hold you all night" or "needing all of you right now."

"What's with the music?" I asked Piper, who was helping me clear my table. She'd started at Blue's a few weeks ago, mostly filling in for me.

"Why? What's wrong with it?" She tucked a strand of her platinum blonde hair behind her ear then blinked. Her long lashes caught on her pink-tinted bangs.

"Every song is about—"

"Don't look now," Piper interrupted. "But your little creeper is here." She widened her eyes for dramatics. "Least he's with his cute brother."

My heart plummeted to my stomach as I peeked over my shoulder, spotting Nick and his brother Hayes up front.

"Nice video by the way," Piper added.

"Guess everyone's seen it by now."

"It's not that bad."

"Yeah, right."

Piper shrugged. "Could be worse. Hey, I'll put them at one of my tables, 'kay?"

"You sure?" I asked.

"Yeah, his mom is a good tipper."

"Thanks." As Piper went over to seat them, I stole another glance. They were standing at the front counter with their posh mom, AKA my therapist Dr. Moore. Nerves rushed through my body at the sight of Hayes. Hadn't he always had that effect on me? But seeing him now, standing there in that electric blue t-shirt, made me think of Drew—and how maybe the butterflies in my belly should've been for him instead of Hayes. I grabbed my tray of dirty dishes and headed to the back, slamming right into my manager, Mark, coming out of the kitchen.

"Whoa, whoa, slow down," he said, looking down at the blob of broccoli and cheese soup that had landed on his white shirt.

"Crap! I'm so sorry."

"Want to go home early?"

"Because I ruined your shirt?"

Mark snorted out a laugh. "No, no. Dinner rush is over." He grabbed a napkin from my tray and dabbed at the spot of yellow on his chest.

"But it's my night to close."

"Piper asked for extra hours."

My phone buzzed in my apron pocket. Drew. It had to be him, saying, *You're still coming over, babe, right?* Mark shifted his weight, waiting for my answer.

"Yeah, okay," I said.

"Good deal."

Was it good? I wished, more than anything, I could talk to Ellie. She always knew what to do. What I wouldn't give to steal a minute with her in the walk-in freezer and ask her, "Should I go to Drew's? Will it make everything better between us?"

"Make sure to restock the serving station before you clock out," he said.

"Got it," I said, rubbing my aching head. I hated my brain, how it never shut off.

Mark nodded then turned toward his office.

After he was out of sight, I plugged in an earbud and scrolled through my phone for a chill radio playlist. I'd had all the country pop I could take for one night. It didn't take long to fall into a perfect rhythm with the music, rolling silverware to the slow, steady electronic beat. But as it played, it suddenly felt familiar, more like a past moment and not just a song I'd heard before. I closed my eyes, trying to remember where I'd heard it before.

As the song hit the chorus, it came back to me in one sharp, swift flash.

It was the night of Sam's party at White Pines Farm. There were so many of us there, dancing by the bonfire. I could see Ellie moving to those same beats, her hair glowing in the firelight... the music was so loud, pulsing through our bodies as we danced with our hands in the air.

But then suddenly, something changed.

We weren't dancing by the fire anymore.

We were at the river. No one went to the river at night. Most people in Waterford were spooked by it, so why were we there? And why was Ellie reaching out for my hand. Why was she *in* the water, calling out for me?

I gasped, opening my eyes.

It wasn't possible. My heart raced like mad.

Ellie and I hadn't gone to the river together that night. I'd gone home early.

"Hello?" Mark said.

I jumped, taking out my earbud. "Sorry. What?"

"Need you to refill these," he said, pointing to the tray of empty sugar caddies he'd just placed on the counter. "And sweep the breakroom too before you go."

I nodded. "Yeah, of course."

My whole body trembled.

"Are you okay?" Mark asked.

"Yeah, all good," I lied while trying to blink away the image of Ellie's pale face in the moonlight against a blue-black river. The last time I'd seen her the night she died, or so I'd thought, was at the bonfire in a haze of oranges and reds, not in the dark by the water. Something wasn't right. Had I gone back to the party that night? Surely someone would have seen me.

Then it hit me—the first letter had said: *I know what happened to Ellie Stone.* What if...

"I'm so ready to get out of here," Piper said, breezing past me in the kitchen.

"Yeah, me too." Could she see me shaking? Feel my anxious energy?

"Not sure I have the energy for your table."

"What do you mean?" I leaned to the side and peeked out

at the dining room at Hayes, who was on his phone. I touched the scab on my temple.

"*She* wants a vanilla latte, decaf, extra foam with soy milk. Nick wants a cookies-and-cream milkshake, extra cookies on top, and Hayes wants a tropical smoothie."

"I can help. I'll make the latte."

"Bless you," Piper said.

As the espresso machine hissed, I sifted through nearly a dozen articles in my brain, trying to remember some detail I'd missed. I'd read them all a hundred times before. They all said the same thing. Girl found at the river. Blue flowers. Cause of death not released. What was I expecting to remember? Some clue that put me there, down by the river, that night?

But thirty minutes later, I was still no closer to understanding why I'd seen what I had.

Are you off work? Drew texted.

I stared at it. The burn in my throat worsened.

"Not now, Drew," I whispered under my breath. It wasn't that I didn't want to be with him, because I did, but as I typed the words, *yes, I'm off,* it finally made sense. Something was definitely "off" with me. Why was I suddenly remembering being at the river when I knew without a doubt that I hadn't gone there that night?

K. Leaving the house now.

I took a deep breath. Maybe I just needed to talk to Drew about it. He was, after all, the one who drove me home that night. Maybe I needed to tell him *everything* from the guilt I was carrying to getting the letters to remembering this strange new scene in my head. Even if things had been different between us lately, I still loved him. I trusted him. And before we could take things to the "next level," I needed to get out of my own head. I texted: *See you in a few* and then closed my eyes, trying to calm my nerves. All I could see was Ellie. There was no way I'd left the bonfire and gone back that night, was there? No way I'd been with her at the river. I would have had mud on my shoes or something. Someone would have seen me coming out of the woods. I took a long deep breath. I needed to open that second letter and see what it said. But it would have to be later. For now, I had to get it together.

I shook it off and headed to the front, slowly sipping my cherry Coke as the sweet syrup clashed with my now stale mint gum.

"Hey, Tori." Nick said, standing at the front counter with his tall, imposing mom. Hayes was still sitting in the booth with his nose in his phone, probably texting Rachel or avoiding me. Maybe both.

"Hey," I said, waving at Nick.

"Sorry about my brother almost running you over."

Dr. Moore glanced up at me.

"It was just a scratch. Besides, I didn't look before crossing."

Dr. Moore handed Piper her credit card. "Still," she said to me, "I'm sorry it happened."

"Thanks."

Nick stepped closer. "Are you going to the conference in a couple weeks?"

I pressed my lips together. "Conference?"

"Yeah, the Young Leaders conference? Miss Taylor said you were on the list at the last meeting."

I hadn't been to a club meeting in weeks. The debate team had always been more of Ellie's thing, not mine. "Don't think so."

"You should go," Nick said, adjusting his glasses on his nose.

"Yeah, you should," Piper said.

"Are you going?" I asked her.

"Yep."

Nick's mom looked up from her purse. I practically could hear her now: *How could you pass up such a great opportunity? And it's in Washington DC for crying out loud!* And what would she think about me and Drew? *You know, Tori,* she'd say, her warm but distant eyes looming over the top of her glasses, *sounds as if you're avoiding something. Are you? Why do you think that is?*

Dr. Moore smiled at me as she placed her hand on her son's arm. "Ready, Nick?"

Whatever. What did she know?

"You really should go," he added.

"Yeah, I'll think about it." I smiled at Dr. Moore.

"Hayes?" she called. "Ready?"

Hayes looked up from his phone, catching me full-on staring at him. He nodded at me, making my face flush with heat again as he eased out of the booth. Flashes of him dabbing his sweatshirt on my cut, his face so close to mine, and of him taking my playground offerings of Rice Krispies Treats and gummy worms all rhapsodized in my head.

"Hello?" Piper said, nudging the back of my arm.

"Yeah?" I asked.

"Um," she said, pointing out the window. "Your ride is here."

Right. My ride.

Chapter 5

THE PARKING LOT WAS dim, lit partially by one street light. I stood at the café door, watching as Hayes crossed the sparse lot toward his Lexus. A few seconds later, I headed outside toward Drew's truck, parked on the other side of the building. My fingers tingled, thinking about gummy worms and see-saws and innocent games of hide and seek. My face flushed again at the thought of being *that girl*, chasing the boy on the school playground.

"Hey," Drew said as I hopped into his red pick-up.

"Hi," I said, eyeing Hayes behind the wheel of his Lexus. His mom was in the passenger seat up front and Nick was in the back.

Drew followed my gaze across the parking lot. "How was work?"

"Fine."

He slipped his hand under my hair. "Missed you."

I inhaled slowly with my eyes still on the Lexus. *What were they waiting for?*

"Hello?" Drew said.

"Hmm?"

"You're a million miles away."

The Lexus *still* hadn't moved.

Drew eased back in his seat, looking from me to the Lexus again. "Something wrong?"

Yes, everything. "No, not really."

The headlights on the Lexus flipped on. Then, finally, it started to move.

"What's going on with you?" Drew asked. It almost sounded accusing. Only almost.

"Long day, that's all."

Drew nodded.

I turned to face Drew. "Nick asked if I was going to the conference."

"What conference?"

"The one Ellie and I were supposed to go to?"

He nodded, but from his blank stare, it was pretty obvious that he had no clue what I was talking about.

"It's also been two months… two months to the day."

He blinked his long lashes, fringed over dark green eyes. "I'm sorry, T." He pulled me in close and ran his fingers up the nape of my neck to the side of my face. We sat there for a while in the parking lot, my head on his shoulder as the heat hummed softly through the vents.

After a minute, he leaned in to kiss me, softly. I closed my eyes and tasted red cherry gummies, not the stale gum lodged under my tongue. As he kissed me, my chest tightened and my ears started to ring. I couldn't breathe. "Stop, Drew. I can't—"

He pulled back. His confusion was illuminated by the glowing dash.

"I'm just so tired."

He rubbed a hand over his mouth. We'd been here before. Too many times to count. He nodded and gave me a tight-lipped smile. He was disappointed and frustrated with me. Again. He put the car in drive and headed toward my house, not his, like we'd planned.

On the way, the nagging feeling inside wouldn't go away. I wanted to go back to playgrounds and gummy worms, to when things were simple and the biggest heartbreak I'd ever felt was over an unrequited crush—not the death of my best friend. Ellie's reflection stared back at me in the passenger side window. I wanted her face out of my head. I wanted her bike out of my garage. And more than anything, I wanted the massive, two-ton boulder I'd been carrying around for weeks out of my gut. I wanted to feel the way I had *before* she'd died, when everything was elementary. Normal.

"Wait," I whispered, as Drew navigated the back roads. "We can go to your house."

"Yeah?" He reached for my hand and squeezed my sweaty palm. "You sure?"

Maybe going to his house would make me feel better and not so alone and in my own head. I moved closer to him, nearly knocking the gear shift with my knee, and breathed in the clean, Irish Spring scent of his skin. "Yeah, I'm sure."

A few minutes later, we pulled into his driveway. My legs shook as I followed him to the back door and then inside, to the dim living room. It felt smaller this time, somehow.

"I messed up," he said, pulling me into his arms.

"What do you mean?" I whispered against his chest.

He inhaled. "I…"

I inched back and met his eyes. "You what?" I waited for his answer in the heavy, growing silence between us.

"I—I should have lit some candles or something. Put rose petals on the bed?"

Rose petals? I didn't want rose petals. My throat went dry, making it hard to swallow. "It's fine," I whispered, following him to his room, which had dirty clothes strewn on the floor and his rock lava lamp glowing on his nightstand. I sat on the edge of the bed as he turned on some music.

He sat down beside me then leaned into me, easing me back on the bed. Even though he'd said it a hundred times before, I waited for him in the warm glow of his room to say it again. I needed to hear those words, to feel the gravity of them, like a confession being offered for the first time. I fought the tears forming in my throat and held my breath, waiting.

When he finally said it, "I love you," my body tensed up more, not less. The words felt empty somehow. I slowly pushed him away, again, both palms against his chest, and for a few seconds, my hands fell in sync with his breathing, moving up and down like a machine. "I can't do this," I said, sitting up.

He sighed, rolling over and throwing his arm over his eyes.

"Doesn't it bother you that we don't talk anymore?" I asked.

He sat up slowly. "Yeah, of course it does, but I've tried talking to you. I've tried giving you space. I've tried everything, Tori. I don't know what you want."

What I *wanted* was to feel like I could tell him anything.

He stroked my shoulder, brushing away a few strands of hair that had fallen loose from my clip. "Talk to me, T."

My eyes started welling with tears. "The night of Sam's party," I said, staring straight ahead at the door, "you took me straight home, right?"

"Yeah. You said you weren't feeling good and you asked me to take you home. Why?"

"Did we go down to the river at all?"

"No."

"Are you sure?"

That night had been so hazy. Dr. Moore had told me that sometimes people block traumatic events from their memory. It made sense, kind of, but even back then, I'd had a sinking feeling there'd been more to it, like maybe someone had slipped me something.

"What's this about, Tori?"

"I don't know."

"Hey," he said, moving to kneel in front of me. "You can talk to me."

I took a deep breath, nodding. I was trying. Really trying.

"Tori?"

"I had a memory about that night, about being at the river with her."

He bit his lower lip. "But you weren't there... at the river."

I stared into his eyes, looking for something in them to ease the hurt in my own soul. But it wasn't there. Not anymore. Maybe it never had been. "I'm sorry, Drew. I just can't do this. I thought I could, but I can't." I stood, stepping away from him.

"Wait," he said, jumping to his feet.

"Everything is just too complicated."

"It doesn't have to be. That's what I've been saying."

He reached for me and pulled me back into his warm chest. We stood there for a while, but I knew it was over. Really over. My throat ached as I tried fighting back the tears, but it was no use. I sobbed into his shirt, afraid of letting him go even though I was the one pushing *him* away, not the other way around. "I should go," I said, quietly.

He held onto my fingers. Slowly, my hand slipped out of his. A whole year together and just like that, it was over. "I just need some time... on my own... to deal with things, okay?"

"Don't do this, T. Come on." He ran his fingers through his messy hair.

I used to swoon over those dirty-blond waves, his eyes, his lips, his everything.

"We've been together for over a year."

"I know," I said.

"And you just want to end it? Now? I don't get it." He rubbed his eye with the heel of his hand.

"I'm sorry."

"Sorry? That's it? You're sorry?" He stepped back, shaking his head. "What did I do wrong?"

"Nothing." I stopped short of saying the whole "it's-not-you-but-me" spiel. "I told you. I just need time." I needed space without him always there, texting, calling, pressuring me to be something I couldn't be for him.

He shrugged. "Well, guess that's it. A whole year and that's it. Done."

"We can still be—"

"Don't say it." He grabbed his keys on the nightstand. "Ready?" he asked, avoiding even looking at me.

"I can walk."

"No way."

Our eyes met.

"Not with some sicko still out there."

My mind flew to the letter in my mailbox. To the something in my woods.

"We might be breaking up," he said, "but I'm not letting you walk home by yourself."

His words made my heart rip apart even more. Was I being selfish, breaking things off now? After he'd been there for me all this time? "Drew?"

He glanced down at the floor.

"I'm sorry." I didn't know what else to say. I rushed over to him and placed my hands on his soft face, pulling him in closer to me... closer and closer until our lips met. He kissed me like he did our first time, a nervous rush that sent fire through my whole body. But it wasn't enough anymore. It just wasn't enough. "I'm sorry," I whispered again, stepping backwards.

"Me too."

He followed me to the back door, pulling me close again. "I don't want to let you go," he whispered.

I didn't look up at him. I couldn't. I was too afraid I'd change my mind.

We stood there a couple more minutes, neither of us letting go, until finally he did. "You ready?"

"I'll walk."

"Tori—"

"I'll be fine. It's literally a five-minute walk. I just need to be alone and clear my head."

"Then I won't say a word. Please? Let me go with you."

"Fine."

As we crossed the street in silence, immense guilt pressed down on me, making it difficult to breathe much less walk the few blocks to my house. I wasn't afraid though. For the first time in weeks, I wasn't afraid of being alone. "I got it from here."

"But—"

"Drew, I can literally see my house from here." I lifted onto my toes and hugged him, breathing him in one last time. "Thanks for... you know."

He nodded. "Yeah, I know."

Even though we both knew it was for the best, walking away from him was harder than I'd expected. It was like that fear of being alone had been replaced, for the moment anyway, with a different kind of fear—the kind rooted in regret. What if I'd just given up the best thing to ever happen to me? I didn't look back. I just kept running forward.

The wind stung my naked arms as I sped through the neighborhood, dodging puddles from the earlier rain. What had I been thinking, saying yes, then saying no? I shielded my eyes as a vehicle with its high beams rounded the corner. I jumped onto the shoulder to let the car pass, and as it did, it spewed a tidal wave of dirty water right in my face. The universe hated me. It had to.

I brushed myself off, wiping wet strands of hair from my face, then flinched at the sight in front of me. I'd been on autopilot, heading, like I had for years, to Ellie's house, not mine. Her light was on in her room, just like it had been every night since it had happened. It was almost as if her mom kept it on, hoping she'd walk through the door any minute, yelling, "I'm home!" But she wasn't coming home. Ever. And somebody out there knew why.

Part Two: Piper

Chapter 6

AS I GOT INTO Dad's old Volvo, I breathed in the faint smell of cologne trapped in faded leather. I liked how it still smelled like him, like he was right there in the car with me. I cranked the diesel engine and sat there for a few minutes, listening to one of his old Lemonheads CDs. I wished more than anything I could go home and see him in his chair with his round reading glasses perched on the tip of his nose. "Heya, Pippa," he'd say. *Heya, Pop.*

Cancer sucked.

I turned up the music and eased out of the near-empty parking lot. The only car left was Mark's old Jeep parked at the back of the building. I liked that about working at the cafe. We closed earlier than most of the restaurants in Waterford. Most days, we were out of there by seven.

But that also meant going home earlier than I liked. So, instead of turning right toward my house, I took a left to cruise through town for a bit, still listening to my dad's CDs as rain splattered against the windshield. It had been raining on and off all day, just enough to fill the lovely potholes our grand city had to offer. It seemed as though I hit every single one of them while weaving along the back streets. I actually hit one so hard that water slapped against my windshield, momentarily blinding me. It was a miracle I didn't hit the curb. I thought I'd lost a tire or killed an axel or something—it was *that* major. The last thing I needed was Mama getting on me for something else I'd done wrong. I pulled off to the side of the road and got out to check the damage.

"I can't believe this!" someone shouted.

I turned around, squinting in the dark at the petite figure

walking toward me on the sidewalk. "Tori?"

She stepped closer. "Yeah. Thanks a lot." She swiped at the matted strands of hair slicked against her cheek. Her light blue t-shirt was almost see-through, hanging on her pointy shoulders. She looked like a drenched chihuahua, standing there in the street, small and shaking.

"I am so sorry. I didn't see you. I swear."

"What are you doing on this street? You live across town," she asked.

I wanted to ask what *she* was doing on the street. Alone. "I thought you were with Drew." I shivered as a chill ran down my spine.

Tori shivered too as the wind kicked up a notch. "He went home." She rubbed her eye, smearing mascara under it.

"And he just left you out here?"

She wrapped her arms around her body and rubbed at her arms, trying to generate warmth. "I'm fine." Her teeth chattered in protest. "I li—live around the corner."

"I know where you live. Come on—get in. You're going to freeze to death."

She nodded.

I had a jacket in the backseat that I handed to her as she got in the passenger side. I also turned the heat up on high. "I feel really bad, Tori."

"It's okay," she said over the Lemonheads. She leaned her head back, burrowing under the jacket, and closed her eyes.

"Did you and Drew have a fight?"

She bit her lip and shrugged. "I like this song," she finally said.

"It's called 'Into Your Arms' by the Lemonheads."

"Never heard of them," she said, her eyes still closed. "Do you think maybe we could drive around for a while?" She peeked through one eye, zeroing in on the big house to her right flanked by tall evergreens. "Don't feel like going home just yet."

"Me neither." It was still early, not even eight yet.

We drove around the block then got back onto Main Street. I had no idea where we were going. Didn't really care. It was just nice hanging out and listening to good tunes with her like old times. We passed by the courthouse and the high school and all five of the fast-food restaurants in our town. At the end of Main, I stopped. "Where to?"

"Take a left."

I nodded, turning onto the old highway leading out of town. My dad and I used to take Sunday drives on that old road. We'd roll down the windows and sing at the top of our lungs. Sometimes Mama and my older brother, Wyatt, would go, but mostly it was just Dad and me.

"Thanks for driving me around," Tori said, tousling her wet hair in the vent, still blowing heat.

"Yeah, of course." I'd always thought she was pretty with her huge brown eyes and those long, thick lashes that looked almost fake. But what made her so pretty was that she didn't even realize she was. One thing for sure was that she was way too good for Drew. A thousand times too good. I wanted to ask her more about what happened with him, but I didn't want to push it either. Not yet. We weren't close like we used to be, which had been her choice, not mine.

"Hey," she said. "Take a right up here, will you?"

"Why?" I asked, staring at the exit sign with symbols for camping and RV parking.

She pressed her hand against her window. "Please?"

I turned on my blinker.

"Then take a left at the stop sign," she said.

My heart dropped. I knew *exactly* where she wanted to go. To the river. "Um, I don't think that's a good idea."

She didn't say anything. She just stared straight ahead.

"I'm not so sure about this, Tori." I idled at the stop sign, checking my rearview mirror. No one was behind me.

"I think I need to," she said. "My head is so messed up right now. I need clarity or whatever."

"And you think going to the river will give you clarity? What if we get killed instead?"

She turned and faced me, wide-eyed. "I just... need to go out there. I need perspective."

"Perspective?" My heart thudded in my chest.

"Yeah, about everything that's happened. It's like I don't know who I am anymore... without her."

I slowly inhaled as we sat there, still idling at the stop sign. "Piper?"

"Yeah?"

"I'm horrible," she whispered over the quiet rumble of the engine.

"Why would you say that?"

"I left Ellie that night. The night of Sam's party. I just left her."

I eased back in my seat. This was about closure for her. She never got the chance to say good-bye to Ellie. If anyone understood that pain, I did. I still sat in my dad's well-worn recliner, still breathed in the fabric of his favorite sweater, still listened to his old CDs, wishing he were still here. Wishing I could have said good-bye, but instead he died in the hospital in the middle of the night, all alone.

I slowly pressed on the gas and took a left, winding down the dark road to the river.

A few minutes later, we pulled into a small lot. Straight ahead was a forest of thick, lush green trees. Just beyond it was the river. "You're sure you want to do this?" I asked, hoping she'd say "No, I changed my mind. It's too creepy."

She nodded.

Neither of us said anything as we stepped out of the car, making our way down the muddy path using the flashlights on our phones to light the way. I followed, staying a few feet behind as she headed to the water's edge where she stood on the bank, staring out at its silvery skim. The rain had cleared and the moon was just bright enough to see without our flashlights. Funny thing was, I wasn't as freaked out as I thought I'd be.

"She's everywhere," Tori said. "It's like she's in the air and in the water. I can feel her all around me, can't you?"

I rubbed my arms, chilled in the wind coming off the river. My thin zip-up wasn't doing much to fight off the fierce cold. "Tori?" I whispered. She had to be freezing in her damp clothes, even under the jacket I'd given her.

She nodded, staring straight ahead.

"Are you okay?" I asked, searching her distant eyes.

The wind shrieked as it sliced across the water. She reached for her hood and pulled it over her head. "I'm not sure," she said, stepping over to a slick log, a fallen tree, lodged in the riverbank.

I followed her, looking over my shoulder every few steps.

"You know," she said, sitting on the flaked bark, "ever since I was a little kid, I've heard people talk about the river curse—

the Waterford legend. Do you believe it?"

I sat down beside Tori and rubbed my arms. On one hand, yes, I believed it with its shrieking winds and deaths, plural. But on the other hand, it was hard to believe something so beautiful could be cursed. The way the moon danced on the water's surface in that moment—it felt peaceful, not menacing or evil.

"Do you?" she asked again.

"My nana thinks it is." I'd heard the stories, too, over the years about the mysterious deaths down by the river. "She told me a few times that the river feeds on people's weaknesses. That it pulls out the darkness in people and makes them act on their true desires."

Tori shook her head. "How exactly does a thing, a place, make someone do something? It doesn't make any logical sense."

"Right?" I let out a breathy laugh.

"Sounds like people passing down ghost stories."

"Yeah, maybe, but she has this album full of newspaper clippings about people who disappeared or died out here," I said.

The wind shrieked again over the water, making both of us flinch.

My body started to tremble from the cold… from the ghosts in the water.

Tori reached for my hand and held it tightly. "Sometimes, at night," she said softly and never taking her eyes off the water, "I lie awake thinking about it. I can't get the image of her out of my head, of her dancing by the bonfire. I still can't believe she's gone, you know?"

"Yeah." It *was* hard to believe Ellie was gone. Even though she and I hadn't been close for a while, it was still strange knowing we'd never see her again. Ellie had always just been there—in the center of it all. But I didn't know what else to say, so I just stayed quiet and let Tori have her time to process. I didn't want to rush her, even though I hated every second of being out there, cursed or not. It still felt like the skin was about to crawl right off my back, the longer we lingered.

"I don't know what to believe anymore," she whispered. She pulled her hand back and used the heel of her palm to wipe her eyes.

We sat there for a few more minutes, both of us staring out

at the black water.

"Come on," she finally said, not a second too soon. "Let's get out of here."

I grabbed a fistful of cold, wet sand and stood, scattering small clumps of it along the water's edge. Off in the distance was a weathered sign posted at the edge of the tree line. I moved toward it, shining my flashlight on it and squinting to make out the words. It said:

KEEP OUT: PRIVATE PROPERTY
White Pines Family Farm

The wind suddenly picked up, rumbling through the trees behind the sign. As we walked back to the car, I could've sworn that I heard Ellie's voice or someone's voice, calling out from beyond the pines from the river.

Chapter 7

"**WANT TO COME IN** for a while?" Tori asked as I pulled into her driveway.

Honestly, I was pretty frazzled after that impromptu trip to the river, so the last thing I wanted was to be alone. I was a little surprised, though, that she asked me to come in. I hadn't been to her house in over a year. "Yeah, okay."

She fumbled with her keys under the yellow porch light, shivering as she fought with the lock. "It's stuck," she said, lifting her finger to the doorbell. But then, she stopped and just stared at it.

"What's the matter?"

Her slender finger hovered over the door cam's tiny black lens. "Nothing," she said, quickly glancing over her shoulder to the dark street.

"You sure?"

She nodded and shimmied her key in the lock. This time, it worked.

"Tori, is that you?" her mom called as we walked into the mercifully warm, if dark house.

"Yeah." She grabbed an afghan from the back of the couch and wrapped it around her shoulders. "Hold on. Let me go talk to her a sec," she said.

I could hear them talking, low murmurs echoing from down the hall. A few minutes later, she was back.

"Is it okay that I'm here?"

"Yeah, of course. She's just watching TV in her room. Want something to drink?"

"Sure."

I followed her into the kitchen, taking a seat at the counter as she started rifling through the fridge. "Want a bottle of water, soda...how about something warm?" She closed the fridge and stepped over to the counter, pointing to the Keurig. "Hot chocolate?"

"Yeah, sounds good."

She opened a drawer and grabbed two K-Cups.

As the first cup brewed, she tapped her fingers on the counter. Her lips were pressed tightly shut. She was deep in thought, like she had been the whole way home.

"You know," I said, second-guessing the invitation to come in. "I should probably go. It's been a long day."

"No, you don't have to. I'm sorry I'm being so weird. It's almost like I've forgotten how to be... normal."

If anyone got it, I did. "I was like that too," I said, over the hiss of the machine, "when my dad died. After it happened, I shut everyone out."

She glanced up at me with those huge eyes of hers.

"I'm not saying that's what you're doing."

She handed me my cup then popped in the next K-Cup. "It kind of is. I broke up with Drew tonight."

I nodded slowly, figuring something had happened.

But then, it sank in. She'd said that she had broken up with him. *Good for you, Tori.* I wanted to tell her that I was proud of her for not being afraid to stand on her own, especially during such a tough time. But is that what Ellie would have said? Probably not.

"I've been totally shutting him out. But every time I tried talking to him about Ellie or the guilt I was carrying, it was like he was trying to dismiss it. Like everything was going to be okay, that it wasn't my fault even though it was. I left Ellie that night, and that's on me. And it will be forever." She pressed her fingertips to her temples and squeezed her eyes shut. "Forever," she whispered.

I sipped my hot chocolate and stayed quiet. Obviously, she needed a sounding board. But where was she when I needed one?

"And then," she said, lowering her voice. "I got some sick letter in the mail last week. You'd think he'd be the first person I'd tell, but I didn't."

"Letter?" I whispered.

"Yeah. At first, I thought it was just a prank, someone messing with me."

"What did it say?"

"'I know what happened to Ellie Stone.'"

The hairs on the back of my neck prickled. "Oh." I shuddered. "What did your dad say?"

"I didn't tell him. Or my mom. I haven't told anyone."

Then why the heck was she telling me? And why didn't she tell her own dad—a cop? I opened my mouth to ask, but she interjected as if she'd heard my thoughts.

"I'm not even sure why I'm telling you." She fanned her face. "Except you were always such a good listener..."

If anything, I was that.

"And you won't tell anyone, right?"

I shook my head. "Of course not. Promise, I won't."

"I guess... I don't know... I mean, I'm going to tell my dad for sure, but..."

"But why didn't you tell Drew?" Because he's all about himself?

She shrugged. "Hold on," she said, stepping toward the living room. A few seconds later, she came back holding an envelope in her hand. She glanced over her shoulder toward her mom's room then said, "Let's go upstairs." She tucked the letter in her back pocket and left her hot cocoa, steaming, under the Keurig.

Upstairs in her room, she flipped on her bedside lamp and closed her door. Under the lamp was a picture of her and Ellie, smiling for the camera. It stung a little to see them together like that. How many pictures had we taken together, the three us during freshman and part of sophomore year when I used to be a part of their group?

"That was the last picture we took together," she said, reaching for the frame. "It was the day of."

They'd taken a selfie, the two of them smiling ear to ear. A glimpse of Ellie's seafoam bike was in the background.

"She rode her bike to my house that morning, like she had a thousand times. It's still in my garage," Tori said.

I shook my head, sitting down next to her on the bed.

"Did you go that night? To Sam's party?"

"No."

She nodded. "I don't remember a whole lot about it."

Suddenly, her big brown eyes glossed over. She blinked a few times then wiped the tears away with the back of her hand.

"What is it?" I asked her.

"I think, maybe, someone at the party might have... roofied me."

It knocked the wind out of me. "Oh my gosh, Tori. That's horrible. Why—why do you think that?"

"Because after getting to the party, everything became a blur. I told the detectives that a few days later, when they called all of us down to the station."

"And what did they say?"

"That we could do a urine test to confirm, but depending on the type of drug, it was probably too late for detection. They said some drugs only stayed in the system for eight to ten hours. I figured, by that point, I'd waited too long."

Again, I was surprised, floored, by how easily she was opening up to me. But like she'd said, I'd always been a good listener, and I'd never given her a reason not to trust me. Plus, we had been close, once upon a time.

Tori let out a hefty sigh. "If only I'd stayed, you know? Then again, I don't remember much about leaving or getting home. I just remember thinking that Ellie was safe with her boyfriend." She put the frame back on the nightstand.

"I'm sorry, Tori."

She seemed so small and broken as she pulled the letter from her back pocket and placed it on her lap.

I stared at it, not sure what to say, if anything.

"It's a new one," she said, eyes still fixed on it. "It came this morning." She rubbed her right eye.

"There's more than one?"

She took a long, deep breath then reached for the letter, picking at the flap and tearing at it little by little. Slowly, she pulled a frayed piece of paper from the envelope and unfolded it, reading the words out loud: "I know the person who did it. So do you."

My breath caught.

She crumpled the letter into a little ball and threw it across the room. It landed by her dresser.

Nerves raced through my entire body. It was all too much—first, going to the river and now this, hearing about the letters. "Who's doing this?"

"I don't know. It just showed up in my mailbox like the other one."

I stood and started pacing her carpeted floor.

"But," she said, "I might know how to find out."

I lowered my eyes to meet hers.

She blinked nervously, then reached for her laptop at the foot of her bed. "Door cam footage," Tori said. "I was going to check it before work, but I couldn't remember the password."

"And you remember it now?"

"Yep. Guess my brain wasn't working earlier."

I pushed out a deep breath then hovered over her shoulder as she logged into her account. After she skipped past security, she started sifting through files of grainy camera footage. Unfortunately, the videos were glitchy because of her spotty Wi-Fi. After what was probably far too long, considering I wasn't the person getting creepy letters, I finally calmed down enough to sit with her. Together, we combed through every single "movement detected" by her mailbox over a twenty-four-hour period.

"There!" She pointed at a grainy figure on the screen.

The camera had caught a partial image of someone—definitely not the mail carrier at 4:02 a.m. There was an arm and torso and a shadowed face covered by a hood. No shoes in the frame. No identifying markers. Whoever it was had been smart or lucky because of Tori's crappy internet. I kept staring at the frozen image of the shadowed face on her screen, unable to look away.

Chapter 8

IT WAS AROUND TEN when I got home from Tori's. No one was around, not my brother or my mom. I figured she was out with her new boyfriend Ray. I hated the sound of it in my head. *Boyfriend.* It was way too soon—it hadn't even been a full year since Dad had died. On top of that, Ray was way too fake and dull compared to my dad.

Ray was a world-class loser, a horrible, comical fill-in for my dad. Most days I couldn't even look at my mom. Couldn't fathom how someone could go from my dad to someone like Ray with his thinning hair and patchy beard, not to mention the thick, black-rimmed glasses that probably weren't even prescription.

An hour later, I heard them come home.

"Please, please, please don't come in my room," I begged under my breath as I heard Mama's heels pause outside my door.

"Honey?" she asked, pushing the door open. "Why are you sitting on the floor? In the dark?"

I turned away from the bright hallway light as she stepped over to the window.

"It's freezing in here," she said, closing it with a soft *thunk* against the sill.

My skin, pale and goose-bumped, had a purplish tint to it in the moonlight. "It's fine." I clenched my teeth to stop the chattering as Mama pulled the blanket from my bed to cover me.

"Piper, honey?" Her eyes were soft, worried.

"Told you, I'm fine. Been a long day."

She squatted, leaning in close. Her breath was warm, tinged slightly with mint gum and nicotine. "Piper?" She lifted my chin so my eyes met hers. "Do you want to talk about it?"

I thought about it for a second, about telling her that Tori and I had gone to the Usman River. By the time I'd gotten home, it had all sunk in—we'd been in the very same place where Ellie had died. Where she'd been killed. Normally, things like that didn't bother me. But this time it had. And then, to see that letter. It was a lot to process.

"Hon?" Mama prompted.

"Babe?" Ray called out.

I shivered at the sound of his voice and at his footsteps as he came down the hall. "I'm fine, Mama. I'm just sad about stuff, you know? I miss Dad so much and Nana too."

"Nana? Oh, Piper, Nana is fine."

After my dad died, my nana got worse, and Mama said it was best to put her in a home. "I know, but I just hate that she's in that place with all those old, senile people."

Mama laughed softly. "She's better off there than being all alone."

Ray stopped in my doorway. "What's going on?"

"Nothing." Mama patted me on the knee and gave me a quick wink. "Just girl talk."

He sighed, rubbing his middle-aged paunch. "I'm starved."

From the smell of his putrid breath, they'd stopped by Cadillac's for a whiskey-on-the-rocks appetizer. Mama cut her eyes at me. Dad was never a drinker. She stood and brushed past Ray. "I'll go warm up some food, and, Piper, keep the window shut. Heat's on."

"Yes, ma'am," I mumbled.

Mama headed down the hall as Ray lingered in the door, staring in that unnerving way of his. He rubbed his thick mustache. "You wanna help pay the bills 'round here?"

Do you? I grabbed my blanket, wrapping it around my shoulders. The guy had some nerve.

"Didn't think so." He sniffed. "Listen to your mama. Don't be rude."

I bit my lip. *Rude?*

As he turned to leave, scratching his balding head, I inched closer to the door and waited until he was in the kitchen before shutting and locking it. Then, I opened my window again, this time climbing right through it and leaving. I closed it behind me, for Mama, not him, and then ran as far as I could from the stench of Ray McDonnel.

I ended up driving to Nana's house even though she didn't live there anymore. She'd moved into Sunnyside after Christmas, but we kept her plants watered and checked on pipes and stuff until we could put it on the market for her. She'd said more than once that I was welcome there anytime.

Inside, it smelled the same as it always had, like stale carpet and dust mites, but it felt more like home to me than my own house at this point. Nana never cared about my piercings or what color my hair was that week. Her place was a safe one. A place where I could be me. One time, my dad and I had gone over there for a visit, and I'd just gotten my nose pierced. Dad wasn't happy about it, but Nana told him to "knock it off." She had wagged her finger at him like he was a mischievous puppy. "Want me to tell Piper about your rebel days back in high school?" They'd locked eyes. "Didn't think so," she said.

Just thinking about it made me miss her even more. I sat on the worn plaid couch and pictured her sitting in her recliner, waving that finger of hers. I needed to go and visit her at Sunnyside. Maybe I would tomorrow or Monday after school, but for now, I just wanted to go to sleep.

I ended up spending the night, wrapped up in a musty, floral-smelling quilt made from Dad's old t-shirts. It had always been my favorite with the obscure band names on it and the colleges he never went to.

The next morning, Mama texted, asking where had I run off to this time.

I rolled off the couch, typing back. *Nana's.*

I'm worried about you, she wrote.

Whatever. I kicked the base of the coffee table. But not worried enough to get in her car and come get me or tell her dirtbag new boyfriend to get lost. It was fine though. She was numbing her pain with booze and a new boyfriend, barely noticing that I'd left the house. *I'm fine.* I added a heart emoji, not that she'd pick up on the sarcasm. *I'll be home later.*

Not that she'd notice.

Chapter 9

MONDAY MORNING, IN THE middle of Honors English, I was called to the principal's office. I kept wracking my brain, trying to think of what I'd done *this time* to get called to the office. Skipping class? Vaping on school grounds? Too many piercings? What was it with this school and its need to deprive its students of personal expression? So what if I had a nose ring and pink hair? So what if I didn't dress or look like everyone else?

Dr. Henderson shook her head at her computer screen then took off her glasses. "I don't understand what's going on here, Piper."

"I'm not sure what you mean," I said.

"You made a perfect score on the ACT. You made a 36, child."

Okay, so I didn't see that one coming, but I also didn't like the way she called me *child* as if I were a first-grader. "Isn't that a *good* thing?"

"Yes, of course, but your grades and the number of absences—just this semester alone—are bleak. Abysmal."

Thanks.

"We've cut you some slack. I know it's been a tough year for you."

She didn't know squat about my "tough" year.

"Losing your father and then one of your friends is more than any of us should have to bear."

My whole body tensed. Ellie wasn't my friend. Not when she died, anyway.

She held my stare. "It's a lot, I know, but you still have responsibilities and your future to think about. If you continue down this path, you'll have to repeat your junior year."

She was waiting for me to say something, probably like: *Oh no, please don't fail me.*

"Piper? Are you listening to me?"

"Yes, ma'am."

"I've emailed your mother this morning to schedule a chat about your grades and absences." She leaned forward and propped her elbows on her desk, lacing her fingers in front of her face. "Piper, you're a bright student. Extremely intelligent. And when you go to class, you excel at every exam. But your grades are suffering from not going and not turning in your assignments. Do you want to go to college, Piper?"

"Not really."

"Your father was a professor, wasn't he?"

"Yeah."

"What was his field of expertise?"

"Cyber Security."

"That's right," she said, clearly trying to be encouraging. It wasn't working. "Don't you want to follow in his footsteps and go to college? Honor his legacy?"

I balled my fists as she talked about my father like she knew him or something. Like she knew *me*. She had no idea what I was dealing with.

"Piper?"

"I don't like computer programming."

"Well, what about art then? You were always such an excellent artist. You could go to art school."

"It's too late anyway. I messed up."

"It's not too late. You can still turn things around."

I stared at her.

"Have you talked with anyone since your dad died?"

I leaned back in the uncomfortable chair across from her plush leather one. Behind her was a large window, looking across the front parking lot with its giant flagpole and massive trees with their brilliant lime-colored buds swaying in the rain.

"Therapist or counselor?" Dr. Henderson prompted.

I shrugged. I'd talked to Ellie and Tori when my dad was first diagnosed with brain cancer during ninth grade. They listened. They cried with me. They helped me cope after he'd come home, gray and weak, from chemo. They were there for me every day, and eventually he got better. For a while, anyway. Then, after Tori started dating Drew during our sophomore year, we stopped hanging around each other. Drew never liked me, but the feeling was completely mutual. Anyway, I never told them that the cancer was back and kicking my dad's ass. Six months later, we lost him. Tori called, offering condolences, but Ellie never did. To be honest, it hurt that she never called. It was the least she could have done.

"Maybe if you could talk to someone," Dr. Henderson said, "you'd see things differently." She shifted her large frame and tugged at her animal print blouse.

She was only trying to help, but I still hated the way she looked at me with that pity in her eyes. I hated her top, too, two sizes too small and that ugly print. "Can I go back to class now?"

She sighed almost disapprovingly. "Yes, you can go back to class."

I erupted from the chair.

"But Piper?

"Yes?"

"Like I said earlier, if you don't get a handle on things, you'll likely be repeating this year."

There were worse things I could think of.

"I'll let you know after I hear back from your mother."

I gritted my teeth and turned toward the door. *Good luck.* All Dr. Henderson would get from my mom would be shallow promises that "things will get better." Promises, broken promises.

Mama had a knack for being passive-aggressive. She'd give me the silent treatment for a few days, feigning her disappointment in my behavior. Then I'd get the blow-up with the "you're better than this" talk. "You have so much potential," she'd say. *More than your brother,* she wouldn't say but would think. We both knew that Wyatt wasn't interested in anything but sports and girls. Dad had known it too. Funny how they'd never been called in to discuss *his* grades.

On my way back to English, the bell rang. Suddenly, the hall was bumper-to-bumper with people. I wanted to keep on walking, to push through the crowd and run for the door, but what good would that do? It would be the last straw, as Dr. Henderson had warned. I turned and headed toward the library instead. I wasn't in the mood to face the social hierarchy of the cafeteria. Besides, Dr. Henderson couldn't possibly expel me for skipping lunch to catch up on my assignments.

I took a seat near the window overlooking the front parking lot and thought about what she'd said, that I could still turn things around. Could I? Could I really? I reached into my backpack for my Lit book, grabbing Nana's album by accident. I'd found it the other night at her house and knew she wouldn't mind if I took it.

"It's all yours," I could hear her say.

It was filled with dozens of newspaper articles, all connected by the river. One of them was about a seventeen-year-old boy who died from unknown causes and was found naked by the Usman River. Nana had always been fascinated, maybe even a little obsessed, with true crime. Even now, her DVR was still set to record every episode of *Dateline* and *20/20,* plus she never missed a chance to read the latest whodunit novel. So, it was no surprise that she'd kept her own book of local mysteries.

"What's that?"

I looked up from the yellowed article. "Oh, hey."

Tori sat down across from me. "Saw you head in here. What are you working on?"

"Oh. You mean this?"

She nodded.

"It's those articles I was telling you about. The ones my grandmother has been collecting for years."

Tori leaned in, examining the headline. "Wow, he wasn't much older than Ellie."

"Yeah, says here he drowned."

She pulled the book closer, reading a few more lines then flipping the musty-smelling page. Tori was quiet for a few minutes, moving from one article to the next.

Deep down, I didn't believe the river was cursed or haunted, and I didn't really think Tori did either, but somehow it was easier to swallow than some of the other theories.

"This one," Tori said, "says female remains were found downstream from the river, near Pine Lake." She looked up from the page. Her face was pale, almost gray as she leaned back in her chair and pushed the album away from her.

I reached across the table for it and put it back in my bag. Luckily, Nana hadn't added any articles about Ellie's death. It probably would have sent Tori over the edge. "Are you okay?" I asked, grabbing an apple from the front zipper.

She nodded, turning to stare out the window. "Just didn't feel like putting on a brave, happy face in the cafeteria, you know?"

I placed the waxy green Granny Smith by her hand. "Same. Plus, I have tons of work I'm supposed to be catching up on. Either that, or I'm going to fail."

"The whole year?" Tori's eyes widened.

"Yeah. Guess I need to get serious." I pulled my notebook from my bag and opened it on the table. In the front pocket was the permission slip for the conference. Maybe an impressive, award-winning speech would get Dr. Henderson off my back. "What did you decide?"

"Decide?" Tori asked.

"About the conference?" I nodded at the form. "Deposits are due this week."

"I haven't asked my parents." She sighed, rolling the apple in her palm. "Mom will probably tell me all the reasons I *shouldn't* go: It's so far away... what if something happens to you?"

For a second, I wished *my* mom cared that much. "Might be good to get away," I said.

"Yeah, maybe."

"We can room together like we did freshman year."

She flinched.

It seemed like an eternity ago, freshman year, when Tori, Ellie, and I first went to that conference. We'd clicked, the three of us, right after making the debate team and then we'd spent weeks together prepping for the conference. We'd had a blast on that trip. "Remember how much fun it was? How free we felt?"

She smiled, faintly. "Yeah, it was fun."

Obviously, we were both working through stuff. Taking a trip wasn't going to magically fix things. For one, I still had some resentment left in me. She'd ghosted me for a boy—and not just any boy, Drew. And second, we stopped being friends around the time my dad died. That was tough to get over.

"Maybe I'll talk to them tonight. I have therapy after school, so that should make my mom happy. She's been on my case about it lately."

At least her mom cared.

"Oh, by the way," Tori said, "I've been meaning to ask... you know the other day when you came over, right?"

"Yeah?"

"Could you maybe not tell anyone about... it?"

"About me coming over?" I asked.

"No, no. I mean about the letter." Tori scrunched her nose all nervous-like.

"Oh, right. Yeah, I won't say anything. I promise."

"Thanks, Piper. I just haven't told anyone yet. I'm still processing things and don't want people gossiping about it. Plus, I still need to talk to my dad."

I wasn't going to tell anyone.

Her secret was safe with me. Her secrets were always safe with me.

Part Three: Nick

Chapter 10

AFTER THE FINAL BELL, Tori bolted down the hall and straight out the side doors to the student parking lot. I was hoping to ask her about the DC trip, but I lost sight of her in the swarm of softball players hanging around the exit. For a split second, I thought about running after her and catching her before she met up with Drew at his truck, but the last thing I wanted was to freak her out and make her think I was following her.

"You just gonna stand there?" Hayes knocked my shoulder as he passed by me.

"Huh?"

"Let's go."

I pushed up my glasses, which were sliding slightly down my nose, and followed my brother through the hall.

"I'm starving," he said as he barreled through the side door. Up ahead was Tori in her bright green coat walking right past Drew's truck. She didn't even look over at him as she hurried by with her head down.

What was the rush? Her appointment with my mom wasn't until 3:30—*if* that's where she was headed. She had an appointment every Monday at that time. And even though she'd missed the last few, Mom still kept the spot open for her.

"Do you have swim practice today?" Hayes asked.

"Huh?"

"Hello? Swim practice?"

"Oh. Tomorrow." I said, following Hayes through the parking lot to his SUV.

"Good. Then we can go grab some food."

"Actually… could you take me home first?"

"Seriously?" he asked, unlocking his Lexus with the key fob.

"Yeah. I have a lot of homework."

"It will literally take less than ten minutes."

"I'd rather just go home." I hopped in the Lexus, losing sight of the bright green coat. I casually checked the side mirror not wanting to make it too obvious by craning my neck out the window.

"What is up with you today?"

"Nothing," I said. "I'm just not hungry."

Hayes stared at me. "Nah, there's something else going on."

"Why is it such a big deal to take me home first? I can walk home," I said, reaching for the handle.

"Relax, would you? I'll take you home."

"You're the one getting worked up over a burger."

Hayes shook his head as he cranked the car and threw it in reverse. I could tell he was miffed at me, but I seriously needed to get home. I had to do something that couldn't wait. Not even for a burger. Five minutes later, Hayes barely stopped the car to let me out in our driveway before he took off again. "Thanks for the ride," I mumbled as he peeled off.

Inside, the house was quiet. Mom was probably out in her office, waiting for Tori to show. I kind of thought we'd pass her on the way home, but either she wasn't coming or she'd decided to take the back streets. It was probably safer that way, not being anywhere near Hayes' vehicle.

But just in case she did show up for therapy, I needed to be ready. I raced upstairs to my room and logged into my computer. It was already 3:20. Any minute now, she'd be traipsing up the cobblestone walkway to Mom's office, if she was coming at all. I slipped on my headphones and took a deep breath, staring at the two frames on my screen. Months ago, I'd installed two cameras, one showing the outside of Mom's office and the other, the inside.

My stomach turned.

It wasn't right what I was doing.

But I was doing it anyway. I had to.

Four minutes later, there she was in her green coat coming up the pathway in front of the old carriage house. She stopped and glanced over her shoulder, probably scanning for Hayes' silver Lexus. *Don't worry. He's not here*, I wanted to tell her.

I leaned in closer to the screen, watching as she raised her hand to ring the bell. The doorbell chimed through my headphones.

In the second frame, Mom swept through the office space, heading toward the front door. Her heels clicked against the hardwood. "Tori, hello. Come on in," she said. Mom, in her three-inch heels, towered over Tori, who was suddenly small, almost like a little kid. Mom stepped aside to let her pass. "How are you today?"

"Good," Tori said.

After they stepped away from the front door, I closed that frame and zoomed in on Mom's office. A second later, Tori stepped into sight with Mom behind her.

"Did you have a good weekend?" Mom asked.

Tori nodded, sitting on the leather sofa.

Mom took the chair across from her and skimmed her notes on her iPad. "So, the last time we met, we ended our session talking about your insomnia. How have you been sleeping?"

"The same. Can't most of the time and when I do, I keep having the same dream."

"What's it about?"

"Ellie... at the bonfire that night." Tori shifted in her seat then tucked her hair behind her ear.

I took a sip of stale Gatorade from the plastic bottle on my desk. It tasted sour. Almost wrong.

"It's okay, Tori," Mom said. "Take your time. I know how difficult this is for you."

Tori nodded then shimmied out of her coat. "It was supposed to be a fun night. A birthday party for a friend. Ellie wasn't supposed to die." She covered her face with her hands and said something, but it was too muffled to make out.

Mom wasn't pushy. She was the opposite, actually. Sometimes Mom would sit there in silence for minutes, giving Tori space to think, cry, or whatever.

"It's always the same," Tori said, dropping her hands to her lap. "She's standing there on the other side of the bonfire, the firelight blazing all around her, almost through her, and she's dancing with her eyes closed. And then the fire suddenly goes out, and everything turns black. I start racing through the darkness, tripping on big, tangly roots and calling out for her. She yells back, asking me to help her, but by the time I find her, it's too late."

"And where do you find her?"

"Back at the bonfire, only now, it's out. Soaked from rain, and she's inside of it… under planks of charred wood. She's trapped there and…" Tori shook her head.

"And what?" Mom asked.

"And drowning. How does that even make sense?"

"I know that none of this has been easy on you."

Mom stood and grabbed a bottle of water from her mini fridge. She handed it to Tori and sat down again. "Do you want to talk about that night at the bonfire?"

"I don't remember much about that night. I wish we would've stayed home. Then Ellie would still be here."

My mom eased back in her chair. "You can't keep blaming yourself for this, Tori."

"Why not? It's my fault she's dead. I shouldn't have left her. Or maybe I should've made her leave with me."

Mom scrolled through her tablet. "The last time you were here, you said that you asked her to leave with you."

"Did I?" Tori rubbed the skin between her eyebrows. "It's patchy, that night."

"If you'd like," my mom said, "we can try a relaxation technique. Sometimes it helps in remembering details."

It was a lot to take in. It was almost too much for me to handle—the intimate details Tori was sharing and my guilt for listening. I was an awful person for doing it. Awful, awful.

"What do you say, Tori?" my mom asked.

"Okay, maybe?"

"It's completely up to you."

"Yeah, we can try it."

Mom nodded. "Tori, I want you to lie down and close your eyes. I want you to take slow, deep breaths as you go back to that day."

"Where do I start?"

"Wherever you'd like."

Tori inhaled slowly, deeply, like she was told. "Ellie came over early that day. She had something she wanted to tell me."

"Good. Do you remember what that was?"

"She never got the chance to tell me because we ended up stripping wallpaper in the guest room all day with my mom.

And then later, Drew came over."

"And that's when you left for the bonfire?"

"Yes."

"Tell me what it was like out there."

"It was beautiful." She took a deep breath, exhaled, and continued. "There was this huge white barn with all these tiny white lights strung in the trees surrounding it. Behind the barn, that's where the bonfire was." Tori lifted her hand. "The fire turned the whole sky this amazing hazy-orange color."

"It does sound beautiful."

"It was. As soon as we got there, Ellie got out of the truck and ran across the field. She just kept running." Tori paused. "Like a moth."

"A moth?" my mom asked.

"Yes, like a moth pulled to light. The fire was amazing. I'd never seen one that huge before. All those tiny sparks in the sky..."

"I want you to think back to that moment... back to Ellie running across the field. Can you see her right now?"

Tori placed her fingers over her closed eyelids and nodded. "Yes, she's wearing her puffy cream coat, but she's taking it off now by the fire. It's warm there. I'm standing with her now," Tori said. "She looks so beautiful. Her hair is loose and falling over her shoulders. She's wearing a black, long-sleeved crop top and her favorite light jeans."

"Good. Now what? What are you both doing?"

"We're laughing. And now we're dancing. There's ten or twenty trucks curved around the fire."

"So, you're dancing... then what happens.?"

"We dance for a long time, an hour maybe. Maybe it's longer, hopping from one truck bed to another. But after a while, my head starts to hurt, so we stop."

Mom typed something on her tablet.

"Ellie is giving me something for my head, aspirin maybe. The water tastes weird as I swallow the pills, but she says it's fine... probably just the hay and smoke we're breathing in. She finishes the bottle of water, and then we jump back into the pick-up to dance some more."

"I see," Mom said.

"After a while, I don't feel like dancing anymore. She's reaching for my hand, trying to pull me into the truck bed again, but I am done. Ready to go."

"Do you ask her to leave with you?"

"Maybe? I think so. I can't remember."

"And then what happens?"

"I'm walking to the barn to go and splash some water on my face and to look for Drew. I remember looking back at her and seeing her in the firelight. I think..."

Tori paused.

Mom leaned forward in her chair.

"I *think* that was the last time I saw her." Tori's voice sounded almost pained by her own indecisiveness.

"And what was she doing? Can you see her?"

"Yes, I can see her... she's talking to..." Tori paused again, but this time, her body jerked.

"Talking to?" My mom prompted.

I leaned closer to the computer screen, noticing how agitated Tori suddenly was, balling both hands into fists.

"It's okay, Tori."

Tori took another deep breath and held it.

"Can you see who she's talking to?"

I couldn't tell if it was an actual nod or not, but it looked like she nodded.

"Tori?"

She opened her eyes and sat up. "I want to stop now," she whispered.

"Of course." Mom leaned forward in her chair, grabbing the bottle from the floor and handing it to her.

She took a long sip of water.

"Tori?" Mom said. "Did you remember something?"

"I don't know. It's all so blurry? I don't even remember making it to the barn or Drew driving me home."

"You've mentioned before that you think someone drugged you... you said that the water tasted weird?"

"Yeah, maybe."

"How does that make you feel, knowing someone might have drugged you?"

She turned and faced the window that overlooked our small courtyard in the back of the house. "Scared. Terrified, actually."

"Yes, I imagine it would be terrifying."

"I don't know if it happened though." Tori paused. "But

then why can't I remember?"

"Like I've said before, there *is* another possibility. Sometimes our minds block traumatic experiences. You did lose your best friend that night."

Tori nodded, biting her bottom lip.

"Okay, how about we take a break," Mom said. "Would you like to? How about we go outside for some air?"

"Yeah, okay."

No, it wasn't okay. I didn't have cameras or audio outside. This was something new. Something Mom hadn't done before. I yanked off my headphones and tossed them on my desk as the two of them walked out of the frame and out the back door of Mom's office.

"Hey," Hayes said, suddenly standing in my doorway.

I slammed my laptop shut, not that the screen was visible from where he stood or anything, but still, the last thing I need-ed was Hayes all in my business. "What the hell, Hayes?"

He stepped back. "What's your problem?"

"None of your business."

He shook his head at me as he tossed a greasy bag with fries and a double-stack bacon burger on my desk. "You're welcome."

Chapter 11

I **DIDN'T MEAN TO** be a jerk to my brother. But lately, he'd been more overprotective than usual, like he was trying to fill our dad's shoes or something. But Dad had been an absent father for years, so I didn't get the abrupt act that Hayes was playing. I liked it better when Hayes was preoccupied with Rachel or soccer, not with me.

"Why are you so mad?" he asked, heading over to my bed and flopping down on it.

A pile of my clean laundry fell to the floor, making my blood boil. "What do you want, Hayes?" I stood, picking up my clothes from the floor.

"Want to play COD or FIFA?" Hayes asked.

"I'm busy."

"Doing what?"

"I have a paper to write for political science."

"That's what made you so mad?"

"What's with the twenty questions?"

He turned on the large flatscreen on my wall and scrolled through my games. "Let's play one round and I'll leave you alone."

I almost expected him to say, "Okay, son?"

"One round then I have to get back to my paper."

"One round."

Two hours later, Mom was calling for us to come eat.

"How are my boys today?" she asked over our plates of grilled salmon and roasted vegetables.

Hayes dominated the table, which was typical. It was fine though. He was better at small talk than I was. He was better at sports and with girls too.

"And Nick? How was your day?" Mom pressed her lips together.

"Fine," I said, poking at the light orangey-pink salmon. I was still full from the greasy burger Hayes had brought home for me.

"Are you looking forward to DC next week?"

"Yeah."

"Who all did you say was going?"

"Miss Taylor and Coach Lyles are going plus three or four juniors, I think."

Hayes looked up from his plate. "Oh yeah? Who?"

"Michael Dunbar, Piper Wells, maybe Tori..."

Hayes straightened his shoulders.

"Maybe a couple others. Not sure."

"That reminds me," Mom said. "Your father emailed last week about taking you boys to London this summer. I said I'd talk to you both about it."

Hayes shrugged. "The new wife going?"

"That I don't know."

I pushed my plate to the side. "Can I be excused?"

Mom placed her fork down on the table. "Nick?"

"I really need to work on my paper."

Mom nodded. "Plate goes in the dishwasher, please."

"Yes, ma'am."

I didn't care one way or the other if I went to London. It's what Dad did. He took us on these over-the-top trips to make up for the divorce. To make up for not being around. Snorkeling in Belize. Skiing in Aspen. Sushi in Tokyo. And now, sight-seeing in London? Sure, why not.

But for now, I had bigger things on my mind than one of his fancy trips.

Upstairs, back in my room, I pulled up the video of Tori's session. I knew I had no right whatsoever to record it. It was a complete violation of her privacy, and my mom's too. And for that, I was truly sorry. But there was something I needed to know. Something about the night Ellie died, and the only way I knew how to get to the truth was through her best friend.

"Morning," Mom said, placing a mammoth cinnamon roll in

front of me. "How'd you sleep?"

I took a bite of the still-warm roll, savoring the sugary icing that oozed like lava. "I love these things," I said, bypassing the question about sleep. I'd been up all night, finishing my paper and going back through Tori's session.

"Homemade. Not the store-bought ones." She smiled then took a sip of coffee. "Everything alright? You've been distracted lately."

"Taking really hard classes this semester."

Maybe she'd buy it even though we both knew that school had never been hard for me. I shrugged, taking another bite of the roll. If she only knew why I was distracted. Maybe I needed to tell her. Maybe I needed to come clean about recording her sessions. But then I thought, *no way*. She'd freak out for sure, go on and on about the legal ramifications. I for sure didn't want that.

"You have swim practice today, right?"

"Yep."

"I'll pick you up after school. I had a cancellation today." Mom patted my arm and smiled. "Oh, did you give any more thought to going to London with your dad?"

My dad. I sighed, checking my phone for the time. "No. Not really."

Mom topped off her coffee then lifted the mug to her nose, inhaling the steam.

"But I will. I promise."

"Sounds good, honey. It's completely up to you."

I took one last bite of my roll then ran upstairs to grab my backpack. Hayes was still asleep in his room, which was across the hall from mine. He'd be late again, but knowing Hayes, he'd talk his way out of it *again*.

Mom was waiting for me at the bottom of the stairs. "Did you wake your brother up?"

"No."

She sighed.

"He's old enough to wake himself up."

She huffed as she started heading upstairs.

"I'm leaving, okay?"

"If you wait a second, I'll drive you."

"I can walk."

"Nick," she said, from two steps up. She turned and stared

at me, rubbing a finger over her lips. It was a tell-tale sign that she was irritated.

"What?" I asked, shrugging my shoulders. "It's not like it's my fault he can't wake up on time." Hayes was always doing something to irritate or worry her. Lucky for me, she was always preoccupied with him.

Chapter 12

"ESSAYS ARE DUE *THIS* Friday," Miss Taylor said in class.

A chorus of groans erupted.

"That's exactly the reaction I expected," Miss Taylor said, leaning against her large wooden desk. "Seeing that no one has started this paper, we're going to the library today to research and write."

I raised my hand.

"Yes, Nick?"

"What if we're finished with the paper?"

"'Course he's done," someone said from the back of the class.

Someone else coughed "loser," making others laugh.

"Then you can work on something for another class or help others find sources. Up to you."

I nodded.

"Alright, everyone, if there are no other questions, grab your stuff and let's go."

I knew the perfect spot—the periodical room on the first floor. It had an old, outdated laminate table with two chairs. No one ever went in there because everyone found articles online these days, but I liked it because the room was tucked in a corner and out of sight. Plus, it was close to the psychology section with hundreds of books on the strange ways our brains worked.

I considered what my mom had said to Tori, about her not remembering the night Ellie died. She'd said that sometimes our minds block traumatic experiences. With that in mind, I headed to the stacks and started skimming titles. One called *Understanding Your Brain* caught my attention. Inside, the topics were familiar, mostly because I'd already taken AP Psychology, but the chapter on PTSD seemed interesting with subheadings on repressed memories and triggers. I kept reading on my way to the periodical room. "People with PTSD often experience intrusive memories of the trauma…"

"Hey," someone said, pulling me from the book.

It was Tori, sitting at *my* table in *my* periodical room. My pulse kicked up ten notches. *What do I do? Sit down with her? Find somewhere else to go?* From the corner of my eye, I saw Miss Taylor approaching.

"Oh, good, Nick. I was just coming to find you." She looked across the room at Tori. "Maybe you can help Tori find some sources, since you said you were finished already."

"Oh, I'm okay, Miss Taylor," Tori said. "I can find my own sources."

"But you can find them faster with Nick helping and then you can start writing. Right?"

Tori scrunched her nose. "Guess so."

"Good. Nick, have a seat and y'all can get started. I'll be around if you need me." She flitted away, answering panicked questions from another girl in our class.

Nerves rushed through my body as I sat at the table, which felt smaller than I'd remembered it. "Sorry about that."

She didn't look up at me.

"Thought I was the only person who knew about this room." I placed my backpack next to hers on the table.

She stared at it.

"So, what's the topic for your paper?"

"Well, I'm not exactly sure. Haven't started it."

"Oh. Okay."

"I don't usually procrastinate. It's just that, lately, well, I don't know." She played with a strand of her hair, twirling it around her finger.

I looked down at the psychology book still in my hand. "What about using psychology as an angle?"

She nodded slowly. "You mean with foreign policy or leadership?"

"Right. Or maybe nationalism?"

She nodded. "That might work."

"We'll have to narrow it down, of course."

She unzipped her Northface backpack, which was the

same as mine, only my zipper pulls were gray and hers were purple. She pulled out her class folder and started reading over the assignment sheet.

"I can help you research. It's kind of my thing."

She shifted uneasily in her chair.

"I can find a few articles for you while you brainstorm." I pulled my laptop from my backpack and waited for it to boot. I could tell she didn't want me there by the way she angled her body away from me, but Miss Taylor had said to help her, so I planned to do just that.

"Thanks," she said, a little softer.

After I logged in, I opened a window with all of my saved files and stared at the CHEM II folder on my screen, knowing that in the folder, archived and coded, were the surveillance videos I'd been storing. All those recordings of her were just a click away. I was a bad person for doing it, no matter what I told myself to rationalize it.

I closed the window and opened the library homepage, going straight to the databases to look for articles. It didn't take long. "I'm finding some good stuff. This paper will practically write itself."

She laughed. "Thanks for helping. Miss Taylor has been getting on to me lately. Ever since... well, let's just say my last paper wasn't my best."

In that moment, it felt as though I knew her, like I'd always known her. It was probably because I listened to her sessions with my mom. After all, apart from that, we'd only ever talked a handful of times in or after class or at the café. We were pretty much strangers. "I don't mind helping. It's fun, researching."

"'Fun,' said no one. Ever."

I smiled, but I felt a little uneasy as the guilt started twisting inside of me.

"Hey," she said. "Can I ask you something?"

I nodded.

"Do you think the river is cursed?"

"What?" I asked, glancing up at her. But she was being completely serious.

"You know, all that talk about the river feeding off evil things, making people do weird stuff?"

"I don't really believe in that kind of stuff."

"What do you think happened that night? To Ellie?"

My heart started to race a thousand beats a minute. How had we veered off topic? We were supposed to be discussing governmental policy, not how her best friend died or the legend of the river curse. I played with my leather watch band, adjusting it to make it looser on my wrist then tightening it again. "Why are you asking me this?"

"I'm sorry," she said.

"I'll... I'll be back," I said, breaking into a feverish sweat.

"Nick?" She looked up at me as I stood. "Are you okay?"

"Yeah, it's fine. I'm good. Just going to pull some books for you."

I raced out of the room and rushed to the bathroom, wondering why the heck she was asking me about that night or about the river being cursed. That didn't even make sense—rivers weren't cursed. It was a stupid county legend. Waterford folklore. I doused my face with cold water, then stared at my reflection in the mirror. Did she suspect me or something? The glass was warped, as old as the mid-century building itself, and it made my whole head distorted-looking. I didn't even recognize the guy staring back at me.

Part Four: Tori

Chapter 13

MAYBE I SHOULDN'T HAVE brought up the river or Ellie, but it was hard not to. She was everywhere, always, in my mind and haunting my dreams at night. She was even in the library periodical room with me. Dr. Moore was right. It was all still too raw. I took a deep breath and closed my eyes, willing myself to get it together. "Just get through the day," I told myself. "Write the stupid paper and get on with it already."

Opening my eyes, I reached across the table and grabbed my spiral notebook from my backpack. But it wasn't mine. Nick's name was written in block letters on the cover. I opened it anyway to borrow some paper, and that's when I froze. Inside, tucked into the front pocket was a thick, cream-colored envelope.

I couldn't catch my breath. My ears were pounding. My heart was racing. Why was there a letter, just like the last two I'd gotten, in Nick's notebook? The envelope was slightly textured, feeling expensive like the others, and on the outside was a clear label, partially covered by the pocket. But it didn't matter. I knew without having to look. My heart pounded so fast I thought I was going to pass out, have a heart attack right there in the periodical room. "Get it together," I whispered.

My hands shook violently as I did my best to steady them and pull the envelope free. I turned it over, playing with the flap. It wasn't sealed. I slid a fingertip under it, freeing the note from inside. It was another message, typed and taped onto spiral notebook paper just like the others. This one said: *Not only do I know who... but I know how she died.*

The letter fell from my hand.

I sat there for a few seconds, stunned, before dropping to

my knees to pick it up. I was terrified he'd walk in and catch me with it. My head whirled as I fumbled with the letter, taking a quick photo then tucking it back into the envelope. *What do I do?* Make a run for it? Leave the library before the bell rang and risk getting detention? Wait for Nick to come back and confront him? I needed time to think. To process.

"Oh, and Nick?" Miss Taylor said from out in the stacks.

I jumped, hitting my head on the table.

"Yes, ma'am?" he answered. His feet were almost to the doorway.

"Here's that book you wanted."

"Oh, good," he said, stepping away from the room to move toward her.

I stood, unsteady on my feet, and quickly placed the letter in his notebook and then in his backpack. "Breathe, just breathe," I whispered, sliding into my chair with just seconds to spare as he re-entered the room with the book in his hands. I glanced up at him from my book, my heart still racing like mad. "Oh, hey." Was his backpack in the same position? His notebook exactly how he'd had it? "Any luck?" I asked, trying to keep my voice from quivering.

He handed me a book with a slick, plastic cover. "This one's a good one. I actually have a copy of it at home."

I nodded, swallowing the huge lump in my throat as the final bell rang. I stood slowly as my legs quivered under my weight. "Thanks." I looped my backpack over my shoulder and turned to leave. *What was he up to?*

Maybe I should have stayed and asked him why he had that letter in his bag, but I needed a minute to wrap my brain around what I'd just found. Maybe more than just a minute. I ran out of the library, setting off the alarm because of the book in my hand. I didn't turn back, not even as the librarian yelled at me. I'd fix it later, tomorrow, whenever. But for now, I needed to get as far away as possible from Nick Moore. I needed to figure out what he knew about that night and why the hell he was coming to *me* and not the police.

I kept running and running all the way to the only place that felt right—my threadbare spot under Ellie's window.

On my way to her house, everything inside me felt rotten and wrong. I kept thinking about Nick's backpack. It was nothing out of the ordinary. In fact, it was almost identical to mine, which was why I'd found the letter. I thought I'd reached into my own bag. It was unassuming, actually, with its black stitching on dark gray canvas, its gray zipper pulls, and its pockets holding pencils and pens and a calculator. But what was far from ordinary was the sick, menacing letter inside of it. And to think I'd almost missed it. Thank God, I hadn't.

After cutting through Ellie's front yard, I took my place among her rose bushes and pulled up the letter on my phone. *Not only do I know who... but I know how she died.* The message used the same font as the others. Ordinary, common.

"Hey, you."

I flinched, dropping my phone in the dirt, as Ellie's mom rounded the corner. Her voice sounded so much like Ellie's. "Hey, Ms. Lisa," I said, trying to catch my breath.

Under the bill of her baseball cap, her face glowed and her skin was smooth. She looked better than she had the last time I saw her, when she had dark purple circles under her eyes and her skin was gray. But the grief was still there, still present in her sad eyes. Maybe bringing up Ellie wasn't the best idea, but was it rude not to ask?

She sat next to me under her daughter's window, which faced the vacant lot next door. "How are you?"

A heavy sigh escaped me. "Been better."

She tucked a strand of black hair behind her ear and leaned against the brick, letting out a deep, solemn sigh. "Tough day?"

Was it that obvious?

"Sometimes, after a bad day," she said, "I sit on her bed and talk to her like she's nestled under those covers, sleeping. It helps, you know?"

As she spoke, her eyes started to gloss over, making mine do the same. Yeah, I did know. I rubbed my eyes.

"Want to talk about it?"

I glanced at my phone, face down in the dirt. Did I want to talk about Nick and what I had just found?

"I know this isn't easy for you." She reached out and rubbed my goose-bumped arm. "I actually went a whole hour this morning without thinking about it, her case, and then I got another email about that conference in DC."

"Yeah, me too."

"Are you going?" she asked.

"I don't know if I can... without her, you know? It was

always more of her thing—debate club, Poli-Sci, the Young Leaders Conference."

"I thought you loved all that too?"

Maybe I had. At one time. Lisa took my hand and squeezed it. It reminded me of how Ellie had done the same the night of the bonfire, her sweaty hand clutching onto mine. "Should I?"

"It's up to you, honey."

We sat there for a few minutes, breathing in the fresh, cool air, neither of us speaking. I'd already told her a thousand times how sorry I was. But I told her again.

"Me too," she said. "Me too. Hey, do you want to come in? I could make us pimento cheese sandwiches. Chloe should be home from school any minute. She'd love to see you."

I hadn't thought about Ellie's little sister and what this had to be doing to her. But I couldn't face her. Not yet. "I should get home," I said, angling to my feet.

"Of course."

She stood and hugged me, smelling of sweet honeysuckle.

As I walked away from her, it suddenly hit me. There was no question about it. I had to go on that trip. I had to figure out what Nick Moore knew about the night Ellie died. The letter in his notebook said that he knew who killed her and how. I had to go to DC and get as close as possible to Nick. The trip was the perfect way to do that.

On the way home from Ellie's, I practiced my speech, saying that it was a great opportunity and that some time away would do me some good... that I needed to do "normal" things again and that it would look excellent on my college applications... yes, that was exactly what I'd say. The hardest part would be sitting them both down at the same time and getting them to agree on anything.

But I had to do it. I had to convince them.

Because I had to figure out if Nick really did know something. And if he did, why hadn't he gone to the police? Why send me letters? Unless... someone had sent *him* that letter.

Chapter 14

TEN DAYS LATER, I was getting on a school van bound for the Memphis International Airport.

"Good morning," Miss Taylor said, tossing her knock-off Louis Vuitton bag in the back of the beat-up white minivan.

I was the last one to arrive. Honestly, I wasn't sure my mom was going to let me leave the house that morning. Even after days of convincing her that everything was going to be okay, she was still "unsettled" by me going to DC. "I get it, Mom," I'd told her. "I really do, but I'll be fine. I promise." And I *did* get it, her need to hold onto me tighter than ever before. Dad had been easier to convince. Mom, not so much.

After that day at Ellie's, I sat them both down later that night and gave them my speech. Mom was a hard no.

"The last time we talked about it, you didn't want to go," she'd said. "And now, all of a sudden, you do? Is this because of the break-up?"

"Mom." I could feel the heat rising to my cheeks. "It's a school trip. It has nothing to do with Drew."

She got up from the couch and came over to where I was standing. She gently stroked my hair. "You've been going through a lot, honey."

"I'll be fine, Mom."

She looked over at my dad, who was sitting on the couch.

"Come on, Dad. Help me out here."

He swept a hand over his mouth then leaned forward, placing his hands on his knees. "It's a chaperoned school trip."

"Yes, that's right," I said, nodding at my dad. He yawned, probably just as tired of fighting with Mom as I was.

"Who is going again?" Mom asked.

"Two teachers and a few students." I hadn't paid that much attention to the names on the list—just Nick's.

"And you're sure you want to?" Mom asked.

It wasn't a matter of *wanting* to go. I had to. "Yes."

"And when is it again?"

"Soon. Like in the next couple of weeks."

"Seriously?" she said, brushing the hair from her forehead. "I didn't realize it was that soon."

"I'm sure it's too late for a refund," I'd added, trying to help my case. The flight and hotel arrangements had been made months ago, before everything with Ellie.

She finally agreed. "Okay, you can go."

"Thank you, thank you, thank you." I lunged in for a hug. Over her shoulder, I mouthed another *thank you*, this one for my dad.

Everything was fine until the morning of the trip when she started back-pedaling, making me ten minutes late for our eight-a.m. departure from the school.

"Come on, Mom. I'll be fine. I promise," I said for the millionth time.

We sped through our neighborhood and rolled through two stop signs just to make it on time.

"Thought you'd changed your mind," Miss Taylor said, taking my bag to place on top of hers.

"My mom was having a hard time with me leaving."

"I understand. But she's okay now?"

We both waved at my mom, who was standing back with the other parents.

"She's fine."

"And you?"

I stared at the pink lipstick on her teeth. "I'm good," I said. It was my canned response for her. Almost every day since Ellie had died, Miss Taylor stopped me either before or after class, in the hall or in the library, just to ask me how I was for the umpteenth time. I already had a therapist. I'd told her that more than once. I suspect it fell on deaf ears.

"Well, good," she said, nonetheless sounding like she'd hoped for something more. "Everyone's already in the van.

Guess we should probably get moving."

There were only four of us going. Our essays, which we'd written in last year's government class, had been selected out of thousands. I still wasn't sure how Nick's was selected since he was just now taking the class. Maybe one of his junior high teachers submitted his paper or something. I glanced at him as I climbed into the van. He was sitting next to Michael Dunbar, and Piper was behind them in the back seat.

"What was that all about with Miss Taylor?" Piper asked as I settled in next to her.

"Oh, nothing." I lowered the bill of my Ole Miss hat and dug in my bag for my sunglasses, not that I needed them with gray clouds hanging low in the sky.

She didn't push it.

Coach Lyles turned on the ignition, sending a cool blast of stale air straight to my face. I leaned over Piper to close the vent.

"Hey, Coach," I called out. "Can you turn on the heat back here?"

Nick, sitting behind the driver seat, turned around and stared at me for a second, then bent down, looking for something on the floorboard. He reemerged a few seconds later, handing me a neatly rolled-up fleece blanket. "My mom put it in my backpack this morning. Said she always gets cold on trips."

Michael, sitting beside Nick, rolled his eyes.

I leaned forward, taking it from him. "Thanks," I said, unrolling the blanket over my lap. What I really wanted to say was, *why did you have that letter?*

We made it to the hotel by seven that night. I stood on the sidewalk in front of the Hyatt and breathed in the fresh, early-April air. Across the street was a quaint, French-style café with a black-and-white awning. In the window was a young couple holding hands and gazing adoringly into each other's eyes. My stomach lurched. Drew and I had been that happy, once upon a time.

I buttoned my bright apple-green coat and sank into the collar like a turtle, hiding my wind-chapped lips from the biting air. It was all for the best. The breakup, our moving on. My phone buzzed in my pocket. Maybe that was him now, calling to say he couldn't live without me. Ha, right. I pulled my phone out and stared at Mom's picture. "Hello?"

"Hi, hon. How was your flight?"

"It was okay. Just got to the hotel."

"I miss you already."

I glanced over at Nick, who was busy wrangling his luggage. "Miss you, too."

Miss Taylor motioned for me to follow her. "We need to check in," she called out.

"Hey, Mom? Can I call you later?"

"Of course, honey. Love you."

"Me too." I ended the call and followed Miss Taylor.

The hotel lobby was packed. A big clock with Roman numerals hung over the check-in counter, showing a few minutes past seven. Coach told us to wait there while he and Miss Taylor checked us in. I sat on a velvety gold couch and watched Nick scroll through his phone. He looked up, catching me. The lump in my throat burned as I quickly glanced down at the new suede boots that I'd bought for the trip. Somewhere along the line, I'd scuffed the left one.

Piper sank down next to me on the couch. She looked pale, maybe even a little green as she wiped the sweat from her forehead. "That cab ride was the worst, wasn't it?"

"Yeah, guess so."

"Maybe I'm just hungry or something. Wonder where we're going to eat."

"I have no idea."

"Hope it's close and doesn't require another cab ride."

Later that night, we ended up going to a small diner around the corner from our hotel. The food was a mash-up of comfort meets gourmet. I ordered the same thing as Nick: tiny sirloin sliders with pancetta along with truffle-infused mac and cheese, all served on a square plate with fancy swooshes and swirls of something. On our way back to the hotel, I ran to catch up with him. "Hey," I said, as casually as possible. "The mac and cheese was amazing, wasn't it?"

"Yeah, it was pretty good."

I smiled. "Oh, I meant to tell you thanks for finding those sources for my Poli-Sci paper."

"Did they work for you?"

I nodded. "Made an A on the paper. You were right. Paper practically wrote itself."

"Told you it would."

"Cool." I picked up my pace, catching up to Piper and Miss Taylor. I didn't want to be too obvious or make Nick suspicious by my sudden interest in him.

"Getting cozy with Nick, huh?" Piper asked, leaning into me as we walked.

"He helped me with my Poli-Sci paper. Just told him thanks, that's all."

"Uh-huh." She rolled her eyes. "Doesn't hurt that he has a cute brother."

"Whatever," I said, suddenly regretting that I'd ever told her about my grade-school crush on Hayes. But whatever. It wasn't like he'd ever break up with Rachel, anyway. Or date me. Besides, the last thing I needed right now was to date anyone—not even Hayes. Especially not Hayes.

After we got back to our room, Piper laid down on her bed. We had adjoining rooms with Miss Taylor, who told us to turn in early. "We have a busy day tomorrow, girls, so don't stay up too late."

"We won't," Piper said. "I'm exhausted anyway. Think I'm jet-lagged."

Miss Taylor left, closing the door between our two rooms.

As I plopped down on my bed, my phone buzzed in my pocket. I hit ignore. "It's my mom again."

Piper shifted on the marshmallow mattress, yawning as she stuffed another pillow behind her head. "Thought maybe it was Drew."

I let out a long, hefty sigh. "Nope. We haven't talked since the night you and I went to the river. Not sure I have the mental space right now even if he did call."

"Makes perfect sense after everything with Ellie."

My shoulders fell. "Yeah, it's been a lot."

"I bet," Piper said.

The way she said it, kind of sad-like, made me wonder if she still was upset with me for not picking up the phone all those times she'd called, needing me. It wasn't right the way Ellie and I had treated her. But now, here we were, getting close again. Could I trust her? I used to.

I glanced at my phone on the bed, thinking about the picture I'd taken of Nick's letter. Should I tell her what I'd found? It was hard holding it in, and besides, she hadn't told anyone about the other letters, not that I knew of anyway. "I found another letter," I blurted out.

Piper sat up, slowly. "Found? Where?"

I bit my lip, second-guessing myself. "Never mind."

"No, no, no," she said, arching an expectant eyebrow at me. "You can't do that. You can't start telling me something and then just say never mind."

She was right. I hated when people did that to me. I stared at her pink bangs, matted to her forehead. "But you can't say anything to anyone. If you do, I swear, Piper."

"I promise I won't. I didn't last time." She crossed her heart. "I swear. What did it say?"

"The same stuff, 'I know who did it.'"

"Oh my gosh, Tori." She took a slow, long sip of the overpriced water from her nightstand and leaned back against the tufted headboard. "What does your dad think?"

"Still haven't told him."

"Are you serious?" Piper swept her bangs to the side.

"Not sure I'm going to. I mean, I'm pretty sure I know who's behind it."

She sat up, shocked. "You do?"

I nodded.

"Well?" Piper's eyes were huge. "Who?"

I sat there, saying his name over and over in my head. It made the most sense, that Nick was behind the letters—but why? For fun? As a prank? But what if he wasn't? What if he was getting letters too?

"Tori?" Piper prompted.

"Girls," Miss Taylor said, interrupting all my second-guessing with a knock on the adjoining door and poking her head into our room. "It's been a long day. I told y'all to get ready for bed. Now, please."

"Yes, ma'am." I rolled off the bed and started digging through my suitcase for my PJs. When Miss Taylor was out of earshot, I looked up at Piper and whispered his name.

Her mouth gaped open in shock, just like mine had the second I found the letter in his folder. She shook her head at me in disbelief, neither of us knowing what to say.

When I got out of the shower thirty minutes later, the lights were off and the room was still.

"Piper?" I whispered, hoping that maybe she wasn't asleep, hoping that maybe she could help quiet the noises in my head. But she didn't answer, leaving me all alone in the dark. Again.

Chapter 15

THE NEXT MORNING, I got up before Piper did. I asked her if she wanted to go to breakfast with me and Miss Taylor, but she mumbled something then rolled over.

"Is she not coming?" Miss Taylor asked out in the hall.

"She's still getting ready. She said to bring her back something, maybe a latte and muffin?"

Miss Taylor glanced at the time on her phone. It was early, not even seven. Our first session wasn't until nine.

"We can do that, right?" I asked.

She sighed through her nose. "Yeah."

Nick was waiting for us in the lobby, already dressed in his slightly-too-big suit, which probably belonged to his brother. "Where's Piper?" he asked, shifting his weight from foot to foot.

"Still getting ready." I couldn't help but to stare at him, trying to figure him out. Was he behind it all or was he a victim, like me?

"Yeah, Michael too." He shrugged.

I glanced at the revolving door, eyeing the café across the street. "Can we try that little coffee shop?" I asked Miss Taylor.

"Sounds good to me."

We crossed the street and followed some woman in a tan trench coat into the café. Techno-pop filtered out of the speakers as we took our place in line.

Nick squirmed, adjusting his navy and burgundy striped tie. "What are you going to get?"

"Not sure. Maybe a chai latte and a croissant."

He blinked nervously behind his thick glasses.

Why was *he* nervous? Was he on to me? Maybe I'd put the

letter back the wrong way and he'd just noticed it that morning.

"Uh," Miss Taylor said, holding up her phone. "I need to take this call. Can you order me a vanilla latte and a bagel? Put everything on my card," she said, handing it to me.

"Wonder what that's all about?" Nick said as Miss Taylor rushed outside to take the call.

"Who knows?" I zeroed in on the freckles on his nose until the tatted-up barista called out for the next person in line.

"Eating here?" the barista asked.

Nick and I looked at each other. He shrugged.

"Sure," I told her. "But, one of the orders is to go." I gave her Piper's order then Miss Taylor's and mine.

After our drinks were ready, Nick and I sat at a table in the corner, talking about my Poli-Sci paper, our up-coming session, and even the weather. I wanted to ask him about the letter in his backpack, but the timing wasn't right. Not yet. I had to build up to it. "Is it supposed to rain?" I asked.

"Looks like it," Nick said over a quiet rumble of thunder in the distance.

I nodded then lifted the slick, ceramic coffee cup to my lips, breathing in a hint of caramel before taking a sip. It was the oddest combination of flavors and not at all what I was expecting from a chai latte. "I think I got your coffee," I said, smacking my lips. "What did you order?"

"Salted caramel latte."

I wrinkled my nose. "Yep. This one's yours." I slid the cup and saucer across the tabletop toward him and inhaled slowly, easing back in my chair. "Ellie used to get those, but I never understood the appeal. I mean, who wants salt in a latte?"

"Me?" he pointed out, pushing the other cup toward me.

"Thanks. You can try it if you want... since I tried yours. It's a chai latte. Trust me, it's good." Trust. That's exactly what I was after, getting *him* to trust *me*.

We held each other's stare for a second.

"Um, no thanks."

"Suit yourself," I said, making light of it. I took a sip then nodded. The frothy, sweet liquid was perfection on my tongue. "Much better."

Miss Taylor was still outside, pacing and nodding as she spoke to whoever was on the other end of the phone. "Can I ask you something?" I glanced from her to Nick. My heart drummed in my chest. *Just say it. Just ask him.* What was the big deal any-ways? I'd told Piper last night. Why would talking to Nick about it be any different?

"Sure, I guess."

I didn't know where or how to start. *Hey, Nick, why do you have that letter in your folder? Did you write it? Are you messing with me or is someone messing with us both?*

"Tori?"

"Yeah?"

"You wanted to ask me something?"

I wasn't ready to ask about the letter, not yet, so I switched gears and blurted out, "Do you think the hurt ever goes away after you lose someone?" I cringed at myself for asking some-thing so personal. I didn't want to go there. Not now.

Nick's forehead wrinkled. "Maybe."

I took a sip of my chai.

"What would you do differently?" he asked. His tone was steely, unwavering. "If you could go back to that night."

My heart stopped. All these weeks of *what ifs* and *if onlys* had been torture. "Not leave her."

He pushed his bagel to the side and nodded.

My head felt woozy and my heart was pounding. "Did you go to the bonfire?" I stared at him from across the table, holding his gaze.

He pressed his lips together and played with his leather watchband.

From the corner of my eye, Miss Taylor was heading back inside. *No, no, no. Not yet.* I needed more time.

"No," he said. "I didn't go."

"Really? I thought everyone did. Your brother did, right?" I pictured Hayes in the back of a pick-up truck by the fire. It was something that I'd remembered recently during my last session with Dr. Moore. She'd done this hypnosis-therapy thing, which kind of dislodged a memory or something. I hadn't remembered Hayes being with Ellie the night of Sam's party, not before that session with Dr. Moore.

"Yeah, I think he went, but I didn't go."

He was lying. I felt it in my gut. Suddenly, I just *knew* he'd written those letters. There was something in the way he squirmed. Something in the way his eyes wouldn't lift to meet mine. He *had* been there that night.

I know who did it. So do you. I know how it happened.

I sipped my chai then placed it back on the table. Yep, he was there that night. He'd practically confessed it in his letters.

He loosened his tie.

"Sorry about that," Miss Taylor said, sitting down at the table. "Is this one mine?" she asked, reaching for the third cup on the table.

"Yep," I said.

Nick cleared his throat. "If it's okay, I'm going to head back to the hotel."

"Oh?" she said.

"I want to go over my notes for my presentation." He stood abruptly, his knee knocking the table and sending my mug to the floor.

Luckily, Miss Taylor was still holding onto hers.

I gasped as my cup smashed on the glossy tile, shattering into a hundred little pieces. Everyone in the café turned to look at us—at my broken cup in a puddle of chai.

Nick stared at me, horrified. "I'm so sorry," he said, his face white as a sheet. "I'll get you another one."

"No, it's fine." I reached down for the mug with trembling fingers.

He reached for it too. "Are you sure?"

"Yeah, I'm sure."

"I'll make you one to go," the barista said, heading over with a broom and dustpan.

"I'm okay. Really," I said as Nick took off, rushing for the exit.

Something I'd said had gotten under his skin.

Game on, Nick Moore. Game on.

Chapter 16

DURING MY SPEECH, I white-knuckled the podium and stumbled on one word, maybe two. Nick, on the other hand, stood up there stoically and ran through his entire presentation without once looking at his notes. Michael's speech was a little less inspired. So was Piper's.

"You were amazing," Miss Taylor told Nick out in the hotel lobby after our session was over. "You all were."

Yeah, right. But I didn't care about my presentation. The whole time I was up there, all I could think about was Nick and getting to the bottom of what he knew.

"Let's celebrate tonight," Miss Taylor said. "Maybe we'll take the subway and go to Georgetown for dinner."

"Can we go to our rooms?" Piper asked.

Coach Lyles shrugged at Miss Taylor. "Fine by me," he said, rubbing his thinning hair. "But I'm going to the next panel on environmental reform policy. Anyone with me?"

Nick raised his hand.

Michael nodded.

"There's one at noon, or maybe it's at one, that I'd like to catch on global poverty," I said. "If that's okay."

Miss Taylor nodded. "Sure, let's meet here fifteen minutes before it starts. Okay, girls?"

"Yes, ma'am." Piper looped her arm in mine then pulled me with her toward the elevators. After the doors shut behind us, she exhaled. "Oh my gosh, Tori, I've been wanting to talk to you all morning." She, almost comically, checked over her shoulder in the empty elevator. "I still can't get over what you told me last night about... you know who."

I thought about being at the café with him earlier that morning and the way he'd acted. Nick was always cool under pressure, except for earlier when I asked him about being at the bonfire. It had rattled him for sure, solidifying—for me at least—his guilt. "Well, then you won't believe what happened this morning."

"Ooh, tell me," Piper said.

I gave her the play-by-play as we headed back to our room.

"Hmm," Piper said. "That is a strange reaction—getting all nervous and wanting to suddenly leave. And he knocked your coffee cup to the floor?"

"Not on purpose, but yeah."

"Well, it sounds like something you said really bugged him," Piper said.

Back in the room, I filled her in on the details, like how I'd found the letter that day in the library with him and how he didn't know that I knew about it. The whole time I was telling her about it, she kept shaking her head.

"Unbelievable," Piper said.

"I know, right?"

"But why?" she asked.

"Why, what?"

"Why write you these anonymous letters? Why not just tell you or the police?"

"I don't know." I glanced down at my phone, at a new text from Miss Taylor, saying: *This session is amazing. Y'all should come down for it.*

But I didn't feel like going. I was still decompressing after giving my own presentation and from the spilled chai incident. "Hey," I said to Piper, "Miss Taylor is asking again if we want to catch that session."

"I'm good," she said.

"Me, too." *Promise we'll catch the next one, K?* I texted her.

She sent back a thumbs-up emoji.

I lost track of time, writing things down in my conference notebook and trying to connect the dots. I jotted down dates that I'd received the letters and what they'd said—best I could remember. For the most part, the words were pressed on my memory. At least I had a screenshot of the last one. While I was writing everything down, Piper had fallen asleep in her bed. Again. She'd been a little off on the trip. Then again, how well did I really know her anymore? Maybe this was just the way she was now, up and down. Tired, not tired.

I jumped at a knock on the door, thinking it might stir her too, but she didn't move. She was deep under the covers, not budging. I scrambled to the door, expecting to yank it open and find a housekeeping cart and someone in a uniform.

"Hey," Nick said.

He'd caught me off guard. "Hi," I said, smoothing my hair.

"I got you this." He held out an extra-large paper cup with a black lid. "Since I spilled yours earlier."

"It's not salted, is it?"

"It's just a chai latte. Anyway, I wanted to say sorry. Again." He pushed his glasses up on his nose then turned to leave.

As he headed down the hallway, I kept picturing the letter I'd found in his bag. Was it still there? Was it in his backpack right now? What was stopping me from saying, *I know it's you. Why are you doing this to me?*

"Who was that?" Piper asked as I closed the door.

I held up the chai. "Nick."

"Seriously?"

Just as I was about to answer her, Miss Taylor texted again: *Where are you two? Session starts in five minutes.*

Crap. "We're late." I put the cup down on the table between our beds then zipped around the room, looking for my shoes and bag. "Are you coming?" I asked, slipping my backpack over my shoulder.

"Can you tell Miss Taylor I'll catch the next one?"

"You're not coming?" I asked, pausing at the door.

"I'm really tired."

Tired? I shook my head, knowing that Miss Taylor was going to be mad. "But you're coming to the next one, right?"

"Yeah," she said, glancing at her phone. "Promise."

Just like I'd thought, Miss Taylor was not happy when I told her in the lobby that Piper wasn't coming to the session with us.

"Did she say why?"

"No, ma'am. Just that she was tired."

She clenched her teeth and inhaled slowly.

Miss Taylor is mad, I texted Piper as I walked into the session behind our irritated teacher. But Piper didn't text back. She didn't respond after the session, either, when I asked her to meet us for lunch in the hotel restaurant.

"I hope she's okay," I said.

Miss Taylor didn't look up from the menu.

"Maybe we should go and see if she's okay," I said.

"Yeah, of course."

After our late lunch, we went up to check on her. Miss Taylor stopped by her room first as I went in to warn Piper. "Piper?" The curtains were drawn, but there was a small gap, leaving just enough light to see the small heap in the bed. "Are you okay?"

She groaned.

Think she might be sick, I texted Miss Taylor.

A few seconds later, Miss Taylor knocked on the door. "Is she okay?" She swept by me, stopping at the foot of Piper's bed. "Piper? Are you feeling alright?"

She lifted her head slightly. "Feel like I'm gonna throw up." She wiped a few beads of sweat from her forehead. "Don't think I can go to dinner. Can I stay here?"

"Of course," Miss Taylor said.

"I'll stay with her."

"No, no. I will. There's no reason for you to miss out on your last night here."

Piper winced as she scooted up in bed, adjusting the pillow behind her head. She swept her damp bangs from her eyes and forced a pained smile.

In just a few hours, she'd be checking out of our swanky hotel room with its thirty-dollar, room-service burgers and into a room way less posh at a local DC hospital. The rest of us would be heading back to Mississippi without her.

Chapter 17

"HOW'S PIPER?" NICK ASKED the next morning.

I sat beside him on the lobby couch, not making eye contact. "I don't know."

"Coach said Miss Taylor took her to the ER in the middle of the night."

I rubbed my swollen, tired eyes. I hadn't gotten much sleep, not with Piper throwing up all night. "Yeah, they left this morning at four."

"What now?" Michael asked, sitting on the couch.

"Guess they're running tests. I don't know much."

Miss Taylor had called the room that morning around eight and told me that she was staying at the hospital with Piper and that I needed to head home with everyone.

"They're giving her IV fluids," she'd said.

"Maybe I should stay," I'd told her.

"No, no. You have a plane to catch in a few hours. I'll let you know as soon as I know something."

"Are you sure I shouldn't stay?"

"Yes, I'm positive. Just head back with everyone this morning. There's no need to change your flight, too. It's too much of a hassle."

But I didn't want to leave Piper. I felt bad, guilty, for thinking she was just being moody when she'd actually been sick. *What a friend*, I berated myself as I started packing and tidying up our room.

And that's when I'd found it.

The empty to-go cup of chai from Nick. I hadn't had one single sip of it, had completely forgotten about it after leaving in such a hurry for the session. Yet there it was, empty on Piper's side of the nightstand. It gave me the strangest sinking feeling in my gut as I held it to the light. What if... no, surely not.

"Isn't that right, Tori?" Nick waved his hand at me in the crowded lobby to get my attention.

"What?" I asked, looking up at him.

"That we're supposed to be at the airport two hours before flight time."

"Sounds right." I glanced at his boyish freckles and nerdy, thick glasses. There was no way he was capable of something like poisoning someone. Was he? But why? Because he knew I was onto him? I was being ridiculous. Paranoid. Maybe he was capable of sending twisted, sick letters, but putting something in my drink? No way.

Then again, I *had* suspected someone of drugging me the night of the bonfire. What if...

"All right, guys," Coach Lyles said, returning from the front counter. "The shuttle is on its way."

In hindsight, I wish I would have stayed. I wish we all would have. But it wasn't like we had a choice.

We left for the airport thirty minutes later. It hadn't stopped raining since that morning, and when we landed, it was as if the black rain clouds had followed us home. I sat alone in the back of the school van, listening to my new French-pop playlist as we headed back to Waterford. Anything was better than Coach's political radio show turned all the way up.

At one point during the hundred-mile drive home on the curvy, two-lane highway, Michael turned to Nick and asked, "I thought this shock-jock guy died years ago?"

Rain spat against the side windows as the van sped down the narrow, rutted-out road. I'd always hated this road, dark and in the middle of nowhere. It had always felt spooky to me, haunted almost. Tall pines flickered by and, every once in a while, the headlights from a passing car lit up the van's interior. Someone, Nick or Michael, had opened a window, letting in a crisp, pulp-sweet air to sweep over us. Then, after convincing Michael that the shock-jock was still alive and still as sanctimonious and dangerous as always, Nick peeked his head over his seat. "Are you cold? Want the blanket?"

His voice was muffled over the music still playing in my ear. I shook my head. I didn't want anything from him. Maybe some answers, but not a stupid blanket.

"You haven't said much."

I removed an earbud. "I'm tired. Worried about Piper."

He stared at me.

What? I wanted to ask. *Why are you staring at me like that? Did you... did you put something in that drink?*

He handed me a shrink-wrapped cookie from his coat pocket then turned back around. I picked at the edge of the plastic wrapper, wondering if he'd tampered with it, too. Still, my stomach growled for it, ached for the hint of cinnamon in the dough. For the sweet, bitter bite on my tongue. I hadn't had anything to eat all day. But I didn't trust him, not one bit, and there was no way in hell I was eating that cookie. I tossed it in my backpack and shut my eyes, hoping that Piper was going to be okay... hoping that the hum of rolling tires would put my mind to rest. I was starting to lose it. Really, genuinely, lose it.

It all happened so fast. Ten seconds, twenty frantic heartbeats, and not one but *two* flips of the van—that's how long it took. And then nothing. Nothing but a slight hiss of the engine and a hint of gasoline in the air. A numbing silence washed over me as I opened my eyes, realizing that we'd landed on our side. Pain seared through my entire body as I tried to wiggle free from the seatbelt holding me in place. It was cutting into my chest and neck, making it hard to breathe. I couldn't move or speak. Nothing came out as I tried to scream for help.

I kept blinking, waiting, and watching sideways through the broken front windshield as feet darted across glass on shiny wet pavement. *I'm here. I'm still alive. Help me.* A pair of black boots stepped over a backpack, alone in the middle of the road. *Was it mine?* I pinched my eyes shut to the bright, blurred headlights in my face and waited.

"Oh, dear God," a female voice said from outside the van.

"Hello? Who said that?" I asked, not knowing if the words actually came out of my mouth.

"Hold on, hon. I'm going to call for help."

I shut my eyes, listening as my heartbeat thudded in my ears. I was still alive. Good. But what about—oh, no. Nick? Michael? "Hello?"

Someone whispered my name. It was faint at first. Not

much stronger the second time. "Tori?"

I turned slowly toward the voice. *His* voice. *Nick.* Pain coursed through my body, strangling every attempt to breathe as I tried squeezing out of my seatbelt to get to him. From what I could tell, the van had crashed against a guardrail or a tree and Nick was somehow lodged under the crushed frame.

"Are you okay?" Nick whispered.

"I'm okay," I said. "You?"

"Think so."

His face glowed ghostlike in the headlights from another car, the one I assumed had hit us. I always hated that highway, but it was the only way back to Waterford from the airport. It seemed like every year there was another wreck, another car or truck on the news, smashed like an accordion. How bad was ours? And where were Michael and Coach Lyles? "Help! Please help us!" I screamed.

No one answered.

I couldn't hold it in anymore. My deep, heavy sobs echoed over the hiss of the engine.

"Hey, it's going to be okay." Nick reached over the seat for my hand.

I cleared my throat and squeezed his cold, clammy fingers. "I'm scared."

"We're going to be fine." He let out a cough, more like a gurgle, and a tiny trickle of blood started pooling at the crease of his mouth. "I can hear sirens now, can't you?"

"Yeah, I hear them," I lied. I craned my neck, wincing through the pain, to see exactly where we were, to see if anyone was out there. Where did that woman go? Had she gone for help? Had I imagined her?

It was eerily quiet except for the engine still hissing. My whole body shook from the cold and the dark and the blood. Nick's, not mine. There was no way I was going to let anyone else die. Not tonight.

I took a deep breath, pushing through the pain to try and release the seatbelt latch. *You can do this, Tori.* I'd never been the bravest or the strongest, but in that moment, I had to be. For Nick.

"Come on," I mumbled, mashing on the release button. Finally, the seatbelt released, dropping me against the inside door of the van with a thud. My arm seared with pain, sending tiny white stars blinking in front of my eyes. But I had to get to Nick. Had to check on him. I climbed over the seat toward him. He was pinned in, nearly swallowed whole by crushed metal. He looked like a little kid, like a five-year-old with broken glasses sitting crooked on his bloodied nose. His eyes fluttered. "You need to stay awake," I told him.

"I need my backpack..."

I stared at him. "What?"

Nick pointed to his bag in the road. "I need it."

There, on the other side of the shattered windshield, which was sparkling like ice in the headlights, was his bag and a lone shoe. I rubbed my tingling arm as a cold gust swept over us, bringing with it a pungent smell of fuel.

"Please?"

My head swirled, pounded, as I shimmied out of the side window and limped across the pavement, taking in the damage and looking fearfully around for Coach and Michael. Maybe they'd gone for help?

Shards of glass crunched under my boots as I waded across the dark road, slick with rain and oil. I looped his backpack over my shoulder and limped light-headed back to the capsized van—tipped over like a dying June bug. My fingers started to go numb as I crawled back through the window. Behind me, bright headlights flickered then went out.

"I'm back. Nick?"

"Did you get it?"

"Yeah." I moved as close to him as I could, reaching out for him in the dark vehicle. "Nick?"

"I have to tell you something," he whispered.

There it was. His confession. The reason he'd wanted me to get his backpack, so he could give me the letters and tell me what he'd done. "What is it?"

"If I die, Tori..."

"You're not." I shook my head, choking back tears.

His shallow breathing rattled between us.

"I'm scared too." I rubbed my eyes.

"Didn't think I'd die like this."

"Stop saying that. You're not going to die. No one else is going to die. The ambulance will be here any minute. I can hear it now," I lied fervently.

"I ne—need to tell you something... Tori... I—"

His voice was so weak, lost in the sound of my brain thudding against my skull. My vision started to blur in the bright orange light. Was that fire? Was the engine on fire? "What do you need to tell me?"

"Tori?"

"You put something in that coffee, didn't you? And in my drink the night of the bonfire."

"I... I..."

I waited for him to say more. "What is it, Nick? Please tell me. I know about the letters. I found one in your backpack. That's why you wanted me to get it for you, right? I know it was you."

He coughed, sending more blood trickling from the corner of his mouth.

"Nick? Stay with me, okay?"

"I'm so sorry, Tori. I'm sorry I..."

He closed his eyes, his head falling to the side like a rag doll. "No, no, no," I whispered. "Stay with me, Nick. Nick?"

Chapter 18

WHEN I FIRST WOKE up in the county hospital, I didn't remember much of anything. I knew that we'd landed back at the airport after our trip to Washington and that we'd started the drive home on that dark country highway. But that was about it.

"Where am I?" I asked the shadowy figure standing in front of the window.

"We'd like to keep her overnight for observation," it said to someone else in the room. Another shadow.

"Observation for what?" I asked as my brain pounded against my skull.

The beeping machines were too loud, echoing in my ears.

And then, that was it. Everything turned black again.

The next time I remembered opening my eyes was a few days later. Mom was curled up in a ball in the chair beside my bed.

"Mom?" I rubbed my eyes, trying to focus.

She stirred, then rushed over to me.

"What happened?" My head was pounding and my whole body ached as I tried to remember. "Where's Dad?"

"I'm right here, kiddo," he said, coming through the door with a coffee in his hand. His face was scruffy, like he hadn't shaved in days. "I'm right here."

"Mom? What happened?" I asked again.

She grabbed my hand and held it to her lips. She kissed it softly.

"Mom," I prompted, clearing my raw, burning throat.

Dad swept in and held a cup of water to my mouth. He angled the straw to my lips and nodded as I drank. "Good girl, honey."

The cool water was like ice on my throat, burning and soothing all at once.

"Enough?" he asked as I leaned back.

"Yes."

He put the cup down and sat on the edge of the bed.

"Please tell me what happened." I looked from him to Mom. "Someone?"

Mom, still holding my hand, sighed like the weight of the world rested on her shoulders. "Your school van was hit head on by a drunk driver. The driver died on impact. Everyone made it out alive—before the van caught on fire."

"It caught on fire?"

Dad nodded, adding to the story. "Michael was thrown from the vehicle but is still alive and in intensive care. Coach Lyles is okay. He was the one who went for help. He has two broken ribs and a fractured collarbone."

"The doctors said you're lucky to be alive," Mom said.

"What about Nick?"

She pursed her lips. "And another passenger from the other vehicle made it out alive too."

"Mom?"

She looked over at my dad, not me.

"Mom?" I asked again. "What about Nick?"

"He's in a medically-induced coma."

Thank God, he'd made it.

She swept her hand over my hair as I tried blinking away the sting in my eyes.

He'd made it.

I shut my eyes again, falling back into a deep sleep.

The next time I opened them, they were gummy and gritty. They felt as though they'd been swollen shut for an entire decade. I rubbed the sleep from them, catching someone standing to the right of me. "Piper?" What was she doing in *my* hospital room and not her own back in DC? "Why are you here?"

Piper angled out of the chair and shuffled over to me. "How do you feel?"

I tried sitting up but fell back against the pillow as the pain shot through every nerve in my body. "Been better—but, wait, what about you?"

"I'm fine. You're the one we've been worried about."

Everything came rushing back to me, the heavy rain, the squealing tires, the van rolling on its side on our way back to school. She'd been so incredibly lucky not to have been in that van with us. "I'm confused," I said, not sure how much time had elapsed. "You were so sick. What happened?"

She lifted her shirt, pointing to a small but fresh scar on her abdomen. "Appendix. It almost ruptured."

Appendix? I touched the aching knot on my forehead. "You had your appendix removed?" My mind jumped back to being in the van with Nick, telling him that he'd put something in the coffee that'd made Piper sick. "I thought..." I trailed off, confused. I'd been *so* sure.

"Yeah," Piper said. "I had surgery last week."

How had I lost an *entire* week? "Last week?"

Piper nodded.

"Tori?" Mom rushed out of the bathroom. "Oh, my goodness. Tori, you're awake!"

"Hi, Mom."

"Oh, honey," she said, swooping in and covering my face in tiny kisses. She smelled like vanilla and flowers, like a breath of summer. With the sterile hospital smell that permeated everything around me, it was a relief. "I've been so worried about you. We all have been."

"Where's Dad?"

"At work, but he's been here every day, checking in on you. How are you feeling?"

"Groggy. Thirsty."

She wiped the tears from her face. "Sweetheart, you had me so scared."

Piper stepped back, letting my mom fuss over me.

I rubbed my eyes, spotting Nick's backpack, not mine, on the floor by the nightside table.

"You've been in and out of it for days, but the doctor said you're going to be fine. Thank God, you're going to be fine."

The backpack held my attention, that sinking feeling returning to my gut. "How's Nick?"

"Doctor said to take things slow and easy right now."

My throat tightened. "Mom?"

"Michael and Coach Lyles are doing okay. Michael had a rough go, but he's better now."

"And Nick?" I repeated.

She reached for my hand and squeezed it as Piper turned to look out the window. The last thing Mom had said to me was that he'd been in a medically-induced coma. "Mom?"

"I'm so sorry." She put her hand over her mouth and blinked as her eyes started filling with tears.

"Mom... why are you sorry? Sorry about what?"

"He didn't make it, Tori."

"No, that's not possible. You're lying."

"Tori, honey, I'm so sorry," she repeated.

"No. It's not true. He can't be...." I couldn't even say the word. There was no way Nick was gone. It didn't make any sense. "How? What... happened?"

"The doctor said he took a turn for the worse."

What did that even mean—a turn for the worse? "You're lying," I repeated, biting back the tears. I turned my face away from her, burying it in my pillow. There was no way he was gone... first Ellie and now Nick? There was no way this was happening. It couldn't be.

Chapter 19

"**LET ME HELP**," **MOM** said, following me up the stairs to my room.

"I don't need your help." I clenched my teeth, wincing through the pain with every single step. "I told you. I'm fine."

Mom didn't respond, which was a good thing because I would have probably bit her head off with one more, *I'm sorry* or *let me help*. The truth was, I didn't know what I needed or how I was supposed to feel.

Mom placed my stuff on my bed then fluffed a few of my pillows. "Are you hungry?"

"No."

She nodded, moving toward the door, then paused. "His memorial is tomorrow. Do you think you'll be up for going?"

"I don't know." My eyes glassed over as I stared at the back-pack on my bed. It was *his* backpack on the foot of my bed, not mine. I hadn't told anyone it was his. I tried a few times, but for some reason, the words never came. What was the point? He was gone. I knew I needed to give it back to his mom, and I probably would. Eventually.

"Okay, hon. Get some rest. If you need anything, let me know."

Get some rest? All I'd been doing for days was resting. Maybe I'd go and return his bag now and tell Dr. Moore that I was sorry, that there'd been a mix up, and that mine had been destroyed in the car fire, not his. We were lucky to have made it out, they'd said. *We.* I grabbed his bag and threw it to the floor. It landed with a loud thud.

From downstairs, I heard, "Tori?"

"I'm fine," I called back to her, easing onto the floor. Every muscle in my body felt bruised and beaten as I leaned against the bed frame, pulling the backpack closer. I had no right. Then again, I had *every* right. If the letter was still inside, it belonged to me.

The first thing I saw in his bag was his laptop, a conference folder with a few handouts from sessions, and his blue spiral notebook. My hands started to sweat as I pulled out the notebook and slowly opened it. But the letter wasn't there. I checked his entire notebook then emptied his whole backpack looking for it. I even flipped his bag upside down, shaking it and spilling eighty-three cents in change, a forever stamp, and four mechanical pencils onto the floor.

It wasn't there.

The letter wasn't in his bag.

What had he done with it? Had he stashed it in his room at home? Did he have more there? I kicked the bag, watching as it slumped over on its side, and that's when I saw it. At first, I thought it was just a seam, the way the bag was designed. But then, as I pulled it closer, running my finger across the stitching, I realized it was a hidden pocket with a tiny zipper. Mine didn't have that. Did it?

My heart sped up as I unzipped the pocket.

There, right in front of my eyes, safely tucked away, was the letter along with a small black journal. I almost missed it. It was the same color as the fabric. My hands shook as I pulled both out, staring at them in my lap. I read the letter first, feeling just as sick as I had the first time. "What were you up to, Nick?" I whispered.

I reached under my bed, feeling for the shoebox that held his other letters, and stashed the latest one inside. As soon as I had the chance, maybe I'd burn them. All of them. Maybe I'd burn his backpack too. And his journal. I picked it up and fanned through its pages. The paper was thick and smelled sweet, and each page had a mere ghosting of graphite as my gaze chased the faint words.

One of the pages caught my eye. It had a list of names, mostly of kids from school. I recognized most of them, like his brother's, but there were a few I didn't. Ellie's name was on it, and so was mine. And someone named Emily—just Emily. *Emily who?* We had a million Emilys at school.

On the next page, notes were scribbled in shorthand or code. None of it made any sense. They sounded like notes on a book or movie: *Cloaked in anger, the character fades into the background... wearing red, watching every move.* A few lines down, he wrote: *Actions that permeate every level of society.* I flipped the page, but something was off, like a page had been ripped out. I ran my finger down the center across jagged edges as Mom called out for me.

I dropped the journal.

"Tori?" she said again.

"Yeah?" I yelled back.

"You got a delivery."

A delivery? I'd been so absorbed with his journal that I hadn't even heard the doorbell ring. I put it back in the hidden pocket then shoved his laptop and folders back in the main compartment. What the heck was that list all about? What was it even for? The throbbing of my incessant headache kept time with my pulse as I hobbled over to the landing.

"They're gorgeous, aren't they?" Mom held up the large bouquet of white and pink hybrid roses in a sea of baby's breath.

"Who are they from?" I asked, working my way down the stairs.

"Don't know." She set the oversized arrangement on the kitchen counter and rifled through the baby's breath, looking for a card. "Oh, here," she said, handing it to me.

I slid the card from the small envelope. "Says 'get well soon. Love, Drew.'"

"That's thoughtful of him. They are stunning."

I nodded, still shaken by finding the journal upstairs in the backpack.

"Oh, and you have some cards here." She pointed to the pile on the counter next to a few other arrangements I'd gotten while in the hospital.

I nodded, moving closer. The roses smelled pungent as I leaned in to admire their delicate petals. Beside them was a smaller bouquet and a "get well soon" card from my mom's office.

"Wasn't that nice of them?" Mom asked.

I nodded.

She grabbed the stack of cards and handed them to me, then kissed my temple. "How about sushi for dinner?"

It was Mom's go-to. It always had been for an A on a spelling test or after a bad run-in with a bully at school. One time we had sushi because my bully, Allie McInerny, made fun of my eyebrows, saying they were thick enough for squirrels to live in. We ate sushi for sadness. Sushi for celebrations. When anything happened in our lives, good or bad, sushi was the answer.

"I'll call it in, okay?"

"Will Dad be home for dinner?"

"I'm sure he will be."

As she pulled up the menu on her phone, I headed to the couch with my stack of cards. I opened the first and the second one. Both were from friends of my mom, sending get-well wishes from the family, but it was the third one in the pile that got me. My stomach plummeted at the sight of the thick, cream envelope with the clear label addressed to me. He had to have mailed it *before* DC. I glanced over my shoulder at Mom sitting at the counter, swallowed by flowers.

"Yes, I'd like to order two California rolls and a..."

I held my breath, tearing at the sealed flap with my fingernail. I pulled the letter, with its frayed, spiral edges, from the envelope and slowly unfolded it.

Someone else was there the night Ellie died.

Part Five: Piper

Chapter 20

"**YOU'RE GOING TO THE** memorial, right?" Mama asked, heading for my blinds. She tugged them open, instantly flooding the room with bright light.

"Shut the blinds," I begged. I hadn't slept in days and the light was definitely not helping my migraine.

She closed them back slightly. "It's in two hours."

"I know." I covered my face with my pillow. I'd seen the posts all over social media. I hadn't planned on going. Didn't want to, but I knew I should. I tossed the pillow to the side and slowly sat up, dangling my legs over the side of the bed.

"It's the right thing to do, Piper." She tugged on her gray button-down shirt that showed her slim torso. She'd lost so much weight since my dad had died. When his cancer came back the second time, it wasn't long before it took him from us. Just weeks, really. I was still numb from *that* service, not to mention Ellie's, and now I had another one to sit through?

"Piper?"

"Fine." I sat up, blinking away the sting in my eyes from the light streaming through the window.

What was one more?

"Good," Mama said then started down the hall toward the kitchen.

Hey, I texted Tori. *Going to the memorial?*

Probably, she wrote back.

Want to go together? I can pick you up. I held my breath, watching as the tiny conversation bubbles bounced. Finally, her message popped up.

Yeah.

Still lying on my bed, I stared at my closet. I needed something to wear, something other than the black beaded dress I'd worn to my dad's service and to Ellie's too. I couldn't bear the thought of putting it on one more time.

An hour later, I showed up on Tori's front doorstep in jeans and a black sweater. I wiped my sweaty palms on my jeans, thinking about everything that had happened to my dad, Ellie, and now Nick.

"Oh, hi, Piper. Come on in," Tori's mom said. "Tori? Piper is here."

As I pulled the door shut behind me, a jab of pain shot through my abdomen. It had been ten days since my surgery but sometimes, like now, it still hurt like hell.

"Hey," Tori said, meandering down the stairs in a black-and-white striped t-shirt dress, black boots, and a messy bun. It looked thrown together, but she was more or less presentable even by Mama's standards.

"How do you feel?" I asked her.

She shrugged. "Thanks for driving."

"Yeah, of course."

Her phone dinged in her hand. She rolled her eyes, hit mute, and dropped it in her purse. "Ready?"

"Sure."

She gave her mom a kiss on the cheek then followed me out the door. "You okay?" I asked her.

"Yeah, just a really hard day, you know? And then..."

I waited as she got in the passenger side of my dad's old Volvo. "And... what were you saying?"

"Oh, nothing. Just that... that was Drew who texted."

"Oh yeah?" I bit my lip and nodded. I really hated that guy. It was his fault Tori and I stopped being friends. "Y'all back together?"

"No. He's just been texting a lot since I got home from the hospital." She turned away, facing the window.

Don't get back with him. Please don't. That guy was the worst. Always had been. The last thing she needed was to get involved with him again. I wanted to tell her that, but instead, I turned up the music and avoided any potential for conflict. Didn't want any—not today.

A few minutes later, I turned into the school parking lot. My breath caught at the sight of the packed stadium. I hated big crowds. I especially hated this one. It reminded me of my dad's funeral with all the students and teachers dressed in black, milling around and crying. Some of them, a lot of them, hadn't even known him. One girl, who was bawling her eyes out, said to me, "I didn't have him in class or anything, but I heard he was a great professor." It shouldn't have made me mad, but it did. Why was she crying over someone she didn't know? I could understand if she'd met him and knew how amazing he was—because he was. Downright amazing.

"I don't know if I can do this again," Tori said, sitting up in her seat.

I took a deep breath, wanting to tell her that if I could do it again after my dad's memorial, she could too. Ellie and her were just friends. It wasn't like she'd lost a parent or anything. But I didn't tell her that. I pulled into the first parking spot I could find and said, "We've got this, okay?"

"I don't know, Piper." She closed her eyes and shook her head.

She wasn't the only one hurting. "Hey," I said. "Maybe we'll feel better if we go and say good-bye." So, it wasn't my best response. It was weak and contrived and I knew it the second I'd said it, but I couldn't give her any more than that.

She leaned back against the headrest. "You know the worst part of it?"

I inhaled slowly, waiting for her to tell me.

"I'm so pissed off at him for dying. I'm angry as hell, and not because we were friends or anything—does that make me a horrible human? It does, doesn't it?" She wiped her nose with the back of her hand. "I'm just so mad that he died without telling me why he sent those letters. I have so many questions for him, Piper." She buried her face in her hands. "I'm such a horrible human," she mumbled.

"No, you're not," I said, placing my hand on her shoulder.

She lifted her hands from her face then flipped down the sun visor to check her reflection. "I'm such a mess."

I reached for a fast-food napkin in the glovebox and handed it to her. If anyone was a mess, it was me. I was just better at hiding it. "Come on," I said. "Let's do this."

Chapter 21

THE SERVICE WAS BRUTALLY sad, not that I'd expected anything different. Practically the entire town had shown up to say bye to Nick. Emily Haskins, our junior class vice president, handed everyone a candle as they entered the stadium, just like she'd done for Ellie's service. Had she volunteered to help with Nick's service too? It kind of made sense though with her dad being a minister. Regardless, it was too soon. Too soon for any of us to sit through another vigil for someone else our age. I tried to remember if Nick had come to Ellie's memorial back in January, but that had been a blur too. Now, here we were in mid-April, back in the same place, probably using the same stock of candles, leftovers from Ellie's service.

After the memorial, we made our way down the steps, filing out of the stadium with the crowd. I had no intention of sticking around to talk to anyone, but surprisingly, Tori wanted to stay.

"Hey," she said. "I'd like to say something to Hayes before we leave. Want to come with me?"

Hayes was standing beside his tall, elegant mom. A long line had already formed by them with weepy people waiting to offer their condolences.

"You go ahead," I told Tori. "I'll be in the car."

"You sure?"

I nodded, spotting my brother out in the parking lot with his friend Sam. "Yeah, I'm good. Take your time though." As I brushed past a small group of girls, I thought about stopping to ask Wyatt how he was doing. It had to be hard on him too, the reminder of what we'd gone through with Dad. But as I started to approach him, he looked the other way. It was fine. We'd never been that close, and after our dad died, we'd drifted apart even further, if that was possible. Then again, it had proven to be just that. I shook it off and ran over to my car, welcoming the quiet inside the old Volvo.

After a few minutes, the parking lot started to thin out some. Tori had managed to squeeze in and talk to Hayes, breaking the line somehow. What was she saying to him? What *could* she say besides *I'm sorry*? She nodded at him then took a step backwards, running her hand through her hair. She'd always had a thing for him. She had since grade school. She'd told me and Ellie one night over a pint of Ben & Jerry's in her room. It was right before the three of us stopped being friends.

"So why are you dating Drew then?" I'd asked her.

"Because *he* actually likes me. Hayes Moore doesn't even know I'm alive."

I wished she'd never gone out with Drew. Never said yes to him. The only person Drew liked was himself.

Tori shifted from one foot to the other and wiped her blotchy cheek while Hayes kept his eyes fixed on his white Nikes, not making eye contact with her. Maybe it was too hard for Hayes to show any kind of emotion. It had been for me. I imagined her saying something to him like, "He was really brave and I'm so sorry for your loss." I'd heard the same platitudes at my dad's funeral, dozens of them, over and over again.

He pushed his shoulders back and turned slightly as his mom leaned into him. She said something, making him step back and nod. A few seconds later, Tori was heading back to the car, pushing her way through a sea of black. I hated how we were all dressed in dark colors again, saying more good-byes.

"Thanks for waiting," she said, getting in on the passenger side.

"No problem," I said, turning the key in the ignition.

She leaned back and closed her eyes. "Lemonheads?"

"You know it."

We sat there for a few minutes, listening to my dad's CD playing where we'd left off. After the last song on the album ended, Tori said in the quiet pause, "I yelled at him. Did you know that? He was dying and I yelled at him. How horrible is that?" She watched as Hayes and his mother crossed the parking lot towards his SUV.

"I'm sorry," I said, not sure what to say. Whenever I got angry at my dad for dying, all I ever wanted was for someone to quietly agree with me, no matter what I said, or yell with me. "Want to drive around for a little while?"

"I think I just want to go home."

"Okay."

We drove through town, passing Nick's house with the RIP signs and candles out front. Our town was too small for two kids to be gone from it. As we passed by, Tori mumbled something into the window.

"Did you say something?"

"I got another one yesterday."

"Another...?"

"Letter."

"Yesterday?" My chest tightened. "What did it say?"

She turned and faced me. "That someone else was there that night."

I pulled over on the side of the road, motioning for the car behind me to pass. "But wait, how did Nick send you another letter after... he died?"

"I don't know. Guess he sent it before he left for DC."

"Are you going to tell the police?"

"Not yet." She leaned the side of her face against the side window.

We sat there for a minute, cars speeding around us. Some of them honked as they passed. I didn't care though. I reached for her hand, gripping her fingers in mine.

"Sometimes, at night," she admitted softly, "I lie awake thinking about it all. I can't get the image of her out of my head, of her dancing in that fiery light. And now, Nick is gone too. Both of them are gone." She let go of my hand. "One minute they're here and then, the next, they're gone."

I nodded, swallowing the burn in the back of my throat and slowly easing back onto the road.

After dropping Tori off at her house, I ended up going to Nana's. I hadn't been back since before DC, and I needed to water her plants and check on her pipes.

Inside, it was dark and dusty as usual. I took my place on the worn plaid couch and imagined her across from me in her recliner.

"Tell me about your day, hon."

"It was awful, Nana. We had Nick's memorial today. It was so sad, you know?" I could see those wild, frizzed curls of hers swaying as she rocked back and forth.

"Those things are never easy," I imagined her saying.

Even though she was the one person in my life who I trusted more than anything, I hadn't told her what I knew. What I'd witnessed that night. I got up from the couch and opened the hall closet, shifting her favorite pair of red church pumps to the side. There was a loose plank of hardwood that I'd discovered years ago as a kid. I used to hide money and my diary in the small hole. Nana told me once that she kept a gun there to protect herself from her third husband, but he eventually drank himself to death. She buried her pistol in the backyard only *after* they lowered him into the ground.

"I'll visit you tomorrow at Sunnyside, Nana," I said, lifting a small box from beneath the floorboard. "Maybe you'll have a good day and recognize me."

Inside the box was a coral-colored phone in a clear case covered with tiny, fake gems. They glistened in the light streaming through the glass panels on the door. We kept the front porch lights on 24/7 to keep burglars away, not that Nana had anything of value left in her house. The only valuable thing, as far as I was concerned, was right there in my lap.

When I'd found it that night, I took it, for safekeeping. You know, just in case. It had been at Nana's house ever since. Turned off, of course. I'd spent weeks trying to decide what to do with it. Did I give it to her parents? To the cops? I finally decided I couldn't give it to anyone, not without implicating myself in her case.

I stared at the dark screen, catching a glimpse of my reflection in the glass. What if I turned it on? Surely no one was still monitoring her account. Her mom had to have disconnected it weeks ago. Right? My own phone buzzed in my pocket, making me nearly drop hers from my hand.

Where are you? Mama texted.

Watering Nana's plants.

I tucked Ellie's phone back in the cubby and stood, shutting the closet door. I always hated leaving Nana's. Even as a little kid, I never wanted to go.

Be home soon, I wrote back.

Before leaving, I sat down in Nana's recliner, touching the

worn arm rests where her hand used to lay. I ran my fingers across the hairline cracks in the leather just like she used to do. "She got another one yesterday, Nana. Another letter."

"What did it say?"

"That someone else was there that night. Nana, I think someone else knows."

Chapter 22

"THERE WILL BE GRIEF counseling this week during the first-shift lunch in the gym," the student worker announced over the intercom.

I leaned back in my desk, thinking about what Dr. Henderson had said a few weeks back, that maybe talking to someone would help. *Want to go?* I texted Tori.

Where? she typed back.

Grief counseling.

I don't know. Maybe?

I stared at the conversation bubbles, waiting for her to say, *yeah, okay*, but then she stopped typing.

I waited for her outside the gym at lunch, but she never showed. I almost bailed myself, but I didn't, hoping that maybe a little therapy would help quiet the ghosts in my head. Maybe talking about Nick's death would help me deal with Ellie's and even my dad's. It was a long shot, but worth a try.

The old gym had a stage on one side, where ten or twelve kids were already seated in a circle, waiting. The hundred-year-old hardwood popped under my feet as I stepped across the floor onto the stage. Behind me, the side door flew open. A tall, youngish woman with bright orange-red hair, the counselor I assumed, rushed toward us.

"Sorry I'm late, y'all," she called out, hurrying to join the rest of us on stage. "I'm Kiki."

The side door opened again. This time, it was Hayes. He paused as the door banged shut behind him. All eyes were suddenly on him.

"There's an open seat right here," Kiki called out to him. "Come join us."

He nodded, slowly making his way to the metal folding

chair beside her. Rachel, his on-again, off-again girlfriend was on his other side. She reached for his hand and held onto it.

Kiki smiled then turned her focus to the entire group. "So, how is everyone today?"

A few people mumbled okays.

"First things first, we're going to take things slow. This is your space and it's a safe one. We will be kind and respectful to one another, got it? Second..."

Hayes pushed his broad shoulders back, nodding, as Kiki outlined her expectations and hopes for the group. She kept on and on about "our space" and about "mutual goals." My only goal was to leave. I'd made a mistake coming.

"Okay," she finally said, ten minutes into the session. "Anyone feel like sharing? It's not required, but everyone is welcome to share."

Jack, Nick's friend also a freshman, raised his hand. His navy and white polo was two sizes too big, hanging on his narrow shoulders. "I'll go first," he said in a quiet, timid voice.

It was almost unbearable listening to him and some of the others talk about Nick. How was this doing any good, dredging up all of these memories just to make us sadder than before we'd come? It made no sense. As we worked our way around the circle, sharing our feelings, it was suddenly my turn.

But I didn't know what to say. Should I bring up my dad and tell them that the ache lets up eventually but that it never fully goes away? Or that some days are better than others? I cleared my throat, glancing for a quick second across the circle at Hayes. "It's hard for a lot of us." I squirmed in my chair. "It's hard to move on like nothing's happened. Like everything's normal. The same. It's not. Two of our people are gone." *Three, for me.* "We'll never see them again in the halls, at football games, wherever. Even though some of us weren't as close to them, we hurt just the same."

A lot of people nodded.

A few smiled at me.

"Do you?" Hayes said quietly, not looking up. "Hurt the same?"

I flinched, fumbling with my words. "I just meant that... I mean, we all are in pain."

"But you said we hurt the same."

"No," I backtracked.

"Because I don't think you have any idea what I'm feeling right now."

"Hayes," Kiki warned. "I know this is tough, but we need to respect everyone in this space, okay?"

He crossed his arms over his chest.

They were all the same—Drew, Hayes, Rachel—all of them were snotty, self-righteous asses. They all thought they were better than everyone.

"Would you like to say anything else?" Kiki asked, looking at me.

"No."

"Hayes?"

"No," he said.

She glanced at her phone. "It's almost time anyway, so let's call it a day, okay guys? And let's try and be kind to one another, yeah?" She smiled, nodding at Hayes.

I stood, making my way toward the stage stairs, but stopped. Hayes was on one knee, rummaging through his backpack. "You know," I said with my voice fueled with a quiet anger, "I was just trying to be supportive."

He looked up at me. "Yeah, well, I'm sick of everyone trying to be something all the time."

"What's that supposed to mean?"

"Forget it," he said, looking over his shoulder for Kiki, who was talking to another student.

"No, go ahead. You *obviously* have something to say."

"You didn't give a crap about Nick, but now, here you are, acting as if you two were friends or something. You weren't. Most people treated him like he was a freak. Well, you know what? He wasn't. He was my *brother*. That's something closer than a friend, although I know you don't have any of those. So, you can take your fake sympathy and go away."

"You have no right—"

"No right? No right to what? Talk to you that way?"

My eyes burned as I fought to keep the tears at bay.

He shook his head at me. "Just leave. You don't belong here."

He wasn't wrong. What right did I have for being there? His brother was gone. But if anyone knew the pain Hayes Moore was feeling, I did. The least I could do was shut up and walk away. I headed to the cafeteria to look for Tori, so I could vent to her about Hayes, but she was sitting with a few of her friends at a table out on the patio, immersed in one of her Russian lit books. That's what I should have done, instead of going to counseling. I headed over to the vending machines and stared at the boring selection of honey buns and peanuts behind plexiglass. Some guy, reeling about something, bumped into me. "Uh, hello?" I shook my head at him, but he acted like he didn't even see me. He didn't even move. He just kept standing there with his backpack digging into my shoulder.

"Did you hear about Miss Taylor?"

"Huh?" I turned to look at him, but he wasn't talking to me. He was asking his friend, Jordan something, who I knew from English class.

"No, what about her?" Jordan asked. He swept his floppy blond hair to the side.

I pressed A2 on the vending machine and waited for my pack of peanut butter crackers to fall.

"She got fired today." The guy pushed his glasses up with his palm. "Sasha Williams saw her being escorted out of the building this morning—by a cop."

"What? No way. Why?"

"No one knows for sure, but—"

The bell rang, cutting them off. I grabbed my crackers and wedged into the traffic, swiping through my phone. There was nothing, absolutely no info, on Miss Taylor.

"Hey," Tori said, running to catch up with me. "Did you hear?"

"About Miss Taylor?"

"Yeah. Wild, huh?

"Do you know why?" I asked, chewing on one of my chipped blue nails.

"No, but I'm shocked. Must be something major to get escorted out of the building."

She stopped with me at my locker, leaning against the one next to mine and propping a foot behind her.

"Missed you in counseling," I said.

"I wasn't feeling it today."

"Yeah, wish I hadn't gone either. Not after that run-in with Hayes."

Tori turned her head and looked at me with huge, curious eyes. "What happened?"

"He's angry."

She tugged on the collar of her retro pink and black pol-ka-dot top. "What did he do?"

"He told me he was tired of everyone acting all sad. Like he has the market cornered on grief or something." I scratched delicately at the tiny stud in the crease of my nose.

Tori nodded.

"He's always been an ass, though. You know?"

She leaned back again, facing the crowd passing by. "Well, his brother just died."

My face burned with heat.

"But you have every right to go to counseling, just like he does. I'll go with you tomorrow."

"I'm not going back."

The bell rang for fourth period.

"If you change your mind."

"I won't." I shut my locker. As we turned the corner to the C-Hall, Tori literally bumped right into Drew.

"Oh," she said, surprised. She stepped back from him, avoiding eye contact.

He ran a hand through his hair and glanced at me.

It made my skin crawl.

"Sorry, T," he said, looking back to Tori. "Didn't see you." He smoothed the front of his olive-green shirt and smiled.

I stared at the small gap between his front teeth.

"Wild about Miss Taylor, isn't it?" Drew said.

"Do you know what happened?" she asked.

"Heard she was stealing from a school account."

"Not what I heard," Wyatt said, nearing us. "She was sleeping with a student."

Drew's eyebrows lifted. "Hadn't heard that one."

"Me, neither," Tori added.

"Well, now you have." Wyatt said, heading into the class-room next to ours.

Drew followed him but then stopped in the doorway to glance back at us. Tori had her back turned to him, so she didn't see that smug smile on his face or the wink he gave me before heading into the classroom. Everything about the guy was wrong. Everything. "Ugh," I groaned.

"What'd you say?" Tori asked.

I started to tell her what a creep the guy was just as Dr. Henderson came on the intercom, saying, "Would the following students please report to the main office: Michael Sanchez, Piper Wells, and Brie Sanderson."

Tori scrunched her nose at me. "What's that all about?"

"Who knows," I told her even though I had a pretty good idea. I'd been falling even more behind in my classes since DC and my surgery. Mama had mentioned having to go and talk to Dr. Henderson "soon." It was probably just another warning for me to get caught up, or else.

"You'd better go," Tori said. "You don't want to piss off Dr. Henderson."

"No kidding. Hey, I'll catch up with you later, 'kay?"

She nodded then headed into her classroom.

As I walked down the hall to the office, I couldn't get that smug smile out of my head. If only Tori knew the real Drew.

Chapter 23

"HAVE A SEAT," DR. Henderson said. "So, Piper, I met with your mother earlier."

Bet that was a real blast.

"She's aware of the difficulties you've been having lately but hadn't realized just how far you'd gotten behind in your classes."

"Yeah, well, it's been a crappy few weeks."

"I understand that," Dr. Henderson said, tugging on her polka-dotted blouse. "That's why I wanted to talk to you today... to make sure you don't fall even further behind. I'm only trying to help."

She kept going on and on in that nasally voice of hers.

I nodded at all the right places and smiled when she paused, waiting for some kind of reaction. But mostly, I just tuned her out as best I could.

"Do you get where I'm going with all this?" she asked.

"Yes, ma'am. I hear you."

"All right then. Be sure to stop by the front desk for your packet."

What packet? I thought as I stood to leave.

"Oh, and Piper?"

"Yes, ma'am?"

"Glad to hear you went to grief counseling today."

That made precisely one of us.

I shut her office door and stepped around the corner to the front desk for my "packet." But Mrs. Doris wasn't at her desk—someone else was. I stopped dead in my tracks, staring at the back of the someone going through the piles on Mrs. Doris' desk. The woman in the navy pant suit paused, slowly straightening her posture. It was almost as if she sensed me standing there. She waited a few more seconds before turning around.

"Hello, there," she said, brushing the front of her navy suit.

"Oh, hi," I said, surprised to see who it was.

Why was Hayes' mom in the school office?

She ran a few fingers over her hair, slicked back in a tight bun. "Can't seem to find the file Doris left for me."

"Okay," I said. I wanted to say more. Say that I was sorry about Nick, but I choked.

"Here you are, Dr. Moore," Mrs. Doris said, coming out of the copy room with a folder for her.

"Thank you," she said.

On the counter was a packet with my name on it. I grabbed it and left, not wanting to stay a minute longer than I had to.

After school, I texted Tori asking if she wanted to hang out. The alternative was going home and facing Mama and Ray, so I begged her: *Please, please, please? I'll buy you a coffee? Don't want to go home—not after getting in trouble with Dr. H.*

"You didn't have to buy me a latte," she said as we pulled out of The Grind's drive-thru. "But thanks."

"Of course," I said. "It was the least I could do after dumping all my stuff on you about Dr. Henderson. Can't believe how much make-up work I have to do."

"Yeah, that is a lot."

"So, where to?" I asked, pulling onto Main.

"We can go to my house if you want?"

The last time I'd been there was the day of Nick's memorial. And, before that, it was the night we'd gone to the river—the night she showed me the letter. We hadn't talked about the letters, not since the memorial when she told me she'd gotten another one. I was just about to bring it up when she said, "Can't believe I *literally* bumped into Drew today."

He was the *last* person I wanted to talk about. "Yeah, that was awkward."

"Right?" she said, shaking her head.

"Have y'all been talking again?"

She took a deep breath. "We've texted a few times."

"Oh yeah?"

"I sent him this really embarrassing text, saying, *You deserve better. Better than some messed up girl haunted by her dead best friend.* He didn't text back at first, which was weird because he'd been texting me a lot, especially after Nick's service. But then I texted him again, saying, *Sorry for everything. I just need time to figure things out."*

"What'd he say?"

"He sent me a thumbs-up emoji." She sighed.

A year together and he sends her a freaking cartoon emoji. Nice.

A few minutes later, we pulled into her driveway. It was kind of weird but nice, the way we'd slipped back into our friendship. I used to hang out at her house all the time with her and Ellie. The three of us would watch Netflix and eat junk food. Ellie would raid the fridge as if it were her own and joke with Tori's cop dad as if he wasn't a cop and totally intimidating. I never understood Ellie's lack of fear.

"Coming?" Tori asked, getting out of the car.

"Yeah." I turned off the engine and followed her to the door.

"Are you sure everything's okay?" she asked as we headed upstairs.

"Yeah, why?"

"You're just so quiet," Tori said.

"It's been a long, crappy day." I reached for her remote on the nightstand. "So," I said, trying to lighten the mood, "what are we watching?"

We ended up streaming two episodes of *The X-Files* and were about to start a third when I got a text from my mom, asking what time I'd be home. If Ray was there, never. I tossed my phone face-down on the bed and turned to Tori. "I can't believe you like this show. It's so old."

Tori shrugged. "Maybe I'm an old soul."

"Yeah, one who believes in aliens."

Tori didn't laugh. She just sat there, staring off into space. "You know what's crazy though?"

"Tell me." I sat up, leaning against her headboard.

"I think he was right."

"Agent Mulder?" I asked.

"No, your brother today about Miss Taylor."

"Why do you think that?"

Tori shrugged. "Why else do you get fired and carted off in the middle of a school day?"

"For stealing money?"

"Yeah, maybe." She hit pause on the TV and faced me. She blinked a few times, biting her bottom lip, which made her two front teeth jut out slightly.

"What is it?" I asked.

"What if she was sleeping with Drew?"

"What?" I reared back. "Why would you say that?"

She inhaled slowly. "I don't know? A feeling?"

I wasn't buying it. She knew something. There was something she wasn't telling me. "Spill it."

She rolled off the bed and went over to her window, staring out into the backyard.

"Tori?"

"I kind of went to his house after Nick's memorial."

Why on earth would she do something like that? But I knew why. Drew had that something about him, a confidence or arrogance that was tempered by his boy-next-door good looks. Tori once said, after they'd first started dating, "I can't believe he picked me. I can't believe someone like Drew actually likes me." She was better than that—better than being the girl who needed to be defined by a boy.

"Drew texted me after the service, and I was so sad," she said, still looking out the window.

Where was she going with this?

"So, after you dropped me off, I went to his house. But not right away. It was later that night. Anyway, his door was open, so I went inside. But he wasn't alone. I saw them together in bed... her hair, his face, her bare back."

"You saw him with Miss Taylor?"

"Well, not exactly. I don't know if it was her or not. The hair was the same color. Maybe. It was dark in the room."

"Oh my gosh, Tori."

"I didn't want them to see me standing there, so I took off." Tori suddenly turned red. "I mean, I never saw her face, but what if it was her and it's been going on for a while? What if someone finally turned them in?"

I sighed, not exactly sure what to say.

"I wish I'd never gone over there. I should have just stayed at home."

Tori's mom knocked on the door, mercifully interrupting. "You girls hungry?"

"No," Tori said, clearing her throat. "We're about to go for a walk."

"Now? Where?"

"I don't know, Mom. Just going out for some air."

Tori's mom, in her posh pink zip-up, straightened her shoulders. She was way trendier than my mom, whose closet hadn't seen anything from this decade. I kind of felt sorry for her mom though. It was almost as if she was waiting for us to ask her to come with us, but Tori just swept past her in the doorway. I smiled awkwardly, still shocked by what Tori had just told me, and followed after her.

Downstairs in the kitchen, Tori paused at the counter, glancing at a vase of sweet-smelling hybrid roses. A few of the petals had started to wilt, drooping sadly to one side. She plucked a stem from the vase then headed to the cabinet, pulling out a Mason jar. "Come on," she said, jar in hand.

"Where are we going?"

Minutes later, we were cutting down Peach Street and over to Church, stopping in front of Nick's house.

"Why are we here?"

"Did you know," she said, pointing to the right side of the house, "that used to be an old carriage house?"

"No."

"Yeah. They converted it years ago."

We stood in front of Nick's mini mansion, both of us staring at it in silence. How had we ended up talking about Drew sleeping with someone to standing in front of Nick's hundred-year-old house? Tori sat down on the curb. I did the same, picturing Nick in his room and Hayes storming around the house, slamming doors or something. Tori started plucking petals from the rose she'd taken from her house. One by one, she dropped them into the bottom of the Mason jar. She pulled a candle from her coat pocket and lit it. Then she placed it onto the petals, watching as the small tealight flickered in the dusk sky.

She said a quick prayer, because, she said, that's what you did when someone died. "You pray for their soul and for their family's healing."

I nodded. "Okay."

"Piper?"

"Yeah?"

"Why do you think he sent me those letters?"

The flame quivered in the Mason jar, catching my eye. I

couldn't breathe, and again, I didn't know how to answer her. As the flame gleamed inside the glass jar, I could feel her staring at me, waiting for an answer. "I don't know."

She looked so sad, so broken, sitting there holding the jar in her hands. She'd been through a lot, losing Ellie and then finding out that the one person, *supposedly*, who knew what had happened to her was gone now too. And, on top of that, she'd caught her ex in the act with another girl, maybe our teacher, a few weeks after their break-up. Yeah, it was a lot to process.

I swallowed the lump in my throat and said a little prayer too, knowing how hollow the words sounded as soon as they escaped my lips. "God, please make it all go away."

"Amen," she said.

Part Six: Hayes

Chapter 24

WHAT WAS SHE THINKING, placing a jar of flowers outside *my house*? It wasn't the first time Tori had come around either. Mom said it was nice of her to pay her respects, but I didn't like it. Not one bit. It was weird and unsettling. After she and her friend left, I went outside to get a closer look at her flower jar. She'd placed rose petals and a small candle inside of it with a note: RIP, Nick. Gone but not forgotten. *How sweet of her*, I thought, and then kicked it so it rolled into the storm drain.

"It's not her fault, Hayes," Mom said as I stormed through the front door a few moments later.

Wasn't it? I mean, it was no secret that my brother was in love with Tori, and I was pretty sure the only reason he went on that stupid trip was to be close to her. At first, I'd convinced myself I was fine, that I was strong enough to handle the meaningless platitudes, the creepy teddy bears and posters from everyone outside our gate, and the "everything happens for a reason" BS. Maybe I wasn't that strong after all.

"You need time to heal," Mom said, almost as if she'd read my mind. It was a hazard of being a therapist's kid.

"I'm fine," I lied.

"You know," she said, following me into the kitchen, "it's okay to get angry or to be sad." Her eyes welled up with tears.

I grabbed the milk from the fridge and gulped it right out of the container. She'd love that for sure.

Sure enough, she sighed loudly and shook her head. "It takes time."

Genius assessment, I thought, wiping milk from my upper lip. "I'm fine."

She tilted her head at me. "Hayes, honey."

"Seriously, I'm fine."

She pulled me into her arms and held me. I could hear her own quiet sobs that she was trying so hard to hold in. "I love you, Hayes," she whispered into my hair.

"Love you, too."

She took a deep breath in then stepped back, wiping her cheek. "I went by the school today."

"Why?"

"To talk to Dr. Henderson. I wanted to drop off some things for Kiki, too."

I held her stare.

"Heard you went to a session. How did that go?"

Didn't she already know? I'm sure Kiki had blabbed about my anger issues and how I'd taken it out on Piper. "It was fine."

Mom nodded at me. "Like I said, it's going to take some time. So, if you're not ready to—"

"Said it's fine."

"Okay. If you want to talk—"

"I don't." I was tired of talking to everyone. Tired of being psychoanalyzed at every turn. "I don't."

The next day at school, I slipped into Mr. Harris' class a few minutes late, just enough to avoid the rote "how are you's." He was showing a World War II film on his ancient projector, the kind that clicked the film through a reel. "Nothing like it," he always said. On screen were black-and-white images of kid's shoes piled high in heaps and emaciated faces with hollowed eyes. The images played against background music that was shrill and too loud. Mr. Harris must have been nearly deaf. Probably as ancient as his projector. I gripped the sides of my desk as the narrator spoke about the Nazi invasion. The narrator sounded a lot like my grandfather with his deep, pipe-smoker voice. The music grew louder, making my ears ring and my head woozy.

After class, I headed to second period and then third, not paying much attention to anything. I almost skipped counseling, but the alternative was going to the cafeteria with all the gawking eyes and sad girls crying superficial tears for a kid they didn't even know. Either way, my options sucked.

The main lights were off in the gym, making the place feel calmer, quieter, with natural light seeping through the old windows. Up on the stage was a smaller group than yesterday. Only four or five students were sitting there with the counselor. Rachel had told me earlier that morning that she had a student council meeting and wasn't going to come, but it didn't matter. None of it mattered. I'd told her the night before that I needed some space. I could barely breathe anymore. I couldn't handle my mom, my teachers, and my girlfriend constantly pressing me about everything.

"Mom says I need some time to process things on my own," I'd told Rachel. Okay, so it wasn't entirely true, but Mom had said I needed time to heal. And I wanted to do it on my own.

"Okay," she'd said. "How much time do you need?"

"I don't know, Rach. How much time does it take for someone to get over his brother dying?"

"I'm sorry," she'd whispered over FaceTime. "I love you."

"I know," I told her.

And that was that. It seemed lately that we'd been on again and off again, but this time, it felt more final—for me anyway.

Now, as I hesitated by the gym door, I felt bad for being mean to her, but it'd be worse if I stayed. It was for the best.

"Hayes?" Kiki called out, spotting me. "Glad you decided to come back."

I'd lost my chance to make a run for it, but did I care?

She waved me over. "Come join us."

As I walked across the gym floor, the door behind me banged shut. Fast footsteps echoed across the floor catching up to mine.

"Hey," a small voice said, a little out of breath.

"Hey..." I said back, realizing who it was, "...Tori."

She looked up at me with her big greenish brown eyes and smiled. At least Piper wasn't with her. Not yet anyway. I stepped onto the stage, taking a seat beside Michael. He was wearing a navy knit hat that covered most of his white hospital bandage, but he still looked pretty beat up. He nodded at me then looked away, the survivor's guilt teeming in his eyes.

"Glad you came back," Kiki said to me.

I gave a noncommittal nod.

"Okay," she said, "Let's get started. Anybody want to go first?"

All eyes were on me, still, except for Tori's. She was sitting across from me and staring at her shoes. If only she hadn't gone on that stupid trip, my brother might still be alive. He only went to be close to her. I balled my hands into tight fists, feeling anger pulse through my whole body.

Kiki nodded reassuringly at the group. "Anyone?"

Everyone stared at the ground. They were all afraid to speak up, probably because I tore into Piper during the last session. I tilted my chin in the air, fighting off the burn in my throat. Maybe Mom had been right after all. Maybe I *did* need more time. Maybe it was too soon. My brother's face flashed in my mind—his goofy, freckled frog face. I cleared my throat. "The last thing I said to my brother was for him to get out of my room—no, actually, I *yelled* at him to get the eff out of my room. That was the last thing I said to him."

Kiki pressed her fingers to her lips and sighed slowly. "Thank you, Hayes. I know you regret those being your last words to him, but you know what?" She ran a hand over her red-tinted hair. "That's what siblings do. They pick at each other and fight over meaningless stuff, but it doesn't mean they don't love each other. He knew you did."

Tori looked directly at me. She'd said that day in the parking lot, the day of his memorial, that he'd talked about me the night of the wreck, but my mom had interrupted us before I'd had the chance to ask what he'd said. I held Tori's stare, my pulse quickening. "What did he say... in the van the night of the wreck?"

She squirmed in her gray metal chair. "Um," she said in almost a whisper.

"It's okay," Kiki said, reassuring her.

She nodded then looked at me again. Man, her eyes were unnerving.

"He said you were... brave. I think he really admired that about you. Looked up to you."

The blood coursed violently through my veins as I clenched my fists again. Brave? I wasn't brave. I felt small and broken. I leaned back in my chair and kept quiet as someone else interjected about Nick. It took everything in me to not stand up and kick a chair over. I sat there, gritting my teeth and not saying another word for the rest of the session, hating the way I was all over the place. "It's to be expected," I could hear my mom say. Even so, I hated going from sad to mad in under sixty seconds—then back to sad again. The yoyo was exhausting.

After Kiki told everyone to stay strong and that she'd see us tomorrow, I bolted out of there as fast as I could, taking the side stairwell to class. But halfway up the stairs, I realized that after all that uncomfortable talk about our feelings, I'd forgotten my bag, and so I headed back down for it.

The door leading to the stage flew open, nearly clocking me in the face.

"Oh, sorry," Tori said, just as surprised as I was. "Did I get you?"

"Nah, it's good," I said.

"Did you forget something?" she asked, stepping out of the way to let me pass.

"My backpack."

"Oh, right." She nodded in the dim stairwell light and started heading up the stairs.

"Hey?" I called up to her, already on the third step. "Can I ask you something?"

She took a step down, meeting me at eye level.

"Why do you keep coming to my house?"

She blinked fast, her long lashes fluttering.

"You sit there on my curb, lighting candles for him or whatever."

She shifted from one foot to the other, just staring at me.

"Why? Why do you do it?" I waited for her to answer me. "Does it make you feel better?"

She pinched her eyes shut then reopened them. "No. Maybe? I don't know, Hayes."

"Well, can you maybe stop doing it?"

She bit her lip and nodded at me.

As she turned to head back up the stairs, I suddenly felt bad. "Hey," I said, letting out a deep, heavy sigh.

"Yeah?"

"I didn't mean to be... I just...."

"I know," she said. "You don't have to explain."

I stood there, not sure what to say next. Thanks?

"But—can I ask *you* something?"

I shrugged. "Guess so."

"You wanted to know what Nick said to me the night he died, right?"

"Yeah?" Now I was the one shifting on my feet.

"Well," she said, rubbing her forehead. "I'd like to know what Ellie said to you the night she died."

My gut dropped. Her question took the wind right out of me. "I—I don't know what you're talking about."

"I saw you talking to her as I was leaving that night. I didn't remember it before, but I'm starting to remember things about that night, one of them being you standing there talking to her by the bonfire."

Why was she bringing this up *now*? I cleared my throat and kept my eyes on the ground, staring at her scuffed white Nikes in the dark stairwell, lit by a window at the top.

"Do you remember what you said to her?"

"I talked to a lot of people that night."

"Okay, but what did you say to *her*?"

I stepped backwards, suddenly unsteady on my feet. "I have no idea."

"No idea? None at all?" she asked.

"No."

The door leading to the stage flew open again. This time it was Kiki. "Oh, hi, guys. Everything okay here?"

Why hadn't I just kept walking? Why did I have to stop? "I - I forgot my backpack."

"Well, you're about to be late for class, so be quick and go get it."

I just stood there, staring at Tori.

"Hayes?"

"Yes, ma'am." I rushed past Kiki, not daring to look back at her or at Tori. Why did she have to bring up Ellie and that night anyway? Why not just leave it buried in the past? I stepped out onto the stage, my mind running in a thousand different directions. How was I supposed to go back to class after all that?

I reached for my bag, exactly where I'd left it. "Big mistake coming today," I mumbled under my breath. "Big mistake."

Chapter 25

AFTER SCHOOL, I WENT straight home and sat in the quiet dark of my room. I didn't bother opening the shades. I just sank into my bed, thinking about Tori and her Mason jar full of flowers and the way she stood there in that stairwell staring at me with those eyes. It made my head swim. She had some kind of effect on me. Always had, ever since first grade. If it hadn't been for Kiki, who knows, I might have slipped and said something I shouldn't have.

I lifted my arm, placing it over my eyes. I was tired of thinking. Tired of being in my own skin. So much had happened in such a short span of time, it was a wonder any of us were still standing. If only we could hit rewind and go back in time. Maybe if Ellie hadn't died that night, then Nick wouldn't have either. I knew it didn't work that way, but Tori got me thinking that the two deaths were somehow linked, like a chain, connected. It was probably a stupid way to think since Nick had been killed by a drunk driver. But there was something about Ellie's death, about that night, that kept nagging at me.

"Can you tell us what you remember?" Detective Ivey had asked me.

Detective Ivey had called all of us down to the station a few days after the night Ellie went missing, and one-by-one, took each of us into the interrogation room. It wasn't called that, but it looked like one with its sterile metal table and the light blinking red on the camera hanging from the ceiling. I'd seen enough crime shows to know what this was. To know that the bottle of water she gave us was to nab our DNA after we drank from it.

"Hayes, take us through Saturday night. How did you get

there?" She was taking the lead, instead of her much older, much rounder partner Jim.

"Like I said, there's not much to tell." I rubbed my eyes and looked over at my mom, who nodded.

"That's okay. Just tell us what you know." She ran a hand over her hair, smoothing fly-aways back in her ponytail. "What time did you get to the party?"

"Maybe nine-thirty."

"And who drove?"

"I did."

"Who came with you to the party?"

"Rachel, my girlfriend." I eyed the camera lens watching me from the ceiling. I'd already told another cop the same stuff less than an hour earlier.

"Were you with Rachel the entire time?"

"Yes, mostly."

"Mostly?"

"Well, she didn't go to the bathroom with me."

The detective narrowed her eyes at the quip. "Did you see Ellie at the party?"

"Sure. Everyone did. She was dancing by the fire most of the night."

"And the last time you saw her was what time?"

"I have no idea. Eleven, maybe? Look, I wasn't paying that much attention to her. She was fine the last time I saw her. Dancing, laughing, I think."

"You *think*?"

I took a long sip of water. "I *think* she was talking to her boyfriend Connor when I left."

"Were you drinking?"

"No."

"Was she? Was Ellie drinking?"

"I don't know."

"There's a lot you don't seem to know," Ivey said.

The red light kept blinking at me. *Tell the truth. Tell the truth.*

The detective leaned back, shaking her head.

Tell the truth. Tell the truth.

My ears whirred and the room spun. I couldn't take it anymore. How—why—was this even happening? One minute everything was fine and the next, our lives were suddenly spinning into something unrecognizable. Why were we even here? My stomach lurched as I pictured Ellie's face in the firelight. *Tell the truth. Tell the truth.*

I leapt from my chair and heaved over the small trash can in the corner.

"You all right?" Her voice was softer now.

No, I wasn't all right. A girl I'd gone to school with since grade school had just been found dead.

"Let's take a short break, 'kay?" Jim offered.

I let my pounding forehead fall to the cool, metal table. The heavy door clicked behind the detectives as they left the room.

When they finished questioning me an hour later, I stepped into a hallway full of other kids who'd been called down to the station for questioning too. My mom told me to wait while she went and talked to someone. Drew was there, and so was Ellie's boyfriend Connor. So was Sam Cox—of course he was. It was his party, after all.

"Hey, now. It's going to be okay," Drew said, holding onto Tori. She'd just come out of the room and was crying into his sweatshirt. "What did you tell them?" Drew asked her. She was sobbing so hard she could barely talk.

We were all freaking out by that point. I'd heard that on Sunday morning, a couple of hunters had found Ellie's body by the Usman River. Not long after that, it was all over the internet: *Breaking News: Waterford Teen Found Dead.* And then, one-by-one, we were being pulled into the police station and being asked what we knew about that night.

"What did you tell them?" Drew asked Tori again.

"The truth."

His eyes flickered as he held her and glanced over at me. The guy was hiding something, that much I knew. Then again, weren't we all?

My phone buzzed on my nightstand, pulling me from that night at the police station. I reached for it, only to be gutted by the reminder on screen for "Nick's Swim Meet @ HHS @ 4:30." Mom must have added it to my calendar weeks ago. I grimaced and hit "ignore" before I stood up slowly making my way across the hall to his room. The door hadn't been opened since we got the news. Mom hadn't been able to go in there. Neither had I.

I pushed it open, breathing in a plug-in air freshener, still fresh in the corner, and sat on his bed, facing his old mahogany desk. All those hours he'd spent sitting there, writing meticulous, grad-level papers and solving impossible math equations. It was wild the way his brain was wired. It wasn't anything like mine.

Nick was different from the other kids in school. He was a little socially awkward—okay, a lot—but I chalked it up to his massive brain. The kid was excessively detailed and neat, everything always had to be perfect, from the pillows on his bed to the food on his plate—vegetables could never touch meats or starches. But other than that, Nick was a pretty normal kid. He had friends. He was on the swim team. He played video games.

We played video games together. Now, we never would again.

I went over to his desk, pulling out every single drawer, one by one, throwing each across his perfectly kept shrine of a room. I tore through old tests, school handouts, and pamphlets and tossed his favorite brand of yellow pencils across his floor. Marbles, paper clips, tubes of half-used Chapstick, tiny green army men, stickers—a hodge-podge collection of his life spilled all over the floor.

"What the hell are you doing?" Mom asked.

I turned to see her standing in the doorway. Her hair was pulled back into a tight, low bun, and the vein on her forehead bulged as she stared at me, angry as hell. She dropped to her knees, gathering up Nick's things. "Get out of here. Now!"

My shoe rolled on a pencil as I swept past her and ran downstairs. I grabbed my keys on the counter and left, not knowing where to go, what to do, or how to be anymore.

Chapter 26

I **DROVE AROUND TOWN** for a while, listening to one of the classic rock stations Nick loved. He'd programmed it in, not that I ever let him listen to it when he was in the car. Now, I turned it all the way up for him, blasting REO Speedwagon as I cruised down Main Street on my way to the soccer fields. There were so many things I still needed to say to him, so much that was left undone.

"No more thinking," I told myself as I pulled into the school parking lot. "No more." I grabbed the ball from my back seat and ran out to the field, kicking it down the left side then sending a shot to the top right of the net, all to do it over and over and over again.

"Hey!" someone shouted.

It was Wyatt, coming out of the fieldhouse with Connor.

"Missed you at practice," Wyatt yelled.

I took another shot on goal. It hit the crossbar. "Yeah, something came up," I lied.

Connor ran after the ball then kicked it back to me. "Want to grab some food with us?"

"Yeah, come on," Wyatt said.

We ended up going to Blue's—the last place I wanted to go. First of all, it was Nick's favorite place, and second, it was where Tori worked. "Hey, I think they're closed," I said from the backseat.

"Nah, we got time," Wyatt said.

The "open" sign blinked at me from the window as I climbed out of Wyatt's Jeep. Before I had a chance to say anything else, he and Connor were lugging me to the front door. Maybe she wasn't working tonight. And even if she was, who cared?

As we headed inside, the manager greeted us then poked his nose into the kitchen, yelling, "Tori, you've got a table!"

Great.

"Got it," she yelled, stepping out from the back.

She stopped in the doorway as soon as she saw me. "Oh," she said, holding my stare. "How many?"

The door behind me chimed. A couple seconds later, someone's arm looped into mine. It was Rachel, wearing a Waterford High Cross Country sweatshirt.

Tori pressed her lips together. "So, four of you?"

"Hey, Lori," Rachel said, squeezing my arm.

"It's Tori," I said.

"Oh, right. Of course."

Rachel smiled in that artificially sweet way of hers then fluttered her eyelashes at me. At one point, I'd probably thought it was cute. Now, it just annoyed me.

"There's going to be at least six of us," Rachel swept a hand through her blonde hair, shaking it so it fell over her shoulders.

Tori grabbed a few more menus. "Got it. Follow me."

Rachel grabbed my hand as the four of us walked to the u-shaped booth in the corner. What was she doing? I'd told her, more than once, that I needed space, and here she was, still acting like we were a thing. Who called her anyway?

Tori tossed the menus on the table as we sat down. "I'll give y'all a few minutes." She turned and sped to the kitchen, where, a minute later, a loud crash echoed over to us. When she came back, she was smiling and completely composed.

"Everything okay back there?" Wyatt called to her. "My sister must be working." He laughed.

I forgot about Piper working there.

"Nope. Just me tonight. What can I get y'all to drink?"

I could feel her eyes on me. I bit my lip, staring at the blurry menu—milkshake? Coke? Sweet tea? I had no idea what I wanted. I started to say something when the bell on the front door chimed again, followed by someone's high-pitched, obnoxious laugh.

"Over here," Rachel said, waving at her best friend Sydney. She towered over the girl next to her, also on the cross country team. Sydney had to be close to six feet tall with long black hair reaching down her back.

They both crammed into the booth with us, squeezing Rachel closer to me. I wanted to leave, to get away from them all.

"Something to drink?" Tori asked me again.

"I'll have a Coke."

"And for you?" Tori asked Connor.

"Same. You doing alright?" he asked her. They knew each other pretty well because of Ellie.

"Hanging in there." She glanced at Sydney, who had cozied up to him.

But it made sense. No one would blame him. It wasn't like he and Ellie had some epic romance. Besides, Sydney had dated Connor first, back in junior high. It was almost as if Tori heard me—*and* agreed with me. She paused for a second then shrugged at the two of them together.

"So," Rachel said, after Tori finished taking our orders. "How was your day?"

"Fine," I said.

She tried her best to keep the conversation going between us, but after I kept giving her simple, one-word answers, she finally gave up. I pulled up on my phone the last soccer game we'd played and watched the footage until our food came. But even then, I kept watching the game while I ate. Occasionally, I looked up from my screen and laughed at a stupid joke that Wyatt made. But, for the most part, I just wasn't feeling it.

After we finished eating, Tori returned to grab a few plates. "You pay up front," she said.

"I'll pay," Rachel offered, taking the check.

I opened my mouth to argue, but she and her friends had already slipped out of the booth and were headed to the counter.

"Nice of Rachel to pay for everyone," Wyatt said, following me outside.

"Yeah," I said disinterestedly, knowing she didn't have a limit on her dad's credit card.

When she finished checking out, she came outside and stood next to me. "Want to hang out for a little while?" she asked, playing with her hair.

She had no clue, never had, when things got dark or heavy with me. Rachel was fun. She was gorgeous and smart—just not when it came to me. "Still need some space, Rach."

"Oh. Right."

She kissed me on the cheek, squeezing my arm. "Still love you," she said, then ran to catch up with her friends.

It was for the best. I kept telling myself that as I got in Wyatt's Jeep, all while the guilt for brushing her off compounded. As if everything else wasn't enough. I couldn't breathe. I felt suffocated and alone all at the same time. Everyone was just trying to help, but no one knew how. *I* didn't even know how. I reached for my phone to tell my mom I was headed home, when I realized I'd left it inside on the table.

"Hey, Wyatt, hang on a minute. I forgot my phone."

Tori was sitting in the booth with her forehead on the table when I walked in. "What a nightmare," she mumbled.

"We weren't that bad, were we?"

She jerked upright and looked at me.

"Forgot my phone." I reached for it across the table, which was still piled high with our dirty plates.

"Oh. Right."

I kept standing there, wanting to say something else. But what? Thanks for the great service? Did Rachel leave you a decent tip?

"Rachel's probably waiting for you," she said.

"She already left." I shifted my weight on my heels, suddenly nervous. Why was I nervous? I twisted the watch band around my wrist.

"Is that his?" She pointed to my arm.

Nick's face flashed in my mind, and I thought about his room, how I'd totally trashed it. I cleared my throat. "Yeah."

"Thought so."

I kept standing there, wanting somehow to bring up earlier when we'd talked in the stairwell. But how?

"I need to lock the door behind you."

"Oh, right. Sorry."

She followed me to the door and stepped outside to grab the chalkboard sign of daily specials.

"I'm sorry about today," I said. *About the way I acted when you brought up Ellie.*

She put the chalkboard sign down, glancing over at Connor and Wyatt in the Jeep. Both were on their phones, not paying a bit of attention to us. Tori nodded, looking up at me with those big eyes of hers, guarded. At one point, they hadn't been. I'd known about her crush on me when we were kids, but now, it was hard to tell what she thought of me. "I was wrong earlier," I said.

"About what?"

"I don't have any right to tell you what to do, but I still don't get why you light those candles for him."

"Yeah, I've been thinking about that since you brought it up. Guess I'm just trying to make peace with it."

She was close—really close—to me and smelled like the petals she'd placed in the Mason jar for Nick. I'd been so horrible to her and to Piper. I'd been horrible to so many people. Haltingly, I admitted, "I... kicked your flower jar into a gutter."

She stepped back, taking a deep breath. "It happens," she said.

"You're not mad?"

"No."

"I wish it was me." I cleared my throat. "That died."

"Don't say that," she said. Her eyes were glossy with tears.

Mine were too, and it made my face burn, letting her see me like that. I didn't know her that well. Not at all, really—not aside from seeing her at school or at the café or when she used to chase me around on the playground as kids. Not as well as I wanted to, then or now. I lifted my hand to rub my eye and when I put it back down at my side, it grazed hers, sending chills across my skin.

"It won't change anything," she said. "All the blaming or wishing that it was us, it won't change a thing."

She was so close that I could see the tiniest of honey-colored freckles on her nose and smell a hint of her spearmint gum. Wyatt honked his horn, making me step back, almost dizzy in the bright light above the door. "I should go," I said, my face flushing again.

Her lips parted like she wanted to say something else, maybe about Ellie again, but then she reached for the sign and said, "Yeah, me too."

As I took off across the parking lot, my mind started to race. What had just happened? One minute I was angry at her, blaming her for my brother's death and for coming around with her jar of flowers. Then, the next minute, I was apologizing to her?

"You alright, man?" Wyatt asked as I got in the Jeep.

"Uh, yeah, all good," I said, holding up my phone. "It was on the table."

"Y'all looked pretty intense out there," Connor said.

"Nah." I played it down, but he was right. There was something about her, something behind those eyes. I'd always been curious about her—about the quiet, smart girl who had a crush on me in elementary school. About the girl who'd been in the car the night my brother died.

A half an hour later, I pulled into my driveway and killed the engine. I sat in the quiet of my car, thinking about Tori. About Nick. About everything that had happened in the last few weeks. I wanted a do-over. A replay. I wanted my little brother back.

"Where have you been?" Mom asked as I tried to slip undetected through the front door. "I've been texting you for over an hour."

"Out," I said.

"No, sir. That's not good enough."

I shrugged and headed to the fridge, opening it and sticking my face in the cool air. I stared at the bottle of champagne in the very back. It had been there for years, a gift from one of my dad's clients, before he left us for the last and final time. Now, all I wanted to do was pop the cork and guzzle it down. Finally make good on his parting gift.

"I need to talk to you, Hayes."

"Don't feel like talking."

Part of the problem with being a therapist's kid was the constant, "let's talk about your feelings." At least that's what it felt like for me. "Tell me how that makes you feel, Hayes." Or, "It's okay to be angry or sad. Are you angry?" Obviously. I waited for it—the impending lecture about crossing the line and destroying her precious Nick's stuff. I deserved some sort of scolding, and I knew it.

"Why did you do that to his room?" She still couldn't say his name, not without choking up. "Were you looking for something?"

"No."

"Were you frustrated about something?"

"No."

"Hayes, I'm only trying to help you."

"I don't need your help, Mom. I'm not your patient." I stepped backwards, shutting the fridge door.

She brushed the hair above her left ear then moved to the counter. "Did you go and see Rachel?"

"What?" I asked, meeting her eyes.

"Were you with Rachel?"

"No. We're not together anymore."

I'd always been the one to talk to her about girls and stuff. Nick never liked talking about *mundane* things like dating or sports, and he kept to himself mostly. Always had. Maybe I told my mom things because it made her face light up when I did. But I couldn't stomach the small talk about a girl, not today. "I'm really tired."

I started for the stairs, thinking our talk was done, when she asked, "Why did you break up?"

"What?"

"You and Rachel? Why did you two end things?"

"I can't deal with this right now." So much for being forthcoming.

The light in Mom's eyes dimmed. "I know, darling. It's hard to let people in when you're grieving."

The way she smiled at me, in that pained, I-miss-him-so-much way, sliced right through me. I kissed her soft, flushed cheek and turned back toward the stairs.

Mom called after me.

"Yeah?"

"I love you." She held my stare for a second then blinked back tears threatening to fall.

"I'll clean up the mess I made in Nick's room, okay?"

"Thank you, Hayes. I just can't go in there right now."

She hadn't set foot in his room since he'd died, other than to stop my tantrum earlier. I hadn't either, not until today. I stood in his doorway, surveying his stuff still scattered on the floor. I'd left behind a huge mess, but so had he, and there was only one of us left to clean it up.

Part Seven: Tori

Chapter 27

"HOW WAS YOUR DAY?" Mom asked, popping her head in my room.

My day? There was no simple answer, not after Hayes had told me to stay away with my little sympathy candles, only to show up at Blue's, all apologetic and, shockingly, vulnerable. "It was okay."

"Was work busy?" Mom asked.

"Sort of. Not really."

"Are you hungry?"

"I ate at work," I lied.

"Okay, Tori." She sighed. "I can tell you don't feel like talking, so I'll leave you alone. But at least tell me, did you go to grief counseling?"

The knot in my stomach twisted. "Yes."

"That's good, hon. Thank you for going."

As she closed the door behind her, I couldn't help but think: What was *good* about it? It wasn't like I felt any better about Nick dying. If anything, my head was even more messed up than before the session. I rolled off my mattress onto the floor, reaching for Nick's backpack under my bed. I grabbed the shoebox next, pulling out his letters. I lined them up in order, studying them, trying to figure out what he was trying to tell me.

I know what happened to Ellie Stone.
I know the person who did it. So do you.
Not only do I know who... but I know how she died.
Then I read the one that came after Nick had died.
Someone else was there the night Ellie died.

141

I opened his journal to his list of names. Maybe one of them was the "someone else" who was there that night. But that didn't make sense. Ellie's name was on it. Of course, she'd been there.

My finger hovered over Hayes' name. Why was it on the list? I closed my eyes, seeing Hayes in the firelight talking to Ellie. He said he had no idea what he'd said to her. Was he lying? Was he hiding something? Was my memory of it even real? I'd only just remembered it in my last session with Dr. Moore. For all I knew, my brain was playing tricks on me, seeing things I hadn't actually seen.

None of it made any sense to me.

Maybe something on Nick's laptop would give me some idea of who this other person was. But as I pulled it from his backpack and booted it, nothing happened. I balled my fists and growled at the stupid thing. It was dead. Dad had tons of charging cables downstairs in his office. Maybe he'd have one that would work.

His desk was filled with half-spent matchbooks, mouse-pads, lightbulbs, highlighters, and some old photos of him and Mom from back when they were happy. I found one photo that looked like it had been taken years ago at a high school or college party. It was a little blurry, but the girl in it was definitely *not* my mother. I leaned on the edge of the desk, studying the writing on the back of the photo. Written in slanted cursive was the name Julia Sands, 03. She looked so familiar, like I should know her.

"What are you doing?"

I dropped the photo and turned around to face my dad standing in the doorway. "You scared the crap out of me."

"Need something?" he asked, scratching the scruff on his face.

I bent down to grab the photo and quickly tucked it in my back pocket. "Do you have a charging cable?"

"What kind?"

"For a Dell, maybe?"

He moved past me, grabbing a brown satchel by the window. He rummaged through it and then held one up, examining it in the light of the window. "This should work. What do you need it for?"

"To charge a computer?"

He laughed. "Well, I figured that."

"My old one. It has a paper on it that I need."

"Okay. Hey, where's your mother?"

Why was he asking me? I hated that they were in such a weird place, and for so long. *Go find her, Dad. Go talk to her.* "I don't know. Somewhere around here."

He gave me *that* smile, the same one everyone gave me after Ellie had first died. The one that said, *it will get better. Eventually.* He squeezed my shoulder then turned to leave.

Back upstairs, I plugged the charger into the laptop, hoping that, first of all, it would work, and second that I wouldn't be prompted for a password. As I waited for it to charge, I pulled the photo from my pocket and studied it under my lamp light. Who was this person? Maybe she was just an old friend. No one too important, probably. I tucked the picture inside one of my Get Well Soon cards and stashed it, for the time being, in my purse.

As Nick's computer continued to charge, I ran a bath in my attached bathroom, lapping my fingers under the hot water and staring at the dark screen on my bed. "Come on already."

It took the same amount of time to fill the tub as it did to boot his computer. I turned off the spout and headed to the bed, staring—seething—at the PIN prompt on the screen. I took a deep breath. What could it be? His birthdate? No, that would be way too easy—or maybe that would be the point of it. No one would ever think Nick Moore would make his PIN his birthdate or something as simple as 1234.

But the problem was, I didn't know enough about Nick to know how he'd think. I didn't know anything about him, not really. I leaned in, almost in a goblin crouch next to my bed, typing and backspacing possible PIN codes. I tried the four-digit year he was born, and when that didn't work, I tried the month and the year. I had one more shot until it locked me out. I tried 0125—the month and the day Ellie died.

My breath caught.

It worked.

My whole body shuddered, first, for getting it right.

Second, for realizing that he'd used Ellie's death-date as his PIN.

What was his obsession with her?

Shocked, I kept staring at his clean desktop, not knowing

what to do next. First of all, I was a Mac person. My laptop had a hundred folders right on my main page. As far as PCs went, I knew just enough to get by on the ones at school, but not a whole lot. Second, I didn't even know what I was looking for. A confession letter right there on his hard drive?

It didn't take long, though, to figure out things and get a basic lay of the land. I just started clicking my way around, finding all sorts of folders and files saved in different places. There were so many—hundreds of files just staring at me. I started combing through folders filled with essays and science notes. I even found a folder with pictures in it. Most of them were random shots of friends at school, church, wherever. It was all a little overwhelming. Right before I was about to give up, I spotted a folder named "CHEM II." I almost didn't click on it, but then I realized something: Nick wasn't in Chem II. He was only a freshman, and all freshmen had to take Biology I.

My stomach churned as I double-clicked on the CHEM II folder.

Inside were more folders, each named for what I figured were different chem labs: Toxicology, Spectroscopy, Chromatography, Globe Atmosphere. I clicked on Toxicology first. Inside was a bunch of files saved as T1, T2, T3, and so on. I double-clicked on T1.

My heart started pounding so fast.

It was some kind of security footage.

I leaned in closer to the screen, recognizing the place. There right in front of me on Nick's laptop was a grainy video of his mom's office. "How are you feeling today?" Dr. Moore asked, stepping into the frame.

My eyes moved from her... to the person sitting on the couch. "Holy..." I whispered.

It was me.

"Been better," I told her.

"That's to be expected, Tori," she said, sitting down in the chair across from me.

I stared at the screen, not able to breathe.

"Tell me about Ellie."

Nick was recording my sessions?

"What about her?" I asked Dr. Moore.

"What are some qualities that made her special?"

My own deep, heavy sigh echoed back to me through the

recording. "Her view of the world." My tiny, broken voice was nearly inaudible on the recording.

"What do you mean?" Dr. Moore asked.

"She was sunshine. A bright light, you know?"

I hit the pause button, not able to listen to one more second of it. Why had he recorded me? I pinched my eyes shut, fighting the rage building inside of me. How could he? I wanted so badly to throw his laptop against the wall and watch the screen shatter.

Instead of destroying it, I started clicking through the rest of the "Toxicology" files, one-by-one. He'd recorded every one of my sessions with his mother. Every single one.

But *why*?

Why had he done it?

I ran to the bathroom, barely making it to the bowl in time to lose my lunch. He had no right.

Chapter 28

MONDAY AT SCHOOL WAS a blur. I walked the halls like a zombie, completely brain-dead after spending the rest of the weekend thinking about those recordings of me and everything Nick had done to violate my privacy. All I wanted was to go home and sleep, especially after realizing what the date was: April 24. Tomorrow would make three months since Ellie had died. But for now, I had to pull it together. I had an after-school ACT prep class that I couldn't miss.

On my way down the hall, Piper caught up with me.

"Want to grab a coffee?" she asked.

"Can't. Have that ACT thing."

"Oh right," Piper said. "Ditch it and come hang out with me instead."

"Can't." I kept walking, too tired to engage.

"Hey," Piper said, grabbing my sleeve and pulling me back. "Everything okay?"

"Just tired," I said, glancing down the hall at Coach Lyles. He was standing outside his classroom door, ushering people inside. He flinched a little as he spotted me. But then he nodded, offering me a small, guarded smile. So much had happened. The wreck. Nick dying. Miss Taylor getting fired. Did he know what happened to her? Why she'd gotten the boot? "Got to go," I told Piper.

"Call me later?"

I waved a hand in the air and hurried down the hall. "Where do I sit?" I asked Coach.

"Anywhere, Miss Henson."

I started for the last open seat in the front row just as Kylie Marshall swept past me and grabbed it. *Great.* I zeroed in on an empty seat in the very back, two rows behind Hayes and Sydney, Rachel's tall, model-thin best friend. She sneered at me as I walked down the aisle between them. Hayes looked up, meeting my eyes. In that moment, I wanted to scream at him right then and there: "Do you know what your brother was doing? Do you? Do you know that he was recording my sessions with your mom? And that he was sending me creepy letters? Do you?"

"Just take a seat, Tori," Coach said.

I didn't even realize that I'd paused. My face flushed with heat as Hayes looked at me. I nearly tripped over someone's backpack on my way to my seat. *Pull it together before you fall flat on your face and make a complete idiot of yourself.*

Coach shut the door and sat down at his desk at the front. "Alright, y'all. We've got an hour. No talking. No getting up and moving around. No bathroom breaks."

I raised my hand.

"Yes, Tori?"

"Are we starting with practice drills?" It was my third time taking the class and he always started with online practice exams. Hayes and a few others, including Connor, looked over their shoulders at me. I hadn't noticed Connor earlier when I'd first walked into the room.

"Yes, Tori," Coach said.

Connor nodded.

I'd been surprised to see him at Blue's with Sydney. Then again, I really wasn't *that* surprised.

"Connor and I are casual," Ellie had told me once. "Not everyone sees the world like you, Tori."

"Which means what, exactly?"

"Sometimes you just have to be free, unfettered."

Ellie loved her ACT-prep words.

Connor turned back around in his seat. Seeing him made my heart ache for Ellie. Did his still ache for her too?

"Okay, y'all," Coach said, "take about fifteen minutes on the practice drill, then we'll go over the answers."

I pulled out my laptop, plugging in the flash drive I'd spent all weekend loading with the CHEM II files from Nick's computer. After I'd first found the Toxicology file, I clicked through a few more of my recorded sessions with Dr. Moore. That's when I found even more of Dr. Moore's sessions, all hidden in that one innocuous CHEM II folder. There were dozens of them, all stored under different lab names. All these unsuspecting kids were confessing their secrets and fears in confidence, and the whole time, Nick was listening, watching, recording them.

I wasn't much better. I'd been listening too, trying to make some kind of connection between the letters he'd sent and his journal notes and the patients he'd recorded. He'd listed names in his journal. Were they his mom's patients? Was one of them the "someone else" who was there at Sam's party? Maybe I was desperate for answers and grasping at straws. Violating confidences. Crossing lines. I pictured the list from his journal: Ellie's name, my name, Hayes, Emily Somebody. Was there *any* connection? Any at all?

I clicked on one of the lab folders I hadn't opened yet, Spectroscopy, but there was only one file in the folder. "That's odd." Odd or not, I slipped my AirPods in and pressed play on the video. It probably wasn't the best idea to watch it now in class, but I didn't feel like waiting either. As the grainy video loaded on my screen, my stomach dropped. It was still so hard to believe what Nick was doing. I shook my head and leaned in closer to the screen, squinting at the grainy video of Dr. Moore's office.

"How are you today?" she asked, slightly out of frame. She was standing at the door talking to someone.

Heavy footsteps strode evenly over hardwood. How many times had I stared at those same worn planks, wishing I was somewhere else? Wishing I was someone else?

"Excited, actually," someone said.

My breath caught. I knew that voice...who was it?

And that's when I saw it. A connection.

The person coming into the frame was none other than Sam Cox.

It wasn't a name Nick had written in his journal, but it was a name we all knew.

I paused the video and went back to the folder to check the date the file had been created. It was January 21st—four days before the bonfire. I chewed on my thumbnail. It seemed so wrong to violate these personal spaces *and* during a class. But I needed answers. I deserved answers. I looked up, feeling someone's eyes on me. It was Hayes staring at me. He quickly turned back around in his seat. It didn't make sense. *He* didn't make sense. Neither did his brother. What on earth had Nick been up to, recording his mom's patients?

I hit play and leaned into the screen again.

There was no way I could wait to watch it later.

"What are you excited about?" Dr. Moore asked. She motioned for him to sit on the couch.

"My party. I've invited you-know-who."

"That's right. Is your date coming?"

"Think so. Maybe."

Sam was that elusive kid at school. Everyone knew Sam, but no one really *knew* Sam. He was beautiful like his Brazilian mother with the same thick hair straight out of a Pantene commercial, olive-tinted skin, and warm, amber eyes. He was carefree, kind of like Ellie, but at the same time, guarded. There'd been rumors that he was gay. Others just said he was picky and only dated models from other countries.

"My mom has really gone all out, you know?"

"And your dad?"

"I don't want to talk about him." Sam's tone shifted, bitter. "I hate him."

The video stopped. It just cut off right there.

"What? No, no, no."

Hayes peeked over his shoulder again. This time, so did Sydney and everyone else in the room.

"Tori?" Coach Lyles asked.

"Sorry. My computer crashed. I didn't hit save."

Why was the file only a couple of minutes long and not an hour like the others? I checked and re-checked it. Had Nick stopped it on purpose? Erased some of it? Had someone walked in on him recording?

"Okay, let's go over the answers," Coach said.

No, no, no, no. It hadn't been fifteen minutes yet.

I leaned back in the desk, staring at the Spectroscopy folder—at Sam's file—on my laptop. All I could think about was Sam's mystery person and the sudden hate in his voice, like someone had flipped a switch. Hayes peered over his shoulder again, squirming in his seat. Did he know what his brother had been doing?

Chapter 29

"**Need a ride?**"

"I can walk." I pulled my cardigan across my chest and headed for the school parking lot.

Hayes picked up his pace to keep in step with me. Why was he suddenly everywhere? "What about Rachel?" I asked.

"What about her?"

"Won't she get mad?" I peeked over my shoulder for Sydney, who was trailing behind us with Connor.

"It's just a ride home," Hayes said, just a smidge awkward.

I glanced up at him, suddenly feeling stupid. "Okay, yeah."

We didn't say much on our way to the parking lot. I'd never been good at small talk. That was always Ellie's strong suit. I was too introverted, always in my own head. Case in point—on the way to his car, I thought about the talk we'd had outside Blue's and the way he'd been nice and vulnerable with me. But then I started thinking about his brother recording my sessions and Sam's and about Nick's broken glasses on his nose the night of the wreck... his backpack with the hidden pocket.

"Everything okay?" Hayes asked, unlocking his Lexus.

"Sure."

"You're just really quiet."

"I'm fine," I said, hopping into the SUV, which smelled like leather and money. It was weird, being only inches from him. I fidgeted with my seat belt, catching a glimpse of Drew's red truck, parked in its usual spot. He was sitting in the back of it, hanging out with some of his friends. Our eyes met across the parking lot. I looked away first.

"That ACT math part was awful, don't you think?" Hayes asked, starting the engine.

"Yeah, it was pretty bad."

As he put the car in reverse, his back-up camera started beeping. He slammed on the brakes, lurching us forward and then back against our headrests. "Sorry about that," he said, glancing in his rearview mirror.

Standing behind the SUV was Connor and Sydney, who held her hands up in the air.

"Sorry, guys," Hayes said, rolling down his window.

Connor stepped closer, leaning into the vehicle. "They let anyone drive these days, don't they?" He laughed, then took a double take at me in the passenger seat. "Hey."

"Hey," I said back.

Sydney wedged in to get a closer look too, then raised her eyebrows at me.

I sank lower into the seat.

"You be careful out there," Connor joked. "Try not to mow anyone else down."

"Ha, funny," Hayes said, rolling up his window.

"Sorry about that," Hayes said to me as Connor and Sydney crossed the lot to Drew's truck.

I nodded, remembering the day he almost ran me over.

"I really am a good driver," he said, easing through the parking lot. As he pulled onto Main, he brought up the ACT prep again. "So, I was about to ask you about that one part..."

He rambled on about a few of the questions, one of which I'd actually done after listening to that super short clip of Sam's therapy session. I nodded as we drove down Main, interjecting here and there with how I'd worked the problem. It was strange, though, sitting there in his passenger seat, discussing analogous structures like we did it all the time, as if it were a normal, everyday occurrence. Why had he asked to drive me home? Okay, so it was *just a* ride, but still, it wasn't like he'd ever offered before.

I'd thought about it a million times, about what it would be like to drive around with Hayes Moore, but that had been before everything with his brother. Maybe now was the time to come clean, to tell him that I had Nick's backpack and laptop and that I'd meant to give it back a long time ago. I opened my mouth to tell him when my phone rang.

"Where are you?" Mom asked on the other end.

"I had a thing... after school."

"Oh, right. The SAT class."

I didn't correct her. I just told her I'd be home in a few minutes.

"Everything good?" Hayes asked.

I nodded. "Just keep going, then take your next right."

"I know," he said.

Right. It was a small town, and we'd both grown up here. But then he drove through the light, completely missing the next turn.

"Did you do that on purpose?" I laughed.

"Swear, I didn't."

"It's okay. You can take the next street."

He turned onto Magnolia, Ellie's street. In late spring and early summer, the thick lush branches hung over the pavement like a canopy. Sometimes we'd ride our bikes in the middle of Magnolia with our heads in the clouds, saying we were going to keep riding until we reached the edge of the sky.

"You're quiet."

I glanced over at him, all serious as he drove down my best friend's street. If only he knew what I was keeping from him. Would he still want to drive around town with me?

He slowed the car, pointing to a tiny terrier, frozen in the middle of the street.

"Oh my gosh. That's Peaches!" I yelled.

He stopped the car.

I jumped out, scooping the dazed pup into my arms. The tiny thing was trembling. "It's Ellie's dog," I told Hayes as I got back in the car.

He drove a couple of blocks then pulled into Ellie's driveway, where Lisa's car sat. Did she even know that Peaches had escaped? Did Ellie's little sister know? "I'll be right back," I said as Peaches licked my cheek.

The path to the front door was overgrown with wild monkey grass and the door itself, once vibrant red, was faded and flaking from the sun. I rang the bell, which was weird since I used to just walk right in. Footsteps shuffled. Curtains in the window wavered.

"Oh," Lisa said, opening the door a smidge to poke her head out. Her cheeks were flushed. "Tori. What are you doing here?" She dabbed at her glistening forehead.

"Peaches? She got out. Almost got hit in the road."

"Oh, wow. I had no idea." She opened the door a little more, just enough to take Peaches from me. Behind her, someone with legs way too long and muscular to be Chloe's darted across the living room into the hall. My face flushed. I'd interrupted her.

"Thanks, Tori."

"Sure. Oh, and tell Chloe hey for me."

"'Course. Thank you, bye," she said, shutting the door.

I stood on the porch, embarrassed and confused. It was totally weird, the way she'd practically slammed the door in my face. As I turned around, stepping back onto the path, something dawned on me—the shoes. Not Lisa's. She was barefooted, but the man's shoes.

"All set?" Hayes asked, as I got back in his Lexus.

"Think so."

"Was she happy to see her dog?"

"She didn't even know Peaches was missing. Think I interrupted her."

"Doing what?"

"She had someone over."

"Do you know who it was?"

"I hope not."

Chapter 30

INSTEAD OF FIGHTING SLEEP, I sat in the kitchen, gazing at the stars outside in the black sky. It was peaceful, all alone, in the quiet hours before dawn... before Dad woke and started his morning coffee routine. Normally, I wouldn't mind his company, but things were different now. I'd realized it after seeing the shoes at Lisa's. And, I'd confirmed it that morning, after seeing the same ones sitting at our back door.

He only bought one kind of shoe, ever—always Nike Pegasus. His latest ones were smoke gray with flashes of fluorescent yellow. There was no mistaking those shoes. And here I'd thought Mom was the one having the affair with her co-worker Will. Did she know about Lisa and Dad? Should I tell her? I pulled the pink and gray Tinkerbell blanket, the one I'd had since I was five, tighter around my body and closed my tired, aching eyes. I was holding onto so many secrets with no one to tell. "I miss you, El," I whispered.

An owl hooted in response, offering a long hoot, followed by two shorter ones.

"Yeah, you get it," I said, slowly falling into a hazy state. The owl kept calling to me, each hoot counting me down, deeper into sleep.

"Can you hear that?"

"Hear what?" Nick asked.

I looked around and saw the owl high in the pines outside the crashed school van. "The great horned owl," I said to him.

Nick nodded. "Tori?"

"Yeah?"

"I need to tell you something."

"The ambulance will be here any minute. I can hear it now. Can't you?"

154

"If I die..."

"Stop saying that." I shook my head, fighting back the tears. The sirens became louder as I fought to keep him alert "Nick?" His eyes were vacant. Wake up. "Nick!"

"Tori?"

Someone was prying me free from the van, pulling me out. "No, stop. I don't want to leave him."

"Tori?"

I gasped, opening my eyes. "Dad?"

"Hey, now. It's okay." He pulled me in close, holding me tight in the darkness.

Bleary with sleep and panic, I asked, "What happened?"

"You had another nightmare."

Right. It was just a dream. I looked around and blinked, trying to focus on the time on the microwave. Was it four a.m.?

"Was it about Ellie again?"

I nodded, crying into his warm sweatshirt. I was too exhausted to tell him what it was really about. Besides, he didn't deserve the truth right now, not when he'd been lying to me and to Mom all this time.

"I'm sorry, so sorry, you're going through this."

Me too. I shut my eyes, listening for the owl, but it was gone. The kitchen was quiet again. Still. "Dad?" I lifted my ear from his chest, from the steady thudding of his heartbeat.

"Yeah?"

"Do they know who did it?"

He stared at me, shaking his head.

I inched back, staring at my dad with his two-day-old scruff and his tired eyes. He'd always been my rock. My hero. Strong and safe. Was he lying to me like I'd just lied to him about my nightmare?

"Let's get you back to bed, kiddo. You've got school in a few hours."

I gripped onto him tighter, seeing a flash of his shoes in Ellie's hallway. I couldn't bear the thought of losing him too. *We* were a family, the three of us. No one else. Just the three of us.

A few hours later, I was kicking my feet free from the mess of tangled sheets and stumbling out of bed to the window, hoping to catch a glimpse of my great horned owl still in the treetops. It wasn't there. Dad's car was still in the drive, but Mom's wasn't. Usually, it was the opposite. Maybe she knew about the shoes too. I grabbed my Waterford High sweatshirt from the floor and slipped it over my head, calculating the minutes before I had to get ready. Maybe Dad would let me be late, on account of my bad night, or let me take a sick day. Either way, I crawled back into bed and started scrolling through my phone, waiting for him to come get me up. Seven o'clock turned to seven-thirty and then eight and still nothing.

Outside, a car door slammed shut and then another. A minute later, the doorbell rang. Dad's footsteps echoed across the hardwood downstairs then stopped. Slowly, I tiptoed to my door, cracking it open to see who it was.

"Hey, Jana. What's going on?" Dad asked.

Detective Ivey and her partner stood in the doorway. She tucked a strand of thick hair behind one ear. "Can we talk, Jacob?"

Dad, wearing a white t-shirt and black Adidas pants, looked over his shoulder, nearly catching me upstairs on the landing. "Um, I'm about to head to the station. We can talk there."

"Won't take but a minute," Jana said.

Dad stepped aside and let the detectives by him. "So, what's up?"

"We found DNA," Jana said, now standing in the living room. "On Ellie's top. It came back inconclusive the first time, but I wasn't satisfied, so we ran it again."

Dad lowered his voice and leaned closer to Detective Ivey. "And what does this have to do with me?"

"The trace DNA on Ellie's top didn't match anyone in the system, but we have a partial match…"

"Okay?" Dad kept his voice low, almost impossible to hear. He mumbled something to her.

"As a cop, your DNA is on file," Jana said. "And the DNA we found matches someone related to you."

The muscles in my back tightened. I felt dizzy, light-headed. DNA? A partial match to my dad's? What was she talking about? I stepped backwards on the landing, making the floor underneath me pop.

Dad glanced over his shoulder. "Can we continue this talk at the station?"

"Yeah, of course."

Dad ushered the two detectives to the door then sat down on the couch, running a hand over his forehead. I did the same, trying to ease the throbbing pain in my temple, but it wasn't working. The detective's words kept pounding against my skull over and over again: *DNA. They found DNA.*

I pinched my eyes shut, seeing that image again of Ellie at the river—the moon spotlighting her pale face in the deep black river. But had I actually left the bonfire that night to go down to the river or was it my mind playing tricks on me? An emotional guilt feeding my imagination? I hated that I couldn't remember anything about that night. Hated, hated it.

Back in my bathroom, I stared at my reflection under bright fluorescent lights. "I don't know what it means... the DNA," I whispered.

"Don't you?" Ellie said.

"No, I don't." I turned on the faucet, letting cold tap water pool in my hands. Was I supposed to know? I splashed the water on my face. Handful after handful, I kept trying to drown out her voice... to get her face out of my mind. *Please just stop this already.* My pale, wet hands shook as water dripped from them like blood. I held them up in the light. Suddenly, they turned black as if they were caked in mud.

I grabbed a towel from the bar and started scrubbing my hands.

Tiny stars blinked in front of my eyes as I scrubbed and scrubbed, trying to keep my balance. What was happening to me?

"Tori?" Dad called from the other side of the door.

I jumped, dropping the towel to the floor. It was clean. There wasn't any dirt on it or on my hands. No mud. No blood.

"Tori?" he called again.

I reached to turn off the faucet. "Yeah?"

"Can you be ready in twenty minutes?"

"Yeah, sure." I held my breath, waiting for him to leave. When I heard his footsteps going down the stairs, I sank to the tile and pulled the clean, white towel over my lap. Why was my mind so messed up?

I couldn't help but wonder: What if?

What if it was my DNA on Ellie's shirt?

What if Nick had been trying to tell me all along that it was me who he'd seen? That I was the one who... killed Ellie? But that didn't make any sense. She was my best friend. I loved her. I'd never hurt her. The second wave hit as I realized what Nick's last letter had said: someone else was there. What if someone else, other than Nick, had seen me?

I stayed in the bathroom for ten more minutes, trying to get a grip, then tossed on some clean clothes from a pile that Mom had left on my desk. It was a ridiculous theory. I'd never do anything to Ellie. The DNA on Ellie's shirt was simple to explain. Maybe I'd borrowed that shirt before. Had a nose bleed or a cut while wearing it. Just because my DNA was on her shirt, it didn't mean I hurt her.

"Tori?" Dad called from downstairs.

I took a deep breath and headed back to the landing. "Yeah, Dad?"

"Hey." He looked up from the living room. "You about ready?"

"Yeah, almost."

"I let you sleep in this morning, but don't tell Mom." He winked.

"Okay."

Dad glanced at his watch. "Need to get to the station."

Something about him was different. Maybe it was just me, reading too much into things. But, as he stood there smiling up at me in our living room, I saw someone other than my dad. He was the same middle-aged guy—trim and fit and nice-looking—but now, he had secrets and a past. There was a side to him that I'd never paid attention to before. He was Jacob, not just Dad, who was now tangled up in Ellie's case with a partial DNA match and an affair with her mom.

"You okay, hon?" he asked.

I nodded.

But, no. No, I wasn't okay. Not remotely.

Chapter 31

I COULDN'T SHAKE IT, the sudden, strange image of my stained hands. It kept looping in my head, like a broken record. So did Detective Ivey's voice: "The DNA we found matches someone related to you."

"Dad?" I asked, getting in his blacked-out squad car.

"What is it, kiddo?"

"What did those detectives want?"

His shoulders fell. "You heard them, huh?"

"Kind of hard not to."

He tapped the steering wheel with this thumb, letting the car idle. "Look," he said, "there's nothing to worry about right now. Not until we know more."

"But they were talking about me, right? It's my DNA on her shirt, right?" I was his only kid, so it had to be me.

"Hey," he said, "there's nothing to worry about right now, okay? You were with her that whole day and then you rode with her to the bonfire. There are a dozen ways your DNA could have gotten on her shirt. It's protocol. They have to follow up on these things." He put the car in reverse, hitting the gas a little too hard.

The car lurched, making my head hurt more.

I eyed the mailbox as he backed down the driveway. What if Nick had been trying to warn me with his letters? Did I need to tell Dad about them? Was it time to come clean? "What do I do?" I mumbled, pressing my head against the cool glass of the passenger side window.

"Did you say something?"

"Nope." I lifted my head, confused by where we were going.

Instead of taking the regular way to school, he was going around the block, passing Ellie's house. He slowed down in front of it.

"What are you doing?"

He pushed on the accelerator. "Taking you to school." Dad glanced at me, offering a quick smile.

"I saw you."

"Saw me?"

I swallowed hard. "Yeah, at Lisa's."

He gripped the steering wheel tighter.

My pulse was fast and erratic. "I've known for a while, about you and mom having problems. But I thought *she* was the one having an affair, not you."

"Tori," he said, stopping at the four-way. "It's not like that."

"Oh, really? So, you're *not* having an affair with my best friend's mom?"

"No, Tori. I'm not."

Instead of turning onto Main Street toward school, he pulled into the First Baptist parking lot. "I promise," he said, reaching for my hand. "I'm not lying to you."

"I saw your shoes, Dad. I know you were there."

He ran his hand through his slightly graying hair. "Okay, okay. I was there, but we're not having an affair."

"Then why were you at her house, sneaking around? And where was your car?"

He opened his mouth to speak, but I cut him off.

"Why are you and Mom sleeping in separate rooms? You're barely speaking to each other."

Dad put the car in park. "Let's take a walk."

"No, Dad. Stop." I pulled his arm from reaching for the door. "I don't want to walk. I just want answers." My whole body shook as he cut off the engine and turned to face me. His eyes were pained, tired.

"You're right." He sighed heavily through his nose. "You need answers."

"Just tell me already."

"Your mom and I *are* going through a rough spot. It happens sometimes in marriages, but I'm not having an affair with Lisa."

"Yeah, you keep saying that."

"I'm looking into Ellie's case, okay? Digging into things I shouldn't. It's not my place or my job. I could get fired or worse. I was just giving Lisa an update. That's it."

I pictured her face, all flustered and splotchy, when she'd opened the door. Maybe I'd gotten the wrong idea. Or, maybe I was being naïve for believing my dad's story. For wanting to believe. Nothing was going to go back the way it was, but I still wanted my family how it used to be.

"I knew they found DNA. Someone who works in that department told me. That's why I was at Lisa's, telling her."

"I don't understand. Why did you go to her first?"

"I wanted her to hear it from me, not someone else." Dad blinked quickly, like he was nervous.

I leaned against the seat, staring out the windshield at the stained-glass windows of the church we used to go to. It had been months since the three of us had gone. "Dad?"

"Yeah?" he said as my phone rang. Mom's face popped up on my screen. "You can answer," he said.

As if I needed his permission.

"Hey, Mom."

"Why aren't you at school? The front office called."

"Dad is bringing me. I overslept."

Her silence was thick on the other end, as if I'd betrayed her or something. Maybe I was betraying her, being there with Dad instead of her. How much had he told *her*? And why were they going through a rough spot anyway? *It happens sometimes* sounded like a lame, shallow excuse to me. "You still there?" I asked.

"Yeah."

"I'm sorry, Mom."

"That's okay, honey. Have a good day."

I slipped into second-period calculus eleven minutes late, right in the middle of an exam. I was supposed to be looking for critical points in the problem, but all I could think about, one equation after the next, was what Detective Ivey had said about the partial DNA match.

"Do you have a question, Tori?" Mr. Choi asked.

"What?"

"Thought you had your hand up."

Piper turned around and glanced at my blank test.

"Piper, turn back around please. We're in the middle of an exam."

"Sorry," she said, grimacing.

Thirty minutes later, I turned in my paper, knowing I'd get a big fat zero, but I literally had bigger problems to solve. Much bigger.

"What's going on with you?" Piper asked after class and on our way to our lockers.

"Nothing. I'm just not with it today, 'kay?"

"Yeah, I can tell. What do you need?"

"A make-up exam, sleep, answers?"

"I can give you the answers, I guess, but I'm sure Mr. Choi will give you a different test."

I nodded, pulling a couple of books from my locker. I didn't need those kinds of answers.

"Oh here, you dropped this." Piper bent down then handed me an envelope.

My stomach clenched. It was the same cream-colored stock as the others. "Where did you get this?"

"It just fell out of your locker. Right now."

"Are you sure?"

"Yeah, why?"

I stared at the envelope in my hand. It just happened to show up in my locker three months to the day? "I have to go."

"Wait!" Piper called after me over the bell.

I ducked into the bathroom and locked myself in one of the stalls, sitting on top of the toilet tank for ten minutes, maybe more, just staring at it. How was it possible that I was getting another letter from him? And at school? Who was helping him? Was it Hayes? Maybe that's what his sudden interest in me was all about.

My phone dinged. It was Piper.

What did it say? Is it another one from him?

I didn't text her back. Instead, I slowly pulled the letter from the envelope. There under clear tape was a new message for me, typed like the rest: *There's more to Ellie's story.*

Chapter 32

"**WE HAVE A NEW** yearbook editor," Mr. Choi said.

Fine by me. It wasn't like I wanted the job anyway or like I'd even shown up for the past few meetings.

Mr. Choi said that we were weeks behind and that we needed to "step up our game, starting *right now*." We all knew what he really meant, that the real reason we were behind was because Miss Taylor had been let go. But none of it mattered to me. I didn't even know why I'd come to the meeting. If anything, I was there for Ellie. I missed her so much, especially with everything going on with my dad. Or maybe I was there to get my mind off the letter... another one of Nick's letters about the night she died.

"Everyone," Mr. Choi said, "our new editor is Piper."

Well, good for her. She'd told Ellie and me last year that she wanted to apply, but Ellie beat her to it, naming me as co-editor.

"Congrats," I told Piper with a weak smile.

"You're not mad, are you?"

I shook my head. Was I mad? No. Confused? Yes. Sick to my stomach? Absolutely. Terrified? Beyond words. But mad about not being yearbook editor? Not at all.

Piper buzzed around the computer lab handing out new assignments, but my head wasn't in the game, not when all I could think about was the letter. Who had put it in my locker? And how? When?

"Hey, Tori?" Piper asked, popping her head over her computer. "Can you come and take a look at this layout?"

"'Kay," I said, trying to sound normal. I rolled my chair over to her work station, staring at a page I had designed weeks ago: "Gone but Not Forgotten."

"I made a few adjustments, but I wanted to make sure you

were okay with it first."

The right side of the spread had pictures of Ellie, smiling, dancing, goofing off, and winning trophies and tiaras. The left-side page, the one Piper must have added, showed Nick, just as honored.

"Well, what do you think?" Piper asked.

"Looks good, Piper."

"Yes, it does," Mr. Choi said, leaning over us.

We spent two hours working on layouts, tweaking the tiniest of details. By five, Mr. Choi called it a day, but Piper said she wanted to stay and finish up one last spread. "I'll lock up the lab," she told him.

Mr. Choi agreed. A few minutes later, he left with a few other students on his heels.

"You don't have to stay," Piper said to me.

But the alternative was going home and seeing my mom. I didn't have it in me to answer her questions about what I'd eaten that day or if I'd gone to grief counseling—I hadn't done either. "I don't mind staying."

She shrugged and went back to her screen. "Oh, hey," she said, not looking up.

"Yeah?"

"Not sure I should bring it up, but..."

I inhaled, slowly, knowing where she was headed.

She swept her pink-tinted bangs from her forehead and leaned closer to her screen. The tiny diamond stud in her nose sparkled in the soft glow of the computer monitor. "It was another one of those letters, wasn't it? The letter that fell out of your locker?" She took off her wire-rimmed blue light glasses and squinted at me.

I nodded.

"But how? You said Nick had sent them, right?"

"Yeah."

Piper pushed back from her station and rolled closer to me. "What did it say?"

I reached in my back pocket and pulled out the folded envelope with its frayed paper and typed message.

She opened it and studied the letter closely, just like I had earlier in the bathroom. Her face paled. "More to the story?"

I nodded, fighting the queasiness in my stomach.

"Hold on," she said as she jumped from her chair.

"Where are you going?" I called as she left the room.

"I'll be right back."

A few minutes later and completely out of breath, she returned. "Yep, it's what I thought."

"What is?"

"There's a security camera in the hall, pointed right at your locker. Whoever *actually* put the letter in your locker should be on camera."

"Well, that's great and all, but it's not like I know how to hack into a security system. Do you?"

"I might know a guy." She winked.

"You know a guy?"

"Want me to ask him?" She rolled back to her station and started typing.

Did I really want someone else involved in this? I reached for my backpack and stood. "I have to go," I said, turning off my computer.

She stopped typing for a second and looked up at me. "I'll let you know what I find out."

I headed down the long, empty hallway, suddenly aware of how alone I was in a big school after hours. Halfway down the corridor, I stopped at the sound of something behind me. "Hello?" I said, my voice quivering as I glanced over my shoulder.

No one was there.

I let out a deep breath.

Get it together, I told myself as I turned back around. My heart thudded in my chest, matching my short, fast steps down the hallway. I peeked over my shoulder again. But again, no one was there. Was I losing my mind? It was probably a custodian in another room buffing floors or cleaning boards. It had to be. Right?

Right. My shoes tapped quickly against the shiny, vinyl-plank floors as I raced to the front door. I took one last look over my shoulder, this time catching a glimpse of someone or something—a dark shadow in the hall. All I could think as I ran out of the school was that I was being followed by the person who'd put the letter in my locker. But there was no way I was sticking around to find out. If I was lucky, maybe Piper's friend would catch him on camera, if he could hack the system.

At home, Mom had already changed into some black leggings and was stretched out on the couch watching Netflix. "How was yearbook?"

I sat down, still shaky from the thought of someone following me in the hall, but I didn't want to tell her in case it was just my overactive imagination. "It was okay. Mr. Choi appointed a new editor though."

"Oh, honey. I'm sorry."

"It's fine. It's not the same without Ellie anyway."

How had everything ended up this way? And why? No matter how hard I tried, I couldn't understand why Ellie had to die. I thought of Piper's yearbook page, seeing Ellie's smiling face frozen in time.

Mom nodded. "I made pasta primavera. I can go and warm it up if you'd like?"

Food was her answer to everything. "Maybe in a little while."

"Okay." She brushed her fingers across my forehead, playing with a few strands of my hair.

She used to do that when I was little, then sing about how I was her only sunshine. *Sing it to me now, Mom.* I put my head on her shoulder, wanting to tell her about everything, including my memory of being down at the river with Ellie, the letters, and even about the detectives coming over that morning. Had Dad already told her?

"Mom?"

"Yeah?"

"Have you and Dad talked today?"

She tensed up.

It seemed like lately, every time I mentioned him, she either flinched, tensed up, or changed the subject. "Are you and Dad okay?"

She sighed heavily, my head lifting and falling with her breath.

"Mom, please just tell me."

"I don't know," she said, pulling me closer into her chest. We sat like that for a few minutes, neither of us saying anything. We just stared at the TV screen, both of us keeping secrets from one another. Both of us afraid to break the silence. "I'll go warm up the pasta," she finally said.

I knew I'd have to eat a few noodles for her. It was the least

I could do. After I choked a few down, I told her I needed to go study. I thought she was going to follow me to my room, the way she hovered, asking me question after question: "After you study, do you want to watch something else on Netflix? We can go and get some ice cream? Bake cookies?"

No, Mom, I don't want any ice cream or cookies. "Maybe later."

"Okay, hon."

As I hiked up the stairs, my phone buzzed in my back pocket. I lifted it out, staring at the screen. It was from Piper. My mouth fell open at the grainy, black-and-white screenshot. She'd done it. Piper had found someone to hack into the security footage. I leaned in, magnifying the photo as big as I could get it, and gasped.

It was Sam Cox.

Chapter 33

I KEPT AN EYE on Sam in the parking lot before school the next morning and then again at the snack machines during break, but he was never alone long enough for me to approach him. I finally got my chance at lunch. I'd been watching him the whole period, waiting for him to break away from his group of friends, when all of a sudden, he jumped up and started heading to the trash bins. He tossed his tray on the belt then walked out of the cafeteria. Just like that.

And just like that, I followed him.

If anybody asked where I was going, I'd just say I was going to grief counseling. Hayes had texted that morning, reminding me that today was the last session. But as I'd hoped, no one asked.

My shoes echoed in the empty hallway as I raced after Sam. All thoughts of Hayes and counseling went away the second I rounded the corner and saw Sam standing there waiting for me—all 6'2" of him. "Why are you following me?"

"What—why would I be following you?"

He narrowed his eyes and stepped closer. "You've been stalking me all morning long. What's the deal?"

"Fine." I took a deep breath and reached into my bag for the envelope. I waved it at him. "Why did you put this in my locker?"

"What are you talking about?"

"This envelope. Where'd you get it?"

Sam furrowed his brows.

"Look, I have you on camera, so it's not like you can deny it. I just want to know where you got it."

Sam leaned in and gave it a closer look. "Oh, yeah." He shrugged and was totally calm about it. "It's not a big deal or anything."

"If it's not, then tell me."

"I found it in my homework."

"What? That makes no sense."

"That," he said, pointing to the envelope, "was stuck in the middle of my notes. When I was out sick last week, a couple teachers left homework and stuff for me at the front desk in the office."

"That's it?"

"That's it."

"Do you have any more?"

"No." His tone was somewhere between bored and incredulous, an unspoken "Why would I?" lingering in the air.

"Are you lying?"

"No, Tori." He eased his shoulders back and shrugged at me. "I'm not lying."

The bell rang and chaos erupted with people moving in a thousand directions, pouring out of classrooms and the cafeteria. Sam said something else, but I couldn't hear him over all the noise in the hall. "What?" I yelled as he turned and wedged in with the crowd, slowly disappearing into the thick of it. What did he say?

"Move it," a senior said, bumping into me.

I stood on my tiptoes, looking for Sam, but he was already gone.

"Hey, we're meeting in the library for English," a girl from my class said, brushing past me. She stopped midstride and turned to face me. "Coming?"

I stared at her braces. "Yeah."

She arched a brow. "Today?"

I blinked. "Right, coming."

On our way down the hall, she offered to let me sit with her and Rachel. No thanks. I headed upstairs instead and sat by the windows overlooking the football stadium since my periodical room was already taken. I settled in and opened my laptop, staring at the black screen. How the heck was I supposed to concentrate on Tolstoy after the confrontation I'd just had with Sam? Was he lying? Did he know more?

I leaned back in my chair, waiting for my computer to boot. A few seconds later, my screensaver popped up. It was Ellie posing in front of my bathroom mirror on the day of the bonfire. What I wouldn't give to go back to that moment and tell her we needed to stay home and chill, to make some more dumb TikToks, eat a tube of cookie dough, binge horror flicks. What I wouldn't do to hit reverse back to the second she barged in an hour late that day. I'd told her, "It's about time you got here."

She had pressed her lips together and shrugged. "Sorry, I got caught up in something. You'll never believe it."

"Believe what?"

She looped her arm in mine and started pulling me up the stairs. "Not here."

"O-kay..."

"I have something I need to tell you." She locked my bedroom door and faced me.

"What did you and Connor do now?" I asked her.

"It's not that."

Mom called out from downstairs.

"It's something else," she said as I squeezed by her to unlock the door.

Why did I have to go and open it? Why didn't I just tell Mom to hang on a second?

I'd thought about that moment a million times since the bonfire. All the what-ifs and why-didn't-Is. I should have asked her what the big secret was. But honestly, I didn't think much of it at the time, and she never brought it up again. I glanced out the second-story window of the library. I wish we'd never gone to Sam's party that night.

"Hey."

I jumped at the voice behind me. I turned and smiled at a girl from my class. "Hey."

"Can I sit here?" Mary Claire asked. "Apparently everyone in the whole school has class here today."

"Yeah, sure." I moved my stuff to make room.

"So, what's your research paper on?" she asked.

"Not sure yet."

She told me about her topic in excruciating detail. I nodded but didn't ask any questions, hoping she'd get the hint that I really didn't care. When she finally paused long enough for me to get a word in, I told her I was headed to the stacks to grab a book. "Watch my stuff, will you?"

She gave me two thumbs up.

I passed by the children's section, wishing I could write on fairy tales or on good and evil in modern children's books—not on Russian literature. I scanned rows and rows of colorful book spines, finally landing on a collection of Grimm's. Some of the titles were familiar like *Rapunzel* and *Cinderella*. I dove right in, reading small snippets of the stories on my way out of the stacks. I didn't make it very far before bumping into someone. "Sorry," I said, not looking up.

"Must be a really good book," he said.

My breath caught at the sound of his voice. I lifted my eyes from the page, meeting his deep blue ones. "Hi."

It was Hayes, standing there all tall and confident and looking like he'd just stepped out of an ad for men's wear in his gray pullover, dark jeans, and fit Nikes. My pulse kicked up a notch as I drew the book to my chest. He looked so much like his mom with the same almond-shaped eyes and strong jawline. What would she think about us standing there together?

"Is your class meeting here too?" Hayes asked.

"Yep," I said, spotting Rachel coming up the stairs. She stopped and narrowed her eyes at me. "Wow."

"What?"

He glanced over his shoulder then turned back to me.

"What's her problem?" I whispered.

"She's not very happy with me."

She turned back around, heading down the stairs.

We both stood there in awkward silence. Did I just turn and leave too? Say, "see you later" or "why are *you* in the Children's section?"

"Hey, do you know where this book is?" he asked. He handed me a small piece of paper with a name and a number penciled on it.

"Tolkien's *The Hobbit*? Yeah, sure."

"Thanks," he said, following me.

After I handed it to him, he sat on the floor.

I sat across from him. "Have you read it before?"

"Nope." He ran his fingers across the cover. "It was one of Nick's favorites. He always wanted me to read it." He opened the book, flipping through its musty, yellowed pages. He sighed deeply. "I told her I needed space," Hayes said.

Confused, I met his eyes.

"Rachel, I mean."

"Oh, right."

"After what happened with Nick," he continued, "I felt suffocated with everyone constantly in my face."

"I get that. It's hard being with someone and trying to act normal. Trying to be what you once were, you know?"

"Is that what happened with you and Drew?"

I balked a little at the mention of his name. "It just didn't feel right anymore. But sometimes, now, I wonder if we were ever right for each other, you know? Anyway, we broke up and then five minutes later he had someone else."

"Seriously?" Hayes asked.

"Well, not *literally* five minutes, but close enough. It felt like it." The image of the girl in Drew's bed, maybe Miss Taylor, with the blonde hair and the perfect curve of her body made me sick, though not as much anymore.

He cleared his throat. "That's awful."

"I tried finding my way back to him after Ellie died, but I just couldn't get there. Then when Nick..."

He nodded then leaned back against the book stack, closing his eyes for a second. "I wish he'd never gone on that trip. At first," he said, opening his eyes, "I blamed you."

A chill ran across my entire body.

"I convinced myself he only went to the conference because of you."

Whoa. All this time, he'd blamed me for his brother's death. I didn't move. Couldn't.

"It sounds awful coming out of my mouth now. I'm sorry I've been so horrible to you."

I thought about his brother's backpack in my room, his journal and the laptop that I'd been holding onto. I'd been awful, too, keeping things from him. "I've been horrible too," I whispered.

"No, you haven't. You're actually the only person who *almost* makes me feel like me again."

"What do you mean?"

"It's like you get what I'm going through because you're going through it too."

My heart panged with all sorts of guilt. I was keeping so much from him. He deserved to know what his brother had done, or, at the very least, he deserved to have his brother's stuff back. "I have his backpack."

He reared back slowly. "What?"

"His bag got mixed up with mine the night of the wreck. I meant to bring it over a thousand times."

His mouth fell open. "Why didn't you?"

"I don't know."

He sat there for a second, shaking his head. "Are you sure it's his?"

"Yeah."

He squinted at me. He was angry. Quietly seething. I could see it flickering in his eyes, feel it in the tension swelling between us.

"And you had it all this time?"

"Yes." I could barely hear my own voice over the pounding in my head.

"I want it back." He stood, his deep blue eyes suddenly a million miles away.

"I really am sorry," I said, jumping to my feet.

"Yeah. You keep saying that." He grabbed the Tolkien book then just stood there. "I want it back today," he said.

I nodded, unable to form words.

Then, he walked away from me, leaving me there to wallow in doubt and guilt and all sorts of gut-wrenching emotions. He'd said I'd made him feel *almost* like himself again. I wanted to run after him and tell him that I *was* sorry, truly, deeply sorry. For everything. But he was already gone.

Chapter 34

OF ALL PEOPLE, I ran into Rachel in the bathroom after school. My head was way too full, too chaotic, to deal with her. I should have turned and left immediately the second I saw her, but like an idiot, I stayed. I kept my eyes to the ground, hoping she'd leave me alone, but of course she didn't.

"It's kind of sad, you know?" she said, checking her reflection in the bathroom mirror.

My stomach turned. I took the bait. "What is?"

"The way you stare at him like a lovesick puppy." She pressed her full, doll-like lips together.

"What are you talking about, Rachel?"

"In the library earlier, the way you looked at him, all pathetic. You know he's just using you, right?"

"Using me?" My voice cracked. "For what?"

She stared at my reflection in the mirror. Her long, blonde hair swayed across her shoulders as she shook her head. "You have no idea, do you?" She stepped closer to me, into my space, staring me down in that unnerving, condescending way of hers.

"What do you want, Rachel?"

"For you to stop stalking my boyfriend. It's sad."

I stared back at her, trying to keep it together.

"He's just using you to get back at me for getting with Drew. To make me jealous or whatever."

I gripped the edge of the sink. Drew? I closed my eyes, picturing the long blonde hair, swaying across a bare back.

"A momentary lapse in judgment. A few actually."

It was *her* long blonde hair and Drew's hands on *her* body. How had I not seen it? I turned on the faucet, meeting her ice-cold eyes in the mirror.

The door flew open. Piper stood there, wide-eyed.

"I was just telling Tori how she should get back with Drew. He's not half-bad," she said, turning off my faucet. "You're wasting water." She turned to leave, side-swiping Piper on her way out of the bathroom.

"Ugh, I hate her," I said as soon as the door shut.

Piper blinked. "What was that all about?"

"Nothing."

"It didn't sound like nothing."

"She's just evil," I muttered. "She's sweet to your face and then she goes in for the kill."

Piper slowly nodded.

I splashed cold water on my face, trying to get the image of her and Drew out of my head. Why Rachel of all people?

"Come on," Piper said. "Let's get out of here."

She drove me home. I should have invited her to come inside, but the last thing I wanted was to hang out and talk about the letter or Sam or Rachel. Besides, I'd promised Hayes I'd deliver Nick's backpack to him *today*.

As she pulled into my driveway, I told her, "Thanks for the ride."

She smiled, tilting her head. I knew she wanted to talk about Sam. She'd texted me a few times during the day, asking what I thought about it. Was I okay? Was I freaking out? Had I confronted him yet? All I'd told her was that I was still processing it all, which was true.

"Talk later?" she asked.

"Yeah, of course."

The house was quiet. I locked the door behind me and headed upstairs for Nick's backpack. Should I return it *with* the letter and journal or without? Should I tuck everything back into place, the way it was? Should I tell Hayes about the other letters his brother had sent me? What about the one Sam had put in my locker? And what about Rachel? Should I tell him what she'd said to me about Drew?

My hands shook as I pulled the shoebox from under my bed, looking for the letter I'd found in the hidden pocket. I put the letter back in its original place, making sure everything, including his laptop, was just like I'd found it. In one way, I was glad to get rid of it all. But in another, I was absolutely terrified to hand over everything to Hayes. What if it all came back to me somehow? What if I'd missed something? What if he thought I planted the letter there? I zipped up the bag, suddenly sweating, then hoisted it over my shoulder. *I'm heading over now*, I texted him.

K, he wrote.

On the way to his house, the conversation with Rachel kept looping in my head. She'd said that Hayes was only using me to make her jealous, that he was using me to get back at her for sleeping with Drew. It was all too much. First Ellie dying and then Nick. Then the break-up with Drew. Drew sleeping with Rachel. The way she'd smirked at me, making sure I knew she'd slept with him—it was all so nauseating. How could anyone ever be with someone like that?

I pictured Ellie shaking her head, saying, "She's not worth it, Tori. She's just insecure and petty. Don't let her get to you." Easier said than done.

The warm sun peeked through the treetops, sending flickers of light to my face. I still had no idea what I was going to say to Hayes. Maybe I'd say nothing at all and just hand him his brother's backpack. That was probably what he wanted anyway.

I took a deep breath as I stood in front of his house.

"You can do this," I whispered.

My legs trembled as I forced myself to walk the path to his front door. I must have changed my mind a million times, one second determined to leave and the next feeling guilty for even thinking it. "Just get it over with," I whispered, reaching to ring the bell.

I held my breath and waited for him to answer.

Where was he? He knew I was coming over. I pressed the bell a second time. Then a third.

"Okay, okay already," Hayes said, opening the door. He bristled at the sight of me then narrowed in on the backpack over my shoulders. "That's it?"

I nodded.

"And everything is inside?"

Yes, Hayes, the letter he wrote me, terrorizing me, is inside with his journal and laptop. "Everything."

He held out his hand for it.

"Look, I know what I did was wrong, holding onto his backpack, but there was a reason."

He lowered his hand. "Enlighten me."

"I should have told you a long time ago, weeks ago, but I didn't because I was..."

"You were *what?*"

I held my breath, looking over his shoulder. I hadn't stopped to think if Rachel was there. "Do you know?"

Hayes blinked. "Know what?"

A loud engine revved behind me. I turned, spotting tail-lights rounding the corner. "Can I come in?"

He glared at me then stepped aside to let me pass.

"Is your mom home?"

"She's at a wellness retreat."

He led me into his pristine kitchen. Everything was super-sized, from the globe lanterns over the island to the oversized fridge to the ten-burner stove. The kitchen matched the rest of his mansion, size-wise anyway. The rest of the house, from what I could see—the furniture in the den and dining room—looked plucked from the 19th century. But his mother's office, which was detached from the rest of the house, was sterile, like the kitchen. "Your house is beautiful," I said, handing him the backpack.

Hayes took it and sat down at the marble island. He ran a finger over the canvas bag. "Why didn't you return it when you realized it wasn't yours?"

My knees felt weak. I sank down beside him, pulling the bag closer to me. I unzipped the hidden pocket and reached inside for the letter. "Here," I said, handing it to him.

"What is it?" He bit his lip, staring at it.

"You don't know?"

"Should I?" His voice was gruff, quivery.

"Open it," I said, suddenly afraid of how my own voice would come out.

He stared at it, not looking up at me.

I pulled the paper from the envelope and handed it to him.

He shook his head as he read it. Color drained from his face.

"There's more."

He stared straight ahead, almost in a daze. "What do you mean, *more?*"

"More letters."

He glanced inside the backpack. "Where?"

"He sent the others to my house. This was the only one in

his backpack."

He shook his head, slowly, as he studied the letter on the counter. "But it's not signed. How do you know it's from him? What if he found it and put it in his bag? You don't know he wrote it." He rubbed the back of his head.

I didn't say anything.

"What do the others say?" he asked.

"The same stuff. I know who did it. And how. And that someone else knows too."

He looked up at me. "Who... who else knows?"

"I don't know." And it was completely freaking me out.

He ran a hand over his mouth.

"Hayes?"

"Yeah?"

"Do you think..." I paused, afraid to even ask it.

"Do I think what?"

"Do you think it would be okay if... I, we, checked out his room? To see, maybe, if there's anything that might tell us something?" It was nervy of me to ask, but if there was something—anything—that implicated me, I needed to know. And I needed to know before anyone else.

"Uh, no way. My mom won't even let *me* go in there."

"You said she's not here."

"Yeah, but it's still not a good idea."

"Why not?"

"It's just not, okay?" Hayes snapped.

Was he hiding something? It *was* possible since I'd been hiding stuff from him, too. I pictured him the night at the bonfire, talking to Ellie. "Is there something you're not telling me?"

He lifted his gaze. His eyes were clouded as he sat there, completely quiet and still, in the middle of his fancy kitchen. "Like what, exactly?"

"I don't know. There's just so much I don't know about you or your brother or about the night Ellie died. And then there's the thing with Rachel. It's so confusing. I mean, I don't think you could hurt her..."

"Why would I hurt Rachel?"

"No. I mean Ellie."

He stood, stepping backward. "You think I had something to do with Ellie's death?"

Deep down I knew he wasn't capable of hurting her, but he

was keeping something from me. I didn't know what, but there was something he wasn't telling me. I kept pushing. "What did you talk to Ellie about the night she died?"

He flinched. "I told you already. I talked to a lot of people that night. I don't remember."

"It's kind of hard to believe that you *can't remember*."

He shrugged. "It was months ago. We were probably talking about the party, the music, I don't know."

"Okay, then, what about Rachel?"

"What about her?"

He stood there waiting for me to answer, but I didn't have it in me to go there. "Nothing. Forget it. I should probably go."

"Yeah, maybe you should."

I covered my face, wanting to hide my frustration, my anger, my vulnerability from him. Why did I have to tell him about the backpack in the first place? No one would have ever known. I lowered my hands, meeting his eyes. "Seriously? That's it?" The tears were brimming now. My throat was achy and dry. All I wanted was the truth, but he wasn't willing to go there. I balled my hands into white-knuckled fists at my sides and groaned. "You're not going to give an inch, are you?"

He didn't move.

"Unbelievable." My shoes echoed on his expensive hardwood flooring as I stomped over to the front door to leave. I reached for the handle then glanced over my shoulder at him. He was just standing there silent and unbending. "Great," I said, pulling open the door and stepping over the threshold.

"Wait."

Chapter 35

NICK'S ROOM WAS PAINTED a deep-sea blue and had a huge window overlooking the garden. His bed, made from a dark-stained earthy wood, anchored the room. The posts were large branches. It seemed more like a kid's room, but maybe that's what he liked—a room straight out of a fantasy novel.

Over in the corner was a desk, carved from the same kind of wood as the bed. I tiptoed over and sank into the chair. On the desk, a few books were open to various pages, waiting to be read. I wondered if anything had been touched or changed since the day he left for DC. I picked up a book, *Sin: The Early History of an Idea,* and read a few notes in the margin. A folder peeked out from under the stack—Honors Seminar: Philosophy. A part of me felt like I was violating his personal space, but another part felt like he'd led me there. I looked around the room for clues, for anything to jump out at me. There had to be something.

Hayes was standing in the doorway, not saying anything as I peered into every corner and closet. Nick's room had two gigantic walk-ins. I felt an urge to wince with every single creak of hardwood, knowing I wasn't supposed to be there, that the only reason I was here at all was because of Hayes' change of heart.

Over by the window was an old trunk, filled with clothes and light jackets. I grabbed a sweater, still fresh with detergent. The mountain-rain smell reminded me of soaked streets and tires skidding on asphalt. His injuries had been bad, but I really thought that he was going to make it. Turn a corner. No one ever said what happened—why he'd taken "a turn for the worse."

Hayes, still standing in the doorway, cleared his throat.

I carefully folded Nick's sweater and tucked it back in the trunk. I stood, stepping cautiously over to Hayes. "I put everything back in place. The way it was."

"Find anything?" His eyes were clouded as he stood there, completely quiet and still.

"No."

He brushed by me, smelling of the same detergent on Nick's sweater. I inhaled, trying not to be too obvious as I breathed in his familiar scent, trying not to forget what Rachel had said: *He's only using you.* I started to leave then turned back around, giving Nick's room a last look. There was another door, one I'd overlooked. "What's in there?"

"Goes up to the attic."

I stepped cautiously to it, grasping my fingers around the ornate metal doorknob. On the other side of the door, the stairwell was dark and smelled of moth balls and roses. My legs trembled as I started my way up the steep, narrow steps. With each one, the old wood popped underneath my shoes, echoing back to me.

"You okay?" Hayes whispered from behind me.

I gave a mute nod. Then, after reaching the top step, I gasped at the sight in front of me.

It was straight out of a Victorian novel with old wooden trunks shipwrecked in corners, a golden-velvet couch, and an antique dollhouse, partially covered with an old floral sheet. Gray light filtered through an oval window in the center of the room, granting just enough visibility to see history stuck in time. Light streamed in on an old armoire, tall and grand but dulled with age. I headed straight for it, pulling open its center doors.

And there it was. Exactly what I'd come for.

My mouth fell open as I stared at the board covered with newspaper clippings about Ellie's death and photos of me and Ellie. There were photos of Sam, too—meaning that most likely Sam *was* involved. There were Post-its too and more pictures of kids who'd been at the party that night. But most of the pictures were of me, so many of me, some I hadn't known had been taken, pinned with precision and all perfectly lined up showing just how obsessed he'd been. I leaned in, blinking at one picture in particular of me and Nick. We were standing outside in front of the school, but who had taken it? And how had it ended up on Nick's board... unless it wasn't Nick's board.

"What the—" Hayes choked out from behind me.

I held my breath. It couldn't be *his* board, could it?

"I should go," I whispered, trying to make sense of what I'd just found.

"Now?"

"Yeah, now." I pushed past him, running down the attic stairs.

"Wait!" he yelled.

I couldn't feel my legs. Couldn't breathe. Couldn't get out of there any faster. My head was spinning so fast trying to connect it all that I nearly tripped over my own feet. I ran out the front door, glancing back at the house, at Hayes, standing in an upstairs window, watching from Nick's room. It was something straight out of a gothic horror film, Hayes the ghostly figure looming in the mansion window.

Part Eight: Hayes

Chapter 36

STOP IT. PULL YOURSELF *together,* I'd thought as she pointed to the letter on the counter. I'd recognized the envelope immediately, the off-white fancy kind my mom always bought. She'd always said it made a difference, the stationery a person used.

"It says," Tori had said in a panic, "that he knows *how* she died."

"But it's not signed," I told her. "How do you know it's even from him?"

I hated misleading her, but what was I supposed to do? Tell her the truth? Tell her that I knew Nick had been writing her letters? Honestly, though, I'd had no idea the level of his obsession with her, and I'd had absolutely no idea about the stuff in the attic.

That was the absolute truth.

I'd known about the letters for a while. I walked in on him one night while he was taping something onto a piece of notebook paper. He was concentrating so hard that he didn't hear me walk through our adjoining bathroom. The weird thing was, though, he was wearing gloves. That's how I knew he was up to something. He carefully, meticulously tucked the letter into one of Mom's thick, fancy envelopes and sealed it with a sponge moistener. Then he unlocked his desk drawer, giving a quick peek over his shoulder as I moved back. Nick lifted the false bottom of the drawer, and there, in clear sight, was a stack of them—four, maybe five envelopes. He placed the latest one on top.

A few days later, when he was at a swim meet, I broke into the drawer, but they were gone. All that was left were a few empty envelopes and extra labels with Tori's name and address on them. So, no, I wasn't *completely* surprised to see one on my kitchen counter. I was surprised, though, about what it had said. *He had known who killed Ellie.* I should have fessed up to knowing about them when Tori asked, but honestly, I was in shock. I thought he was sending her secret admirer love letters, not I-know-who-killed-your-best-friend ones.

I stepped back from Nick's window, watching a last flash of Tori's red Nikes disappear around the corner. I grabbed the baseball from his shelf and threw it across the room, shattering his nightside lamp. Mom would just love that. I sat on his bed and stared at his desk. All those nights he'd spent sitting there, typing, printing out, and taping sick messages onto paper—to do what exactly? If he knew who killed Ellie, why not just tell Tori or go to the police? Why taunt her? I knew my brother could be a little off, strange at times, but this was beyond strange. It was criminal.

As I ran back downstairs to the kitchen for Nick's letter and backpack, I heard Mom's heels clicking on her bedroom floor. I hurried out of there as fast as I could, before she had a chance to see me. I thought about going straight to Tori's house and telling her that I was sorry. Telling her that I knew Nick had been writing her letters, but I couldn't. Not yet. I needed time to think about it all. Time to let it sink in.

I ended up parking at the bank across from the high school, staring at the letter for hours. It was hard to comprehend. Hard to believe he was capable of being so cruel, toying with her like that. And that board in the attic? That was a whole other level of demented with all those pictures of Tori and Ellie. It didn't make any sense.

If he was capable of stalking her with letters, what else was he capable of? I leaned back, trying to push it out of my head. No, there was no way. But the thought kept coming back to me as I read his words: *Not only do I know who... but I also know how she died.* Tori had also said that someone else knew, but who? Who else was in on this?

"Hayes?" Mom called as I tried to slip undetected through the front door. "Where've you been?"

I stopped at the foot of the stairs and back-tracked to the

kitchen. "Out," I said.

"I saw Tori leaving the house when I came home earlier," she said, filling her glass with tap water.

My head spun.

With her free hand, she brushed the hair above her left ear then moved to the counter, where the letter and backpack had been. "Are you two seeing each other?"

"What?" I asked, meeting her eyes.

"I was surprised to see her here, that's all."

"No, we're not."

"The thing is," she said, then stopped. "Never mind."

"What is it, Mom?"

She shook her head. "It's nothing. I was just curious why she was here, I guess."

"She had something of Nick's she wanted to return."

"Oh?"

Did I tell her about Nick's backpack, now in the trunk of my car? "Just a folder."

"A folder? Could I see it?"

Had she seen his backpack on the counter? Along with the letter? Did she know about the letters?

"Hayes?"

"I told her to keep it or whatever. It was just a folder with a bunch of math problems in it."

The light in Mom's eyes dimmed. "That's too bad."

"But I can ask her for it. If you want."

"Would you, please?"

"Sure." I started heading for the stairs when she called me back. "Yeah, Mom?"

"Did Tori say anything else?"

I bit my lip. "Not really. Why?"

She held my stare for a second then blinked, offering a quick smile. "No reason."

She was holding back something. I was sure of it. But then again, so was I.

Chapter 37

THE NEXT DAY AFTER school, a dark, unmarked police car with tinted windows was sitting in my driveway. She'd done it. Tori had gone to the police about the board in the attic... about the letters. I couldn't breathe or think. What did it mean for me? For my mom? My whole body shook as I parked beside the car, contemplating whether or not to back up and make a run for it.

Why did she have to go to the police?

Maybe the police weren't there about Ellie or Nick. Maybe it was for something completely unrelated. It *was* possible. I took a deep breath and slowly made my way to the front door, remembering the last time the police had come to my house— the night of the wreck. Now the cops were back. So was the tightening in my chest.

"Oh, good," Mom said, lifting a hand to her throat, "you're home." She nodded reassuringly as I stepped cautiously through the front door. Two cops in suits, not uniforms, were sitting in the living room, left of the foyer. Mom was across from them, sipping Earl Grey on a tufted leather sofa identical to the one the cops sat on. I stepped across the hundred-year-old hardwood, holding my breath.

Both detectives stood and introduced themselves. I remembered the lady, Detective Ivey, from the night we'd all been hauled down to the station after Ellie's body had been found.

Mom patted the couch cushion. "Come sit, Hayes. The detectives would like to ask you a few questions about the night of Sam Cox's birthday party."

My heart dropped. She *had* called them. "Okay," I said, trying to get a grip... trying to get my story straight. It had been months. A lot had happened since then. What exactly had I said

186

that night at the station?

Detective Ivey smiled as we sat. Her partner, the big cop, was stuffed into a white dress shirt and gray pants that were way too small for him. She flipped through her notes for a few seconds and then smiled up at me. "Hayes, can you take me back to the night at the bonfire? You said you saw Ellie that night. Can you remind me about that?"

I rubbed my suddenly sweaty palms on my Adidas joggers and nodded. "It's been a while, but yeah. She was dancing by the fire most of the night." I glanced at our huge fireplace centered on the back wall. Its mantle was overcrowded with pictures of Nick and me. I lowered my head, fighting the urge to get up and run right out of there.

"Did you talk to her?" Detective Ivey asked. "Because someone mentioned seeing you and Ellie talk that night."

I looked up at her. *Someone* mentioned it?

"But the funny thing is," she continued, "it's not here in my notes anywhere."

"I think she just asked me where Rachel was."

"We have a witness saying that you two looked pretty heated, like you were deep in conversation."

"Heated?" I asked, trying to keep my voice steady. I shook my head. "I don't remember it being heated."

Mom put her hand on my knee. I stopped talking.

I remembered that night clearly. How could I not? The night of the bonfire was the first time Ellie and I had really spoken to each other, aside from "hand me that beaker" or "hey, good game." We'd known each other for years, though, from passing each other in the halls at school. I liked Ellie all right, never had a problem with her, but that night, she really pissed me off.

"Hey," she called across the orange embers sparking into the night sky. "Come here a sec."

Rachel was still in the barn with her friends, not that she dictated who I could or could not talk to. But if she saw me talking to Ellie, I'd never hear the end of it, and I was not in the mood to have her go on and on about it all night.

"Come here," Ellie repeated. "I need to talk to you about something."

I jumped into the truck bed and stood there, inches from

Ellie, alive and electric. She moved to the country-rap blend as I huffed impatiently, waiting for Rachel to spot us. "What is it, Ellie?"

She stretched to her tippy-toes and leaned into my ear. She smelled like woodsmoke. "Tell your creeper brother to back the eff off. He follows Tori around everywhere. He's even here tonight."

"No, he's not." When I'd left the house earlier that night, he was in his room, playing video games and yelling at someone through his headset.

"Yes, he is. I *just* saw him." Ellie pointed to the other side of the fire where Tori was clutching onto Drew. Tori's dark chestnut hair was glowing fiery red. "He was just over there. Anyway, tell him to back off or if he doesn't, it *will* get ugly. I mean it, Hayes," she said, jabbing her finger into my chest.

I gritted my teeth and jumped from the truck bed right into the path of one very suspicious girlfriend. I'd never given her a reason to be suspicious. Maybe she'd felt me pulling away from her, which made her grip onto me even tighter.

"What did *she* want?" Rachel sneered.

"Nothing," I said. "You haven't seen Nick here, have you?"

"Nope." She squeezed my bicep and nudged closer as we headed to the barn, away from Ellie in the firelight and away from Nick, who was allegedly lurking in the shadows.

As I sat there in the living room with pictures of Nick plastered everywhere on the walls and the two cops sitting across from me, I kept thinking about what Detective Ivey had said, that Ellie and I looked like we were having a heated conversation.

Mom patted my knee. "Detectives, if there are no further questions..."

"Actually," Detective Ivey said. "Hayes, would you remind us, please, what you and Ellie talked about the night she was killed."

I tapped my thumb on my lip. For whatever reason, I'd lied about what Ellie and I had talked about that night. Even back then, all those weeks ago, I'd been protecting Nick, but why? Had I subconsciously suspected him of something? Now was my chance to come clean about what she'd said that night, about the letters, about all of it.

"Hayes," Detective Ivey prodded, "even the slightest detail could help us with our investigation."

I looked out the window to my Lexus parked in the driveway. Inside was Nick's backpack. Were they going to ask about it? About the letter? Was that why they were there? Were they waiting for *me* to offer it up? If I gave them the letter, that would mean giving up my brother? What good would that do? He was gone. Why taint his memory with something that he might or might not have done? I needed more time.

"Hayes?"

"Hmmm?"

"How about you just take us through that night again. Start with when you first arrived at the party."

I gave her a play-by-play, like she asked, and stuck to my original story, which involved me heading back to the barn with Rachel after I'd talked to Ellie.

"And then what?"

"We stayed for maybe an hour or more, I guess."

"Did you leave the barn or stay there the entire time?"

I glanced over at my mom, who remained completely calm. "Am I in trouble or something?"

"No, no," Detective Ivey said. "We're just following up on a few leads."

The timing seemed convenient—a blink after Tori had found that stuff in my attic.

"So, Hayes, did you leave the barn?"

"Um, I stayed there with Rachel."

"The entire time?"

"Think I went to the bathroom, but yeah, other than that, the entire time."

She ran through some of the same questions one more time, just phrased a little differently, then stood abruptly. "Okay, thanks for your time."

Did she know I'd left the barn? That I'd gone back to the bonfire to look for Ellie? I'd only wanted to tell Ellie to go easy on Nick, but when I got there, she wasn't there.

On my way back to the barn, I backtracked a little. It was just for a few minutes, to check out Ellie's story about Nick being there. If he was at the party, like she'd said, I didn't want her giving him a hard time. He could fend for himself, of course, but he was still my little brother, so I went looking for him. For just a minute. I stood in the dark on a slight hill overlooking the woods. Music echoed from across the field where the bonfire was still blazing, and that's when I saw two figures running out of the woods. The first was Nick. Running after him was Sam. I didn't tell the detectives, then or now. They hadn't asked.

They hadn't asked about the letters or the board in the attic either. Maybe Tori hadn't snitched?

After they left, I went upstairs and sat on my brother's bed. I never asked Nick about that night, why he was in the woods with Sam or why he was running from him. I tried remembering if I'd seen Ellie or anyone else out in the dark woods, but I couldn't remember. Maybe I didn't want to. Maybe I was chicken shit, afraid of the truth. But the funny thing about the truth, like secrets, is that most of the time, both have a way of surfacing no matter how hard you try to keep them buried.

Chapter 38

THE NEXT DAY AFTER last period, I waited for Tori at her locker. She'd been ignoring my texts, so I didn't have much of a choice but to confront her in person. Maybe I deserved to be shut out, but I really needed to talk to her. One thing I couldn't figure out was why she hadn't gone to the police from the start.

"Hey," I said as she approached.

She flinched as soon as she saw me.

"Can we talk?"

She glanced over my shoulder at the after-school hall traffic. "I'm not sure that's a good idea."

"The police came to see me," I said in a low voice.

She tugged down on her crop top then gripped the straps of her backpack. "What did they say?"

"Not here."

"... Okay."

Neither of us said a word as we walked down the long hallway, which seemed endless. I probably should have said something to her about how we'd left things, but I didn't know how to say it. Or what to say.

She stopped at the door leading into the band room. "We can go in here. The band is practicing in the auditorium today."

Inside the stale-smelling room were rows of metal chairs and music stands. The back wall was mostly windows, one of which had a crack.

She poked her head into the drum room. "Good," she said, checking it out. "No one's in here either." She leaned against a metal desk pushed against the wall and dropped her backpack onto the floor.

"I've been texting you," I told her.

"I know."

"I had nothing to do with it. You have to believe me."

She studiously avoided eye contact. "Do I?"

Sunlight streamed in through the dirt-caked window, making her dark hair auburn. I leaned back, watching her nervously play with a strand of it. "I swear I had no idea."

"I don't know what to believe anymore. I'm a wreck. I haven't slept in days. It's been consuming me, the letters and that awful board. Maybe I *should* go to the police."

"I thought you already did. Thought that's why the cops came over yesterday."

Tori took a deep breath and shook her head. "I haven't told them anything."

Then who did? And what made them come to my house?

"Hayes?" She waved a few fingers at me.

"Sorry, what?"

"What did they want?" she asked.

"They asked more questions about that night. Made me go over everything again. Said they were following up on things."

She rubbed her arms, shivering. I took off my hoodie and handed it to her, instantly second-guessing myself. But it was just a sweatshirt. That was it. A hoodie didn't have to mean anything. She peered up at me with those intense, searching eyes of hers, and then slipped it over her head. It nearly swallowed her.

"Thanks," she said, curling her fingers in the sleeve.

I shrugged then glanced out the cracked window that overlooked the football stadium.

"Oh," she said, reaching for her backpack. Tori started rummaging through it with the fervent energy of a squirrel. "Here," she said, pulling out a bundle of envelopes, all the same size and color. "Take them. I don't want them anymore."

"What am I supposed to do with them?"

"I don't know. Burn them?"

I took them from her, studying the clear label with her name and address typed on the front. "So, these were mailed to you?"

"Not exactly *mailed*. There's no stamp or anything. But this one," she pointed to the one on the bottom of the stack, "showed up in my locker the other day."

"Wait." I stepped back, confused. "It just showed up? What does that mean?"

She swept a thick strand of her dark hair behind her ear. "It means someone put it in my locker."

"And? Who was it?" I asked.

"Sam."

"Are you sure?"

"Yeah, positive."

"How do you know that?" Why was Sam putting one of these letters in her locker? "How did he even get it?"

"Caught him on the school camera. Then I confronted him. He said that he found it in his homework and it had my name on it, so he dropped it in my locker."

"Do you believe him?"

"I don't know."

My mind raced with a thousand possibilities. Did I tell her what I knew? What I saw? Did I tell her that I saw my brother coming out of the woods with Sam that night... that Sam was chasing him?

She rubbed the back of her neck then pulled her laptop from her backpack.

"What are you doing?"

"You need to see to this."

I moved closer, hovering over her shoulder, as she pulled up a file.

"Here," she said, handing me one of her ear buds.

She hit the play button on the grainy video she'd pulled up onto the screen. "How are you?" someone asked in the background. Someone else cleared his or her throat. It was hard to tell. Then, a tall, slender figure moved into the frame, her heels clicking in a familiar way on the floor. "No way," I breathed at the sight of the light hair slicked back into that tight bun at the nape of her neck. It was my mother. "What the hell is this?" I mumbled.

The video kept playing.

"I'm excited, actually," a guy said, walking over to the couch.

I leaned in, squinting at the video and waiting for the guy to sit so I could see his face. My mom was obviously in a session with someone. But with who? And why did Tori have a recording of it?

"What are you excited about?" Mom asked.

The guy looked up. It was Sam.

"My party. I've invited you-know-who," he said.

"That's right. Is your date coming?"

I glanced up at Tori.

"Think so. Maybe. My mom has really gone all out, you know?"

"And your dad?"

"I don't want to talk about him. I hate him."

The video stopped.

"Why do you have a recording of my mom in a session with Sam Cox?"

"Your brother was recording her sessions, including mine. I found them on his laptop in his backpack."

I cleared my throat, suddenly burning. It was hard to believe Nick would do something like that. I thought I knew my kid brother. Okay, so he was far from perfect, but this was getting tougher and tougher to stomach. *What the hell were you doing, Nick?*

"Why... why would he do that?"

Tori shook her head. "I don't know, but I copied the files onto my computer."

"Is there anything else you're keeping from me?"

"Anything else *you* are?" she snipped back.

A distant clanging of cymbals and a few horns blaring filtered back to us as the band started shuffling down the hall. Practice was over. So was our discussion for the moment, anyway.

Chapter 39

LATER THAT NIGHT AT home after Mom went to bed, I crept up to the attic to study the disturbing creation my brother had made. There were so many pictures, random shots of people who'd been at the party that night along with Post-it notes galore with names on them—Ellie, Tori, Sam, Rachel, Drew, and Emily—Emily who?

I sat down on the dusty velvet couch in the attic and stared at Nick's tangled web. I couldn't decide if he was a creepy, strange kid tucked away in an attic obsessing over Ellie's death or if he was actually involved in this mess. It didn't help that he had photos of Tori too. I thought I'd known him. I never, ever, thought he was capable of something like this. And why was my name on Nick's board? Because I'd talked to Ellie that night? And what about Drew? And who was this Emily girl? Vice president Emily? I pulled my phone from my pocket and texted Tori: *Who is Emily?*

What do you mean?

On Nick's board, there's a post-it with the name Emily.

I have no idea. It's in his journal too.

What journal?

Check his backpack. Hidden pocket.

I'd stashed his bag in the armoire, but I hadn't gone through it again, not since she'd first brought it over. She'd said there was a hidden pocket, but where? I unzipped the top, staring at his laptop. What the hell was he doing recording Mom's sessions?

Check the pocket where the letter was, Tori typed.

There it was. Right where she said it would be. I didn't recognize it. The journal was soft to the touch, small, and black, with a strong smell of fine-grain leather. Inside, almost every one of the pages was filled with cursive writing. It was no doubt his handwriting. I'd recognize it anywhere. I found the page with the list she was talking about. Underneath the list was some more writing: *The character fades into the background, wearing red, watching every move.*

What the heck was this?

You find it? Tori texted.

Trying to make sense of it. I stared at the conversation bubbles on my screen, waiting for her to text back.

Can I call you?

Yes, I wrote back. My phone rang almost immediately. "Hey," I answered on the first ring.

"I was thinking about something."

"Okay. What is it?"

"Your brother told me in DC that he didn't go to Sam's party, but what if he was lying? What if he did go?"

I stayed quiet on the line, screaming in my head that he did go. Just tell her the truth. Tell her he was there. Tell her you knew about the letters too.

"What if Sam's mystery date was your brother?"

"Wait. You think Nick and Sam were a thing?"

She was quiet on the other end for a few seconds.

"Hello? Are you still there?" I asked.

"Yeah, I'm here. But it's possible, right? What if Ellie found them together that night and one of them snapped and killed her to keep her quiet? What if that's the 'someone else was there' part of his letter? Maybe he couldn't keep it a secret anymore?"

"I don't know, Tori." My ears were ringing now. It was all coming at me so fast, her theories and her wild speculation. She thought my brother and Sam were a thing? What the heck?

"Maybe..." she said.

"Maybe what?" I prompted.

"Maybe Sam did it, afraid of his dad finding out about them. It lines up with Nick's letters, saying he knew who killed Ellie. Maybe Nick couldn't live with the guilt anymore of knowing Sam had killed her. Maybe he used the letters instead of going to the police."

I closed my eyes and rubbed my aching head. It made sense, sort of. Except, I thought my brother was in love with Tori. In fact, I was pretty sure of it. I took another deep breath and let it out slowly into the phone. "But I think he was more into you than Sam. And what about the board in the attic? The other names. It's not adding up."

"Right. And it doesn't explain the DNA," Tori said.

She said it so quietly I almost didn't hear her. "What DNA?"

Tori sighed on the other end of the phone.

"What is it?" I asked her.

"I overheard my dad talking to the detectives. They found DNA on Ellie's shirt, a partial match to his. Mine, I guess."

"Yeah, but that's not a big deal. You were around Ellie all the time."

"Yeah, maybe. So much for my theory. I don't know, Hayes. Maybe we should just go to the police. Maybe I should have gone to them from the start. Why I ever thought I could handle this on my own is beyond me."

Go to the police? A surge of panic ran through me. I needed to talk to my mom, to see what she thought we should do. I was afraid of exposing my brother and my family too soon—before we had all the pieces. Okay, yes, he'd written those horrible letters, but had he really been part of a cover-up or the murder itself? "Let's wait a little longer." I wasn't sure what more time would do. Delay the inevitable? I didn't care though. I needed more time to figure out what Nick had been up to. "Please?"

"Okay," she said. "We can wait."

The next morning, Mom met me at the base of the stairs, smiling. "Morning, Hayes. I made you pancakes."

"What's the occasion?"

"No occasion." She tousled my hair like I was five then said, "Can't I make my handsome son breakfast?" It was code for, *sit down. Let's talk.*

I followed her into the kitchen. My brain was foggy from being up most of the night, tossing and turning with dread, but my stomach nonetheless growled at the stack she placed in front of me, oozing with maple syrup. The more things changed, the more they stayed the same.

"When's your next soccer game?"

Soccer game? It was the last thing on my mind. I swiped through my phone as she sat across from me with her own plate of egg whites and fruit.

"Haven't talked to you in a while."

"Yeah."

"Anything new?"

"Nope."

"Mind putting the phone down?"

I glanced up at her. She wasn't mad or anything. In fact, she looked kind of sad. Maybe a little lonely. I took a swig of OJ and told her that the next game was Monday at five. "You're still coming, right?"

"I might be a few minutes late, but I'll be there."

My phone dinged on the table with an alert. I wanted to reach down and check it, but how horrible would that be—to not even give my mother five minutes of my life to talk about school and stuff. Things had been hard lately, but she deserved that much.

"Did I hear you up in Nick's room last night?"

I froze. Would she get pissed again if I told her yes?

"It's okay if you were, Hayes."

I took a bite of my pancake.

"I'm sorry I was so awful to you the other day. I was just surprised to see you treating his things like that, but I get it. I'm angry, too."

My phone dinged again.

And again.

"What is so important this morning?" Mom asked.

"Probably a group chat or something."

Then her phone started going off too. She eased up from the table and grabbed her phone off the counter. Both of us fell silent as we read variations of the same news alert, likely blasted to the entire town of Waterford. I stared at my phone in disbelief, and the pancakes turned uneasily in my stomach. I couldn't believe the headline or the headshot underneath it: *Charges filed against former high school teacher for alleged affair with student. Possible connections to the Ellie Stone murder case.*

I stared at the mug shot. It was Miss Taylor. She looked like she hadn't slept in days or weeks. She had always been so put together, but in that police photo, she was a mess. Under her photo was her full name—*Emily* Taylor. I pushed away from the counter and ran for the front door.

"Where are you going?" Mom called after me.

"Pick up, pick up, pick up," I mumbled after calling Tori's number. I stepped outside on the front porch just as she picked up on the other end.

"Can you believe it?" Tori asked.

"No, I can't."

"It's weird, right?" Tori asked.

"'Weird' is one word for it." I closed my eyes, seeing Nick's handwriting—the black marker on the pale yellow Post-it with the name *Emily*. And now, *Emily* Taylor, our Poli-Sci teacher from Waterford High had been arrested after an alleged affair with a student. "Who's the student?"

"I overheard my dad talking to another cop earlier."

"Yeah, and?"

The silence was thick on the line. "Tori?"

"It's Sam."

"Are you sure?"

"From what I overheard, they brought in Miss Taylor late last night. She admitted to being in the woods that night with Sam, breaking things off. She also said that someone took a photo of them. The flash spooked her and she ran to her car at the park entrance. She said Sam chased after whoever took the photo."

My breath caught in my throat.

"Here's the thing," Tori said. "Ellie's phone was never found. They're looking for the phone at Sam's house."

But what about Nick? Where did he fit into this? I sat there for a minute, thinking about my brother and why he never said anything. And why the hell did he send Tori those letters? "Hey, are you still there?"

There was a long silence on the other end and then I heard a muffled voice, like she was covering the phone with her hand, talking to someone.

"Hello? Tori?"

"I have to go. I'll call you later."

Chapter 40

THE NEWS ABOUT SAM spread fast. By Monday, the halls were thick with talk and guilty verdicts. Everyone was saying that they'd known all along it was Sam who had hooked up with Miss Taylor. It was all a part of the "river curse"—the lust and dark desire crap. By lunch, I'd had it. I wanted to punch a wall, or better yet, all of them. They had no clue what they were talking about, saying Sam had killed Ellie and Nick too. Where had that come from? It was a car accident. A drunk driver had killed my brother. I wanted to leave, get in my own car and drive for miles.

But I didn't. Mostly because Mom told me to "stay put and ignore it all." Easy for her to say. She wasn't in the middle of it, dodging questions about stuff no one my age needed or wanted to deal with. During gym, I hit the track, plugging in my ear buds and cranking up the angriest music I could find. It helped, until Rachel showed up. At least she didn't talk. She just ran, her long legs keeping decent pace with mine.

We ran for a half hour against a cool breeze, never saying a word to each other. I stopped first and sat down, stretching my quads. One lap later, she joined me, sweat glistening on her forehead.

"Crazy about Sam, eh?" she asked, breaking a peanut butter protein bar in half and handing me a piece.

And there it was—another person bringing it up.

I nodded, meeting her eyes.

She wiped the sweat from her forehead.

"I still can't believe it. Sam and Miss Taylor? Guess it makes sense though..."

Don't even breathe the word curse.

"She's like twenty-two or three and—"

"Can we maybe not talk about this?"

"Yeah, of course."

I glanced up and saw Tori's friend, Piper, trying to finish her laps. She swept her pink hair from her eyes and shook her head—was she shaking her head at me?

"I've always liked running with you," Rachel said.

I took a deep breath. "You know we're not together, right?"

She smiled, shaking her head lightly. "Of course, silly. Friends can still run together." She popped the rest of her protein bar in her mouth. "Can I ask you something?" She shifted slightly on the bleachers, watching as Piper slowly rounded the corner.

"Guess so."

"What's the deal with you and Tori anyway?"

"What do you mean?"

"Are you two a thing now?" She pressed her lips together and shrugged. "I mean, I know you two have a connection or whatever because of Nick, but is there more going on?"

Did I really owe her an explanation? After what she'd done? After she'd cheated with Drew? It was probably my fault though. I'd pulled away from her after Nick died. Maybe even long before that. I'd shut her out. Drove her to him. So, it wasn't like it was a big surprise or anything when I saw them in his truck. I never told her I knew. I just told her I needed space. And then Tori started coming around, and I was curious about the bookish, quiet girl who'd dated Drew for almost a year. About the girl who'd had a crush on me in grade school. About the girl who my brother had been obsessed with.

Rachel cleared her throat. "I mean, it's none of my business if there is something going on, but I'm pretty sure she's back with Drew."

"What are you talking about?" Tori had never said anything about her and Drew being back together. Not that she had to tell me anything about who she was dating. I gritted my teeth, suddenly pissed that Rachel was telling me this.

She swept her damp hair from the side of her face. "Yeah, she and I had a nice little chat the other day after I saw you two in the library together. I told her that things weren't over between you and me."

"But they are."

"They don't have to be."

"Yeah, they do. I know you cheated with Drew, and I also know Tori would never get back with him."

"Did *she* tell you about me and Drew?"

The bell rang. I stood, clenching my hands into tight fists. *She didn't have to. You just did, Rachel.*

Later that night after my game, Tori texted, asking if I was okay. We'd started texting each other more and more. It made sense though with everything going on in our lives. We were both dealing with a lot. And it wasn't like we had an official playbook on how we were supposed to handle everything, so talking to each other helped. But as I stared at her text, I wasn't sure how to answer it. Was I okay? Was anyone right now? *Guess so*, I answered. *What about you?*

Want to FaceTime?

I stretched out on my bed. My whole body was sore and tense. I was absolutely exhausted—mind and body. *Sure*, I texted back. A couple seconds later, my phone rang.

"Hey," she said.

I flipped on the small table lamp for some light. "Hey."

"How was the game?" She loosened her hair from a clip then adjusted her glasses.

"I didn't know you wore glasses."

She took them off. "Only at night to read."

"Oh," I nodded. "We lost. Coach should have canceled it. None of us had our heads in the game, not with Sam as a person of interest."

Tori rubbed her eye, smearing make-up under it. "I'm sorry.'"

I grabbed my phone and carried her with me through the jack-and-jill bathroom to Nick's room. I kept the lights off in his room and sat in the bright moonlight streaming through his window. He used to sit at his desk, staring, sometimes for hours, out that window. I'd never asked him what he was thinking about. Maybe if I had...

"Hayes, you still there?"

"Yeah, I'm here."

"It's dark. Where are you?"

"In Nick's room."

"Want me to let you go?"

"No." I actually liked talking to her. Every time I tried backing off or she did, it made me miss her. But was it weird, liking the same girl who my brother had been obsessed with? Liking the same girl who dated the guy my ex had been cheating with for months? "So, I have a question."

"Okay?"

"You and Drew, you're not back together, are you?"

"No. Why?" Tori asked.

"Because Rachel said you were."

"Yeah, well, I wouldn't trust a word that girl says."

I nodded. "I know about her and Drew."

Tori cleared her throat. "Did she tell you that?

"No. I kind of already knew. I saw them together in his truck a couple times and then when you told me he cheated, I put two and two together."

"Technically, he didn't cheat. We were broken up. Or maybe he did. Who knows how long it was going on between them."

I sat in Nick's chair, propping the phone on his desk. "What do you mean?"

"I don't know. Something he said about messing up."

I nodded, not wanting to push it.

We sat in the dark together. She'd turned off her light too and had put some chill music on, not anything like the raging stuff I was listening to earlier. "What is this band?"

"Do you hate it?"

"Opposite, actually."

"Explosions in the Sky."

"Noted." I leaned back in Nick's broken gaming chair. Mom had promised Nick that she'd get him a new chair, an expensive ergonomic one. She'd never done it. My knees knocked the underside of the desk with each rock and tilt of the chair.

"What's that knocking sound?"

"Nick's chair."

I kept knocking my knees against the underside of the desk, until something popped, cracked almost.

"Hayes?"

"I think I broke his drawer." Mom was going to have a fit. I crawled under the desk to check out what I'd done. "Hey, Tori?"

"Yeah?"

"Let me call you back, 'kay? I need to fix this drawer before my mom comes in here and loses it."

"That's fine."

I hung up and used the flashlight on my phone to inspect the large crack where the raw wood had split. Something else caught my eye too, a piece of paper maybe, taped to the underside of the drawer.

I pulled it free. It was an envelope, cream-colored and thick like the others. This one, though, wasn't addressed to Tori. Inside was a typed message taped on paper like the others. My heart lurched as I read the words. This one said: *I know who killed Ellie. It was me. I killed Ellie.*

It was signed, Nick Moore.

Chapter 41

Mom was in the kitchen wiping down her pristine marble countertops that gleamed under the bell-shaped bar lights. I imagined sliding the thick envelope across the slick countertop and her reaching down for it, her long, slender fingers, slowly, carefully, pulling out the confession from her son. But I didn't have the guts to show it to her. Not yet, anyway.

"Where are you going?"

"Out."

"Now?"

"It's eight o'clock, Mom."

"Out where?" she asked. "Hayes?"

The desperation in her voice stopped me in my tracks.

"I know you're upset about Sam. We all are."

Yeah, except I was *literally* holding a confession in my back pocket that could clear him. "I need air."

"Don't stay out late."

I couldn't breathe or swallow or even make eye contact with her. I couldn't get out of there fast enough. The last thing I wanted was Mom to follow me to the door, asking more questions—ones I couldn't answer. How did you tell your mother that your little brother had confessed to killing someone?

Or did she already know?

Somehow, I managed to get out of the house and into my car without blurting out what I'd found, but it was hard keeping it in, not telling her right then and there in our kitchen. I mean, she was my mom. Nick's mom. She needed to know. She deserved to know.

I drove for over an hour on country back roads, listening to sports talk on FM radio. I ended up not far from White Pines—the place my brother had allegedly, according to his confession letter, killed our classmate. But why did he do it? What reason did he have? I pulled into the park entrance and drove to the lot closest to the water. It was quiet out there with the engine off and my windows rolled down. I sat there in the dark, staring into the black trees guarding the river, questioning everything.

Someone must've forced him to write the confession. Maybe the real murderer? But who hated Nick that much to force him to do such a horrible thing? Sam? I needed to start looking for clues. But what if it really was Nick... if it was him... no, he wouldn't have... right? *What do I do? What do I do? What do I do?*

My phone lit up with a text.

You never called me back, Tori wrote.

I stared at the message, the tightness in my throat still there, maybe worse.

Everything OK?

No.

Want to come over and talk about it?

Come over? I glanced at the time on my phone. It was only nine o'clock.

Nick's letter was sitting in the passenger seat. Should I go to Tori's? Give her the letter that was most likely meant for her anyway? Or should I drive it to the police station? Or back home to Mom? I slammed my fist on the steering wheel a couple of times, pain searing up my arm.

I somehow ended up at a grocery store, aimlessly walking the aisles. I ended up spending almost thirty bucks on the most random things. My brain was so muddled, unaware of anything around me. I got back in the car, dumping everything I'd just bought into the passenger seat. I stared numbly at my loot then texted Tori: *Still want me to come over?*

Yeah.

K.

When you get here, go around back, Tori texted.

I needed to tell her. I had to.

Ten minutes later, I was standing in her backyard, lit by soft white bulbs strung across the trees leading to a small shed.

"Hey," she said, poking her head out the door. "Glad you came."

It took everything I had not to collapse right there on her lawn.

"You're shaking." She led me inside the small shed that was dimly lit by a lamp in the corner. The place had just enough room for a couch and a side table, not much more.

"Cool place."

"Ellie and I used to hang out in here. Haven't been inside for months." She sat on the couch. "What's in the bag?"

"Oh," I said, handing her the Piggly Wiggly sack. "For you." I sat beside her, too afraid to look her in the eye.

"Oh my gosh," she whispered, running her fingers through the bag filled with a hundred different kinds of fruit snacks.

In grade school, she'd had a new kind every week. Welch's, Disney-themed, fruit-bursts, you name it. And every week, she gave me one or two packs, sometimes three. The way her face lit up when she offered them to me had been cute, but it had also been annoying to a kid getting ragged on by the other boys, who sang, *Hayes and Tori, sitting in a tree, k-i-s-s-i-n-g.*

"I can't believe you did this," she whispered. "Thank you."

What had I been thinking?

Soft string lights filtered in from outside, giving just enough light so I could see the contours of her face. *Tell her. Tell her now. Tell her what you found under Nick's desk.*

She cleared her throat. "So, what's going on? You wanted to talk?"

She was so close to me, making my head dizzy with all sorts of thoughts. I placed my hands on my knees and leaned forward. "I can't do this," I whispered.

"Do what? Talk to me?"

Come on. Say it. Tell her. "It's just that..." I couldn't say it. Couldn't tell her that Nick had confessed in another one of his letters to killing Ellie. If I'd told Tori the truth, I'd be betraying Nick. I needed to keep his secret. For now. "I just don't have the head space right now for this."

She eased back into the soft couch cushions. "I get it. It's a lot to deal with. I still can't believe it about Sam either. I thought maybe I'd done something to Ellie."

"You?"

"Yeah."

"What do you mean?" I took a deep breath.

"You know the other morning when I had to get off the

phone real fast?"

"Yeah... I was wondering about that."

"Well, my dad was telling me about a new development in the case. That when the detectives ran Ellie's shirt again for evidence, they found a partial DNA match to my dad. I figured it was my DNA."

"Yeah, you mentioned that before."

"Well, my dad told me that it wasn't mine. I'm guessing they found something else, something connected to Sam."

I turned to face her. She was so close to me and her breath was so warm on my neck. The whole room was suddenly spinning.

"Still can't believe it all."

I nodded as the shed suddenly filled with bright headlights.

Tori looked at the window. "It's probably my dad."

My heart rate rocketed.

"It's okay. Let's just go outside on the swings."

I could barely breathe as I followed her. She settled into a tire swing hanging from a thick oak branch. I sat on the top step of the deck, across from her. Exactly a minute later, the patio door creaked open.

"Tori? You out here?"

"Hey, Dad."

I stood and faced him. He was a little intimidating in his uniformed black shirt and olive pants with the shiny badge clipped to his belt.

"Hey, kiddo," he said to Tori as she swept in beside me.

Something in me stirred at the sound of his deep, heavy voice and at the "hey, kiddo." I'd heard it before. I rubbed my eyes, trying to remember that "hey, kiddo" and that distinct rasp. He stepped toward me, getting a look at the guy in his backyard with his daughter. My breath caught in my throat as I stared at him. I knew him—not as Tori's dad, or a cop, but as someone who'd been in my house a long time ago.

With *my* mom.

"Hey, kiddo," he'd said. I was three, maybe four. He and my mom were in my parents' room. He was shuffling around, bare-chested, pulling on a boot. Then another.

"Hayes, this is my dad," Tori said.

I leaned forward, holding out my hand to him. "Nice to meet you, sir."

"Jacob," he said, lifting his hand from his weapon to shake my hand. "You alright, son?"

"Yes, sir."

We were about the same height. The last time I'd seen him, hunched over and hobbling around in my mom's room, he towered over me. "I should get going."

"Yeah," he said, "you should. It's late for a school night."

I nodded, trying my best to keep it together. "Yes, sir. It was good to meet you."

"I'll walk you to your car," Tori offered.

As we headed to the driveway, a thousand thoughts raced through my mind, including the random memory I'd just had of her dad and my mom together. What the hell had that been about?

"Sorry about that," Tori said.

"Don't be."

"He's harmless. I promise."

My head was spinning. I should have never gone over there.

"Are you okay?" Her eyes were filled with worry.

"Yeah, hey, we'll talk later." I turned away and made a move toward my SUV.

"Wait," she said.

I glanced at her over the hood of my SUV, thinking about what she'd said about them finding the DNA on Ellie's shirt. She'd said it was likely Sam's. It had to be Sam's if they arrested him, right? But *had* they actually arrested him or were they just holding him for questions?

But why had Nick confessed to killing Ellie? It was Sam's DNA on her shirt, right? It didn't make sense. A light in one of her upstairs rooms flipped on. Was her dad up there, spying on us?

Tori noticed too. "Guess I should go. Talk later?"

"Yeah, later."

As I drove off, I tried to piece it together. All the tiny, fragmented pieces—all the lies and secrets—nothing fit right. And then again, *everything* fit.

Chapter 42

ON MY WAY HOME, I kept replaying the day Tori had come over with Nick's letter in his backpack. She'd explained what he'd been doing to her. Tormenting her. I didn't want to believe it, that he was capable of being so cruel. But he was, and I'd missed all the signs.

The house was dark and quiet. Mom was probably in bed already. I unlocked the front door and stepped across the foyer, pulling Nick's confession letter from my back pocket. "Mom?" I called, nearing her room, where a sliver of light shone under the door. Good. She was still awake. "Mom?" I asked, pushing the door open.

"Hi, honey." She took off her readers and sat up in her massive king-sized bed. It was the same one Tori's dad had stumbled out of all those years ago. "Glad you're home."

I placed the now creased envelope in front of her. She looked up at me, her gaze catching mine.

"What's that?" she asked, holding my gaze.

"Did you know?"

"What are you talking about?"

I waited as she opened it. Waited as she read it. Her face contorted. I recognized the fear in her eyes as she looked up at me for a brief moment. The fear of thinking that Nick could be capable of killing someone. Her eyes welled with tears as she looked away from me.

"Did he do it, Mom?"

She shook her head, suddenly incapable of words.

Say something, I screamed inside my head. She was my mother, the adult here, and yet she couldn't say a damn word? She threw back the covers and got out of bed, putting her hands on my shoulders.

"Did he do it, Mom?"

She shook her head again. "No," she said firmly, yet almost as if she were trying to convince herself of it. "There's no way he'd ever do something like this."

But he'd confessed to it and there was DNA at the crime scene, a partial match to the man I'd suddenly remembered being in my mother's bedroom at one point in time.

Tori's dad had *brown* eyes. My mom and dad were both blue-eyed. So was I. Nick's eyes were brown, like Jacob's. Same shape too. It wasn't full proof of paternity, but I'd paid enough attention in biology to understand patterns of inheritance. It was rare for two blue-eyed parents to have a brown-eyed kid. It wasn't impossible, but it was rare. And his mannerisms, the way Jacob walked across the deck—he and Nick had the same gait. I'd never paid attention to that before, the way people walked, until it was right in front of me. "Mom?"

She stepped back, nearly falling on the bed.

"Tori said the DNA they'd found was a partial match to her dad's. We also have Nick's confession letter."

"What are you saying?" Mom asked.

"I know about you and Tori's dad." I gripped the bedpost as she stared at me, mortified, guilty, devastated but—oddly—calm. "Is... was... Nick his son?"

She sat on the edge of her bed, looking down at the hardwood. "Yes."

I leaned against the wall, noticing how small and frail she was in her white nightgown.

"It was a mistake. I ended things," she said. "Then I found out I was pregnant." She drew in a long, deep breath and shook her head slightly. "Your dad was so happy about having another child. It made us closer, for a while."

"Until he started cheating again."

"Yeah. Your dad left us a year later and Jacob started coming around again. But then we ended it. For good."

"Does Jacob know Nick was his?"

"I never told him."

"Did Nick know?"

"I don't know," she said.

"But why would he kill Ellie? It doesn't make sense."

"I don't believe he did. I just can't."

"Do we go to the police? Take his confession letter to

them?" I balled my hand into a fist, wanting to punch it through the wall.

Mom stood up, steadying herself on the dresser. "I need to make a phone call."

I assumed it was to call her attorney or maybe it was to tell Jacob. Did that mean I needed to tell Tori? Or would he? I didn't want her to read about it in the news or hear it from someone else that the person who'd admitted to killing her best friend was actually her half-brother Nick—not Sam.

"Hayes, honey?"

"Hmm?"

Mom drew near to me, pulling me into her arms. "I'm going to figure this out, 'kay?"

I wanted to believe her, but she'd been lying to Nick and me our entire lives. All I could think was, as she rocked me in her arms, *what other secrets was she keeping*? And what, exactly, did "figure it out" even mean?

Did it mean that she was going to destroy evidence?

Did it mean that she was going to let Sam take the fall for something my brother had confessed to doing?

Did it mean that I was going to have to live with another lie?

Part Nine: Piper

Chapter 43

THE THING ABOUT BEING invisible is that no one sees you in the most obvious of places. I was there the night of the bonfire and saw what happened. I know it all.

"I just can't believe it," Tori said. She'd come over the day the news hit about Sam and was sitting cross-legged on my bed, scrolling on her phone. "Sam? I mean, really?" She tossed her phone down and leaned against the headboard.

No official charges had been filed, but he was now the number one suspect.

"Yeah, it's wild," I said.

She glanced up, biting her lip.

"Have you talked to Hayes about it?" I asked her. "What does he say?"

She shrugged. "We've talked a little. It's hard for any of us to believe."

"Yeah. My brother is having a hard time with it too."

It was true. Wyatt had been torn up after the news hit. It made me want to tell him that Sam didn't do it, but then he'd start asking questions, like how do *you* know?

Wyatt and Sam had been friends since, well, forever really. Mama always liked telling the story about the two of them in preschool, when Wyatt pushed a bully off the see-saw and told him to leave Sam alone. The kid listened, left Sam alone after that, and they'd been friends since.

Tori reached for her phone again. "Maybe I should call him."

I shrugged.

"It's all so complicated. I never know what to say or do when it comes to guys."

She didn't have the *best* track record with guys. Drew was the ultimate creep, and Hayes, well, he was broken and wishy-washy. It wasn't his fault though. It was mostly his mother's, the way she coddled him. But, Drew, he was the worst.

I never told Tori what happened with Drew and me, but I'd told Ellie. She just laughed. Didn't believe it when I told her what Drew had done to me in the art studio after class one day early in our sophomore year. "You're lying," she'd said. "Why are you trying to start crap?"

But I wasn't lying. I was being real with her.

"Help me with these brushes, will you?" he'd asked after everyone, including Mr. Sims, cleared out for lunch.

I was in the back of the studio, washing my brushes in the large basin sink when he came up from behind me. I figured he'd just bail and leave me with the entire clean-up, but he stayed. As I ran my fingers under cool water, watching the bristles bleed down the sink in muddy greens and rusted oranges, he caught me off guard, stepping in close behind me and wrapping one arm tightly across my chest.

I dropped the brushes in the sink and wrestled free from his grip, pushing him away from me.

But he pulled me back and kissed me. His breath was vile as he leaned all his weight on me, wedging me back against the sink and pressing his fingers into the skin of my neck.

"Stop." I dug my nails into him, but he was stronger and bigger than me. "What are you doing?"

He untucked my shirt and moved his hands over my chest. His breathing was heavy and soured. "Stop," I said louder, but he didn't listen.

Stop.

Please stop.

Stop!

But he didn't.

The door opened. A girl from our class, Mary Claire, walked in, wide-eyed. She cleared her throat, staring at us. "Forgot my bag."

Drew mumbled something, backing away from me.

"Hey," I managed.

"Are you okay?" she asked.

"She's fine," Drew said. "Just pissed because we got stuck with clean-up today."

She held my stare for a few seconds and then reached down for her bag under the table. "Are you sure?"

I nodded, unable to speak.

"Okay," she said, slowly turning to leave.

"Talk about timing, huh?" Drew asked when she was out of earshot.

"You're disgusting," I choked out.

"What is your problem?"

"*My* problem?" I couldn't breathe.

"You wanted it just as much as I did."

I kept my eyes fixed on his shoes, relieved with every step he took away from me. I held my breath, waiting for him to disappear.

Now, sitting on my bed, facing his ex, I thought about telling her. But what good would that do? It had happened ages ago. And like she'd said, things were long over with him. Besides, Ellie didn't believe me.

"You're lying," she'd said when I told her Drew had "come on to me" in the art room after class. I was building my way up to telling her what he'd actually done when she said, "You've always been jealous of Tori. Why can't you just let her be happy?"

I was floored by her casual dismissal. Silenced by her choice to believe the good in him over me. She didn't believe me. Why would Tori?

"I should go." Tori stood and headed for the door.

Maybe I'd end up telling her, eventually. There was a lot more I was keeping from her. A lot of secrets that were starting to surface, but I wasn't saying a word to anyone. Not yet anyway.

Chapter 44

A FEW DAYS AFTER the news about Sam hit, he was in my house and talking to my brother about it. I didn't mean to eavesdrop on their conversation, but my brother's door was open, and it wasn't like they were whispering or anything. When I heard Sam say how horrible it was, sitting in that interrogation room for hours and hours being accused of the most "god-awful" things, I couldn't help but stop and listen.

"What did they say?" My brother's voice was low and strained.

"That I killed Ellie."

"But why would they think that?"

"Because of Emily," Sam said.

"Emily?" Wyatt's voice raised an octave. "Emily told the police you killed Ellie?"

"Not exactly, but you can't tell anyone. My parents hired this intense lawyer who says I can't talk to anyone since it's still an open investigation."

"So, you're *not* in the clear?"

"All they said was I was free to go. That cop, Ivey, got called out of the room, and, an hour later, she said I could go. She told my lawyer I needed to stay close. Like where the hell would I go? Mexico?"

"So, wait, back to Emily. What did she tell them?"

"Are you sure no one is home?"

Wyatt's gaming chair rolled across his wood floor. I ducked into the bathroom at the end of the hall and hid behind the door, waiting as he scanned the hallway then peeked into my room next to his. After he slipped back into his room, I tiptoed back to my post.

"My parents are at work and who the hell knows where

Piper is," Wyatt told Sam. "She's never here."

"You sure?"

"Yeah, man. No one is here."

Being invisible had its advantages.

Sam sighed heavily. I could almost feel the weight of his breath on my own shoulders. I hated that I'd kept quiet about it all, let him suffer for hours in that interrogation room, but I couldn't come forward with what I knew. I just couldn't.

"Emily couldn't take it anymore. She caved under all the pressure. They knew she was seeing a student, so she fessed up to that weeks ago, you know, and got fired for it. She said that they've been investigating her ever since."

"Did they know it was you?"

"Not when she first got fired."

"Wait," my brother said. "How did they find out?"

"There was a photo."

"A picture of you guys?"

"Yeah. Someone sent it to Dr. Henderson, who, as the principal, had to take it to the police."

The room fell silent as my brother, who was not the sharpest guy on the planet, pieced things together. "So, the picture..."

"It was dark, grainy, but you could see it was Emily. The other face, mine, was blurred, but I was wearing my WHS soccer jacket from this season."

Wyatt mumbled something under his breath.

"Anyway, she confessed to meeting *me* in the woods the night of my birthday party to break things off. That's when someone took the photo. She got spooked and ran to her car, and I went chasing after whoever it was who took the photo."

"Can't believe you never told me," Wyatt said.

"I never told anyone. I promised Em. It's stupid. I'm eighteen and she's twenty-three, but whatever. It's over. It was over before anything started."

"So, you two never..."

Sam didn't respond and whether he shook his head or nodded, I couldn't see from my spot in the hallway.

"So did you catch whoever took the picture?"

"Nope."

I pressed my shoulders back against the floral wallpaper, staring at the oversized blooms on olive-green paper. In a way, it made me feel like I was back in the woods that night, surrounded by all the whispering trees and thick foliage.

"I chased after *someone*, but I lost whoever it was. I never saw the person, only a shadow."

"So, the cops think it was Ellie who took the picture?"

Way to go, Wyatt. I really needed to give my brother more credit. He was keeping up just fine.

"Yeah, and they think I caught up to her, took her phone, and then killed her to keep her from telling on me and Em."

"But if you killed her and took her phone, why would you turn around and send the picture of you guys to the principal months later? That makes no sense."

"That's what I said. But they had explanations for that too. They said it was to throw them off or that maybe she'd tossed the phone in the woods and that's what made me snap and kill her. Then someone else found the phone later and sent the picture."

"But they let you go... why?"

"Said they had a new lead, but that *we're not done here.*" Sam lowered his voice to mock the detective's.

"What's the new lead?"

"Hell, if I know. I'm sure someone will leak that to the press too. I'm so screwed... murder suspect, *affair,*" he air-quoted, "with a teacher. All my mom has done for days is cry."

The front door creaked open and then slammed shut. "Hello?" my mom called out.

My heart nearly leapt out of my chest. Lacking any other option, I turned and raced into my room. It looked like I'd have to sneak out my window and crawl to the front door—without getting caught. But I was good at not getting caught. Really good.

Chapter 45

THE NEXT DAY AFTER school, Tori and I met in the computer lab to finish up the yearbook. A few others were there too, working to finalize their layouts. We worked late, until we couldn't see straight anymore.

After everyone called it a night, Tori popped her head over the computer monitor. "Hey," she said. "I heard Sam is off the hook."

"Where did you hear that?"

Tori rolled her chair over to my computer. "My dad. He told me Sam was cleared, for now, but that's it."

"He didn't say anything else?"

Tori leaned back against her chair and tugged on her hoodie strings. I admired how pretty she was without even trying. She didn't need make-up or trendy clothes to have style. She just exuded it without knowing she had it. Ellie, on the other hand, was a try-hard—at everything.

"Well, he did say there was a new lead, but that he couldn't talk about the details... yet. He's been under a lot of stress lately. I think..."

She stopped and did that biting of her lip thing again, contemplating whether to trust me. I leaned in. "Yeah?"

"I think my parents are done. You know, divorcing."

"Why do you think that?"

"It's been over for a while now, but this morning, I overheard them fighting in the garage. Couldn't hear what they were saying, but it was bad the way they were yelling at each other. Really bad." Tori rubbed her suddenly watery eyes. "My mom said she hated him and what he'd done to us."

"What does that mean?"

"I have no idea, except..."

I glanced at my computer screen, at the glossy image of seniors in the student section at a volleyball game. If I acted disinterested, like it didn't matter if she told me or not, then she'd be more likely to spill. That was my theory, anyway.

"I think he's having an affair with Ellie's mom."

I couldn't help but bug my eyes out at her. "What? What is it with this town? It's like everyone cheats."

Tori's face reddened. Maybe it was a little insensitive for me to say, with the whole Drew and Rachel thing still fresh, but with all the sneaking around—Waterford was all set for a two-hour *Dateline* special.

"I'm sorry, Tori. I really am."

"I don't know for sure. He told me he was just keeping Ellie's mom in the loop with the case, but there's *something* going on with him."

How did I tell her that I knew what it was? That yes, her dad had cheated before and that Nick knew about it? That Nick had told Ellie that night in the woods that he wasn't in love with Tori because... Tori was his sister. When he'd said it out loud at the water's edge, I nearly fell over the small bluff and gave myself up right then and there.

"Shoot. I have to go," Tori said, staring at her phone.

"Everything okay?"

"Family meeting." She flashed me her phone with a text from her dad. "Guess I'm about to find out." She rubbed her eyes, still red from earlier. "I'll call you later."

I wanted to ask her more, but it was only a matter of time before it all came out. If I'd learned anything over the past few months, it was patience. After she left, I locked up the computer lab and then headed home too.

Walking to my front door, my heart jumped to my throat as someone said, "Beautiful moon" behind me.

I turned at the deep voice coming from the shadows. "Who's there?" Tall evergreens stood shoulder to shoulder, like guards in the night. A tall figure stepped forward, pointing to a hazy halfmoon hanging low in the purple sky. "What the hell, Sam? You scared the crap out of me."

"All I said was beautiful moon."

"Yeah, well, you're creeping in my bushes, so there's that." I eased the grip of my keys, its metal teeth cutting into my palm.

"You know... I was thinking about something, Piper." He stepped in front of me, blocking my path to the front door.

"My brother's probably inside."

"He is. But I came here to talk to you. Not him."

"Oh, yeah? About what?" I stood straight and jutted out my chin as if it somehow made me larger, fiercer. It didn't. He was tall and imposing with thick, broad shoulders and deep, serious eyes that held mine.

"Let's take a walk."

"I really should go inside. I have a ton of homework."

"You're not afraid of me, are you? You're practically my little sister."

Only I wasn't. "To be honest, you *are* kind of freaking me out."

"Don't be an idiot. I'd never do anything to hurt you."

"What do you want, Sam?"

"Told you, to talk." He nodded at me to follow as he started heading for the elementary school across the street. "Not going to ask you again, Piper."

There was something in his voice. Something almost chilling but sad at the same time. I knew he'd never hurt me. But I still stayed a few feet behind and pressed the record on my phone, just in case.

He didn't say anything else, not until we got to the swings. He sat down, gripping the rusted chains and kicking at the dirt under his feet as he swayed back and forth. "You know," he finally said, "when I was in that interrogation room, I had a lot of time to think. I was there for hours. Did you know that?"

I took a seat, leaving an empty swing between us.

"They kept telling me that I was the one who killed Ellie that night at my party. You know what reason they gave me?"

"No." My voice sounded so small, like I was three again out there on that playground.

"They said it was because Ellie took a picture of me and Emily and that I chased after her and killed her because of it. Crazy, isn't it?" He stared with his thick, heavy brows furrowed over intense, penetrating eyes. "But you know what?"

"What?"

"I don't think Ellie took that picture of me and Em. I think you did."

My head spun. Tiny little stars danced in front of my eyes. "That's crazy. I wasn't even there that night."

He didn't say anything.

"I *wanted* to go, but Wyatt wouldn't take me."

"I saw you."

"No, you didn't." My whole body trembled.

"Yeah, I did. I saw you with those kids from band. And I saw you go into the woods that night too. Want to know what else? I think you saw an opportunity and took it. I think you saw me and Em in the woods and you took that picture of us.

"That's ridiculous."

"You think so? Tell me then, if Ellie took the picture, how did she send the photo to the school weeks after she died? Did she send it from the grave?"

I dug my heels in the dirt and kept my eyes down.

"I didn't tell the cops you were in the woods that night. Almost did, but my lawyer told me to keep my mouth shut. Lucky for you, I did. But there's one thing I need to know." He stood and started pacing in the dirt. "Why'd you take the photo?"

"I already told you, I didn't."

"Cut the crap, Piper. I know you did. I just don't get *why*. What have I ever done to you?"

He stopped pacing. His beautiful face was contorted. Anguished. Hurt that his best friend's little sister could do something so awful. But he was wrong. I hadn't taken the photo—sent it, maybe—but I didn't *take* it.

"And don't give me some morality bull because we both know you didn't do it for that. So why? For fun?"

"Like I *said*, I didn't take it." I pulled my phone from my hoodie pocket, careful to angle it so he couldn't see me hit pause on the recording. "Here, look through it. You won't find anything."

"That doesn't prove anything," he said. "But you know what? Deep down, I know it was you. And you know what else?"

"Please, Sam, enlighten me."

"I know that *you* know what happened that night."

We held each other's stare, two elks locked.

"You're delusional, you know that?" I hopped off the swing, breaking eye contact first.

"We both know it's true."

"Whatever, Sam. You don't know anything."

But he did know. Somehow, he knew that I had sent the photo. Ellie had taken it. I sent it weeks later after the trip to DC. Sam had wanted to know *why*, but I couldn't tell him the truth, that I didn't want him and Miss Taylor together. That I hoped she would get fired.

And she did.

Chapter 46

TORI STOOD FACING HER locker, completely zoned out. She looked a mess with her hair slicked back in a knotted pony-tail and dark circles under her eyes. Not that I had any room to talk. I'd slept at Nana's again and had just enough time to hurry home before school and take a quick shower before Ray woke up. The last thing I wanted was to see his face. It took me less than twenty minutes to get ready and get out of the house. At least I'd made an effort with some concealer and mascara, but as I ran my tongue over gritty teeth, I realized that I'd forgotten toothpaste. I popped a mint in my mouth and headed over to Tori. "Want one?"

Tori looked at the aqua tin in my palm.

"Do you want one?" I repeated.

"Sure." She plucked a tiny mint from the tin and placed it on her tongue.

"Everything okay?" I asked her.

"Yeah, why?"

"You left in a hurry last night. Everything go okay?"

Tori shrugged. "Oh, it was nothing."

"You sure?"

She leaned sideways, looking around my shoulder. "Yeah... I have to go."

"Why?" I turned and saw Hayes coming toward us.

"See you later." She blinked a few times then slipped into the crowd, heading in the opposite direction of him.

One minute, she couldn't get enough of the guy, and the next, she was avoiding him. He hurried past me, bumping my shoulder with his oversized gym bag, trying to catch up to her.

I pulled my sweatshirt hoodie over my head and followed too, staying two steps behind. He took the side stairwell that led down to the auditorium. I waited a few breaths then slipped in after him. His footsteps echoed on the stairs as he chased the sound of her boots. I slipped my shoes off and followed in my threadbare socks, feeling the cold floor leech heat from the balls of my feet.

"Tori, wait!" Hayes called as he raced after her down the stairs.

At the bottom of the stairwell, the auditorium door banged shut.

Okay—apparently, she wasn't waiting.

A few seconds later, it banged shut a second time as he followed after her. I tiptoed down the last flight of stairs then slowly inched open the door. They were standing close to the stage, only a few feet away from me.

"Are you mad at me or something?" Hayes asked her.

From where I stood in the dark stairwell, I could see and hear them perfectly.

"I'm just really tired right now. I have a lot going on." Her tone was strained.

He nodded. "Yeah, I get that."

"But," she said, glancing up at him. She bit her lip. "Why'd you ghost me?"

Hayes stepped back. "What?"

"I've called and texted you. You could've at least texted me back," she said. "I mean, what the hell was that the other night with your stupid fruit snacks?"

"I'm sorry. I've just..."

"What's going on?" she asked.

"I—I need to tell you something." Hayes sucked in a deep breath.

"Okay, then tell me."

"I found something the other day, something of Nick's, and I've been trying to make sense of it all." Hayes dropped his bag to the floor and unzipped the side pocket, pulling out an envelope. "Here," he said. "I found it under his desk." His hand trembled as he handed it to her, but she just stared at the envelope, not taking it from him.

"What does it say?"

My heart pounded a million beats per second as I waited for it.

Hayes pulled the letter from the envelope and slowly unfolded the piece of paper. "I found it the night I came over to your house. I wanted to show you then, but I panicked. Chickened out. It says who did it."

Tori took the letter from his hand and stared at it. Her eyebrows furrowed.

"I kept thinking about what you said, about the police finding DNA on Ellie's shirt."

My knees buckled.

"I didn't call or text you back because I needed time to think," Hayes said as the warning bell rang.

"Time to think?" Tori said, lowering her arms to her sides. The letter fell to the floor.

"I had to talk to my mom."

"Your mom?"

Hayes stared at her, offering a slight nod. Then, they just stood there, eyes locked in the dimly lit auditorium, neither able to look away.

"I have to go," she whispered.

"Wait." Hayes grabbed his bag and the discarded letter on the floor.

I inhaled slowly, trying to calm my breathing as I eyed the letter in his hand—the one from Nick, saying who did it. What did it say? Whose name was on that letter? Why couldn't he have just read it out loud? And whose DNA had the cops found on Ellie's shirt?

"I have to go to class," Tori said. She ran down the stage steps and started making her way to the main door of the auditorium, which was across from the gym.

Hayes followed after her again.

But I didn't follow either one of them.

I'd heard enough for the time being, even though I wasn't sure what it all meant. What I did know, though, was that something had shifted. Things were starting to close in around us—and it wasn't good. I pressed my forehead against the cool cement wall and kicked it. Not good at all.

Chapter 47

AFTER SCHOOL, I HAD to run to catch up with Tori in the parking lot. She didn't stop by my locker like she usually did. "Hey," I called, finally falling in step with her.

"Oh, hey," she said, rubbing her eyes.

"Did something happen?"

She clutched the straps of her backpack and squinted at me in the bright sunlight. "Can you give me a ride home?"

"Yeah, sure." I unlocked the Volvo from a few cars away.

"Actually," she said as we walked, "can we ride around for a little while first?"

"Yeah, okay," I said. "What'd you have in mind?"

"Maybe we can stop by the river?"

My stomach clenched. *The river?* I was game for driving, but not for driving there. Why on earth she kept wanting to go to the place her best friend had died was beyond me.

"I know. It sounds ridiculous, right?"

I almost said, "Yes, it does," but then I stopped. While I didn't want to go, I kind of understood why she did. Sort of. I thought about all the nights I'd spent in Dad's chair. He loved that reddish-brown recliner. He'd spent more on it than on his car, or so he used to joke. "That supple Italian leather is as smooth as butter," he'd say when I sat in it. Now, it was in the corner of my room. I figured the river was the place where Tori felt connected to Ellie, just like Dad's chair was the place I felt closest to him.

"I just need to go there. Clear my head."

"Okay," I said as we both got in the car.

We grabbed lattes first, then I took the back roads to the river, winding along the old highway with the White Pines entrance. There was another way to get there, but this way was quicker. A few minutes later, I pulled into a parking spot and put the car in park.

"You coming?" Tori asked.

I looked up from the dash and over at Tori, who had gotten out of the car already.

"Yeah, coming."

"We don't have to stay long," she said.

I followed her down the tree-lined path right to the water's edge. She reached for my hand and squeezed it. "Thanks, Piper. You've been a good friend to me."

As she let go of my hand, she turned and headed for the fallen tree trunk, black and rotting. I stayed put, staring out at the water, remembering.

Remembering how Ellie and Nick had fought that night— exactly where I was now standing.

Sam had been right. I did go into the woods the night of his party, just like he'd said. I found the perfect spot overlooking the river and stayed up there, hidden but still close enough to see both the water's edge and the bonfire in the distance. For the longest time, I just sat there, gazing at the stars and listening to people laugh and sing in the background. I didn't want to go home or to Mary Claire's. I wanted to stay there and watch things unfold, even if it was at a distance.

"Hey, Piper?" Tori called from the tree trunk.

I blinked, trying to shake it off. *Keep it together, Piper.* "Yeah?" I stepped over to her.

"You asked earlier if I was okay, right?"

"Yeah."

"Well, I'm not." Tori rocked gently back and forth. Back and forth.

"What's going on?"

Tori, with her big solemn eyes now flooded with tears, looked up at me. "It was Nick."

"What was Nick?"

"Nick confessed to killing Ellie."

"What do you mean he confessed?" I pictured the letter Hayes had in his hands earlier.

"He said in a letter, like the others he sent me, that he was the one who killed Ellie."

I didn't know what to say.

She cradled her head in her hands, still rocking.

But he hadn't killed her. I was there. I saw them fight. I saw him push her down, and I watched as she fell back, hitting her head on a rock. But she'd gotten up. She had blood trickling down the side of her face, but she got up.

Ellie had yelled at him, and that's when he ran off.

She teetered on the riverbank, possibly wobbly from the fall, but most likely, it was from the water I'd spiked. Ellie sat on the bank for a few minutes, just staring out at the calm surface. I almost went down there a few times to tell her I'd spiked her drink to make her look like a fool in front of everyone. She deserved that for ditching me, for not believing me about Drew, for bad-mouthing me.

But every time I started to go, something stopped me. Maybe it was a lingering anger or resentment or the image of Drew I couldn't get out of my head. The last time I almost got up, I stopped at the sound of voices.

Ellie heard them too and ran partially up the bluff, hiding behind an old, thick oak. At first, when I saw him emerge from the trees, I didn't know who it was. His face was shadowed, but when he turned around, I saw that it was Sam. A few minutes later, Miss Taylor showed up, coming from the park entrance.

I flipped onto my stomach and crawled closer to the edge of the bluff.

"I can't do this anymore," Miss Taylor had said.

He shook his head at her, obviously upset.

"Don't do this, Em. Please."

"We need to stop this, whatever *this* is, before it goes anywhere. I'm your teacher, Sam."

"Yeah, but I'm eighteen now."

"You're still my student for the next five months."

"I'll quit and take my GED."

"Don't be ridiculous."

She pushed him away, but he pulled her back in. She didn't fight it. She didn't fight it either when he leaned in and kissed her. That's when the flash went off.

From the bluff's edge, I could still see Ellie standing behind the tree. She didn't move, but Miss Taylor did. She panicked, rubbing her eyes and escaping to her car in the parking lot. She left Sam there, confused as he ran in the wrong direction, away from both Miss Taylor and Ellie, back toward the bonfire.

So, no, I wanted to tell Tori, Nick hadn't killed Ellie that night. After he knocked her down, she got up. And Sam hadn't killed her either. Neither one of them had killed Ellie, even though Nick had confessed to it. Maybe he thought he had. I opened my mouth to tell Tori that, but I stopped, suddenly afraid.

"Piper?"

"Yeah?" I gasped, choking on the chill coming off the water's surface. It hadn't seemed that bad, when we reached the water's edge. Now? It was suffocating and arctic.

"There's more."

"More?" I swallowed the lump in my throat.

Had they found *my* DNA on Ellie's shirt? I glanced over my shoulder, expecting the SWAT team lined up behind us, but it was all clear. No one was on the riverbank, other than the two of us. At least not yet.

I glanced at the fist-sized rock by her feet and thought about doing the unthinkable. What had I become?

Chapter 48

IN THE SECONDS AFTER Tori had said, "there's more," in that sliver of a moment in which I'd nearly lost myself in the darkest place I'd ever known and almost picked up that rock and thought about doing only God knew what, she said, "he wasn't in love with me." I stepped backwards, momentarily taking my eyes off the rock wedged in brown, swollen sand. "Hayes?"

"No, his brother Nick. *Our* brother. Hayes' and my brother Nick."

"Nick was your brother?"

"Half-brother, yeah. I wonder," Tori said, tucking her wind-blown hair behind her small ears, "if Ellie found out somehow and that's why he killed her. Maybe she was taunting him with it or something and he snapped?"

"Wait," I said. "How did *you* find out?"

"They found DNA on her shirt, a partial match to my dad's. My dad and my therapist had a kid. Can you believe that? My dad and Hayes' mom?"

What? Was that what her family meeting had been about?

They'd found *Nick's* DNA on her shirt.

Nick's DNA... not mine.

I sat in the sand, the cold seeping through my thin leggings. She moved from the log and sat beside me, looping her arm in mine then resting her head on my shoulder.

"But I don't feel any better knowing. Is that awful? All these months, all I wanted were answers. To know who took her away from us. But now, all I feel is numb."

"No, it's not awful," I whispered, staring out at the water. "Knowing who did it doesn't bring her back."

"But they always say it brings closure. I don't feel like it's closed though. Just the opposite, actually."

"Have you talked to your dad?"

"He doesn't know I know."

I leaned back, confused. "But I thought—"

She stood, dusting the sand from the back of her jeans.

"But wait, then what was your family meeting about?"

"He and Mom wanted to tell me they were separating. Mom said something about cheating, about not being able to come back from it. I thought *she* was the one who was cheating, but it was my dad the whole time. I pieced the rest together after talking to Hayes earlier today."

"So, Hayes knows?"

"Yeah, and soon the whole world will too, I'm sure."

"The DNA, is it confirmed? It's Nick's for sure?"

"Think so. If it's not yet, it will be soon enough."

Soon enough kept repeating in my head as Tori and I walked back to Dad's Volvo in the parking lot. Had I made a mistake letting her walk away from the river? But as we drove away from it, it didn't matter anymore. Like she'd said, soon enough the whole world would know.

Thirty minutes later, we pulled into her driveway.

"Thanks for taking me to the river," Tori said.

"Yeah, of course."

She reached for her backpack on the floorboard then stopped.

"What's wrong?" I asked.

"Did I ever tell you I found a journal in his backpack?"

My pulse kicked up. "A journal?"

"The night of the wreck, before he died, Nick said he needed his backpack. He begged me to get it for him and that he needed to tell me something." She was struggling to get the words out. "When I woke up, I was in the hospital. And his backpack, it was in my room..."

"You're not making any sense."

"I'm... I know. I can't stop thinking about what he was trying to tell me that night. Do you think he knew he was my brother?"

I tried evening my breath. "I don't know."

She reached for her phone, pulling up a picture.

"What is that?" I asked, as I glanced at her screen.

"It's a page from his journal. There's a list of kids from school."

I blinked, trying to read the faint writing. "A list for what?"

"I don't know. Maybe who he thought killed Ellie… or who was there that night."

Was I on it? I squinted at the names, gray and slanted and tiny. "But he said *he* did it, right?"

"Yeah, but look here." She leaned in close, pointing to her screen. "It says, 'cloaked in anger, the character fades into the background, wearing red, watching every move.'"

Forcing a breathy laugh to hide my panic, I shook my head and said, "Sounds like he was writing a story or something."

"Maybe," Tori said.

"What else would it be?"

"I don't know, Piper." She held my stare.

The lump in my throat returned. I swallowed it, acting as cool and casual as possible.

"It's just all so confusing, you know?"

I nodded.

"Anyway," she said, then let out a long, heavy sigh. "Wish I knew what he was trying to tell me." She reached for the door handle then sat there for a few seconds more, staring at me like she wanted to ask me something. Finally, she pushed open the door. "Thanks for the ride."

There was something in the way she looked at me, as if— no. There was no way she was playing me.

"Any time," I said.

I watched her walk across her yard to her front door then backed down her driveway. It was weird. *She* was being weird.

Instead of going home, I drove by Nana's, but her neighbor Jack was out on his front stoop, surveilling the neighborhood. So, I kept on driving, thinking about that look in Tori's eyes. I looped around the neighborhood one more time before going home to face my mother.

Inside, there was a smattering of small white Chinese take-out boxes on the counter.

"Get any cashew chicken?" I asked Mama. I was trying my best to sound as normal as possible, like I hadn't just thought about using a rock to quiet the only friend I had.

"No, but there's General Tso's."

Of course, she'd ordered Wyatt's favorite, not that I was really all that hungry anyway after what happened at the river.

"Your principal called me today."

"Again?"

"She said you weren't making the progress in your classes like she'd hoped. She wants us to meet with her tomorrow."

"Okay." I grabbed a couple of fortune cookies and started to head to my room.

"Piper!" she called.

I stopped midway down the hall. "Ma'am?" I said just as the front door opened. It was Ray. It was the one and only time I didn't mind seeing his ugly face. It saved me from Mama's lecturing.

"Hey, hon," she said to him.

I shut my bedroom door and tore off the plastic wrapper of one of my fortune cookies, imagining the little paper saying, "something unexpected will come your way" or worse "you hold a secret someone will discover." Instead, it told me to "fol-low what calls you."

My dad's chair was calling from the corner of my sage green room. I'd picked the wall color when I was ten and was well over it by eleven, but I'd been too lazy to change it. Now, I just lived with it, like I lived with all the unfinished paintings I'd started. All those canvases and sketches that I'd started and then abandoned were in my closet, under my bed, on my book-shelves. I hadn't painted since... Drew.

I yanked the blanket from my bed and plopped onto the Italian leather.

Luxurious, Pippa, isn't it?

I'd always loved how he called me that. No one else did. Only him. But what would he say about everything I'd done? I was flunking out of school. I'd spiked my ex-friend's drink with a roofie. I'd gotten my teacher fired. And that wasn't even the worst of it. Somewhere along the line, I'd turned into a horrible, deplorable human and done things that couldn't be forgiven.

I sat in Dad's chair, waiting for Mama to come and have "a talk" with me, but she wasn't in any hurry now with Ray there. I started thinking about the page in Nick's journal instead. My paranoia was starting to eat away at me, little by little. What if Nick had written it down somewhere that he'd seen *me* that night? And that after their fight, he'd come back to check on her and found *me* with her?

But why had he written that confession? Why confess to something he hadn't done? Why cover for *me*? I broke a second cookie in half, pulling the paper from inside. "The fortune you seek is in another cookie." 'Course it was. I tossed the fortune to the floor and turned on the TV to numb my brain with some documentary on the History Channel. I curled my knees into my chest and eased back into the recliner, suddenly too exhausted to think about misguided fortunes.

I'd dreamt of that night so many times. Each time, the images grew sharper. The blaze of the bonfire, brighter. The rotting algae in the water, blacker. The red of her hoodie, bolder. When I saw her emerge from the edge of the woods, it stunned me. From my spot on the bluff, I watched as a girl—was it me?—stepped slowly, carefully, into the river. She was going directly into the freezing water. It made no sense. And then I saw the body surface and the girl in the red hoodie struggling to pull the body from the water. I didn't move. Didn't dare to blink as her heavy breathing filled the night air, competing with the music and voices in the background.

She pulled the limp body ashore and turned toward a flash of lightning that lit up the sky above the water. A storm was coming, though it was still far enough away in the distance. The girl fell to her knees beside the body and clasped her fingers over her own mouth, staring at the pale-blue face in front of her. Then, suddenly, she stood back up, peeking over her shoulder into the dark trees behind her. The girl in red ran away, leaving behind the body on the bank, all alone and discarded.

"What do I do? What do I do?" My heart thudded in my chest as I waited for her to come back.

The dream was always the same.

The girl in the red was always me, running, disappearing, re-emerging.

The girl returned, now holding flowers in her hand. The girl was me, kneeling over the too-still body, feeling desperately for a pulse. "Wake up, Ellie. Please wake up." A small gasp escaped her lips. I reared back, shocked, as her eyes fluttered open. "Ellie?"

She stared up at me with a sudden fear and terror, and then, not a second later, it was gone. Her eyes, blank. The life in them, extinguished. "No, no, no, no." I swept my fingers across her forehead then stopped at the small gash on her right temple. It wasn't deep, not deep enough to have killed her. "No," I whispered again, sitting back on my heels, shivering. My clothes were soaked. The t-shirt under my sweatshirt, my red sweatshirt, clung to my skin. What had I done? I stared down at Ellie.

What had I done?

I took her cold fingers in mine and sang to her like I had to my dad as he lay dying from the cancer that had ravaged his body. He loved Etta James. Maybe Ellie would too, out there at the water's edge.

What had I done?

I stayed with her for as long as I could. I had to close her eyes, though. I couldn't handle her staring at me like that, frozen in that last, agonizing moment. I covered each eye with a wild blue flower. It seemed fitting somehow. I'd once read somewhere how blue blooms were known to have a calming effect on people. Maybe she'd sleep well. I crossed her arms over her chest and then stood at the sound of something behind me in the woods. "I'm sorry," I whispered. "I have to go now, but someone will come for you soon. I promise."

It had started to rain, only slightly though. I glanced over my shoulder, and stopped, somehow shocked at the sight of her small body at the river's edge... somehow shocked that my hands were covered in her blood.

I started running as fast as I could, tripping on thick roots and loose rocks in the woods. Cold rain hit my face, burning like embers from a fire. My senses were on high alert, flinching at every twig snapping under foot and every whisper echoing in the trees. *How could you? How could you? How could you?* I ran from the voices, but they only grew louder as I tried to make it to the roadside. "I'm sorry," I yelled. I was so close to the road now, but the wind was relentless, pulling me back. I'd almost made it when someone grabbed me from behind. "Let go of me!" I screamed. "Let go!" *Let go. Let go of me.* I fell to the ground and pulled my red hood from my face, staring up into Ellie's pale, lifeless eyes. They were filmy, algae coated, dead.

"Piper?" she asked.

"I'm sorry, Ellie. I am so sorry. Please let go of me—"

"Piper!"

I opened my eyes, gasping for air. It wasn't Ellie pulling at me but my brother. "Wyatt?" I shook my head, confused. Wyatt shook me, calling my name. I wasn't in the woods by the river. No sand. No water. No body. I exhaled, releasing all the fear from inside my body. I was in my room. "I was dreaming?"

He nodded, eyes wide and mouth gaped.

"What?" I asked.

"What did you do?"

"What do you mean?"

"Piper, what the hell did you do to her?"

Chapter 49

"Leave me, alone, Wyatt."

"No way. Not after that."

He chased me down the hall and out the front door to my car. "It was a stupid dream, that's it," I told him over the hood of Dad's Volvo.

He swept a hand through his shaggy hair, thick like our dad's used to be. He had the same midnight-colored eyes as Dad too, large and deep set, and the same squared jaw. Every time I looked at him, my heart still hurt. "Let it go, Wyatt." I got in the car, hoping he'd go back inside the house. He didn't. He got in the car with me. "What the hell?"

He grabbed my arm. "Sam said something was up with you."

"Sam?"

"Yeah, remember Sam?"

I blinked.

"He told me you were the one who took that picture of him and Miss Taylor."

"He's lying. I didn't."

"Are you in love with him or something."

"No, Wyatt, I'm not in love with him."

"Piper, come on. You can talk to me." His eyes softened. He could be nice when he wanted to be, when he wanted something from me. "What's going on with you?"

"Don't you think you're overreacting just a little?"

His eyes widened again. "You were just yelling in your sleep how sorry you were... *to Ellie*. You don't think I should be *just a little* freaked out about that?"

Sweat trickled down my back as I shrugged at him. "I had a bad dream. That's it."

Both of our phones dinged at the same time. His face lit up in the dark as he checked his phone, the bright screen casting harsh shadows. "Holy..."

"What? What is it?"

He shook his head, turning his phone toward me. It was a news alert: "New DNA evidence in the Ellie Stone case." I reached for my own phone, pulling up the story. It said, "Recent DNA evidence is connected to Nick Moore, a Waterford teen who died in April from a fatal car crash on Highway 25."

Thank God. I sighed with relief.

"Piper?" Wyatt asked in the quiet of the car.

I couldn't face him. I couldn't look him in the eye.

"What are you not telling me?"

It did no good to tell him. None whatsoever. He didn't need to carry around my guilt, my secrets.

"Piper!" Wyatt reached across the seat and grabbed my arm.

His fingernails pinched even through my sweatshirt. I hated how I teared up almost instantly.

"Tell me."

"Fine."

He let go of my arm but never took his eyes off me.

"Okay, fine. I was there that night."

"And?"

"And I saw Nick and Ellie down by the river, fighting about something, Tori, I think. He pushed Ellie down, but she got up. And then he took off. That's when Sam showed up with Miss Taylor. But you can't tell anyone. You have to swear you won't."

"What difference does it make now?"

"It doesn't, but please, just swear that you won't say anything. To anyone."

Wyatt narrowed his eyes at me.

"Swear it. On Dad's grave."

"Okay, okay. Fine. On Dad's grave."

I leaned my head against the seat, staring at the article still pulled up on my phone. It was over now. Finally. The DNA on Ellie's shirt was Nick's, not mine. I'd been so afraid that my DNA had landed on her shirt, implicating me. But it was Nick's blood that had been found on her top. It made sense. They'd fought and he'd pushed her down that night, so it added up.

But he hadn't killed her.

"Wait," Wyatt said, facing me. "Who sent the photo to the principal?"

My throat tightened. Sam had been right: I had. I wanted Miss Taylor fired for what she'd done to me the year before, or more like what she *hadn't* done. After what happened with Drew in the art studio, after trying to tell Ellie what he'd done, I went to Miss Taylor. But she downplayed it, making it sound like we'd had sex and that I was regretting it or something. I told her that, no, that wasn't it at all, but she dismissed it—me—like Ellie had. She said she'd file a report, but she never did. Wasn't it her job? Her duty?

"Piper?" Wyatt asked.

"I don't know."

He held my stare as the German Shepherd from next door barked in the yard.

"But you can't say a word to anyone that I was there that night. I mean it, Wyatt. Not a word to Mama, not to Sam, not to anyone."

"Yeah, I got it." He reached for the door handle. My shoulders started to ease as he got out of the Volvo. I sighed slowly, deeply, staring at the park swings across the street, swaying in the night air. It was like Ellie was over there, Nick too, whispering, *liar, liar, pants on fire.*

"Hey, Piper," Wyatt said, leaning back in the car. He reeked of chili pepper and sesame. "Just one more thing."

"Yeah?"

"Why didn't you say anything to the cops or call 911?"

"What do you mean?"

"If you had nothing to do with it, why didn't you tell the police what happened?"

My insides quaked as he stood, his hands resting calmly on top of the car.

"Shock? I was totally freaked out."

He didn't blink.

He just stared at me, like he knew. "Don't stay out late," he said, then slammed the door shut.

Chapter 50

THE MORNING AFTER MY run-in with Wyatt, I was back in the principal's office. Someone who was also back was Dr. Moore. I'd seen her a few times since at the café, picking up her cauliflower crust pizza with feta and extra tomatoes. But now, seeing her in the front office again in another one of her designer suits, this one plum colored, she looked different somehow. Maybe older? Sadder, if that was possible.

Dr. Moore sat down beside me and smiled. "How are you?"

"In trouble, I think."

She swept her French-manicured fingers over her blonde hair and glanced up at the principal's door. "First offense?"

"I wish."

"Honesty helps."

Does it? I thought as Dr. Henderson opened her door.

"Good morning," she said, waving at Nick's mom to join her.

As I waited for my mom to show, I kept replaying the conversation I'd had with Wyatt about Nick and Ellie. All he had to do was keep his mouth shut about me being there. It wasn't a lot to ask, but would he? I pulled out my phone and started scrolling through Instagram, not because I cared what people had posted, but because I needed a diversion. Anything but this.

Twenty minutes later, Mama swept into the front office right as Dr. Henderson's door opened. "I appreciate your time," Nick's mom said, stepping across the threshold.

"Of course. Tell Hayes we're thinking of him."

I hadn't thought about how Hayes was handling the news. It couldn't be easy for him.

"Thanks again," Dr. Moore said. As she turned, she nearly bumped into my mama, who was suddenly dowdy and plain in her pale-pink blouse and gray pants. She was small, too, compared to Dr. Moore and not just in size. Maybe it was the three-inch heels or the old money that made the doctor seem grander. Whatever it was, my mama didn't seem to notice.

"Hello, Julia," Mama said. She placed her hand on Dr. Moore's arm and said, "How are you?"

Stupid question.

"Well, I've been better." Dr. Moore offered a smile.

"Of course." Mama shook her head, obviously pained by her too—casual *how are you?* "Look, if there's anything I can do… anything at all, just let me know." Mama motioned for me to get up and join her.

"Thank you, Jennifer. I appreciate it. It's been difficult, to say the least. Hard on Hayes, especially."

I tucked my phone in my pocket and stood behind my mom, who grabbed my hand.

"I can't imagine what you're going through," she said, as if holding onto my hand would keep me safe. Keep me from dying or from being a part of the scandal.

Dr. Moore nodded. "I'm handling things." Then, she fixed her eyes on me and said, "Besides, the truth has a way of coming out."

I cleared my throat, glancing away from her.

"Have a good day," Dr. Moore said. "Oh, and Piper?" She stopped at the front desk, grabbing an armful of books and packets. "If you need someone to talk to, I can refer you. I know some excellent therapists at Willow Falls."

My stomach dropped.

"Bye, now," she said, pushing back her shoulders and taking her exit.

"Give me just one quick moment," Dr. Henderson said to my mom before ducking back into her office.

"What was that all about?" Mama whispered.

"What do you mean?"

"With Nick's mom."

I was hoping she hadn't noticed. "No idea. Why?"

Mama smoothed her graying brown curls. "Seemed a little odd to me, that's all."

"All right," Dr. Henderson said. "Sorry about that."

I bit a fingernail, anticipating the lecture about how my second chances were about to run dry. I followed Mama into the wood-paneled office and held my breath as she leaned in and whispered, "Let's turn things around, K? Make your daddy proud."

She got me, right in the heart.

I got lucky. Dr. Henderson gave me "one last shot" along with ten hours of community service. No detention or suspension for skipping classes. "But if you blow this," she'd said, "the next time, I won't be so lenient. You have so much potential, Piper, so let's turn things around." Then, she sent me off to English while she and Mama talked some more.

I should have been grateful or happy, but all I could think about in English was what Mama had said about Dr. Moore, about her acting *odd*. After class, I went straight to the bathroom and hid out in one of the stalls. It probably wasn't the smartest idea after just getting reamed about skipping class, but the whole run-in with Nick's mom was making me uneasy. The way she stared at me when she said, "the truth has a way of coming out" was downright creepy.

I sat on the back of the toilet tank and thought about that page in Nick's journal, the one with the list of names on it and the weird message about someone in red, watching, fading into the background.

What if... what if Nick's mom had found the journal before he died? What if he'd written somewhere in that journal that he'd seen *me* that night? I could see Dr. Moore now, with her plumped-up collagen cheeks and full lips, saying, "The truth has a way of coming out. Right, Piper?"

Chapter 51

I HELD MY BREATH for days, waiting for that knock on the door. It finally came a week after the run-in with Nick's mom in the school office.

"Hey, Piper," the female detective said, acting as if we knew each other. She shielded her eyes from the sun. "I was hoping we could talk."

"About what?"

"The night Ellie Stone was found."

"Who is it?" Mama called from the kitchen. Her quick footsteps padded across the hardwood as she called my name.

"Hello, ma'am. I'm Detective Ivey with the Waterford Police. This is my partner, Detective Daniels. We were just telling Piper here that we'd like to talk to her about the Ellie Stone case."

Mama placed her hand on my shoulder. "Oh?"

"We've been following up with some of the kids who went to the party that night. Do you mind if we come in for a few minutes?"

Mama gently squeezed my shoulder. "Sure, come in."

The detectives moseyed over to our lovingly worn leather couch. I sat across from them on the matching loveseat while Mama stood by the mantle, teetering from one foot to the other.

"Like I was saying," Detective Ivey said, "we're just following up on the night of the bonfire."

"But I didn't go that night," I said, running my fingertips along a few of the delicate creases worn into the leather.

The detective flipped through her notepad, skimming her notes. "Are you sure about that? I'm talking about the night of Sam Cox's birthday. The bonfire?"

"Yeah, I know what party you're talking about, and I told you, I didn't go."

"Well, you see, I have it in my notes that you did go."

My heart raced. *Keep it together.* "Who said that?"

"Couple of people, actually."

"Like who?"

"Does it matter?"

I stared at her, trying to figure out her game plan.

"Can I get you some coffee? I just made a fresh pot," Mama said in her timid, I'm-a-little-uncomfortable voice.

"No, ma'am, but thank you," Detective Ivey said.

I glanced over at my mom, fidgeting with the pearl button on her white shirt. I was so glad Ray wasn't around for this.

The detective followed my eyes. "On second thought, I'd love some. Black, one sugar?"

Mama nodded, turning toward the kitchen.

"I wasn't supposed to go," I said as soon as she was out of ear shot. "Sam is my brother's friend, and I begged my mom to let Wyatt take me, but she refused. So, I snuck out and went anyway. I just didn't want to get into more trouble."

"More trouble?" Detective Ivey asked.

"I've been having a hard time at school and stuff. Ever since my dad died, things have been hard."

"I'm sorry about your dad."

"Cancer." I swallowed the obscene-sounding word, tasting the bitterness of it in the back of my throat.

"Is this him?" Detective Ivey reached over the armrest and picked up the frame on the side table.

I nodded and waited for her to put it back in its place.

"So," she said, readjusting her weight on the couch, "then, you *were* there that night."

"Yeah, guess so."

She wrote something in her notes. "For how long?"

"Not long. Maybe an hour?"

"Did you see anything suspicious?" she asked.

"Like what?"

"Like someone talking to Ellie who usually didn't. Something like that."

I shook my head. "Don't think so."

"Why'd you only stay an hour?" The detective looked up from her notes.

"Because it wasn't any fun, so I left."

"Do you know what time you left?"

"No."

"How did you get home?"

My mind whirled in a thousand different directions, wondering who had told her I was there—Wyatt? The kids from band who had given me a ride? Sam? I didn't have to tell the detectives anything, not if I didn't want to. I knew my rights. And what was with all the questions anyway? My eyes stung as I glanced at my dad's picture. Why did I have to bring up my dad?

"You all right?" she asked, pressing her lips together.

"Why are you here?"

"What do you mean?"

"I thought you had DNA on Nick Moore, so I'm not sure why you're asking *me* all these questions."

"How did she die?" Mama asked, walking back into the room with a small tray.

The detectives glanced at each other.

"We haven't released that information yet," Detective Daniels said, taking one of the cups from Mama.

"It really is a shame losing those kids. Can't imagine the heartbreak of those two mothers."

"That's why we're being thorough, ma'am," Detective Daniels said. "Ellie's family deserves answers. So do the Moores. We just want to make sure we have the *right* answers, not just convenient ones."

"Wouldn't call DNA evidence *convenient*," Mama said, handing a cup to Detective Ivey.

"No, but the DNA in this case only places Nick at the scene. It doesn't necessarily prove he killed her," Detective Daniels said.

"So, you think someone else did?" My voice suddenly sounded small.

Detective Ivey sipped her coffee then placed the cup on the table between us. "We're still investigating."

"You're looking for the smoking gun, so to speak," Mama added.

Detective Daniels pursed his lips.

"Isn't it true that police only solve six-in-ten murders, meaning nearly half go unsolved?" Mama asked, obviously pleased with what she'd learned from her true-crime books. It was the only thing she and Nana had in common.

"Well," Detective Ivey chimed in, "that's not the case here, ma'am. Which leads me to my next question, actually." She reached down and pulled a sheet of paper from her oversized bag. "Piper, do you have a red sweatshirt with a hood?"

Mama's gaze snapped to me.

"No," I answered as calmly as possible.

"You sure about that?" Detective Ivey asked, looking at my mom, not me.

"What's this all about, Detective?" Mama asked.

"Just asking everyone who was there that night."

"Why?" Mama fiddled with her pearl button again.

"We have DNA evidence that places Nick with Ellie that night, but we also have reason to believe someone else was involved. Someone in a red sweatshirt." The detective reached across the coffee table, handing me the sheet of paper. Mama leaned over my shoulder.

I blinked a couple of times trying to focus on the blurred lettering, which was a little distorted from the copier. But even with the bad photocopy, I knew exactly what I was looking at. I recognized his handwriting from the journal page that Tori had shown me.

I didn't mean to do it. It was an accident. We fought, but I didn't hurt her on purpose. I pushed her and she fell backwards, hitting her head on a rock. But she got up. I swear she did. When she didn't come back to the bonfire, I started to worry, so I went back to check on her, just to make sure she was okay.

That's when I saw someone in a red hoodie hovering over her body. They'd pulled her from the water and placed a small blue flower over each of her eyes. I think whoever pulled her from the water heard me in the woods because it scared them off. That's when I went to check on Ellie, but there was no pulse. No life left in her. She was dead. I bit my lip so hard that it bled. I cried, begging God to make her wake up. To wake me from the nightmare. All I could think about was that I'd killed Ellie. The blow to her head had made her fall into the water and drown. It was all my fault.

"Are you sure," Detective Ivey said to me, "that you don't own a red sweatshirt with a hood?"

I glanced at her. "Even if I did, which I don't, owning a red hoodie doesn't mean anything. All this means is that someone was there—*if* it's even true. For all I know, it could be a made-up story. Pure fiction."

Detective Ivey took another sip of coffee. "No, you're exactly right, Piper. But if someone else was there, they could have seen what *actually* happened that night—after Nick left Ellie by the water. You see, there are a few things that just aren't adding up for us."

"Like what?"

"Well," she said, "*that* I'm not at liberty to say."

We stared at each other for a minute.

"You're welcome to look in my closet," I offered, "but you won't find a red hoodie." They could search all they wanted, but I was smarter than that. Any evidence that could implicate me—Ellie's phone, the bottle of Rohypnol, the clothes I wore that night—all of it was at Nana's under the floorboard. "Go ahead," I said, sinking back into the couch cushions.

Detective Ivey stood.

"Down the hall," I said, "second door on the right."

She nodded.

As they rifled through my things, I tried to figure out why they'd landed on me. Nick hadn't mentioned my name in that journal entry, and there was no description either, other than someone in a red hoodie. Someone had to have given me up. Sam? Probably. Wyatt? Maybe. But the "who" didn't matter. What did matter at that moment was changing the narrative—and fast.

Chapter 52

HIS ATTORNEY WAS ONE of the best, at least according to the six o'clock news report. So, I didn't feel that bad about what I'd done. After an "anonymous" tip had been called in, two Waterford detectives found Rohypnol in the back of the suspect's closet along with a red Adidas sweatshirt and the victim's cell phone. The family had called in defense attorney Alexis Thorpe. The news said that the victim, Ellie Stone, had Rohypnol in her system and that, ultimately, it suppressed her respiratory system, causing her to drown.

Of course, I knew all this. I saw it firsthand.

All I'd wanted was for her to look like a fool in front of everyone. I wanted her to slur her words and fall over her own feet, not to actually die. It was supposed to be a mean prank, a little dose of revenge, for picking sides and for abandoning me when I needed her and Tori the most. But I let it go too far.

After Nick had pushed her down, Ellie got up just like he'd said. So, thinking she was fine, he left and went back to the bonfire. But Ellie just stood there in the woods, staring out at the water, dazed. A few minutes later, Sam and Miss Taylor showed up. Ellie was still in the woods, hidden, as Sam and Miss Taylor fought, and that's when Ellie snapped the photo of them. The flash had freaked them out, sending Sam and Miss Taylor running in opposite directions.

While all of this was happening, I was hiding out on the bluff, watching.

After everyone left, Ellie just stood there in the woods, staring out at the river.

The haunted, cursed river.

I pictured it all now in my mind, thinking that I could have saved her.

But I didn't. I let her die, which meant that I killed her.

I saw her go into the water.

I saw her struggle.

I saw her arms flail above her head as she gasped for air... her head bobbing up and down, finally disappearing beneath the black water's surface only to reappear again minutes, too many minutes, later. That's when I stood and ran down to the water's edge.

But I kept watching, thinking she'd swim back to shore any minute. She called out *to me* to help her, but I didn't move. I stood there on the bank, watching her drown. Watching her take her last breath, muffled by the water that was slowly infiltrating her lungs and suffocating her.

I just watched.

I heard something rustle behind me in the trees, and when I glanced over my shoulder, I saw Nick. Or maybe that was later, *after* I'd pulled Ellie from the water. *After* I'd found her phone and tucked it in my pocket. *After* I'd placed those small blue flowers over her eyes. I'd plucked the flowers months earlier and had put them in my pocket. They were still there from the last time I'd worn the hoodie, pressed inside a small journal, now soaked, that my dad had given me. The truth was, I couldn't remember exactly when Nick saw me. I just knew he had. And when Tori told me in DC about the letters she was getting, about someone knowing who killed Ellie, I knew immediately that they were from Nick.

I just didn't know he thought *he* had killed her.

I thought he knew I had.

Things were starting to close in around me, but I couldn't go down for it, so I did what I had to. I changed the narrative.

A few days after those two detectives came to see me, I sneaked into Drew's house and planted the evidence from under Nana's floorboard in the back of Drew's closet. It was easy hacking into his security system. And, of course, I'd washed the red hoodie multiple times to rid it of my DNA and had wiped down Ellie's phone and the pill bottle too. Anyway, I'd hoped the detectives would put two and two together and conclude that it was the best friend's boyfriend who did it—he'd drugged her with the worst of intentions and then left her for dead.

It was pretty easy, planting it. I skipped school and went to his house. No one was home, and he didn't have a guard dog or nosy neighbors, so it was no big deal. It seemed fitting, poetic somehow, to end it all that way. It cleared Nick's name, and at the same time, ruined Drew's. It was a win-win for everyone, and with Drew taking the fall, everything could go back to the way it was with Tori and me—before he and Ellie had messed everything up. So, yeah, it was definitely a win for everyone.

Almost everyone.

Part Ten: Tori

Chapter 53

"IT'S HARD TO BELIEVE he would do something like that," I said from where I sat on the small bluff overlooking the Usman River.

"Really?" Piper furrowed her brow. "Because I think he's totally capable of it. You said yourself you thought someone drugged you that night. Now you know."

The rippling water down below caught my eye as sunlight shimmered on its surface. Maybe there was some truth behind the curse of the river, bringing out a deep, twisted darkness in people. Maybe it had pushed Drew to do the unthinkable. Or maybe I just needed something more to understand the cruelty behind his actions. But I still didn't get why he killed her. "It doesn't sit right with me," I said. "I thought I knew him."

"Do we ever really know someone completely?"

I turned and faced her. Her pink bangs fluttered in the sharp breeze coming off the water. "Maybe they got it wrong. First, they thought it was Sam. Then it was Nick. And now, Drew? I feel like they're grasping."

"It makes sense though. Sam was only a person of interest. They were interested in Drew from the start."

"How do you know that?"

Piper rubbed her nose.

"Piper?"

"You said yourself he was called in a few nights after the bonfire."

"Yeah, but so were a dozen others who were at the party that night."

"Apparently they were suspicious of him from the start. Who knows how many times they called him down to the station to question him? And it's not like he was honest with you all the time." She shrugged. "You told me yourself he was cheating on you with Rachel."

We were broken up. It wasn't cheating, I wanted to say.

"And what about him taking you home early that night? About you not being able to remember anything?"

The wind shrieked across the water, as if it were trying to tell me something. I crossed my arms over my chest. "Maybe your Nana was right."

"About what?" Piper asked.

"The curse of this river."

Piper nodded. Her gaze was now fixed on the water. Something in her shifted. Her shoulders relaxed as she stared almost trance-like at the water, almost like she'd forgotten I was there. "Nana says it makes us do things we normally wouldn't. Feeds us with doubt and anger and whispers evil things to us."

The hair on the back of my neck stood as she spoke. It didn't sound like she was still talking about Drew. Suddenly, I pictured her grandma's book with all those newspaper clippings... the last one about those two girls who'd gone missing near the lake... buried in a field of blue flowers.

Piper's phone rang. "Oh, crap," she said, blinking fast. "I need to go."

"Go?"

"Yeah, I told my mom I'd meet her for dinner 'to talk,'" she air-quoted.

"Oh, okay."

I followed her down the steep bank then veered off for a second to the water's edge. If only I knew what really happened that night, maybe I'd finally find peace. Find a way to quiet the noises in my head. Maybe then, I'd stop sitting under Ellie's window, blaming myself for what happened to her. But this whole Drew theory didn't sit right. He was a lot of things, but a killer wasn't one of them.

"You coming?" Piper called from the edge of the path.

I glanced up at her as she shifted from one foot to the other. She was nervous and fidgety, not at all like her normal self. Something was definitely off. "Yep. Be right there!" I stood slowly and turned one last time to the water. I breathed it in, closing my eyes and giving into it—the absurd, foolish idea that the river could somehow consume people. *Go ahead*, I thought.

Do whatever it is that you do. At this point, I had nothing to lose.

After Piper dropped me off at my house, I didn't feel like going inside to face Mom or Dad. I needed to talk to someone—just not one of them. I ended up, of all places, at Hayes' house. At first, when he opened the door, he just stood there and stared at me.

"Hey," he finally said, breathlessly.

"Hi." So much had happened. So many secrets had been kept from each other. Could we even find our way back? "Can I come in?"

He swept his hand over his mouth. "Yeah, of course."

I followed him inside, fighting with every step the urge to turn back around and run out the door. The last time we'd talked was in the stairwell, when he showed me Nick's confession letter. "I'm so confused," I whispered.

"Confused?"

"How did we go from Nick confessing to Drew getting arrested?"

Hayes looked over his shoulder, maybe for his mother, then said, "Come with me."

"Where to?" I asked, but he'd already turned and was headed up the curved staircase. I followed him up the stairs and then down the long hallway straight toward Nick's room. My insides churned, remembering the last time I'd been there.

Hayes stopped in his brother's doorway and waited for me to catch up.

The room was exactly the same. It probably would be forever. I stood there in the center of it, suddenly paralyzed by every emotion possible: fear, dread, doubt, guilt, anger—you name it. I could barely breathe as each one hit me. It was still so hard to believe that I had a brother and that I'd lost him before I even knew him as one. I was full of worry too. Why had he confessed to killing my best friend?

"Tori?" Hayes asked, moving toward the attic door.

I nodded. I needed a second. Maybe two. It had taken everything inside of me just to stand on his doorstep and ring that bell. I hadn't planned on revisiting the attic.

Hayes stepped over to me, reaching for my hand.

My body eased at the warmth of his palm.

But at the top of the steps, he let go and went to open the antique armoire. "My mom comes up here every night," he said, facing it. "She just stares at this board for hours. Says she won't stop until she knows the truth."

"But they cleared his name, right? They're saying Drew's the one who killed Ellie, not Nick."

Hayes turned around. Behind him, Nick's collage of photos looked like the backdrop to a movie set. He handed me an envelope. Was it another confession? Another one of his letters?

"What is this?"

"It's a certificate of paternity. Nick must've found it in my mom's files. She blames herself for what happened that night. She said Nick was only there that night to talk to you. To tell you..." Hayes rubbed his forehead. "I can't believe he carried that guilt around for so long, thinking he killed Ellie." He handed me another piece of paper from the armoire, a bad photocopy of a handwritten note.

My heart dropped at the slanted writing.

"It's from his journal. My mom tore it out before he went to DC."

I read over the words. They blurred the more I read.

It was an accident... I pushed her and she fell backwards, hitting her head on a rock. But she got up... I saw someone in a red hoodie hovering over her body. They'd pulled her from the water and placed a small blue flower over each of her eyes... I went to check on Ellie, but there was no pulse... I bit my lip so hard that it bled... It was all my fault.

I stepped backwards, dizzy. "Why do you think he sent me those letters instead of just telling the police?"

"No idea. Maybe it was his way of confessing, hoping you'd figure it out and turn him in. I think he was too scared to do it himself."

"It was a pretty cruel thing to do, sending me those letters." I glanced at all the photos. I swallowed, slowly fighting the nausea as I walked over to his board. There were so many photos, from a home photo printer for sure, but one in particular caught my eye. It was of me and Ellie, taken the night of the bonfire. Someone had taken it on their phone. Maybe Nick had pulled it from someone's Instagram. I hadn't noticed it the last time, probably because it was partially hidden behind another picture. "Can I have this one?"

Bailey

Hayes stared at me as I pulled it free. "Why?" he asked. "What is it?"

"A picture of Ellie and me... from that night."

He leaned over my shoulder. Had he spotted what I had? Had he seen the blurry image of the hooded person standing in the background, almost unrecognizable? Almost unnoticeable? "That's not Drew," I whispered.

We both flinched at the sound of heels clicking against the wood floors below in Nick's room.

"Hayes? Honey? Are you up there?" his mom asked as she came up the steps. "Oh," she said, stopping in the attic doorway. "I didn't know you had company." She nodded at me. "Hello, Tori."

"Hi."

She swept past us then shut the doors to the armoire. "I'd rather you two not be up here."

I slipped the photo in my pocket, hoping she didn't notice. "Sorry," I said. "I should get going anyway."

"I'll walk you out," Hayes offered.

"No, it's okay." I placed my hand in my pocket, feeling my fingertips slide over the slick photo paper. "I'll call you later."

On the way home, I texted Piper to ask how dinner went. She said it went fine.

Heading to visit my grandmother now, she wrote.

She'd asked me a dozen times to come and meet her Nana at Sunnyside. I thought about going over there now as I pulled the photo from Nick's board out of my pocket. There was just something about that grainy, blurred image in the background that was bothering me. I ran home and asked Mom if I could borrow the car for an hour.

"Where are you going?" she asked, looking up from her iPad on the kitchen counter.

"To hang out with Piper."

She nodded at her purse on the table. "Keys are in my purse."

Fifteen minutes later, I pulled into the nursing home's parking lot, looking for Piper's pale-yellow Volvo. It was next to a random blue van. I reached for my phone on the passenger seat, so I could text Piper that I'd decided to come and meet

256

Nana. The only problem was, my phone had died. But it was fine. Piper had invited me more than once to come and meet her Nana and to hear all about the river curse and her album full of stories.

I stopped at the front desk to ask what room Mrs. Wells was in. An older bearded guy in scrubs pointed his large finger down the hall. "Last room on the right," he said. "But most everybody is in the main hall watching *Rocky*." He nodded at a room over my shoulder.

"Thanks," I said. "I'll check it out."

He was right. Most everyone was in the main ballroom watching *Rocky* on a large screen. But not Piper and her Nana. I scanned the room three times before heading down the hall to Nana's room. When I heard Piper's laugh, I slowed down outside the door then stepped quietly inside. They were talking behind a seafoam-green curtain, which separated the room in two. Nana's roommate wasn't there. She was probably watching *Rocky* with the rest of the old people.

"I miss the way things used to be," Piper said. "Mama is with Ray all the time. It's like Dad didn't even exist."

"It was hard on all of us, Cami," Nana said. "Losing him like that. No explanation. No reason as to why."

"Nan, it's me. Piper. Remember?"

"Of course, I know that, child."

Who was Cami?

Nana cleared her throat. "Now tell me, whatever happened with that new fella of yours."

"Nan, I'm not seeing anyone."

"Nonsense. The last time you were here, you were going on and on about that boy. Oh, what was his name? Nick, was it?"

"I wasn't seeing him," Piper said quietly. "I told you last time that *he had seen me*."

My stomach plummeted. The drumming in my ears was so loud, I swore they could hear it.

Nana laughed. "Well, that makes no sense at all, child. What do you mean he saw you? Saw you doing what?"

I held my breath. *Say it. Say it, Piper.* I swept my finger over the slick photo, still in my pocket. It was her face in that picture. I was sure of it. Her blurred face, shaded by the hood. She'd said that she hadn't gone to the bonfire that night, but now I had proof, literal proof in my hands, placing her there. How was it even possible? All this time she'd been so nice to me... so supportive, and yet...

"Nothing. Don't worry about it," Piper said. "Want to watch *Wheel of Fortune*?"

I knew right then that the conversation was over.

"Yes, that sounds nice, Cami."

Who the heck was this Cami person?

A loud round of applause echoed from down the hallway, signaling that the movie was probably over. I needed to leave before Piper realized I was there, but I also wanted to stay and ask Nana questions. But now was not the time. As I slipped out of the room and into the dim hallway, the photo felt like it was burning a hole in my pocket. I'd gone through so many posts from the bonfire that night. I'd never seen any with Piper in them. Then again, I'd never looked for her.

Maybe Nick had been the real genius, finding the one photo to place her at the party that night—and in a red hoodie of all things. Had he realized what he'd found, or was it just a coincidence that he put that photo on his board?

Chapter 54

WHAT ARE YOU DOING? Hayes texted a few days later.
Nothing. Why?
I need you to come over ASAP.
Right now?
Yes. Door is unlocked. Come up to Nick's room.

My mind flew from one thing to the next. What was so urgent that I had to come over right then, at that exact moment? Whatever it was, it had to be important.

Ten minutes later, as I passed by the old carriage house, I stopped to glance at Dr. Moore's office door. It looked like it had a fresh coat of paint, maybe a brighter shade of red. I inhaled the brisk spring air then zoomed around the walkway to the main house, doing exactly what Hayes had said to do—go straight up to Nick's room.

But it felt strange turning the doorknob to his house and walking in like I belonged there. "Hello?" I called out, stepping over the threshold. I swallowed uneasily as I breathed in hints of a fresh linen candle. It flickered on the marble countertop. My mom would have freaked about having a candle burning with no one around. "Hello?"

Hayes appeared on the top landing. "Hey. Come on up," he said.

"You have a candle burning, you know."

"Yeah, it's fine."

I climbed the steps, watching as he shifted nervously on his feet. "What's going on? What's so urgent?" I followed him down the hall to Nick's room. Again. *Not the attic...* But he stopped short of the attic door and pulled out Nick's desk chair for me to sit, instead. On the screen in front of me was a paused video. "What is this?" I asked even though I knew exactly what it was—another one of Nick's recordings in his mom's office.

"It's from today. Just a while ago."

"You recorded a session? Today? Why?"

"Something Sam said to me at school today, it kind of freaked me out."

"What did he say?"

"It wasn't anything I hadn't heard before, but we were talking about Drew getting arrested and he said he didn't think he did it. When I told him my brother didn't do it either, he said he knew. Then he told me..." Hayes glanced up at the door, listening for footsteps.

"What is it?"

"Hold on," he said, then sped across the room to shut and lock the door.

I cleared the tickle in my throat.

"That whoever killed Ellie killed Nick too."

I met Hayes' eyes and held his stare.

"I know it was wrong, but when I saw him go to my mom's office, I pulled up Nick's old surveillance stuff to see if I could still log in."

"And?" I asked.

"And it worked."

We exchanged glances.

"Listen," he said, hitting the play button.

Dr. Moore curled her hand over her ear, sweeping her hair back. Sam closed the door behind him then moved to the center of the room where she was standing.

"How are you, Sam?"

His hands were shaking slightly and his breath was short. "Not good." He stepped back, redirecting toward the door. "Maybe we should reschedule. I'm not feeling it today."

"Of course. Whatever you'd like."

He stopped in front of the door and inhaled.

"Sam?"

He didn't turn around to face her. "If I tell you something, it stays here, right?"

"Yes, always."

"The cause of death..." he said quietly, almost inaudibly. He rested his forehead against the caramel-colored wood.

"Ellie's cause of death?" Dr. Moore asked.

"No. Nick's."

"Okay... what about it?"

"He didn't die because of the car accident."

Dr. Moore moved toward him. She reached out her hand but hesitated and dropped it to her side. "What do you mean?"

"So much has happened," he said, turning around to face her. "I don't know what to believe anymore, you know? There've been so many news stories, theories, posts, police interrogations—including mine—that I don't know what's real and what's not anymore."

"Okay... but you said that Nick *didn't* die from the accident." Her lip trembled. "Then what? How did he die?"

Sam started pacing the floor, mumbling something under his breath.

"Sam?" She was now just as visibly shaken as he was.

He took a deep breath, staring at her. "I followed her."

Dr. Moore didn't ask Sam who he'd followed. No prompting for a name. She just nodded, gripped the back of the chair to keep from collapsing, and motioned for Sam to sit.

He sat on the couch, in his normal spot, placing his elbows on his knees and resting his head in his hands.

"Go ahead," she said, easing into the seat across from him.

"I just don't know what to do."

"Tell me what you know. You said you followed someone."

"I saw Piper sneaking out of her bedroom window the other night. I was headed over to see her brother when I noticed her. I was curious, so I followed her."

"Why were you curious?"

Sam shrugged. "I don't know. I mean, there's always been something off about her, even before their dad died."

"What do you mean by off?"

"Most of the time, she was fine, did normal little sister stuff, like trying to hang out with us. It was annoying, the way she was in our space all the time—in the kitchen when we got snacks, in the den when we played video games, in the backyard... always there. Sometimes, she'd just stare at you... with this blank, completely freakish stare."

Dr. Moore nodded. "So, you followed her?"

"Yeah. She ended up going to her grandma's house, which was strange to me since Wyatt told me their Nana was in a home. But Piper just opened the glass slider in the back and went in." Sam paused, almost as if he were afraid to continue.

Dr. Moore took a deep breath. "It's okay. I know this is hard for you, but you need to keep going."

It was hard for her too. I'd never seen her so nervous and twitchy. She kept shifting in her seat like she wanted to get up and shake it out of him.

"Shit," he said.

I looked up at Hayes, wide-eyed and scared. He was standing at my right shoulder, just as fidgety as his mom in the video.

"She didn't close the door all the way," Sam continued, "so I slipped in and followed her inside to confront her or something, but then I saw her in her grandma's bedroom, sitting on the edge of the bed. She started talking to her, only there was no one there." He rubbed his arms.

"It's okay, Sam. Keep going. What happened next?"

"She started talking to her. She said, 'Hey, Nana,' to absolutely no one. 'You're looking good today.' It was like she thought her Nana was really there. Then she said, 'Nan, I did something you would think was really bad. You know how I told you what Drew did to me, right? Well, I got him back, Nan. Real good.'"

Dr. Moore nodded.

"Then," Sam continued, "she was like, 'yes, ma'am. Can you believe it? But something had to be done. They were getting close, sniffing around, Nan. I couldn't let them find out what I'd done to Ellie or to Nick.'" Sam looked up, meeting Dr. Moore's wide-eyed stare.

Her lips parted with a small gasp.

"It was the strangest thing the way she was talking to her grandma, when there was no one there. It freaked me out, Dr. Moore, and it rattled me, too, what she said about Nick."

Dr. Moore slowly leaned back in her chair. His revelation had stunned her into a deep, contemplative silence.

Hayes pressed pause on the video.

I didn't know what to say. "Is there more?"

"No. After that, he clams up. He tells her he wants to leave and that it was a mistake that he came. It pretty much ends there. That's when I texted you."

"What do we do now?"

"I don't know that there's anything we *can* do."

"I need to tell my dad."

"No. You can't tell him I recorded my mom's therapy with Sam. She'll lose her license or worse. Besides, it's hearsay. We don't know if any of this actually happened."

I reached into my coat pocket, pulling out the photo still inside it. I tapped on the blurry image of the girl in the dark hoodie. "She was there the night of the bonfire... wearing a red hoodie."

"It's too dark to tell. Besides, she could have taken it off. Someone else, like Drew, could have put it on later."

"So, then what? We do *nothing*?" My voice was high-pitched and shaky. He was my brother, our brother, and we were supposed to do nothing?

Hayes sat down on Nick's bed and cradled his head in his hands. "I don't know. I don't know what to do."

Chapter 55

IT TOOK A FEW days, but after Sam went to Dr. Moore, she finally ended up doing what she should have done years ago. She came to see my dad. I was walking back from Ellie's house when I saw headlights in the driveway. I hid at the side of the house, hoping they'd stay on the porch so I could hear them.

"Hi, Jacob," she said, standing on the doorstep.

He squinted at her, haloed in the yellow porch light. "Jules... what are you doing here?" He glanced over his shoulder then pulled the door shut behind him as he stepped out onto the porch.

"Can we talk?"

He nodded. "Did you want to go somewhere?"

"No, this is fine for now. I just need to get it out, before I chicken out and change my mind again." Her four-hundred-dollar heels tapped on the wooden porch as she treaded carefully, carrying years of guilt, regret, sadness in each step. "I'm sorry," she finally said.

He nodded at her, unable to meet her eyes. He already knew. He had to know.

"I've been saying that a lot lately. To Hayes, especially. But I've owed you an apology for a really long time, Jake. I should have told you years ago that Nick was your son."

He flinched at the word "son." "Why didn't you tell me I had a son? All these years and I had no idea."

"You know why. You went back to Kate," she glanced at the door and paused.

"She's not home."

Dr. Moore nodded. "You went back to your wife and I went back to Daniel. It's what we agreed on."

"When did you know... that he was mine?"

Dr. Moore leaned back against the porch railing with a heavy sigh. "I had a paternity test done early on. Nick must have found it a few months back." She inhaled slowly, trying to compose herself. "I'm pretty sure that's what started his obsession—*interest*—with Tori—with the pictures, the following her around, the letters."

The letters. My heart dropped. I never told my dad about them.

She tried her best to explain the letters and the board in the attic, doing her best to protect, preserve, their son's image. "I don't think he meant to scare her like he did. I think, in his complicatedly wired mind, he was helping her to the truth while processing it all himself."

Dad shook his head in disbelief, or maybe shock. "By sending her those letters?"

"No, that's not what I mean."

"Then what *do* you mean?"

She pressed her perfectly manicured fingers to her forehead. "I don't know what I mean. Look, he'd just learned you were his father—that's a lot for anyone to process. I think the night that Ellie died, he was going to tell Tori. He just never got the chance. And then... Ellie died, and he thought he killed her."

Dad squeezed his eyes shut.

"He knew someone else was there that night," Dr. Moore said. "He saw someone, and I think he was trying to figure out who it was. Maybe he thought it was Tori. It tears me up inside to know that, for months, he thought he was the one responsible. He must have been so terrified, carrying that around with him."

"So, you think the letters were his way of confessing?"

"Yes, I do. I found his journal the night before he left for DC. He'd confessed right there in his own writing."

"So, you were the one who tore out the pages?"

"I had to. I had to protect our son, but then..."

"But then what?"

"It's going to sound so awful, Jake."

"Just tell me."

"I wrote one of the letters."

"What?" Dad stared at her in shock.

"I only did it to protect our son. I never believed, not for one second, that he killed Ellie. When my contact from the police station said they found DNA evidence on Ellie's shirt, that's when I dug up the journal pages. He'd written in his journal that when he went back to check on Ellie that night, he bit his lip so hard it bled. I was so terrified of it being his blood, his DNA, on her shirt."

"And so you wrote Tori a letter? I don't understand."

"I wrote it to plant doubt. All the letter said was that there was more to the story. I wanted to make sure that *if*, and probably when, Tori went to the police to tell them it was Nick all along, that at least they would know there was more to it. I knew from his journal that someone else had been there—someone else more capable than Nick of killing Ellie. And so, I stuck the letter in a homework packet left for Sam Cox in the main office, hoping he'd think he got it by mistake and give it to her. And he did."

"Unbelievable," Dad muttered, barely audible.

"But now, none of it matters. All the blame has been taken off of Nick. His name has been cleared. He's been vindicated."

"Then why are you here, Jules? Why are you telling me all this?"

Dad's phone rang. He reached for it in his pocket and silenced the call. It was probably mom.

"I'm sorry he scared her, and I'm sorry she had to find out about him being her brother the way she did... and you too, Jake. I wanted to tell you, so many times over the years, but the timing was always off. Maybe if I had, our son would still be alive."

"What are you saying?"

"I think Nick was killed because of something he saw the night Ellie died."

Dad shook his head. "No, he died because of a drunk driver."

"I don't think he did, and I also don't think Drew was the one who killed Ellie. I think the person who actually killed Ellie also killed Nick to keep him quiet."

Dad stared out at the front yard, trying to process what Dr. Moore had just dumped on him. There was a lot to connect. But if anyone could do it, he could. He was, after all, a cop. Then again, how had he not seen it? All those years with Nick walking around town—how had he not seen himself in his own son's eyes? But he had to have known the *second* Detective Ivey showed up on his doorstep with a partial DNA match. Why not fess up right then and there?

"So, what's your theory?" Dad asked.

"It's not mine, actually."

"Okay, then whose is it?"

"I can't say," she trailed off. "But there's someone you need to look into. I just don't know how to prove it, not with all the evidence stacked against Drew."

"I'm in narcotics, Jules. It's not my case."

"No, but it is *your* son, our son, who was killed. Your daughter's half-brother. We owe it to them to at least try."

"Who am I supposed to look into?"

"Ask your daughter."

My knees buckled. How did she know? Had Hayes told her what we'd done? What we'd seen?

As Dad and Dr. Moore stood on the porch, I couldn't help but think about Piper and her shadow looming in that photograph. I needed to tell him.

She'd said something at the river the other day, about it making people do things they normally wouldn't. How it fed people with doubt and anger and made them do evil things. But I wasn't about to accept that. I needed to expose her for what she really was. The only problem was, I didn't have any concrete proof.

Chapter 56

AFTER DR. MOORE LEFT, I stayed outside for a while, thinking and rocking on the tire swing in the backyard. I finally headed inside almost an hour later to face my dad.

"Hey, kiddo. Where've you been?"

"Dad, there's something I need to tell you."

He eased up off the couch and slowly walked over to me, smoothing his disheveled hair. "Okay. What is it?"

"I heard you before, outside talking to Dr. Moore."

He nodded and leaned his weight on the back of the sofa.

"She said you needed to ask me, right? Who to look into about Nick's death?"

Dad scratched his bristly cheek, barely able to make eye contact with me. I didn't know who he was anymore. The person I thought he was wasn't in this room. But it didn't matter. What he'd done was in the past. And now, we needed to work through our current problems. We had to move forward. For Nick.

Dad nodded as if he'd heard me.

"You need to look at Piper." I reached into my coat pocket and handed him the photo from the night of the bonfire. "That's her, right there in the red hoodie."

"Okay..."

"I think she planted that evidence at Drew's house."

"That's a pretty big accusation. Did she tell you she did that?"

"No, not exactly."

"Tori, what does that mean?"

"She didn't tell me, but I just know she did it."

"How do you know?"

What was I supposed to say, that it was a gut feeling? And

that Sam overheard her talking to herself, confessing? "Dad, can you just look into it? Do what cops do?"

He sighed heavily through his nose. He always did that when he was frustrated or mad. "I can look into it, but the evidence against Drew is pretty solid from what I hear. Is there anything else, other than this photo, for me to go on?"

I shook my head, not wanting to bring Sam into this. He'd have to tell his story, but like Hayes had said, it was a secondhand account. It was hearsay. As I started to walk off, defeated, I stopped. "Check the cameras at the hospital the day Nick died."

"What? Why?"

"When I woke up that day, Piper was standing at the foot of my bed. When I asked her what she was doing there, she was acting all weird."

Dad nodded. "Weird how?"

"I don't know. Just weird, guilty. That was the morning Nick died, and when Mom told me, Piper just looked out the window. She didn't cry or even look like she'd been upset at all. She didn't seem shocked or bothered by it. Not one bit."

"Tori, you were on so many pain meds. You'd just been in a serious wreck... your state of mind was..."

"I know, not clear. That's why I'm saying check the cameras. Check for her in the halls. Check Nick's time of death. Just check." I rubbed my aching temples. I hated how unclear my memory was. For so long, I'd assumed Piper had been there that day for *me*, to comfort *me*, but maybe she had been there for another reason.

Nick had been getting better, stronger by the day. Maybe it had caused Piper to panic because he knew too much. Maybe the cameras would catch her slipping into Nick's room that morning. It would only take a few minutes to snuff the life out of him.

In my mind, I replayed what Sam had said about Piper talking to her Nana. She'd said that "something had to be done. They were getting close, sniffing around. I couldn't let them find out what I'd done to Ellie or Nick."

"Check the cameras, Dad. Please?"

He did.

A couple of days later, Dad called me into his office downstairs to tell me what he'd found, which was nothing. There was nothing caught on camera. In fact, the entire morning's footage didn't exist. It had been erased or had never been recorded to begin with. Dad did tell me that they'd called Piper in for questioning. He said that she had shown up dressed in all white from head to toe and wearing bright red lipstick. "It was odd," he said as I sat down in the chair across from him.

"See?" I said.

He smoothed his black Narcotics shirt and nodded.

"What did she say?"

"She told the detectives that it was 'an interesting story, but that it was pure fiction and unless they had any 'hard evidence,' they couldn't hold her. Then she got up, pushed the metal table, and strutted out of the interrogation room with her mother."

"And that was it?"

"That was it. They didn't have anything to hold her."

Dr. Moore had been right. The evidence was stacked against Drew. Piper had been too careful. Too conniving. Too clever.

"So, what do we do now?" I asked Dad over his stacks of folders and old books.

"I don't know, Tori. I need to talk to Ivey and Daniels. It's their case and as far as they're concerned, they've got their guy. I'm just not sure they're going to waste the energy chasing down this theory anymore."

I pushed my hands against the armrests and stood, frustrated. Drew wasn't their guy. If Dad wasn't going to help me with this, I'd figure it out on my own. "What would they need?"

He shrugged. "A confession."

Piper was never going to confess to the police. Not in a million years.

Dad stood and rested his large hand on my shoulder, gently squeezing it. "I'll talk to them, Tori, but you need to be prepared to let this go. I know you want justice for Ellie. We all do. But you need to let the system work."

I swallowed the raw burn in my throat. What he was saying was all true, even if I didn't want to hear it.

Chapter 57

I COULDN'T SLEEP. IT had been days, weeks, even months since I'd slept through the night. Everything about the bonfire kept gnawing away at me, night after night, as I tossed and turned in my bed. I wanted nothing more than to hit re-wind... to go back to that night and do it all over again.

How do you make peace after something so tragic? I texted Hayes from under the covers. *How do we move on knowing what we know?* I reached out across my quilted comforter, brushing my fingers over my pillow and waiting for him to write back.

"Make her confess," Ellie said in my head. "Make her tell you what she did to me and to Nick. That's the only way you'll get any peace, T. And you know Drew didn't do this. You know what Piper is capable of."

"But how do I make her tell me?"

"You'll figure it out. You always do."

I scrolled through my phone, looking up ways to "make peace after tragedy." One article said to travel, read a book, exercise, or wear a color that makes you happy. Another one said to spend time in nature. To pray. To listen to music. Yet another said to do something creative or symbolic. I moved from one website to the next, searching for the answers I needed to move on.

We just do, Hayes finally texted back. It was four a.m., so I was surprised to see his text pop up on my screen.

I think I have an idea, I typed.

It didn't take long to get things rolling. I ordered a few things online for store pick-up and sent out a handful of e-vites. When I typed in the date of the event, May 25, it hit hard because that was exactly four months to the day.

She'd been gone for four months.

Sixteen weeks.

One hundred and twenty days.

The morning of my big idea, Mom woke to find me sitting at the kitchen table, hunched over my lemongrass tea.

"What's all this?" she asked. She picked up one of the flattened paper lanterns on the kitchen table and held it up to the kitchen light.

"It's to find peace."

"What do you mean?" she sat down across from me, rubbing sleep from her eyes.

"Lanterns provide light, right?"

She nodded.

"I thought it would be healing, I guess, to get a few people together and release these at night for Ellie and Nick. Some people say the light leads the way forward and pushes away darkness. It's like a path, the lantern shows us a way forward."

"That's beautiful, Tori."

I shrugged. "I read it online somewhere."

"Still, it's a lovely sentiment. When are you doing it?" she asked, tucking a strand of her caramel hair behind her ear. She looked refreshed, happier than she had been in a while. I was glad for her, even if it meant my parents were separated and time-sharing me and the house.

"Tonight... at the river."

Mom looked up at me surprised. "At the river?"

"It's fine."

She cleared her throat. "Well, if you need any help, let me know." She stood, shuffling over to the coffee pot.

Even though Nick hadn't died out there, I did believe, deep down, that he died *because* of the river... because of what happened to Ellie out there. Maybe it was morbid to hold the memorial in the place Ellie had taken her last breath, but I wanted to release the darkness that was still lingering and send it into the sky with the white lanterns.

"This is perfect," Hayes said later that night.

I nodded, scanning the small group by the fire. I'd invited a few of Nick's friends and a handful of Ellie's too, including

Sam and Wyatt. Connor was there too, playing a few songs on his guitar. I rubbed my goose-bumped arms in the cool air and smiled up at the dozen or so glowing white lanterns dotting the night sky. "Maybe now this place will be at peace."

"This place or you?"

"Both?"

"You don't really believe it's cursed, do you?" Hayes asked.

"No. Maybe. I don't know."

"You don't sound too convinced."

We sat down on the blanket together in front of the bonfire we'd made and leaned back on our elbows to watch the lanterns float higher and higher. "But don't you think it's weird how many bad things have happened here over the years? There are all these stories..." I paused, something catching my eye. It was Piper, walking towards us on the bank.

Hayes turned to follow my stare. "What's she doing here?"

"I invited her."

"What? Why?"

I sat up. "It's all about finding peace, remember?"

"Hey," Piper said. "Sorry I'm late."

"It's okay." I jumped up and handed her a paper lantern. "I saved one for you."

"Thanks," she said. "Good turn-out."

"Yeah, it is." The crowd around the fire clapped as Connor finished the song he'd been playing.

"You invited Sydney?" Piper asked.

"Connor asked if she could come."

"Oh," Piper said, and tilted her head. "Isn't that a little weird since Ellie and Connor were a thing?"

I'd been so preoccupied that I hadn't even thought about it being weird. But was it? "I think Ellie would be okay with it."

Piper shrugged.

"What? You don't think so?"

"You're probably right. I mean, no one knew her better than you did." She scratched the small diamond stud in the crease of her nose and held my stare as Connor started playing another song on his guitar. She nodded to the beat. "I like that song," Piper said. "Stairway to Heaven." She stood there for another minute listening before heading over to the river's edge to release her lantern.

"Everything okay?" Hayes asked, still seated on the blanket.

I sat back down beside him and watched as Piper released her lantern. "You don't think it's weird that Sydney is here, do you?"

"Not really."

Piper stood at the river's edge, gazing up at the sky as her lantern drifted higher and higher. She slipped her hands in the pockets of her white joggers and teetered in the sand.

"Should I go and talk to her?"

Hayes twisted his brother's watch on his wrist as he studied Piper. "Looks like she might be leaving."

Piper had turned away from the bonfire and was heading in the opposite direction of it.

"But she just got here," I said, watching her walk down the bank. "Wait a second..." She wasn't leaving—she was going into the woods. I tucked my hand in my pocket and felt for my phone. "I'll be back, okay?"

"Want me to come with you?"

"No. I'll be fine." My heart pounded even faster as I stood and ran after Piper.

By the time I caught up to her, she'd made it to the top of the bluff and was standing way too close to the edge. She was so close that her toes were hanging off it. I peeked at my phone in my pocket and pressed record. "Hey," I called out. "Be careful up there."

She leaned slightly forward over the edge, making my insides turn.

"They're beautiful, aren't they?" I asked, pointing to all the lanterns in the sky.

She sat and dangled her legs off the ledge.

I sat down beside her and stared into the dark water churning below us. Dad said that all I needed was a confession.

"How are you holding up?" Piper asked.

"It's been so hard, all these weeks, you know?"

She nodded.

"Did you hear that Drew's out on bail?"

"What?" Piper asked. "How?"

"His attorney said the Rohypnol found with a random red sweatshirt and Ellie's phone was circumstantial. She said it proves nothing other than he was there the night Ellie died along with every other kid in Waterford." I took a deep breath, praying I could keep it together. "She's saying it's a set-up."

Piper's gaze snapped to me.

"I mean it kind of is, isn't it?" I said in a small, prodding voice.

She didn't speak.

Now was my chance. I needed to say it. I needed to confront her with what I knew. I fisted my hands, took another deep breath, and slowly exhaled. *Do it. Now.* "I know what you did, Piper. I know it all."

Piper squinted and shook her head at me. "What are you talking about?"

My whole body trembled. My ears whirred. "I know what you did."

"Oh yeah? What did I do?"

She swept her pink bangs away from her eyes and waited for me to speak.

But my words were lodged in my throat.

"What is it that you *think* you know?" Piper asked. "That I planted evidence? So what?"

"I know what you did to Nick."

Suddenly, everything about her demeanor changed. Her shoulders dropped and she stared down at the river with little to no expression on her face. No shaking hands. Nothing. I had no idea what to do next. Maybe I needed to say it again?

"I did it to protect you," she whispered, still gazing down at the water.

"To protect me? I don't get it. You killed Nick to protect me? From what?"

"There's no way to prove that I had anything to do with it. There's no hospital footage. I took care of it."

My stomach dropped.

So, it was true. It was all true what Sam had heard.

"You took care of it?" I mumbled under my breath.

She nodded. "I learned a lot from dad over the years," Piper said, her face blank of all emotion.

My eyes burned with tears. The rage inside of me was brimming to the surface. "He was my brother. Why—*how*—could you do something like that?"

"Nick knew what you did to Ellie."

"What *I* did to Ellie? What are you talking about, Piper?"

"He was closing in on you, and I was the only other person who saw what you did that night."

"You're not making any sense."

"Okay, then let me be clear," she turned to face me. "*You* killed her. You killed Ellie and Nick saw it."

I scoffed. "What are you talking about?" I stood, too fast, my feet teetering on the edge. Tiny stars blinked around my head as the memory flashed back to me again... my hands shaking in the moonlight... the river below.

Piper stood too. "It's true. It happened right here. You were fighting about something. Actually, you were fighting about Hayes. You said that she had feelings for him and you fought. You pushed her right here, making her go over into the water."

"You're lying," I said, rubbing my temples and seeing a flash of Ellie from that night in the moonlight, yelling in my face. No. It wasn't true. There was no way. "No. I went home."

"That was after you pushed her."

"No," I repeated. "You're lying. You're twisting everything. *You* killed her. You put those blue flowers over her eyes to connect her death to those girls in the next county, didn't you? To make the police think it was a serial killer. Then, when you found out that Nick saw *you*, you killed him to keep him quiet."

"You might think you know what happened, but you don't. So, before you go and turn over to the police what you're recording right now in your pocket, you might want to reconsider. Because I recorded you too." She pulled out her phone, searching for something. "Here," she said, handing it to me. "And don't worry about deleting it. It's backed up."

I stared at a video, dark on her screen. "What is this?"

"The truth." She reached over my shoulder and hit the play button. My whole body went numb at the sight of Ellie and me on the bluff. My hands were pressed against her chest... shoving her backwards, and I was yelling at her that I *hated* her. The river was in the background down below, angry and dark.

"Stop," Ellie said, shoving me back.

I fell to the ground, landing on my backside. I got up, wiped my muddy hands on my pants, and started yelling at her again.

She lifted her hand to the side of her head and wiped at the large spot of thick, drying blood. She held up her bloody palm and told me to stop, but I kept coming at her.

"There's no way," I mumbled, eyes locked on the video. It had to be a doctored video. Hadn't Piper just admitted to knowing about this stuff?

But in the clip, I kept yelling, saying that I *hated* how perfect Ellie was and how she always got whatever she wanted. "And now you want Hayes?" I screamed at her.

"What are you even talking about?" Ellie yelled back.

"I know that's what you wanted to tell me earlier at the house." The wind shrieked in the background. "You're in love with him, aren't you? Was that what you were talking to him about earlier?"

"I don't know what you're talking about, Tori. I'm not in love with Hayes. And besides, he isn't even yours. You're with Drew. He's with Rachel," Ellie yelled. "And no, that's not what I wanted to tell you earlier. I—"

I cut her off. "I know about your mom and my dad, Ellie. You always have to have what's mine. You take whatever you want, and I'm sick of it."

It wasn't possible. I'd had no idea about an affair, maybe some suspicion, but that was later—after Ellie died. I rubbed my temples, not understanding any of it. "It's not possible," I said under my breath as I struggled to refocus on the video.

In the video, Ellie shook her head at me, confused.

"You always take everything I have," I slurred.

"Tori," Ellie said as the wind whipped at the loose dark strands of hair around her face.

"You take *everything*—you want my dad because yours left you and you want Hayes because Connor doesn't love you. You *know* how I feel about Hayes. Why him?"

"He doesn't even talk to you," Ellie shouted.

And then, there, on the small screen, I gave Ellie one last shove while yelling, "I hate you!" I pushed her so hard that she stumbled backwards right off the bluff overlooking the river down below. And then, I just stood there, frozen, staring at my shaking hands.

That's where the video ended.

I dropped the phone and fell to my knees as Piper bent down to pick it up.

"There's no way," I whispered. "She was my best friend. I would never..."

"Well, apparently you did."

"No. It's not real. The video is fake."

"It's real, Tori. That's really you and Ellie, and deep down, I think you know it."

"No. The last time I saw her, she was by the fire, talking to Hayes. Then I left. Drew took me home." I pinched my eyes shut, seeing her hand covered in blood. Then I saw my own hands, covered in mud and shaking in the moonlight, and the water below... her muffled cries for help echoing back to me... oh, no. What had I done?

Surely, I'd gone down to the river to help her. I wouldn't have just left her, right?

I gripped a handful of cold wet dirt and screamed under my breath. "It's not real. It can't be." I slowly opened my eyes, afraid to face Piper.

But she was gone.

"Piper?"

My legs trembled as I stood, calling out to her again, "Piper?" I ran along the bluff then stopped to peer over the side. A few people were still scattered below on the riverbank, but where was Piper? I stared out into the black water. Was it actually possible that I'd pushed my best friend into the river and had blocked it out all these months?

Was it true?

And if it was true, then what did that mean for me?

Chapter 58

AFTER SEARCHING THE WOODS for Piper and not being able to find her anywhere, I went back to the river's edge, trying to remember what had happened after I'd pushed Ellie. Did I really just go back to the bonfire and ask Drew to take me home? Was it really just that simple? As I neared the fire, now a small, smoldering pile of glowing wood, I looked up into the night sky. The white paper lanterns were now all gone. So was my hope that I'd find peace any time soon.

"Hey, there you are," Hayes said, approaching from behind.

"Have you seen Piper?"

"Why? What happened? Did you confront her?"

I didn't know what to say. I touched the edge of my phone in my pocket and glanced up at him, shaking my head... too afraid to speak.

"Tori, is everything okay?"

"Can you take me home? Please?" My hand trembled as I gripped my phone, slick in my palm.

"Yeah, of course. I'll be right back. Let me grab my stuff."

As soon as he turned away, I pulled out my phone, still recording. I hit pause and stared at it. *What now? What do I do now?*

Twenty minutes later, Hayes pulled into my driveway. I sat there quietly, staring at the house in front of me. It was the same two-story colonial as always, not having changed much, if at all, in the sixteen years that I'd lived there. But what had changed was the girl about to cross over that threshold. How was I supposed to go inside and face my mom with her million and one questions about how the night had gone? *Oh, it was fine. And guess what? Guess who killed Ellie? It wasn't Piper like we thought.*

I needed more time to process what I'd just learned.

"Are you sure you're okay?" Hayes asked, breaking my trance.

"Yeah, I'm okay. Thanks for driving me home."

"Sure."

I reached into my purse for my keys and grabbed something else along with them—something I hadn't seen or thought about in a while. I held it up in the glow of the dash, staring at the slightly bent photo, white creases in the old paper through half of the frame.

"What's that?" Hayes asked.

I handed it to him. "I couldn't figure out who this was for the longest time."

Hayes flipped it over and read the back. "Julia Sands. That's my mom."

"Yeah. Makes sense now," I said.

He nodded. "Still can't believe everything that's happened."

"Me neither."

"Are you positive everything's okay? You've been so quiet since we left the river."

"Tough night," I whispered. "A lot harder than I thought it was going to be."

As he leaned in to hug me, I breathed in the fabric of his shirt, slightly tainted by the smell of smoke. I'd always had it bad for him... but bad enough to do what I'd done? "I should go," I said, slowly pulling away.

"Hey," he said as I stepped out of his SUV. "It's going to be okay."

But was it?

I treaded slowly across the front yard and waved as he backed down the driveway. As soon his taillights disappeared around the corner, I changed directions and headed to the woods behind my house. For so many months, I'd thought someone had been lurking in those trees, watching me. I'd been so afraid of the monsters in the dark. Still, I ran through the woods, creepier and darker than they'd ever been, and hurried down the path to the only place I knew to go—to Ellie's window.

"Hey," I whispered, slightly out of breath. I leaned against the cold hard brick and inched my way to the ground. Her face was so clear in my mind with those bright green eyes of hers and waves of dark hair falling over her pale shoulder. Where did I even start?

"At the beginning," I imagined her saying.

"Right. The beginning. So, there's this video…"

Earlier, when Piper had pressed the play button, I didn't want to believe it was real, but the sinking rock in my gut had told me otherwise. For months, I'd been starting to remember tiny fragments from that night—and all along Nick had known. He'd been trying to tell me that he knew it was me.

I know what happened to Ellie Stone.

I know the person who did it. So do you.

Not only do I know who… but I know how she died.

Nick must have seen me push Ellie, like Piper had said, and the only reason he didn't turn me in was because he'd found out that I was his half-sister. But why would Piper kill him to protect me? It didn't make any sense. If he were going to turn me in, wouldn't he have done it right after it happened? I rubbed my eyes, so confused. But wait—then why had Nick confessed? "Ellie, what am I not connecting here?"

"Nick thought he'd killed me. But I didn't die from a blow to the head, did I?"

"No. You died because I pushed you over the bluff into the water."

"But I drowned because of the Rohypnol suppressing my respiratory system."

I leaned my head back against the brick. Right, that's what Drew's attorney had said. "Oh my gosh," I whispered as it hit me.

Piper hadn't killed Nick to protect *me*.

She'd done it to protect herself. She thought Nick's letters were about her.

This whole time, she'd been keeping me close to find out what I knew. She'd been playing me, and there wasn't a damn thing I could do about it. If I went to the police and told them that Piper had killed Nick, Piper would give them the video of me pushing Ellie into the water. She'd played the game perfectly. And even though she was the one who drugged Ellie that night, and probably me too, I was the one who pushed Ellie over the bluff. I was the one who had pushed Ellie to her death.

"I was the one."

I sat there under my best friend's window and sobbed into my hands.

"I was the one... it was me."

"Tori?" someone said quietly.

I jerked back and squinted into the darkness. Had Piper followed me? "Hello?"

Ellie's mom stepped out from behind a row of thick evergreens. How long had she been there? What had she heard?

"Is everything okay?" she asked.

"I'm... I'm sorry," I said.

She pulled her gray cardigan tighter around her thin body. "Sorry for what, hon?"

"I didn't mean to bother you."

"Sweetheart, you're not bothering me. Your dad texted all worried about you. He said he saw headlights in the driveway, but then you never went inside the house."

My dad? I hadn't even thought about him and his part in all this. I clenched my teeth as Ellie's mom sat down beside me in the grass. The thought of them together made me sick. My dad had always been my hero, my protector, but he was just a liar and a cheater. The more I sat there and thought about it, I realized something. Wasn't this all his fault? If he hadn't slept with Ellie's mom and hadn't had that affair with Dr. Moore, none of this would have happened. I closed my eyes, remembering what I'd said on that video. I'd told Ellie, right before I'd pushed her over the bluff, that she always had to have what was mine. Was I *that* threatened? Was I *that* worried about my family being broken that I killed her?

"But she was my best friend," I whispered. "I loved her."

"Oh, Tori, I know you did. Come here." Ellie's mom pulled me into her chest. "It's not your fault," she whispered into my hair.

"I have to go," I told her, suddenly getting to my feet.

"Let me at least drive you home."

"I can walk," I said, still unable to look her in the eye. "Sorry again."

"No need to apologize."

If only she knew.

I left her sitting there in the cool, damp grass as I ran like hell to get away from her. The last thing I needed was to confess everything and tell her that I was the one who killed her daughter.

The guilt kept pushing me faster and faster until I was deep in the woods. When I reached the edge where I could see my back door, I stopped and pulled out my phone. In my hand was a confession. Piper had admitted to killing Nick. But what she held in her hands was just as damning. If I took her down, she'd take me down with her. Hadn't she said as much? I shivered at the thought of the monsters lurking in the shadows behind me, but as I glanced over my shoulder, I realized that the only monster in the woods tonight was me.

And then I did what I had to.

I hit the delete button.

Epilogue

NOW YOU KNOW MY secret, the one I've been carrying around for months. It wasn't some blue flower serial killer or the river that killed Ellie that night. It was one of her own friends. Maybe I should feel guilty for my part in all of it, but I don't. And I especially don't feel bad about Drew going down for it. As for Nick, I did what I had to in order to survive.

At least now, the town is on its way to finding normal again.

If only I could.

Just the other day, Dr. Moore stopped by for a visit. She said it was good that I'd checked myself into Willow Falls. It's not the first time though. I've been here before. Anyway, she told me I was here because of the guilt gnawing away at my insides. "Eventually," she said, "the truth will come out."

Hayes had said the same thing a few days after Tori's little gathering at the river. On the last day of school before summer break, I ran by the art room to get a few things—my old brushes and some paint. As I headed down the hall, I overheard them talking in the stairwell by the auditorium. The door was propped open, so of course, I hung back to watch and listen. It was what I did. It had served me well in the past and would doubtlessly continue to do so well into the future.

"Do you think we'll ever know the truth?" Hayes asked her.

Tori inhaled slowly, looking up at him. "You mean who really killed Ellie?"

"Yeah. Do you think she's capable of killing them both?"

It was no big surprise that they were talking about me.

"I don't really know," Tori said.

He pulled her closer into his chest, resting his chin on the top of her head. "We have to stop blaming ourselves for what happened. My mom said there's a lot under the surface with

Piper—something that started *way* before you and Ellie."

She rubbed her eyes. "You're right."

"Eventually, it will all come out. Maybe not today or tomorrow, but one day it will."

I stepped back, fighting the urge to scream that *she* did it, not me. *She was the one who pushed Ellie over the bluff. She was the guilty one.* But Tori just stood there, staring at the ground. I thought about the night I showed her the video and how surprised she was. But was she really all that surprised? My theory all along was that she knew exactly what she'd done. Maybe the river did have something to do with it, pulling something truly wicked from deep down inside of her that night. And as the orange flames flickered in the background against that midnight sky, she did exactly what she set out to do. I couldn't help but wonder now if it was all worth it, all that tragedy. And for what?

"One day," Hayes repeated.

One day it will come out.

Maybe Hayes and his mother were right. Maybe it would, eventually. But I wasn't telling. And it didn't seem like Tori would either.

Now, as I turned back to my easel, which was facing the window overlooking the courtyard, I added another dab of orange to my canvas. I was doing my best to capture it—the bonfire the night Ellie died. When I'd left that night, I remember thinking that I'd never seen anything like it. It was almost as if the bonfire had come to life in a powerful, angry rage, a fire goddess dancing, swaying, stretching her arms higher and higher into the night sky. I'd never seen a fire burn as brightly as it did in that moment. It was almost as if it were speaking a hellish promise. And now, I was doing my best to recapture it.

"Piper?"

I kept my eyes on my easel, on the fire goddess with her blue-orange tendrils of hair against a black sky. From her mouth came sparks of orange-embers, spitting out all the burning littles lies we'd been telling.

"That's a lovely painting, dear."

"Is it?"

The woman in the white coat nodded.

I had to agree. I especially liked how I'd dotted in that tiny sliver of sky beneath the heavens, two shooting stars.

"Are you ready for our group session?" she asked. "We have someone new joining us today."

I looked up from the blue-hued embers on my canvas. A tiny bit of joy sparked from deep down inside of me. Someone new?

"Yes, I'm ready."

Acknowledgments

Everything about this little book has been a surprise to me from its conception to its conclusion. Even the way the book came about was a surprise; it formed from the scraps of another novel I'd been working on at the time. Some of the characters from that other novel landed here, taking on a brand-new existence. I had no idea what they would do or where they'd take me. In fact, I had no idea who "knew it all," not until the characters led me there; the novel wasn't mapped out or plotted as I'd done with my previous books. The process for this book was messy and organic; it was fun and frustrating. It was something I hadn't tried before—using four characters to tell four different sides of a story. But I took a chance and am grateful that my publisher, Geoff Habiger, did as well.

I'd like to say thank you to Geoff for taking that Friday afternoon meeting with me in November 2022 and for seeing something in this odd little book. When I finished writing it, I had no idea what to think. Geoff had vision and patience from the start, and for that I'm grateful. I'd also like to thank my good friend and graphic designer Melinda Posey who understood my vision from the start and who worked tirelessly until we got the cover just right.

I'd also like to thank my beta readers and editorial team: Eunice Tan, Emmeline Arehart, Josie Munday, Abbey Orwig, Sam Poore, Samuel Stettheimer, Dana Viveros, and Mattie Washington. Without these readers and their invaluable input, Burning Little Lies, as it is, wouldn't exist. A novelist I admire, Lisa Jewell, once said: "People might think that writers are possessive of their work, think that no one but them can possibly know how it should be. Sometimes the writer is the least able to see the solution and sometimes the editors are the geniuses." Thank you to my team of geniuses for all the solutions, big and small.

And a huge, colossal thank you to my family—to my husband and kids who were (mostly) patient and understanding during all those hours I spent in the office toiling away at this book. And to my mom and dad, my biggest supporters: thank you for never doubting me when doubt was all I had in front of me.

Finally, I am grateful for you all, the readers, new and old. It can be a little daunting as a writer to send a book out into the world after pouring weeks, months, and even years into a project. We can only hope that people will like what we've done. I hope you enjoyed it.

About the Author

Christine H. Bailey teaches creative writing and first-year writing at a private university in Tennessee. Before teaching English, Christine worked as a journalist, a marketing/public relations writer, and a freelance editor. She is the author of five YA novels as well as several academic articles and short stories.